PRAISE FOR DAVID RICE

SONG OF TIANANMEN SQUARE

Utterly fascinating...powerfully affecting...lyricism and immediacy.
— Robert Farren in *The Irish Times*

A gripping and all too realistic novel about the Tiananmen Square massacre.

— Chris Patten, last governor of Hong Kong

David Rice has recreated the sights, sounds, smells and above all the emotions of Beijing in the spring of 1989

— Jonathan Mirsky, reporter for *The Observer*

THE DRAGON'S BROOD

I trust this book, because of what it says about Chinese faces....
Rice is a keen observer.

— Jonathan Mirsky in *The Irish Times*

A fundamental impression of truthfulness... my respect for an enjoyable, enlightening and important book.

— Tony Parker in *The Sunday Times*

SHATTERED VOWS

Despite the anguish it portrays, *Shattered Vows* is an immensely heartening and encouraging book.

— Robert Nowell in *The Sunday Times*

Well documented and at the same time an outcry for changing the present disastrous policy.

— Professor Hans Küng

I know no study ... that compares with this. No one has researched the subject as well as David Rice. No one has listened ... with such wisdom and sympathy.

— Peter de Rosa

THE POMPEII SYNDROME

THIS IS DAVID Rice's sixth book and third novel. A native of Co Down, Rice is founder and director of the famous Killaloe Hedge-School of Writing (www.killaloe.ie/khs), which hosts weekend workshops for beginning writers from around the world. He has worked as a journalist on three continents, and has also been a Dominican friar. In the 1970s he was an editor and Sigma-Delta-Chi award-winning syndicated columnist in the United States, before returning to Ireland in 1980 to head the Rathmines School of Journalism (now DIT). In 1989 he was invited to Beijing to train journalists on behalf of Xinhua, the Chinese government news agency, and to work as an editor with *China Features*. He was in Beijing during the massacre of Tiananmen Square, and later returned to secretly interview 400 of the young people who had survived the massacre. This led to two books, *Dragon's Brood* and the novel *Song of Tiananmen Square*, which was read for a full week on RTÉ, Ireland's national radio. His books have been published in Britain, Ireland, Germany and the United States. Rice's No. 1 bestseller *Shattered Vows* led to the acclaimed Channel 4 documentary, *Priests of Passion*, which he presented. At present he divides his time between Ireland, London and Cologne, where he is researching his next novel, based on a little-known incident from the Nazi era.

ALSO BY DAVID RICE

SHATTERED VOWS

KIRCHE OHNE PRIESTER

THE DRAGON'S BROOD

THE RATHMINES STYLEBOOK

BLOOD GUILT

SONG OF TIANANMEN SQUARE

THE POMPEII SYNDROME

DAVID RICE

MERCIER PRESS

WHAT YOU NEED TO READ

MERCIER PRESS
Douglas Village, Cork
www.mercierpress.ie

Trade enquiries to Columba Mercier Distribution,
55a Spruce Avenue, Stillorgan Industrial Park,
Blackrock, Dublin

978-1-85635-534-6

10 9 8 7 6 5 4 3 2 1

Mercier Press receives financial assistance from
the Arts Council / An Chomhairle Ealaíon

The poem *'Windscale'*, is reproduced by kind permission of Faber & Faber,
London.

Strange Fruit Music and words by Lewis Allan © 1939 – Edward B
Marks Music Company – Copyright renewed; extended term of copyright
derived from Lewis Allan assigned and effective July 21, 1995 to Music
Sales Corporation – all rights for the world outside of USA controlled by
Edward B Marks Music Company – All Rights Reserved – Lyric repro-
duced by kind permission of Carlin Music Corp., London NW1 8BD

Printed and bound by J.H. Haynes and Co. Ltd, Sparkford

For
Catherine
Thorne

Those who tell me we are not [vulnerable] are the ones who do not have the security and intelligence information which, for my sins, I carry.

– David Blunkett, British Home Secretary, quoted in *The Observer*, 16 December, 2001

When stupidity comes upon a state, all is over.

– Hilaire Belloc

Human beings learn as much from catastrophes as laboratory rabbits learn about biology.

– Bertold Brecht

PROLOGUE

'SOUND,' YORKSHIRE TELEVISION film director Nancy Harris says. 'Camera.' Father Frank Kane, Dominican friar and eminent historian, turns from Mount Vesuvius, where it rears beyond the ruins of Pompeii's forum, and faces the television camera. His white robes move in the breeze.

'In the afternoon of April the third,' the mellow voice says, 'in the year AD 79, life was going on as usual in this bustling town. People paid little heed to the rumbling and the plume of smoke that came from the volcano – they had become used to it, indeed, bored by it.

'The shops were open, their sliding doors pulled back, and people were buying fruit and bread and wine for the evening meal. A little dog sauntered along, sniffing the hitching posts and lifting his leg in salute.

'In the brothels the first customers were choosing their girls and settling down with them in the tiny cubicles. Over in the bakeries the loaves were being pulled out with a long stick, while slaves turned the nearby millstones to grind the flour for the next day's batch of loaves.

'But there was to be no next day. Within a few hours everyone in Pompeii would be extinct, buried under many feet of red-hot ash. The bread would be found, still uneaten, two thousand years later. The little dog would be found, still trying to run, but turned to stone. The young men and women would be found, still clinging to each other nineteen centuries later, on the narrow brothel beds.

'One moment life was going on as usual. Just hours later it was all over. There was nothing. No living thing. No Pompeii. Just a smooth and smoking plain of grey-black ash.'

'Cut,' Nancy Harris says. 'Nice going, Frank. Let's have coffee, everyone.'

The sun filters through her hair, creating a halo effect. A horde of youthful Japanese, led by an oriental Mary Poppins brandishing a folded red–and-white umbrella, stops to gaze, first at Frank's graceful white Dominican habit, then at Nancy's cluster of blond curls.

The sound engineer breaks out the thermos and plastic cups; the camera operator puts a dust cover over camera and tripod. As the four sit on a couple of broken pillars cradling their coffee, Frank tugs his mobile phone from his deep habit pocket and switches it back on. Almost immediately it rings.

He presses the green answer-button and puts it to his ear. Whatever he hears makes his eyes open wide in horror.

'Are you all right?' Nancy leans across to him.

Frank shakes his head. It is as if he has been struck dumb.

But all this is later. *Much will happen first.*

PART ONE

1

THE AGUSTA A-109E helicopter was a great white shark that swam through the blue Galway sky. It circled twice as if scenting prey, and the beat of its rotor was the thudding theme from *Jaws*.

The wheels came down, the helicopter banked and sank slowly towards Ballybrit's new theme park. As always, Detective Sergeant Jack Stokes – known to his colleagues as Black Jack – marvelled at the delicacy with which the massive machine settled on the ground, next to the four white Humvee four-wheel drives with the gilt crescent on their doors.

All Sheik Aboud's transportation was white and gold, even the private jet stabled up at Knock Airport in County Mayo – pure white from nose to tail, except for the gold crescent moon on the tail fin. Even the jockeys who rode his famous horses to victory at Royal Ascot wore white and gold. Papal colours too, come to think of it – but that would be just coincidence.

The crowd applauded as the tall, white-robed figure stooped under the lashing rotor blades and ascended the platform, along with the heavy-set, power-dressed man in dark suit and red tie, who was Black Jack Stokes' ultimate boss, the Minister for Justice. The other suits were bodyguards for the sheik, Stokes guessed. They stood around the platform, dark glasses and dark faces scanning the crowd, wires going from their ears into the neck of their jackets.

'Your sheik does it in style, doesn't he?' Black Jack nudged his partner, Detective Garda Des King. 'Everything white and gold. Look – even the chopper matches.'

'What d'you mean, *my* sheik?'

'Aren't you married to one of them?'

'So Leila's from Gaza. What the hell's that got to do with anything?'

'They're all the same, Des. Y'need to watch out for those Arab boyos.'

'Jack, that's not even funny. And it's not fair, either. We need to talk –'

'Hold on there. Wait till we hear what Flaherty has to say.'

When Black Jack said 'hold on', you did. Although he invariably spoke quietly, the Northern Irish accent gave an edge to whatever he said. Perhaps it was the authority that came with his forty-seven years and an effective policing career. Perhaps it was also the six-foot-plus build of the man, the cut of the jaw, or the grey edging the dark hair. There was a lot that was dark about Stokes – the sallow skin; the black eyes; the Mediterranean good looks. He could have passed for an Arab himself.

Armada Spanish, people sometimes said, but that was hardly likely in a Belfast man. It was understandable that his colleagues called him Black Jack. Not to his face, though Stokes was well aware of it. And didn't mind in the least.

The Minister for Justice had moved to the microphone. This first phase of Ballybrit's Great Eastern Theme Park was unique, Mick Flaherty began by telling the crowd.

'And we can thank Sheik Aboud for every brick of it. And for the truly brilliant concept itself. This much I can promise you – before long people will be bypassing Cairo to come here to The Great Eastern Theme Park!

'And why not? Because here, you can tour the Pyramids, the Taj Mahal and Beijing's Forbidden City, without ever having to go there. Models perhaps, but so realistic you'll think you're there. And you'll be able to look inside them too.

'But it's not all the Far East – there's the Eiffel Tower and even Westminster Parliament. And we'll be able to view our very own power stations, like Ardnacrusha and Moneypoint, with everything working just like the real thing: cutting-edge technology has made these stunning replicas possible.'

And as for the rides: computers, Flaherty said, had created the most incredible realism ever achieved – 'rides that would make those Disneyland efforts look like the jaunting cars in Killarney. You'll be controlling your own spaceship to Mars; you'll be walking on Mars itself. There are simulators here that will let you pilot a supersonic fighter and shoot down your enemy – or get shot down yourself.'

Flaherty went on to praise Sheik Aboud as a great Irishman – 'It's an honour to have him as one of us these last few years.' He spoke of the employment the park had already brought to the region, and about the tourists who would soon be flocking there all year round.

And what an honour it was for himself, Flaherty, to have got the theme park for Galway: 'But then, I know that it's up to me to look after the people who elected me.'

Just one more thing and Flaherty's cup would be full: 'I've nearly persuaded the sheik to take his transport museum out of England and set it up over here. It's one of the most famous in the world, and people come from all over to see it. I've told him the Lake District already has all the museums it can cope with, whereas we badly need one here in Galway. Well, I intend to keep working on our sheik here, that I promise. Watch this space.'

'Our boss has the gift of the gab, hasn't he?' Des King said.

'Gift of the garbage, more like,' Stokes muttered. 'An' it's about the only gift he has. Except for the ones he gets off the sheik.'

Now Sheik Aboud rose to speak.

'Jaysus, he looks like Jesus,' a woman in the crowd said.

With his soft brown beard and piercing dark eyes in a face of utter serenity, Sheik Aboud did resemble the classical portraits of Jesus.

But the voice belied the face: it was one of those plummy Home Counties accents that are cultivated at public schools. If it weren't for the white robes he wore – unusual for the sheik – this could have been an upper-crust Englishman. That's how he usually looked, in the society pictures from Royal Ascot and Epsom: mostly Sheik Aboud was dressed in a racing gentleman's grey topper or jaunty trilby and elegant tie. The papers were always running pictures like that, of Sheik Kemal Aboud leading in yet another winner, trained at his world-famous stud farm across in County Kildare.

But the sheik had chosen to live in the west of Ireland, and now he was telling his listeners of his love for Galway, whose people had made him so welcome since he had arrived there ten years earlier. 'As you know, I have always used my wealth to create employment here. It has been my way of thanking you.'

'Wouldya listen to that, now,' Stokes muttered to his companion. 'Sure isn't he using his money to cut himself off from those same Galway people? High walls and bodyguards. Amn't I right?'

'But wasn't there a kidnap attempt some years back?'

'Aye, there was, I'd forgotten that. So maybe he needs those goons up there.' Stokes surveyed the suits and shades up on the platform.

'Entrance is free to everyone today,' the sheik was telling the crowd. 'Enjoy yourselves, my friends. And meanwhile we'll do some thinking about that museum. Who knows? Your Minister for Justice can be a persuasive man!'

***

THE MODELS WERE astonishing. Stokes and King filed from room to darkened room; in one, peering at a gigantic model of the Ardnacrusha hydroelectric station that suddenly became transparent so you could see the turbines churning and the water roaring through. And tiny people walking around. There was even a blue sky above, with clouds moving slowly across. And the hills at the back, with the shadows of the clouds moving across them.

In the next room was a model of Westminster Parliament which again became transparent to let you see into the Commons chamber, where a debate was in progress. It was hard to tell which parts of the model were solid, and which were simulated by holograms or computers.

That Westminster model gave Stokes a twinge of concern as his training kicked in. Was it wise, or even responsible, to show the interior of such a building? It would be a godsend to any dive-bombing terrorist to know exactly where the Commons chamber was. Or the prime minister's office, for that matter.

As they walked out to the car, the sheik's helicopter pilot was tying down the rotors of his machine. A competent-looking young fellow, he wore a pilot's uniform – dark-blue officer-style cap, dark slacks and white shirt with blue epaulettes at the shoulders.

'What d'ya think of that?' Stokes said as they passed. 'Told you the sheik had style. Even the flunkies have uniforms.'

'C'mere, Jack. That wasn't fair what you said back there.'

'What'd I say?'

'That the Arabs here all need watching.'

'I didn't mean any harm, Des. Don't be so friggin' sensitive. Sure don't I think the world of Leila. *And* her cooking, by the way!'

'Still, it hurt Jack. Leila's a million miles from that rich bastard back there. And so's her people. I can tell you, the Arabs I know here, especially the Muslims, are the finest people I've ever met. *Ever.* They're honest, they're upright, they're decent. They could teach us so much. And they hate terrorism as much as the next man.'

'Des. I'm sorry. Look –'

'And none of them's rolling in money. I mean, Leila's father's a cardiologist, but you'd hardly get rich in Ennis.'

'Sure I know that, Des.' Stokes got into the car and started the engine.

'And did you know he gives a chunk of his income every month to Oxfam and the Red Crescent, because Muslims are supposed to give alms? It's one of their five duties. Leila told me that.

'Another thing – that sheik's from Saudi Arabia – well Palestinians are as different from him as the Irish are from the Swiss. People think Muslims are all the same – let me tell you, they're as different from each other as Christians are. I wish you could meet Leila's family.'

'Well, maybe I will then. I was out of order, and I'm sorry I said what I did. It's just – I'm under a bit of pressure these days. But sure so are you. Maybe I really should meet your in-laws.'

'Why not? It's time they met you. At least they'd know what a hoor I have to work with!'

'Aha, the bitter word.' A chuckle. 'Where'd I be without you, Des King? Keepin' me in line the way you do. Why don't you ring them right now? Set it up for this week. Go on ahead, Des.'

Des King shrugged, pulled out his phone, spoke briefly, and then listened intently. He turned to Stokes. 'Leila's mother's inviting us for Sunday afternoon. But, her husband has just come home and she says he wants a word with you.'

'Put it on loudspeaker.'

The voice was gently guttural. 'Detective Stokes? Ali Mansour speaking here – the father to Leila. How are you, detective? I have been hearing all about you.'

'It must have been godawful, if you were listening to our Des.'

A chuckle. 'No, Detective. Desmond is very complimentary in regard to your good self. But he has occasionally mentioned your concerns about terrorists – of course, spoken strictly within the family, I hasten to assure you. And it is in that regard that I have something to tell you now.

'I have just come from the hospital, where we have a young Middle Eastern chappie in with breathing problems. He collapsed in the street outside that new Eastern Theme Park in Galway – the one that is actually being opened today, I believe.'

'Sure aren't we just coming from there.'

'I hear it is very wonderful. Well, anyhow, someone called an ambulance and they brought him to A&E in Galway. As it could have been a cardiac issue, they wanted to admit him for observation. But they had no beds, so they sent him here to us in Ennis.

'Look detective, I am not sure exactly what I am trying to tell you, except that this young chappie is totally and completely terrified. *Totally terrified*. I have been to many places in the Middle East – such as Baghdad and Lebanon – and I have seen many terrified people, but this is the worst case I have ever seen.'

'Has he told you what's spookin' him?'

'We can get no information out of him whatsoever – where he has come from, or where he was going when he collapsed. Or what has caused him this terror. But detective, I know a frightened man when I see one. This is one who seems to be looking at death right in the very face.'

'And he's from your part of the world – like, the Middle East?'

'That is why I thought you would be interested.'

'Look, I'll be down soon as I can. I wouldn't be treading on any toes down there – the anti-terrorist squad's not too territorial.'

'Then you will come? To tell you the truth, I had been hoping you would. You may get no further with this young man than I myself am getting, but it would be worth trying – as a policeman you will know how and what to ask. And if there is something out there that is causing this level of terror, you need to know it. People who cause terror are terrorists, are they not?'

'I'll be down first thing in the morning, then. Nine o'clock alright?'

'That will do nicely, and I shall be awaiting you at the hospital – the cardiac unit. Goodbye until then, detective.'

Stokes switched off the phone. 'Now what the frig's all that about? Listen Des, I'd like you to come along tomorrow. Pick you up at the house. Seven-thirty ok?'

2

H IS MOBILE RANG as Stokes eased his Toyota Prius out of the right-angle bend north of Gort. Des King pressed the loudspeaker, and they pulled in to the side. It was 8.10 a.m.

'Detective Stokes? Ali Mansour here. I have rather bad news for you. The chappie you are coming to see has vanished. He is not here in the hospital any more.'

'Well fuckin'hell's gates – oh, sorry about that, Doctor. When did this happen?'

'Early morning – about twenty-five minutes past three.'

'Did nobody see him go?'

'That is the mystery. The people at the front desk say they never set eyes on him. We can only conclude that he used one of the service doors at the rear of the hospital.'

'And nobody saw him heading for the door? None of the night staff? That's bloody weird, so it is. Tell you what Doctor, we're on our way to Ennis anyway. Why don't we just keep going, and we'll go into the whole thing when we get there?'

'Great. All this is very worrisome, and we really need

to talk it over with someone like yourself. Is Desmond coming with you?'

'Your son-in-law's right here with me. We'll be there in less than an hour.'

'I look forward to seeing you then.'

***

DOCTOR MANSOUR MUST have seen the two gardaí arrive as he was waiting for them on the steps of the hospital. He was a tall, handsome man in his fifties, somewhat like a younger Colonel Gadaffi but with a far kindlier face. Stokes warmed to his smile.

'You are being kind to my daughter, I take it?' he said to Des King with a smile, as they shook hands.

'When she deserves it!'

Mansour chuckled. 'Ah, then I am very satisfied – she always deserves well. My daughter is a very very fine girl.'

'So tell us about this here Houdini,' Stokes said, as Mansour led them down the long, white corridor to the cardiac unit.

'Let me begin from the beginning, Detective Stokes.'

'Jack'll do. Forget the titles.'

'Well Jack, he was hyperventilating in the ambulance on the way down, so they skipped casualty and brought him directly here.'

'You say he's told you nothing?'

'Actually he spoke four words in Arabic – *Min Fadlak Laa Ta-da-hom* …'

'Meaning?'

'*Please don't let them* ... And then he stopped, because he started hyperventilating again. But when that was brought under control, he did not finish what he was trying to say. And he never spoke again.'

'*Please don't let them* ...' Stokes pondered the words as he took out his notebook.

'I happened to be doing the rounds, so I was examining him. That was when he spoke.' Mansour led the men into his office, where there was a large cluttered desk, and on the wall a giant relief diagram of the heart.

'Could he've been on drugs?' Stokes asked, as the men sat down.

'Toxicology checked that for us – blood and urine tests. Absolutely clean.'

'You say he was terrified? How did it show?'

'He presented with typical indications – there was copious sweating, dilated pupils, and that hyperventilation I already told you about. But there was also extremely inappropriate behaviour – he screamed when someone pulled back a curtain; he was continually jumping at the banging of doors – hospitals of course can be very noisy places. By the way, can I offer you coffee? Or perhaps tea?'

'Whatever you're having yourself,' Stokes said, and Des nodded agreement.

Mansour ordered coffee down the intercom on his desk.

'Certainly sounds inappropriate,' Stokes said.

'Astonishingly so. Even footsteps made this young man jump. When people came near he cringed in the bed.'

'Could he've been just a bit of a head banger?'

'You mean psychological problems?'

'Aye, like – a looper. Space cadet. Y'know.'

'Oh, indeed and we thought of that too, and got a psych consult done. In so far as one was possible with someone who won't speak. Or cannot. Dr Murray concluded that there was nothing wrong there, but that this was a very badly frightened young man. She too used the word *terror*, and she would not use such a word lightly.'

A young woman carried in a tray with plastic coffee cups and milk and sugar.

'Well, if we've got a terrified young fella on the loose,' Des King said, 'we're going to have to find him – before whoever he's terrified of does.'

Stokes nodded and turned a page of his notebook. 'So what did he look like? Could you describe him for us?'

'Well, he was clearly from the Middle East – probably Saudi Arabia.'

'How'd you know that?'

'The words he spoke in Arabic. I recognised the idiom and the accent.'

'Sure I could tell a Derryman if I heard four bloody words out of him. Anyway – ?'

'The beginnings of a moustache – this is a very young man – about seventeen or eighteen. Curly black hair. Quite small build – about 160 centimetres tall.'

'Stokes did a rapid calculation in his notebook. 'That's about five foot four, isn't it? Or maybe five five. Wearing?'

'The usual blue jeans. And I think – I think perhaps a grey shirt. Footwear, I have no idea, but perhaps Nurse Spillane could tell us that. Oh by the way, the clothes were gone from his locker when he disappeared. But the hospital gown which we had put on him was gone too. And his admission card. The whole thing is very strange.'

Stokes folded his notebook. 'Thanks Doctor. I'm glad we came. And we appreciate this information.' He handed a card to Mansour. 'That's my mobile number: if there's any developments, would you ring me right away?' He stood up to shake hands. 'Well, I believe we're having dinner with yez on Sunday? We're looking forward to it, aren't we, Des?'

'One moment Sergeant, I have not yet quite finished. There is another mystery. Because of the disruptive behaviour caused by the young man's terror – remember this is a cardiac unit where quiet is essential – we had to put him out to a single room in the corridor, on telemetry.'

'What's that?'

'It means that he is connected to the unit's central monitoring system, so that the duty nurse in the cardiac

33

ward can immediately see on her screens if all is well. But here is the point – she could also immediately see if the leads were pulled off. Well, almost immediately. She had gone to check on a nearby patient, but in those few seconds he was gone.'

'And this was all at three in the morning?'

'Three twenty-four to be exact. Our duty nurses keep very precise records.'

'Aye, that's a bit of a mystery. Do y'know what's just occurred to me now – did this fella leave of his own accord? Or could he have been abducted? Maybe by whoever he was scared of?'

'We can find nothing on the CCTVs. Either in the corridors or in the car park. There might just be a couple of unmonitored ways to reach the back doors to the hospital – the service doors – but they would be very complicated, and only known to people working here. And besides, the service doors are always kept locked. This rule is very strict. So no one could have come in that way.'

'So how does our man get out, then?'

'There are panic bolts on the inside.'

***

THE GARDA CAR purred past Barefield on the bypass to Galway, and accelerated effortlessly up to the legal 100 km/h. Stokes loved the sound of that Prius engine, and loved its power and acceleration – it was in a different league to the ten-year-old Carina sitting in his driveway.

But enjoying its hybrid power didn't make him exceed the speed limit. He relished what lurked under the innocent-looking bonnet of that car, but he believed in rules.

'So what d'you think, Des? Whole thing's a bit weird, isn't it? By the way, I liked your father-in-law. I think we'll get along the best.'

'Well, we certainly don't have much of a description to go on, do we – of the fella who did the runner.'

'Indeed an' we don't. By the way, I was thinking, that boyo's from the Middle East. And he collapsed right outside the theme park. Ten to one he works there.'

'It's a possibility.'

'Know what you'll do right now, Des? Give the doctor a ring, and ask him could he find out if they're missing any workers from the theme park. Would you do that?'

'Sure. But why don't we just ring directly?'

'Because that fella was scared shitless, right? So if he *was* working at the theme park, odds on he was scared of something *in* there. Now we wouldn't want to be putting them on their guard there, would we? The gardaí checking them out or anything. No, better leave the doc do it. And he's not to mention us, or say the boy was scared.'

Des King put the phone on loudspeaker, punched in the number and asked for Doctor Mansour. The gently guttural voice came on, and Des put the request. Mansour was happy to oblige.

There was silence in the car for a few minutes, each man occupied with his thoughts.

'I know what you're thinking, Des,' Stokes said. 'You're like all the rest of them – you're thinking I've got a thing about terrorists. C'mon now, admit it.'

'Well, you *are* pretty gung-ho about it. You know that yourself.'

'And you're thinking there's nothing to it, right? What would terrorists be doing in a place like this? Is that it?'

'Certainly isn't, Jack. It's not like that at all. You go on about that gut feeling you get – well I actually buy into that. I've only been with you – what – a couple of months, but I've seen your instincts at work, and I've seen them proved right. A couple of times now. No, I'm glad to be part of this. It's just, I sometimes wonder at how strongly you feel about terrorists. It's more than just doing your job.'

'You're right – it *is* more. A lot more. Alright Des – try to imagine a wee boy walking down the street in Belfast. He's not yet ten. A bomb goes off somewhere behind him, so he starts to run. Then another bomb goes off ahead of him and the street fills up with smoke. Were y'ever in a bombin', Des? Or feel what it does to your eardrums? So the wee boy starts running back the other way. Then another bomb goes off ahead of him again. In the end he just stands there, shakin'. And lookin' at the cars lining the street beside him, wondering which one's going to blow up next.

'That wee boy was me, Des. And d'you've any idea what terror really means? You can't even begin to imagine it till you feel it yourself. It's the feeling you get when you know you're going to be dead in ten seconds' time. *Dead*, Des – d'y'hear me? *Raw meat*. Like those children in Algeria, when the men moved from one to the other, cutting each child's throat. Terror's what the last child feels – while he waits. Actually, while *she* waits. Last one was a wee girl.'

The Prius slid into Gort, and Stokes changed gear to go through the town. Des was silent.

'We lived in one of those mixed estates in Belfast, and one night we were all sitting in the front room – the telly was on and I was trying to do my homework, and half watching the telly. A brick came through the window, and then a machine gun sprayed the wall just above our heads. We thought we were all finished.

'And I think my father must have known terror before he died. He drove a black taxi, and the Shankhill Butchers got him. He must have known terror when they started taking him apart. That's why we moved down to Shannon, by the way.'

'God, Jack. I never knew –'

'Do y'know how they define terrorism, Des? It's "the use of extreme violence to intimidate a population, including the innocent, for political gain". Well, that's why I joined the gardaí. I know what terror does to the innocent. I know it from first-hand experience.'

The road to Clarenbridge was a silver ribbon unwinding before them in the sunlight.

THE PHONE RANG just as Stokes pulled into the car park of Galway Garda station.

'Sergeant Stokes? Ali Mansour here. I have been ringing the theme park, and they say they are missing no one.'

'Thanks Doctor. Now, could you help us a wee bit more? Two more things?'

'I would be very happy to oblige, Sergeant.'

'Thanks indeed. Look, so they're missing nobody at the theme park. Or they *say* they're missing nobody – which isn't quite the same thing. But there's bugger all more we can do there right now. Hold it a minute.'

Stokes unplugged the phone, put it to his ear as he climbed out of the car.

'There's two other places employ most of the Middle Eastern people here, and both belong to Sheik Aboud, who owns the theme park. He's got that Trucial Software plant up in Tuam, and then there's that Castle Patrick where he lives. I hear tell there's quite a staff there, and they're all from the Middle East. No locals employed.

'Would you phone both places and ask are they missing anyone? I'd really appreciate it. Shot in the dark, I know, but it's all we've got to go on right now. Oh, and don't mention us, of course.'

3

AT BUCKLEY'S PUB in Tuam, County Galway, conversation suddenly stopped. Owner Tony Buckley threw his eyes to heaven. 'Christ, would y'look what's coming!' he muttered.

Tessie Kane was barefoot, and in a nightdress. She stood at the door, gazing from one customer to another. 'Has anybody seen our Eileen? I'm looking for my sister.'

'Ring the nephew, Rose,' Buckley called to his wife. 'Tell him get up here fast.'

Tessie shuffled up to the bar and climbed onto a stool beside a rather daunted sales rep. 'Have you seen Eileen?' she asked him.

'Tessie,' Buckley said gently, 'Eileen hasn't been around for twenty years. She died in America, don't you remember? But Martin's around –'

'You were always a liar, Tony Buckley. Like your father. Don't you dare tell me a thing like that!'

'Tessie –'

'And give me a whiskey while you're at it. A large Paddy with no ice!'

'Tessie –'

'Do as you're *told!*' She glared at Buckley, who, shrinking visibly, put a glass to the upturned bottle and pressed twice. 'And no ice, do y'hear? That's what sank the *Titanic*.'

Tessie sat in silence with the whiskey in front of her. The murmur of conversation rose again. But not as high as it had been – Tessie's presence had a somewhat dampening effect. She sat staring into her whiskey, while the sales rep gazed morosely into his Guinness. Buckley occupied himself with polishing glasses. Always liked to look busy, did Buckley.

The door opened and people nodded to the tall, well-built young man with thick, heavy-framed glasses, who came across to Tessie. The glasses gave him a slightly owlish look. He looked in his late twenties.

'C'mon, Tessie,' he said quietly, putting a gentle hand on her arm. 'I'll take you home now.' The accent was American.

Tessie got off the bar stool without a word.

'I'll fix up for that, Tony,' the young man said, pointing to the untouched whiskey. He coughed, drew out an inhaler and put it to his mouth.

'That's OK, Martin. It's on the house.'

'Thanks, Tony. You're one good guy.' The man took Tessie by the elbow and she shuffled quietly out to the street.

Buckley sighed as he took the whiskey glass off the counter. 'All I can say is, thank God for young Martin. Poor Tessie's getting worse by the week. But this is the first time she's ever done that. Hard to believe she was once such a power here in town.'

'Who is she when she's at home?' the man on the stool asked.

'Tessie Kane. She was a solicitor here, and a county councillor. Got an awful lot done. Could make the old archbishop dance to her tune – clergy were terrified of her. She's a sister of that TV priest, Father Kane. You know the man I mean – he's sorta like Sister Wendy, only his line is history. And y'know yer man Seamus Óg O'Kane – the county councillor who goes on about the aliens – the refugees? He's a half-brother, calls himself O'Kane instead of Kane to sound more Gaelic. Tessie's a bit like him too, tongue like a razor. Or used to have. It's terrible sad really.'

'So what is it?'

'Has to be Alzheimer's. That's what people're saying. Getting worse, and Martin's started paying for home help while he's out at work.'

'Who's he, anyway?'

'Martin Gutman. The sister's child, born in the United States. Invalided out of the Marines. Some kind of accident. Did you see the inhaler? And the specs? Came here to live with the aunt, a couple of years back, and works at Trucial Software, just up the road. She's lucky to have him with her – more a son than a nephew. Only thing is, he's a bit religious and that annoys the hell out of Tessie. The same Tessie was never gospel greedy.'

OUTSIDE THE MASSIVE walls of Castle Patrick, Jack Stokes and Des King sat in Stokes' Toyota Prius, and watched the white-and-gold helicopter climb out and away. Minister for Justice Mick Flaherty was in the helicopter, getting a ride home after an agreeable weekend with Sheik Aboud. He would have needed the break after the exertions of declaring the theme park open. Flaherty was a regular guest of the sheik.

'God, I'd give my right arm to search inside those walls,' Stokes muttered. 'But how d'you do that when your boss is the owner's best pal? Or how could you even get a spy inside the place when everybody there's from the Middle East? When the sheik even flies in his own electricians and plumbers?'

Des King pressed a button on his phone, and talked for some moments. He turned to Jack. 'About Sunday's dinner, Leila wants to know if Deirdre still has to go to Dublin. Remember she said she'd try to postpone it? Leila's parents really want to meet her.'

'They'll have to wait, I'm afraid. Her tutor's over from England – only chance to meet. You know what the Open University's like. Though what they'd know about Irish mythology in bloody Cambridge I'd like to know. So it'll be just you and me at the dinner. By the way, tell Leila I hope her mother cooks as good as she does! Come on, let's go or we'll be late meeting Kennedy.'

Stokes started the engine, put the car in gear, and accelerated away.

A HALF HOUR later Stokes was sitting with Des King, sipping coffee in Superintendent Kennedy's office at Tuam Garda station. Instant, of course – what could you expect? Stokes preferred the real thing, and liked to grind his coffee beans. Coffee snob, his wife called him.

'There's nothing really to go on,' he said to Kennedy. 'Nothing. It's just that that bloody sheik's filled the place up with Arabs, all working at his computer plant and the theme park, or over at his castle. With so many Muslims in one place there's bound to be some extremists among them, and I'm beginning to get a bad feeling about the whole set up.'

'Arrah, I wouldn't worry about the computer plant. It's highly specialised stuff they do there, so Sheik Aboud has to bring specially trained people in to do it. I hear they make software for Airbus, stuff for flight simulators, that sort of thing. It'd be fairly confidential stuff, I'd say.'

'But why all from the Middle East? Well not all, but most of them. And none of the rest are Irish. There must be some trained people in this country – or trainable people – if the sheik bothered to bloody well look.

'And what about all the work permits? Och, don't tell me – I know the answer to that myself. *Flaherty*. He's the sheik's message boy. Minister for Justice, me arse! Minister for Passports, more like!' He put down his coffee cup. 'Noel, I'm worried. Look at what we have here – swarms of Middle Easterners, and not a bloody check on any of them.

'A sheik in a castle behind high walls, with a crowd of his henchmen, and not a local man let near it. Bar Flaherty, of course. Then the sheik's computer plant, and no Paddy in there either. And now this bloody theme park in Galway – same thing.'

He ran his hands through his military-type crew cut. 'And I'm supposed to be looking for terrorists! My hands are tied with that fucker Flaherty and I couldn't get a search warrant from Judge Farrell even if I caught him in the hay.'

'But Jack, there's another reason for that too,' Kennedy said. 'With this O'Kane bastard stirring up things against the immigrants, everybody's on their tippy toes. Flaherty can't be seen to go along with O'Kane – so maybe it's not that he's trying to oblige the sheik. He could be scared of being seen as another racist.'

'Aye, now you could be right there. Anyway, there's no evidence to justify a search warrant. There's bugger all to go on. Friend of Ireland, our sheik. Friend of the government. Friend of County Galway. But I just have a gut feeling.'

'There's a young American fella here in town,' Kennedy said. 'Works at the computer plant and could well be a help to you. Ex-US marine. He seems sound enough, and I can vouch for that because I've known him personally for the last couple of years. He's done a lot of voluntary work – like helping out with the lads' basketball when he has the time. Soccer, too. Things like that. I'd really trust him.'

'What's his name?'

'Martin Gutman. His mother was from around here – she died years ago in America. Martin came over to Tuam a couple of years back, for a holiday with his aunt. And just never went back. Of course he'd have his citizenship from the mother. The aunt's gone a bit funny lately, but he's really great with her. Better than a son would be. He's a good man.'

'OK, let's set up a meeting,' Stokes said.

***

THE PHONE RANG in the day room as Kennedy walked the two men out to their car.

'It's for you, Superintendent,' a garda called from his desk.

'I'll take it here. Hold it a minute, lads.' Kennedy put the phone to his ear, listened intently for several minutes. 'I'll be out there in ten minutes,' he said. He turned to the man at the desk. 'The Hanging Tree, Willie. Another suicide. Set up the cordon, will you – scene-of-crime tape, and a garda at each gate. Nobody gets in. Understood?'

'Right away, Super.'

'And will you look after the rest? Pathologist, morgue, oh, and get on to forensics in Dublin, in case it's foul play.' Kennedy turned to Stokes and King. 'Better come with me, lads – this could concern you. Another young fellow's just hung himself, and he just might be an Arab. Mediterranean type, they said. Like yourself, Jack!'

'What's all this about a Hanging Tree?'

'I'll tell you about it in the car.'

The men climbed into the Super's Avensis, Des King up front with the driver. The car took the main Galway road, and then almost immediately turned west down a side road.

'So,' Stokes said, as he settled in. 'This Hanging Tree?'

'You're not going to believe this Jack, but there's a tree a few miles down this road, and five young fellas have hung themselves from it in the last couple of years. This'll be the sixth now. People are calling it the Hanging Tree. And they're saying there was another spate of hangings there years ago. Back in the 1930s. And maybe during the Famine. And it could have been a gallows in 1798. So they say.'

'Wouldn't they be better cutting it down?'

'A German owns the estate and he says no. Says they'd just use another tree. He's a contrary bollix, anyhow.'

'Five – no, six? That's kinda spooky, all right.'

'It's spookier than that, Jack. They say around here that any young lad who goes there to hang himself *walks* the whole way, and in an absolutely straight line, right up to the tree. There was one seen walking through the middle of a farmyard, carrying his coil of rope. Nobody stopped him, and it was only afterwards they realised where he was headed. People here are uptight over the whole thing. They'll be even more jumpy after this one.'

'Hey, doesn't this road go out to the sheik's place?

Castle Patrick? We came in this way this morning, didn't we, Des?'

'We turn off soon,' Kennedy said. 'The tree would be about four miles from that castle. Different estate altogether. By the way, *I* don't subscribe to all this thing about the Hanging Tree – I think it's all just copycat stuff. Young men are killing themselves by the dozen anyway – it's pretty bad here in the county. So I suppose they might as well add a bit of drama while they're at it. That's all there is to it.'

'Aye, sure there's suicides all over the country these days.'

'By the way, I didn't tell you – this isn't going to be pretty. He dropped so far the noose tore the head right off him.'

***

THE HANGING TREE stood in the centre of a small clearing far into the wood, black, gaunt and leafless against the fresh green backdrop of the surrounding oaks. It too might have been an oak, but there was no way of telling, except from its massive girth and height. It could have been hit by lightning. Or maybe died from shame, Stokes thought momentarily, as he crossed the clearing towards it.

A stench hung in the still air.

The yellow tape was not yet in place, and the body lay on the grass below the tree. The top of the spine protruded from the jagged neck. The body was bloated, stretching the blue jeans to bursting point.

But where was the head?

Stokes looked up, and lurched with shock. Eight feet above him the head gazed down, and now turned slowly to fix its bulging, sightless eyes on him. The noose had lodged itself right inside the mouth, below a Saddam-like moustache, so that the white teeth gripped it in a sort of snarl. Red sausage-like things hung from the torn neck. Stokes closed his eyes and turned away.

'I'll make a guess,' Kennedy said. 'He slipped before he got the noose under his chin. Or maybe he had it in his mouth while he was tying the other end to the branch. Anyhow the noose held him by his upper jaw instead of his chin. Did the job just as well though, didn't it?'

'I suppose the drop pulled the head off,' Des King said. 'I wonder why he used so much rope.'

'Maybe he just wanted to make sure.' Stokes thought for a moment. 'Y'see, these poor fellas are amateurs, and wouldn't know how much rope to use. Only do it the once, y'see. Any suicide note, by the way?'

Kennedy shook his head. 'Nothing at all in the pockets. First thing they checked.'

'So are we sure it's suicide?' King asked.

'I'd have no doubt,' Kennedy said. 'I mean, look up where the rope's tied – one of the very top branches. It would take two men to get him out along that branch, and it wouldn't hold the weight of two, never mind three.'

'But look at his hands – they're badly cut. And the shirt and jeans are all torn. Couldn't that indicate a struggle?'

'It could. But then it could also be from forcing his way through all that gorse and bracken to get here. Especially if he went in a straight line through everything. Not that I'm inclined to believe that old nonsense, as I said, but it could be copycat stuff.'

'Looks as if he's been here a wee while,' Stokes said. 'I'd give him a week anyway.'

'At the very least, Jack. Anyway we'll leave that to the pathologist – do you want to wait for her, by the way?'

'No, we'll be off. But would you do us a favour? Would you get a photo of that face up there – what's left of it – get it to Dr Mansour at Ennis Hospital? See if it matches a fella did a runner out of there. I'll be in touch with the doc anyway. And let us know if there's any developments.'

'Certainly will. Come on and I'll drop you back.'

4

$\mathbf{Y}$*ORKSHIRE MORNING CLARION* news editor Will Davis swivelled the computer screen
sideways, and leaned back in his chair. He wished
he were younger, looking at the long legs in the denim skirt
sitting across from him. The gentle tock-tock of newsroom
keyboards was just audible through the glass-panelling of
his office.

'You've heard of Freshpark, Meg? It's one of those
nuclear plants in Cumbria, up the coast from Sellafield.
I want you to do an in-depth series on the whole nuclear
industry, but focused on Freshpark. Key to our future,
that sort of thing. You know how Greenpeace and that
lot are kicking up. And the Irish are upsetting people as
usual. Well, we could present Freshpark as it really is.
Not as the carpers show it. That is, if things *are* as safe
as they're saying. On the other hand, if they're not, I'd
want you to take on Freshpark and show it up. What do
you say?'

'But, isn't that Brian's job?' Meg Watkins said. 'I mean,
he's your science editor.'

'Brian's tied up with this global-warming series. It'll

keep him busy for quite a while. I've talked to the newsroom about it, and they agree you should do it. A joint effort between News and Features. You've got a science degree, haven't you? So what's the problem?'

'Will, I just couldn't. Please, not now. Honestly, I'm not ready. I need a bit more time.'

'You've had plenty of time. You've got to get back in there. What's happened to my hard-nosed reporter?'

'You know damn well what's happened. And I need time –'

'We don't *have* that kind of time, Meg. Now you're taking this on. Is that clear?'

'Will, don't ask me –'

'I'm not asking you. I'm assigning you. Have you got that?'

Meg stood up. 'Whatever you say.' She lifted her briefcase, clicked it shut, and walked out of the office.

Will watched her walk through the newsroom. God, how that woman carried herself. She was near the door when he called her back.

'Come in and sit down, Meg. I want to talk to you.'

'I'd rather stand, if you don't mind.' An angry tear glinted at the corner of her eye.

'Please just sit down, will you, for God's sake. And close that door behind you.'

Meg sat down in silence.

'Listen to me, Meg. You're far and away the youngest we have here – what are you? – twenty-five? – but you're far and away the best we have. Or certainly *one* of the best. Potentially, anyway. You write like an angel, and you can ferret things out like no one else can. That's why I'm giving you this. It's a big one, but it's *time*.'

'Will, I'm not ready.'

'That's because you've stopped believing in yourself. And I know why. But so do you. I know what you've been through, and that's why I'm hammering into you how able you are. I don't often give praise, as you well know. But maybe you need to hear some now, so you can put all that behind you. I'm asking you to take this on. Trust me, will you?'

Meg sighed. 'I don't seem to have much option, do I?' She took out her diary. 'How much time can you let me have?'

'Good. I knew you'd do it. Look, if this is to be a thorough job, it's going to take quite a while. I've arranged for you to have all the time you need. And you can work out of home as much as you want – you've got your laptop.'

Will paused and leaned towards her. 'But I mean thorough,' he resumed. 'The whole nuclear industry, remember, but focused on Freshpark. You'll have to do in-depth interviews – directors, workers, experts, scientists, retired personnel. The lot. And the opposition too, of course. Greenpeace. Friends of the Earth. You know who I mean. Find out what's really bothering them – and find out the answers. If there aren't convincing answers, we want to know why.'

'Can I start Monday? I need to visit Grace at my mother's this weekend. You know that mother's looking after her now don't you, since – since what happened with Colin.'

'Monday's fine. And Meg, you could make a nation-wide impact with this series, if you do it well. We're pretty well a national paper now – don't let the name *Yorkshire* fool you. Remember the *Manchester Guardian*? It grew so big nationwide they dropped *Manchester* from the title. We'll be doing the same soon.

'By the way, you should really sit down with Brian when he gets back from the States. As science editor he could fill you in about Freshpark, and save you a lot of time. In fact you should stay close to him all the time you're working on this – he could point you in the right direction whenever you need it.'

Will stood and put a fatherly arm on Meg's shoulder as he walked her to the door. 'I know it's been a hellish eighteen months for you. Just start believing in yourself again. *We* all believe in you.'

***

MEG FELT CALMER as she stepped into the lift. She slightly resented Will's incursions into her private life, but his words had helped. And she couldn't deny that she needed them. Those final months before she left Colin had eroded that tiny scrap of self-confidence that had been all she had ever possessed. Given her a breakdown, actually. She could still see him sitting by the window in their little flat, reading out an article of hers in that prissy, mocking voice that he used to inflict on his grammar-school pupils.

'Pathetic!' he might snort. 'Not even grammatically correct – do you realise that? It's pure and utter journalese, with a capital J. How do you ever hold down that job?'

Or Meg might come home and find one of her news features lying open on the coffee table, the page red-inked like a butcher's apron, with any repeated words circled and linked with red lines. And a teacher's mark at the bottom, two out of ten. And the comment – 'Work of an amateur'.

One part of her knew it was jealousy – envy, rather. The envy of a lower-middle-class man for a public-school girl – a Roedean girl, at that. And one nearly half his age. The envy of an embittered forty-year-old who could never have made it into print and knew better than to try. Who had failed as a teacher, failed at anything he had ever put his hand to. You could say he'd even failed as a car driver, which was why he had been in the wheelchair.

It was only envy, but it had still worn Meg down. And down and down. The man had genius – the genius to nit-pick with deadly exactitude, and the genius to hatch each nit into a louse. And the insight to fasten on Meg's already wretchedly low self-esteem and make it hit zero.

It wasn't just Meg's writing, either. Colin would sit there, endlessly puffing his Rothman's cigarettes, and sneer at her clothes. 'You're going out in that skirt? With those legs? You'd embarrass Grace if she were old enough.'

The thing was, Meg only had to look in the mirror to see her legs were good. But from childhood she had learned not to believe mirrors, not to believe her own eyes, not to trust her own judgment. And anyway, a man who kept at you and at you could make you doubt anything – legs; cooking; writing; parental skills.

So why did she stay with a man who obviously hated her? Because love conquers all, and she had loved him. He'd come around, she had told herself – he would if she loved him enough. And he had been a good father to Grace: even from the wheelchair he could bathe and feed her. Wasn't a failure there. He truly loved Grace, so maybe if he was capable of that love he could come to love Meg too.

Yes, there were times when Meg had thought of leaving. How could she not? But in the end, when all confidence is taken from you, even the confidence to leave is gone. That's why it all went on for so long.

It wasn't until Will had told her to go and see a doctor because she was losing so much weight and that doctor had sent her for counselling, that Meg realised she could actually leave.

She finally did and then regretted it, after Colin got cancer. That caused her the worst grief of all: if Meg hadn't left, Colin might never have died. The possibility that it was the stress that brought on the cancer. But no, that wasn't true either: the cancer was in him before she left, but neither of them had known that.

Stop it! Just stop going over old ground, Meg told herself for the hundredth time, as she headed down the street from the *Yorkshire Morning Clarion*.

***

'SO, MEG, WHAT do you need to know?' Brian Mottram lifted his pint of bitter. 'Cheers, by the way.'

'Cheers!' Meg lifted her G&T. 'Just brief me about Freshpark. What exactly is it – what exactly is in there. You know, you should really be taking this on – not me.'

'Well, I can't, and that's that. I've got this series on global warming, and it's going to take quite a while. I have to do more research in the States. Anyhow, you have the experience for it.'

'That's what Will keeps telling me. God, I hope he's right. I don't know why he picked me for this.'

'There's something you should know about Will. He's been around a long time and he's got a reputation for sudden enthusiasms, and dropping them just as suddenly.' A chuckle. 'Can include women, by the way – well, occasionally! But there's one thing Will sticks with. Over the years he's had a habit of zeroing in on someone very young, but with talent, and pushing them all the way to the top. Like with Kate Atkinson – she's now the *Guardian*'s top business writer. Looks like he's picked you this time.'

'Well, I only hope I can live up to his expectations. Anyway tell me, what's so special about Freshpark? I think I already know the answer, but I want to hear you say it. Let me put it to you, for the sake of argument, that it's just another nuclear power station. Right?'

'Wrong. Freshpark doesn't even create electricity like other nuclear plants – it used to once, but not any more. What it does is to take in used-up nuclear fuel from power stations all over the world, even from as far away as Japan, and reprocess it. They've got a special plant called Thule for doing it.'

'Reprocess it?'

'What they call spent fuel – what's left over after a nuclear reactor's been operating. Every year they replace about one third of the core of the reactor with fresh fuel. But there's still lots of goodies in the spent fuel, and Thule separates them out to be used again. Especially plutonium. There's other stuff too.'

'And then they send it back to Japan or wherever?'

'Not quite. Only some of the stuff's useful – like plutonium – and they have to bake it together with uranium to make little pellets of fresh fuel. They do that at a special factory that they call their Crox Plant.'

Meg sipped at her G&T. 'That seems a sensible way to do things. Using the same fuel twice sounds rather like renewable energy. So why all the scaremongering?'

5

'WHO ARE YOU? What do you want?' Tessie Kane stood in the Georgian doorway, arms akimbo.

'I'm looking for Martin Gutman,' Jack Stokes said.

'What do you want him for?'

'I've – I've business to discuss with him.'

'Well, he's got no business with you. I don't want any strangers coming here, upsetting our peaceful home. Get out of here. Go on, get –'

'Who is it, Tessie?' Martin Gutman came to the door, peering over Tessie's head at Stokes.

'It's some – *man*,' Tessie muttered, turning on her heel and going back in. A door inside slammed.

'Sorry about that.' Martin smiled ruefully. 'She's not herself these days.' He extended his hand. 'Hi! I'm Martin Gutman.' Good handshake – firm, confident. Big fella. Warm smile. A man you might take to.

'Stokes. Jack Stokes. Garda Síochána.' He grinned. 'That's "cops" to you! Special Branch. Look, could we talk somewhere?'

'Sure. Come on in.'

The front room had the fusty atmosphere of a room rarely used.

Martin moved a pile of newspapers from an armchair and sat down opposite Stokes. 'Get y'anything? There's beer –'

'No. Thanks all the same. Look, I was talking to Superintendent Kennedy up at the station yesterday. He thinks you might just be able to help me. You work at that Trucial Software plant, right?'

'Sure do.'

'Can we talk in confidence?'

'Sure can.'

Stokes hesitated. 'Supposing I asked you to keep your eyes open up there? For anything that might be, well, odd, is what I'm trying to say.'

'Not sure I get you. Sergeant, isn't it?'

'Detective-Sergeant. Look, there's a helluva lot of overseas people working at that computer plant. Mostly from the Middle East. Now, if I told you my job's a watching brief on – I suppose I'd better say it – on potential terrorists. And I just wanted to ask you –'

The door burst open and Tessie came in, brandishing a frying pan like a lethal weapon. She pointed it at Stokes. 'I want him out of here! Get out of here, you!' She lifted the frying pan.

Jack Stokes sidled past Martin, out through the front door and down the steps as fast as his legs could carry him.

'Don't you come back here!' Tessie hissed, and flung the frying pan after him. Stokes ducked and the pan clattered onto the street, narrowly missing a passing car.

The door slammed, and Martin caught up with a visibly shaken Stokes. 'Hey, I'm real sorry about that. As you can see, I have all the terrorism I need right here. C'mon, we'll go round to Buckley's. A drink might steady you.' He lifted the frying pan from the street and left it on the house steps. 'Tell you what – you go on over and wait for me. I'll try to calm her down and I'll see you there in about ten minutes. OK?'

'Grand.'

***

THERE WERE ONLY two customers in Buckley's pub – elderly locals with tweed caps stuck to their heads. Buckley himself was watching Sky News.

Jack Stokes settled himself in a corner to wait for Martin Gutman. He was ever so slightly annoyed with himself that he had mentioned his terrorist quest so soon. Should have pussyfooted around for a bit, surely. Why hadn't he? Well, the Super had spoken so highly of this Gutman fella. And *he'd* known him a few years. No, that wasn't it. It was Martin Gutman himself – there was just something about him. Something sincere. No, more than that. As if he had suffered terribly, and come through it. No, more than that: you don't just take to somebody like that, unless you get a good feeling about them. And

Stokes, who otherwise worked rationally through things, had found that when your instinct tells you something that strongly, you go with it.

The two men at the bar greeted Martin warmly when he came in. That was a good sign.

He came straight across to Stokes. 'Pint?'

'Aye. Please.'

Martin went across to the bar, chatting to the two locals while he waited. Finally he came back with the Guinness, plus a sparkling water for himself. 'Hardly ever touch liquor,' he said, in reply to Stokes' raised eyebrow. 'Gives me headaches, since I was ill a while back.' He sat into the corner. 'So tell me about these terrorists.'

'Let's keep our voices down, if you don't mind. Though there's nothing to tell really. I've no reason to suspect anything. Or anybody. It's just, there's so many young lads here from the Middle East, all gathered together – not just at your computer plant, but at that theme park down in Galway – that, well, if there *were* any terrorists, that's where nobody'd notice them. That's about it, really.'

'And you want me to keep my eyes open, right?'

'Aye. Just that.'

'Sure. But to tell you the truth, the computer plant seems an OK sort of place to me. They're a decent enough bunch. Different from us, of course: all those prayer mats and stuff. They're all highly skilled, I'll tell you that. But they seem OK guys. But sure, I'll keep my eyes open. Now that I'll be watching closely, maybe I *will* notice something. Leave me your number and I'll get back to you.'

'One other thing – are you missing anybody up at work?'

'Not that I know of. But then there's a lot of guys working there, and I wouldn't know them all. So I wouldn't necessarily know if someone went missing. Why?'

'There's a fella hung himself the other day. Could be an Arab.'

'Yeah, we heard about the hanging. Pretty awful, everyone says.'

And there's a young Saudi-Arabian gone missing out of Ennis hospital – he was a patient there. He was scared of something, and did a runner. Or somebody took him out, we don't know which. All three of the sheik's places, including your plant, say they're missing nobody. But maybe they're just not telling. Would you check it out for us? But – very discreetly.'

'Sure. Be glad to.'

Stokes handed him a card. 'And anything you notice: let *me* judge if it's important, alright? We can meet here any time. I don't think I could face that lady again, if you wouldn't mind.'

'I don't blame you.' Martin chuckled. 'But it was funny, you ducking that frying pan. She's my aunt, by the way. Getting worse by the day. She'll have to be in care soon. Sad, really. She was one helluva woman.'

***

'CALL FOR YOU, Jack,' Des King called across the day room. 'It's the Super in Tuam.'

Stokes pressed the speaker on his desk.

'Bit of a development here, Jack.' There was a tinge of satisfaction in Kennedy's voice. 'Hanging Tree, remember? Well, first of all, it's not the man who disappeared from Ennis hospital. They sent up a nurse, and she's certain they're two different people. So that's that anyway. But wait – you're not going to believe this: we have what might be a suicide note. And it's in Arabic.'

'Can you get it translated?'

'Already did. Man here in town did it for us.'

'An' it says –?'

'*I cannot go through with this.*'

'That's it?'

'All that's in the note. But there's more. Remember there was no note at the scene? And the cut hands and the knees? Well, young Hennebry here reminded me that a few parts of the estate wall still have broken glass cemented into the top – smashed bottles and the like. You know the stuff – illegal nowadays. So maybe that's what cut the hands, or the shirt, or the jeans, if your man tried climbing over it.'

'Good thinking.'

'So we sent five or six men to each spot where the wall has broken glass, and just blitzed the ground around it. Went through it with a toothcomb. Inside and outside the wall.'

'And?'

'Nothing on the ground, bar a few cider cans – some of the local yobbos drink there from time to time. But on top of the wall there were a few fibres – could be from jeans or a shirt. And what could be blood on a couple of them. But there was also a bit of brown paper, caught on a glass shard. Might have come out of a shirt pocket. We almost missed it. Damp, sure, but biro doesn't run.'

'The suicide note.'

'You bet.' Kennedy was enjoying this. 'So then we took out an ordnance-survey map – one of the large-scale ones – and drew a straight line from the tree to the spot where we found the note.'

'You're killin' me. Go on will ya!'

'And projected the line further – straight as a die. Want to know where it led?'

'The sheik's castle.'

'Got it in one, Jack.'

***

'JACK,' STOKES' WIFE called. 'Come here till you see this.' Stokes came into the room, an open folder in his hand. He took off his reading glasses to peer at the TV screen.

'It's that O'Kane politician,' Deirdre said. 'You know, the county councillor who goes on about the immigrants.'

Stokes sat down to watch, the folder on his knee. It was one of those talk shows, and Seamus Óg O'Kane was at his rabble-rousing best. Or worst.

'Sure our climate is all wrong for the blacks,' he was intoning. 'I met a black fella the other day and he told me he hates this place – the rain and the cold and the fog. I told him he was dead right and he should go home.

'We should repatriate the lot before it's too late, before they flood us with black babies that'll make Ireland a black country. Or yellow or brown, for that matter.' O'Kane guffawed. 'Now if there was green fellas – little green men – I wouldn't mind a green country so much!'

A couple of other political types were struggling to get a word in, succeeding rather poorly, and the presenter was milking it for all it was worth.

'For God's sake, that's pure fascism,' one of them spluttered. 'You could go to jail for that!'

'I'll not go to jail Niall, and y'know why? Because I'm only saying out loud what everybody else thinks.' There was some half-hearted clapping from the studio audience. 'And I'll tell you something else. There's one thing worse than the blacks, and that's those Saudis and Arabs and whatnot. They're not just trouble – they're dangerous. Half of them are terrorists, but you don't know which half, and that's the problem.

'If we don't want ourselves blown up, then we have to get rid of the lot of them.'

'Look, councillor, you can't use this show to say things like that,' the presenter interrupted.

'Well, I've just said them, haven't I? One thing we're going to have to do, and that's for sure, is have a dossier on every Arab in the country. It's the only way to flush them out.'

Stokes sighed. 'It's assholes like him make my job impossible. I'm supposed to be looking for the one or two terrorists who just might be hiding here, passing themselves off as genuine Muslims, and hiding among them without anyone knowing. Sure my job's well nigh impossible – it's delicate enough to have to question immigrants at any time, but this O'Kane scrote makes everything I do look like persecution.'

He stood up. 'It's hard enough without his carry-on. I've that bloody sheik filling the place up with more and more Arabs and nobody knows what he's really up to. I've a young Arab lad in terror of something and now gone missing. And another fella hangs himself – probably Arab as well. And of course they tell me nobody's missing from any of the sheik's three places. But what if they're just saying that? Kids awake? I promised them a story, but this bloody dossier's had me tied up.'

'Don't keep them up too long. And then come down and relax. Promise?' Deirdre put an arm around his waist. 'I want time with my Black Jack.'

***

'YOU'RE LIKE A dog with a bone, Jack, do y'know that?' Superintendent Moran said. 'You bloody north-erners are all the same. Do ye ever let up?'

'I left Belfast at seventeen, Super. I'd see myself as a Clare man. A Shannon man.'

'Who are you kidding Jack? You've got that stubborn streak they all have up there. The weasel inside you. Scratch a northerner, and what do y'find inside? Nails. Iron nails, rattling through your veins.'

'Know somethin', John-Joe? *You're* the bloody racist – why don't you just link up with that O'Kane frigger? And mebbe start a campaign to keep us northerners out.'

'Arrah, I wouldn't want to do that now Jack,' Moran said with a chuckle. 'Ye can be useful bastards at times. But by God, ye never let up. I mean you keep after that bloody sheik, who's your boss' best buddy, when there's no shred of evidence of anything.'

'Alright, then. Maybe it's not evidence, but there's circumstantial stuff that's all pointing in one direction.'

'So list what you have.'

Well, there's the young fella, scared shitless of something, goes AWOL from Ennis hospital. When he collapsed it was outside the sheik's theme park. And he had a Saudi accent.'

'Go on.'

Then there's this other young fella hangs himself. Leaves a note in Arabic – *I can't go through with this*. By the way, forensics sent his DNA to the Yard. Might be something there, but we haven't heard back yet. Oh, and I told you about the line on the map, that points straight to Castle Patrick.'

'Ah Jack – not that superstitious bloody nonsense again. Don't give me that.'

'Fact is, he *did* walk in a straight line, at least from the wall to the tree. They found the trail through the undergrowth. Copycat maybe, but he did it.'

'How about outside the wall?'

'Roads and grass fields, mostly. Not so easy to trace.'

'There you are then. No real evidence. And Flaherty pushing us to leave the sheik alone. Why don't you just back off, Jack?'

'Aye, but how do I ever *get* any evidence if I don't stay on it? Tell us that now.'

'How do you know there's any evidence to get?'

'I just have a gut feeling about it.'

'For God's *sake*, Jack.'

'My gut's been right before, Super.'

'Then let your gut find something that'll justify a search warrant. And then we'll see.'

***

THE CREW OF the Castletownbere trawler *Brandon* were hauling in their nets about 100 miles west of County Clare, when the body tumbled out along with the fish. Skipper Marty Harrington saw it first. It was almost the colour of the fish – blue jeans, grey shirt, silver-blue face.

When they lifted it out from among the dancing fish, it sagged as if there was no skeleton inside. The right arm was missing from above the elbow.

6

THE STENCH OF sulphur befouled the air like the fart of a colossus, as Father Frank Kane gazed down into the crater of Vesuvius. A wisp of smoke curled upwards. Cinders crunched under his feet. He turned to the camera, while the soundman held the boom just above him: 'This is the mouth from which death came forth,' he said, 'on that catastrophic day in AD 79. A plume of death rose slowly into the air, and people down on the plain glanced up with mild interest. They were used to their mountain and its moods.

'One of those watching was a man called Pliny, known as the Younger Pliny, because he had a famous father, and he has left us an account of what he saw.

'Pliny was perhaps the earliest journalist in history. Two thousand years before anyone had ever heard of journalism, Pliny was certainly the first eyewitness to write down his impressions of a world ending.'

Frank went on, 'He has told us how the smoke rose above Vesuvius like a monstrous pine tree. Let me quote Pliny: "It rose to a great height on a sort of trunk and then split off into branches, I imagine because it was thrust upwards by the first blast and then borne down by its own weight so that it spread out. Sometimes it looked white, sometimes blotched and dirty, according to the amount of soil and ashes it carried with it.'"

The camera zoomed in as Frank concluded: 'Of course the people who gazed on that pine tree, white and blotched and dirty, were gazing on the very instrument of their doom, only they did not know it.'

'Cut!' Nancy Harris called out. 'All right, Frank, I want the remainder with you looking down towards Pompeii. Tim? Camera over here please, so we have Naples in the shot as well, right below Frank. All right?'

Frank looked down towards the distant glinting grey that was Naples. Smog as usual, but you could still see the bay curving beyond the city, with that intense cobalt blue that only the Mediterranean seems to muster. He was glad he was in shirt and trousers – the filth and the cinders would have made short work of his white Dominican habit.

'Sound,' Nancy said. 'Camera.'

'Down there,' Frank resumed, 'in what are now practically the suburbs of Naples, were the towns of Pompeii and Herculaneum. On that day in AD 79, the people went cheerfully about their business – that is, if they weren't watching the mildly interesting fireworks display from the mountain. And they were cheerful – Pompeii was a cheerful town, well fed, easy going, with lots of available sex. A good place to live, according to their standards!'

The camera zoomed in again as Frank turned full face to the lens. 'Yet every moment death was coming closer,' Frank said. 'A Valkyrie riding the sky, and they could all see it coming. But they did not want to see it. The incredible thing is that the people down there knew it could happen. Or should have known. Earthquakes had damaged half the town only fourteen years earlier, and there had been ample warning from earthquakes since then. Hot ash had fallen on Pompeii only the day before, so that many people had left the city for safety.

'But the people all came back. *They came back.* They simply couldn't believe anything really terrible could happen – life and streets and brothels and bakeries don't just suddenly cease to be.

'Or don't they? These people learned, if they had a few moments in which to learn, that things sometimes do cease to be. In fact, whole worlds can cease to exist, along with the people in them. But, for these people, extinction was unthinkable. It's what I call "the Pompeii Syndrome" – because something is unthinkable, you do not think it. You *cannot* think it.

'The Pompeii Syndrome is not confined to Pompeii. As a historian I find it present in every catastrophe throughout history: people on the verge of their own extinction invariably refuse to think of it. Precisely because it is unthinkable.'

***

JACK STOKES TURNED from his computer in Galway's Garda station and rubbed his hands. 'Getting somewhere, Des. This here email from the Yard – they've an ID on that fella from the Hanging Tree. Name is Issam Q-u-t-b – don't ask me to pronounce it. Arrested around the time of those London bombs, then released. Aged twenty-seven, and a computer programmer – well, was. Member of some fundamentalist club near Finsbury in London, till a year ago, then he went off the radar. Club's suspected of links to terrorists, but nothing's ever been proved.'

'Well, that's a step forward, anyway.'

'It is an' it isn't. All still bloody circumstantial, and that's frig all use. Well, right now anyway, but if we just keep on building … By the way, did y'ever hear of somebody called Omar?'

'Omar Sharif?'

'No, Des. Just Omar.'

'New to me,' Des King said. 'Who's he when he's at home?'

'Dunno. It's in this email, says he's a leading terrorist, and that he just *might* be in Ireland. It's only one possibility – but we're to be on the alert. Would you follow it up? There's very little detail in the message, but ask HQ to get on to London, and you might come up with a bit more.'

'Sir!' King snapped a mock-military salute.

'Wait, there's one other thing you could do for us, Des. While you're onto the Yard, would you ask them to do a profile on that Sheik Aboud? I think he was reared in England, so they'd be able to get some information. Tell them it's only routine, but to keep it confidential.'

***

'WILL, I CAN'T *do* it.' Meg was weeping into the telephone. 'I'm not up to this job. I have to quit.'

'Meg –'

All Will could hear were sobs.

'Meg, listen to me –'

'It's no *use*, Will.'

'I'm coming over. Right now. I was just leaving work anyway. I'll be there in twenty minutes.'

***

WHEN MEG OPENED the door of her flat, Will found her quietly crying.

'Come on,' he said, putting an arm around her shoulder and leading her to the scuffed leather sofa. 'Now what is it?'

'I'm finished as a journalist, Will. I can't do it any more.' The voice was small.

'Don't talk shite. You're a Roedean girl, remember!'

'It's *true*.'

'It's rubbish. I'll tell you what's wrong with you. That fucker of a husband sucked you dry of every scrap of confidence – he set out to give you that breakdown, and if he was still alive he'd just love to see you like this now.'

'What if Colin was right? I wasn't a good wife to him, you know – I left Colin to die. I'm not doing a great job of being a mother either – my own mother has to look after Grace. Will, I can't even take care of my own child. And Colin always said I couldn't write for toffee, and I think he was right.'

'So what you do now is prove him wrong. Listen Meg, I gave you Freshpark so you'd do just that. It's a biggie, I know it. But that's why I gave it you. Make a go of it and you'll never look back.'

Meg rubbed her eyes.

Will took her hand in both of his and squeezed it gently. 'Y'know what my wife told me yesterday? She's got a lover, as I think you know. Well, she told me, go and get one for yourself. And then she said, but who'd have you now?

'See what I mean, Meg? That's what we're all up against. People always try to destroy your confidence, and it's worse when it's someone you love. And should love you. Remember Oscar Wilde – "Each man kills the thing he loves"? You simply don't let them do it.'

Meg looked up. 'So why do *you* stay?'

'The children. Why else? Anyway listen, Meg. You're bogged down with all this scientific stuff here. Leave it for the moment, and go up to Freshpark to see it for yourself. Then all this will mean something.' Will waved at the files scattered on the table and floor.

'Now, I've got something for you. You know those

invitations Freshpark send out from time to time? Usual PR stuff – guided tour for journalists? Well one came in for Brian Mottram yesterday, and he's in America. So why don't you take them up on it? Go up there this weekend. You'd enjoy it: they wine you and dine you and put you up in that special hotel they have on the site. And give you the Grand Tour. That'd be the way to start. When you get back you'll have a better idea what this stuff is about.'

A wan smile. 'Whatever you say, Will. Alright, I'll give it a try.'

'That's my girl.'

***

'SO WHAT IS the most worthwhile thing in life?' Mansour's soft guttural voice fell pleasantly on the ear, and the man exuded a gentle confidence. The kind of surgeon you wouldn't mind trusting your heart to, Stokes thought. Which indeed was Mansour's métier.

Stokes and King were sipping mint tea with Mansour while his wife and her two daughters cleared up after the meal.

The couscous and lamb had been delicious. A drop of wine wouldn't have gone amiss though, Stokes thought. And it would have been nice to get a better look at the women: those veils were a bit of a turn-off. Meant to be, of course. Still, that's the way.

'Most worthwhile thing?' Stokes pondered the question. 'Aye, well it isn't money, that's for sure, though I could do with a wee bit more. Love, maybe? Happiness? I don't rightly know.'

'Money, love, happiness – they are all a bit elusive. They are fine when you have them, but they are like eels that can slide from your grasp. No, I am talking about something you can do, or not do, as you choose.'

'Fight for justice, maybe?' Des suggested.

'It could be,' Mansour said. 'But I am telling you what I think it is. I am convinced that the most important thing in life is relieving someone's suffering. Or preventing it. That is what makes us human. Indeed it is what you do as a policeman, when you begin to think about it.'

'You might be right, there.' Stokes thought for a moment. 'Is that from the Koran? Isn't that what you call it?'

'That is indeed where I learned it. Almsgiving is a duty, like prayer or fasting. Or pilgrimage. Well, what is almsgiving but the relief of suffering? Compassion is the key to Islam: we call God *al rahman al raheem* – "most compassionate, most merciful".'

'Well then, tell me Doctor –'

'Ali.'

'Tell me, Ali, where do these terrorists get their notions? You wouldn't call them exactly compassionate now, would you? This whole Jihad thing …'

'The Jihad's an obligation to fight the evil within ourselves. So we become pure and honest and compassionate.

When the Prophet came back from war he said, "Now the Greater Jihad begins – the Jihad within each of us." It is the hardest fight of all: that is why it is called the Greater Jihad. Whereas we fight enemies only to remove oppression or injustice – that is the Lesser Jihad.'

'Just like us, then?'

'Exactly. We have more in common than we know, Jack. And by the way, when we talk of terrorists, which terrorists do we mean? When an American-built missile is deliberately slammed into a block of Lebanese flats and kills fifty women and children, is that not terrorism? And how do you cope with terrorism on such a scale as that?

'Or if you were a young Palestinian and saw your father stripped naked and humiliated, and saw your family dumped in a squalid refugee camp for generations – remember that's ethnic cleansing – and have no hope of ever *ever* leaving, but staying there until death, could you possibly be tempted to strap dynamite to yourself and take as many of your persecutors with you as you could?

'Of course that would be terrorism, but you would be responding to decades of terrorism all around you. You would not even need all that preaching about martyrs going to heaven.'

'Not that different from how we felt in Northern Ireland, then.'

'Only a great deal more terrible, Jack.'

'So it's never as simple as the media make it out to be.'

'Far from it. Let me ask you something, Jack. Did you ever see a decent Arab or Muslim in a Hollywood film?'

'Come to think of it, no.'

'Because there are not any. Film after film has systematically degraded us, stereotyped us as decadent, backward and evil, to a man. So that the two words "Arab terrorist" go naturally together. Remember that movie *Executive Decision*? Where the terrorists are monsters who pray before killing passengers, and who quote the Koran to justify their killing? Have you seen it?'

Stokes nodded.

'Now, tell me, did you ever see a film about decent Arabs, trying to live honest lives of care and compassion? The kind of lives that come from truly following Islam?

'Or did you ever see a film about Moorish Spain, when Arab culture literally saved civilisation, while Europe turned savage in the Dark Ages? Did you ever hear a mention of Ibn Rushd, the Arab scholar who preserved Aristotle and Plato for the world?

'And the worst thing of all is that when the terrorists look at these films, and see us portrayed as total savages, right across the board, they say, well what's the point of even arguing with the West?'

'I take your point.' Stokes was thoughtful.

***

A PRETTY ROAD, thought Meg Watkins, as she

drove northwards along the tortuous A595 that follows the Cumbria coast, hemmed between sea and mountain. One to be enjoyed, provided you weren't in a hurry.

Glimpses of the Irish Sea, and the last of the evening sun glancing off it. Hills and dales and hairpin bends – outer rim of the Lake District. And tiny hamlets where the road narrows between sandstone houses straight out of a calendar, a couple of the houses with signs for Grisdale Auctioneers. Somebody had told Meg you could see the Isle of Man on a clear day, but it wasn't there that evening.

And neither was little Grace. Once more Meg's conscience gave a twinge – was she neglecting Grace by coming up here? But this was work. If only Mother wouldn't whine so much about looking after her. But what alternative was there? Meg had to earn for them all. And Grace and Mother would never fit in Meg's tiny Leeds flat. Well then, get a bigger one. No, because Mother wouldn't leave that nice house in Cawood. Thought of herself all her life, and not likely to change now.

Meg's thoughts were forever turning to Grace. And then to her own mother's whining. And then back to Colin – if only Meg had been more understanding. More patient. More loving. He might be alive today. If only Meg could stop this cycle of brooding …

The light was fading as the MG gurgled by Ravenglass, then the signpost to Sellafield – that was the other nuclear site in the area, but not the one that concerned Meg. She was heading for the far more famous Freshpark, a good nine miles further north.

Finally here was the sign, indicating the side road to the village of Freshton and its neighbouring nuclear plant, Freshpark. The village had that tatty jaded seaside look – shabby bay windows overlooking the sea; red telephone box; glimpse of a church steeple; an official-looking sign pointing to Freshpark, and a couple of speed bumps you wouldn't want to miss. Up, and over. Up, and over. A sharp turn to the left, under a stone railway bridge, then sharp right again. And suddenly, there It was …

Meg found a gateway and pulled in. She stared in awe across the twilit fields. A panorama of power filled the darkening horizon. Freshpark was a chess set built for Titans – massive cooling towers floodlit against the evening sky, random chimneys like gigantic pawns, pagoda-shaped castles and bishops and even knights, and things that could have been ringèd kings. Orange plumes of smoke. A tall tower with a bulge at the tip, like a toadstool. Hadn't there been two of those towers in the photos, Meg recalled. Well, one of them must have been taken down, or else it was hidden behind something else.

She gazed and gazed. For her, Freshpark would never again be just a place name.

Meg turned the ignition key, eased the MG out onto the road. And now for this Freshton Manor they all talk about – this marvellous hotel run by the nuclear plant exclusively for its official visitors.

That MG was the love of Meg's life – well, after little Grace. She had splurged on it shortly after leaving Colin, as a sort of investment in herself. The counsellor had suggested it – said it could help her confidence. And it had been worth every penny, if only for the admiring glances that came her way when the top was down. 'Going topless,' she called that.

If only she could have believed in those glances. She always felt that the people who threw them could never have guessed how awful she really was inside. As Colin had said, if people really knew her...

***

MEG FELT LIKE the young bride in *Rebecca* coming to Manderley for the first time – and just as nervous – as the MG swung around the curved drive, and there beyond the beeches rose the red-brick pile of Freshton Manor.

Mullioned windows; soaring chimneys; geraniums in grecian urns lining the steps. It only needed the doors to swing open and the butler to emerge. Which was almost what happened. Not a butler but a hotel manager, oleaginous, elegant in striped pants.

'Ms Watkins? Ah, indeed. Welcome to Freshton Manor. I do hope you'll enjoy your stay with us. I'm John Parker. Delighted.' A click of fingers. 'Giles will park your car and see to your bags. Giles?

'And now, if you'd like to sign our visitors' book?

And then, perhaps a little, ah, something to make you welcome, after you see your room? Dinner will be in an hour.'

The bar smelled of leather, and glowed with mahogany and maroon watered-silk walls. Two men turned from the counter, visibly brightening at Meg's approach. One adjusted his tie. They wore dark business suits and Parker introduced them as journalists from London and Glasgow.

'A whisky, Ms Watkins?' Parker at her elbow. 'We haven't quite fifty-seven varieties, but we do have many. From the Highlands and the Islands.' He indicated wall-to-wall bottles.

'I think I'd settle for a beer. Perhaps a half of bitter?'

'Splendid choice. We have our very own here. Especially brewed for Freshton Manor.'

Meg felt the weight of the world lighten ever so slightly. Just getting away can be a therapy in itself. And then she remembered Grace again. Maybe I should be with her tonight, she thought, instead of all this. No, no, maybe not. There's this job to do, and it puts food on Grace's table. And mother's. Anyway, I'll phone later.

***

DINNER WAS GRACIOUS at Freshton Manor. Game terrine with Cumberland sauce, the toast kept warm in crisp little serviettes. Spring salmon from the Freshton River – caught right in the hotel grounds, they were assured – with new potatoes and peas. Pudding unpronounceable, but seeming to Meg a *marron glacé* with a hint of whisky. And throughout, a lightly-chilled Montrachet.

'The same meal served to the late queen when she opened Freshpark here, all those years ago,' someone told Meg. 'Except she was Princess Elizabeth then.'

There were just Meg; the two journalists; the deputy director of operations for Freshpark, a Mr Hodkins; the environmental site manager, a Dr Jarrold; and an elderly, uppercrust sort of chap called Sir Bertram Nicholls, who reminded Meg slightly of her late father. He was the one who had mentioned the queen.

Conversation was mostly about Freshpark: and it struck Meg that these people seemed to know exactly what they were about, and had the confidence to carry it through. Meg, herself devoid of confidence, was impressed with it in others. If these were a sample of the people running Freshpark, then Freshpark seemed to be in safe hands. Of course that might be just a first impression. Well, there'd be time to find out.

But there was pain among these people at the downright bias from some of the media. 'Not your people,' Hodkins hastened to tell Meg. 'The *Clarion*'s always been fair to us.'

'The worst troublemakers are certain foreign governments,' Sir Bertram said with considerable anger. 'Especially, and unforgivably, the Irish. They've taken us to

Europe on the flimsiest of grounds. Of course they'll get nowhere with that. But distributing those iodine tablets was flagrantly dishonest – the tablets were useless *and they knew it*. Sheer, downright propaganda. All they did was frightfully upset their own people, as well as deceive them. They seem an extraordinarily dishonest, brazen bunch of – of power-mongers.'

'Well, we always knew that,' the journalist from Glasgow said.

***

'HELLO, JACK. CONOR Fitzsimons here.'

'Hello, Superintendent.' Stokes was pleased to hear from his former boss. 'You're in Bantry, I take it? I heard you'd moved down among the heathens. Tough lot those west Corkmen I hear.'

'Bantry it is, Jack, for my sins. Listen, there's something down here might interest you. You're still on that roving beat, aren't you – terrorists and all that?'

'For *my* sins, Conor!'

'Listen. There's a body here in the hospital morgue, and the people here don't know what to make of it. Came up in a net, a hundred miles west of Clare. One of the boats out of Castletown. Could be foul play, so they're coming down from the Technical Bureau. Reason I thought you might be interested is – you know that leather patch you get on jeans? Well the one on this man's jeans is in Arabic. At least that's what we think it is.

'Look, could you come down? There's quite a bit more to tell you, and I'd like you to see things for yourself.'

'I'll be down this afternoon. And Conor, thanks for thinking of us.'

'If you could make it around three, the scene-of-crime lads'd be there then.'

'Three, it is. Cheerio Conor.'

***

'FRESHPARK LOOKS ALMOST beautiful in the morning sunlight,' Meg wrote in her first article for the *Clarion*. 'Concave cooling towers throw orange smoke against a blue sky; a gigantic silver sphere glints, hundreds of feet in diameter; the Thule plant, in its beige-and-red livery, could be a hospital without windows, although a thousand times more vast.

'Appearances can deceive, of course, and Freshpark's glorious morning could well be as in Shakespeare's sonnet – soon to be clouded over. It is the things that actually go on beneath that orange smoke, and inside that silver sphere, and deep within that Thule plant, that must give us pause.

'However first impressions, at least, are reassuring. Inside Thule itself there is the hush of hospital corridors, except for a continuous gentle double beep which could be from some life-monitoring medical equipment. In fact that sound is the key to Thule's own safety monitoring.

'This is where they separate the plutonium from the spent nuclear fuel. We were assured that safety is paramount here. Before we even moved within Thule, we were given special safety socks and shoes, and a badge that monitors any possible radiation. There are even life-buoys on the walkway above the pool where the spent fuel is stored – it's kept deep under water in a concrete reservoir the size of two football fields, and all of it under Thule's roof.

'Next door is the Crox plant, where they bake the plutonium and uranium into tiny pellets the size of peanuts. They told us you could hold a few in your hand and they wouldn't do you any harm. They even showed us the pellets – not in our hands, but behind glass. It struck me that, if the pellets were that safe, why were we not allowed to hold them? Wouldn't it be a brilliant way to demonstrate safety? I actually put that question to our guide, and was told that no risks, even the tiniest, are ever taken. It's what they called *a total safety culture*.

'Certainly, before we finished our tour, the stress on safety was so pervasive that I found myself asking – what exactly is all the fuss about?'

***

THE MORGUE SMELL was in Jack Stokes' nose and throat – that cocktail of formaldehyde and incipient decay which, once smelt, is never forgotten. He stood looking at the shattered body of a boy of about seventeen.

The pathetic beginnings of a moustache were hardly visible against the blue-grey skin. A piece of bone showed through the stump of the right arm.

Something about that poor little bag of bones resonated with Stokes, in a way he could scarcely understand. As if this child-man was – was what? Was asking him for help?

But how can you help the dead?

'He can't have been more than twenty-four hours in the water,' pathologist Dr Maeve Boulton was saying. 'I won't bother you with the reasons for concluding that, but one of them is that there are absolutely no signs of decay. And he hasn't been chewed up by marine life. Except for the arm.'

'Any ID on him?' Stokes asked.

'That's an interesting point,' Superintendent Fitzsimons interrupted. 'There wasn't a single thing in any of the pockets. Nothing.'

'This poor fellow could have come off the Cliffs of Moher,' the pathologist said. 'What you're looking at is quite literally a bag of bones. There's hardly a bone that's not shattered. Into tiny bits – you can see for yourself. This body fell, and probably from a very great height.'

'What we don't understand,' Fitzsimons put in, 'is how the body drifted that far out. And in such a short time. Maybe you know that most Cliffs-of-Moher victims wash back up around Doolin?'

'Any theories?' Stokes asked.

'None so far.'

'Suicide? There's been a lot of it lately.'

'All I can state for the moment is that death is consistent with injuries from a fall,' Dr Boulton said. 'So far, it could be suicide or murder. If it's murder, he could have been killed first, and then thrown from a cliff. A rule of thumb is that if a body is dead when it enters the water, it usually floats. That's because there'd be no water in the lungs. Now, this body was caught in a net – but, was it caught deep down, or was it on or near the surface? I doubt if the fishermen could answer that.'

'I take it the scene-of-crime unit took samples? I'm sorry I missed them.'

'They came early, Jack,' Fitzsimons said. 'Earlier than they said. But they certainly took away lots of samples, and some of those might throw some light on things. They even took DNA to send to Britain if need be.'

'Fingerprints?'

'Absolutely.'

'And of course I'll be taking away my own samples,' Dr Boulton added.

'So what can we hope to learn from them, Doctor?'

'Well, the nail scrapings can often indicate if there was a struggle – you know, someone's skin under the nails.' She thought for a moment. 'No. Won't be much help this time – there'd be very little after twenty-four hours in the sea.'

'Pity. Might have ruled out suicide. You'll take pubic hair?'

'You've been around, Sergeant! Yes, I'll be taking that too. You know this could even be a sex case. He's a good-looking boy. Or was, poor little dickens.'

'Pictures?'

'First thing SOC did.'

'Digital?'

'Both. Digital *and* film.'

'Aye. Right, so.' Stokes turned to Fitzsimons. 'Conor, could you email a picture of this wee boy up to Doctor Mansour at Ennis hospital? There's just the chance it might match someone who went AWOL from there a while back. Sure I know a cadaver mugshot isn't the world's best likeness, but it's all we've got. If the doc sees *any* likeness, ask would he come down, or send somebody down, to do a formal ID. It's just a possibility, mind. Now, what about these here jeans? With the Arabic or whatever?'

An orderly produced a heavy manila evidence bag, and turned it over to show its transparent window. Behind it the jeans had been folded to show their small brown-leather waist-patch. All Stokes could discern were squiggles.

'There's nobody here can read it, unfortunately,' Fitzsimons said. 'Dr Sa'id could, but he's on holiday back in Egypt. But there'll surely be somebody down the town.'

'Could you get us a photo of that patch?' Stokes asked.

'No problem. Harry'll do it right away. Digital OK?'

'That'll be fine. And when he's done the photo could he attach it to the email going to Doc Mansour? Say I asked would he translate it. Alright?'

'Leave it to Harry. Be done straight away.'

'Well, we'll be off then. Listen, thanks everybody. I appreciate you calling us in on this.' Stokes took a last look at the shattered body of this child-man. No more than a teenager – couldn't even manage a moustache. 'Poor wee bag o' bones. Wonder what happened him? Will we ever know?' For no reason at all he felt a prickling at the corner of his eyes. And what could only be the beginning of a lump in his throat. Something that hadn't happened in years.

***

BILLIE HOLIDAY WAS on Lyric FM as Stokes' car came north through the Oranmore roundabout, a few miles south of Galway. Broadcaster Paul Herriot was presenting some sort of special on her life and tragic early death. She had only seventy cents in the bank, Herriot was saying, when she died of drugs and cirrhosis of the liver.

So many ways to do yourself in, Stokes was thinking, as he half listened and half brooded. The slow ways like drink or drugs, and the quick ways like cliffs or hanging trees. Plenty of time to think when it's slow. But what if it's quick? They say your whole life flashes by in an instant. But sure how does anybody know?

So when that wee bag o'bones went off the Cliffs of Moher, what did he see on the way down? Or what did he think? Would he regret jumping? Would he've wanted to go back up? He'd have had a few seconds.

The fella off the Hanging Tree would've had fewer. Nanoseconds, maybe. Any time at all to think? Before – *THUNK*. Suddenly Billie Holiday's fresh, sensual voice was singing *Strange Fruit* –

> Southern trees bear a strange fruit
> Blood on the leaves and blood at the root
> Black bodies swingin' in the Southern breeze
> Strange fruit hangin' from the poplar trees

AS THE CAR came through the roundabout in Galway, on a sudden impulse Stokes turned off where the sign said *Tuam*, and headed northward, straight for the Hanging Tree. He wasn't sure why.

***

'SO WHY DID you go there?' Deirdre wanted to know. She had been a bit miffed when Stokes got back late, but they were both soon over it. That was the way with them. And now, meal over, children in bed, they were having a cup of tea by the fireside.

'Dee, I honestly don't know. Just – I don't know what got into me. I had to see the Tree again. C'mere, am I losing it? Losing my objectivity? God I hope Des doesn't notice it, if I am. Or the Super.'

'Did you learn anything at the Tree?'

'I just sat on a stump and thought and thought.'

'About what, love?'

'About what's going on here. Going on all around us, and nobody even noticing. That poor boy going off the Cliffs of Moher, and young fellas walking to this Hanging Tree. And that sheik looming behind it all like some kind of evil genius.'

'Now you don't *know* that, Jack. Really. Do you?'

Stokes sighed. 'No, I suppose I don't. Look, you're the one with the intuition. Could that be what's going on with me, that I just have a really strong gut feeling about it?'

'Course it could. By the way, you know there were hanging trees outside most Irish towns and villages? In the old days, just like in Mississippi. Nothing special about them.'

'That from your dissertation?'

'I've come across it in my research. It's more than just myth, though. The Celts used to hang people for ritual reasons, then bury them to mark boundaries. Human sacrifice – that Latin writer Strabo mentions it, and so does Julius Caesar. But it's not just back then – the English had hanging trees all over the place. Until relatively recently. For rebels and criminals, sure even for stealing a sheep. Some of those trees would still be standing. Nothing so special about them. Sure isn't there a Gallows Hill just up the road from here?'

'Aye, there is, surely.' Stokes shuddered. 'Do y'know, Dee, sometimes I wonder are we all walking in a straight line towards some bloody Hanging Tree – the whole damn lot of us. The whole world, I mean. And carrying our own rope, and not even knowing it. Am I out of my mind, Dee?'

***

'YOUR SATURDAY PIECE was pretty good,' Will Davis said, as he hung up his jacket at Meg's. 'Brilliant description of Freshpark. Conveyed how stunning it is. But, ah, nothing really critical to say? Pervasive safety culture? That's it? Come on now, Meg.'

'I genuinely was impressed, Will. By the place, and by the people I met there. They came across as competent and trustworthy.'

'How was the dinner?'

'Good food and good conversation – both.'

'I thought it might be.'

'What are you getting at?'

'They didn't buy you with a dinner, did they?'

'Oh for God's *sake*, Will – give me a break. What do you take me for? Do you think I come that cheap?' Meg stood up, eyes both angry and tearful. 'Your arrogance amazes me. How *dare* you say that to me. You know me better than that.'

'Of course I do. Obviously they didn't buy you with a dinner – I was only teasing. Actually I wanted to see what you're like when you're angry, because you rarely are. You're at your best when you're angry. You should try it more often.'

'It was a rotten thing to say, and I'm really hurt.'

'Alright, Meg, I'm sorry. I really am. It was over the top, and I apologise. But there *is* something I want to put to you, and please don't get upset.'

'What?'

'Sit down, will you? Let me explain something. They were all men there, weren't they?'

She nodded.

'And they were a lot older than you, yeah? And they were scientists and engineers – all professionals and authority figures, weren't they?'

'I suppose they were. Why?'

'Here's why. Meg, you have a brilliant critical faculty, if you could only realise it. But you popped it in your pocket over there at Freshpark, didn't you? And you know why? Because they were all authority figures. And you've a problem with authority figures.'

'I certainly do not!'

'Yes you do. Listen, deep down you're a strong woman. I've been around you long enough to know that. It's just that somebody somewhere ran off with your self-esteem and that wasn't today or yesterday. It was long before Colin – I'd take a bet on that. And it was somebody in authority did it to you. And that's why you have a problem with authority figures.'

'Well, you're one yourself, aren't you?'

'No, I'm not, as a matter of fact. I'm a friend – if you'll allow me. And a mentor. Why do you think I gave you this Freshpark thing? To draw out that critical faculty in you. And then to get you to trust your judgment.'

Meg still felt cross, but somehow not as cross as she should have been.

'Just don't take these people at face value, Meg.' Will went on. 'Dig deeper, OK? And from now on, I want you to question everything you hear in the line of duty. Everything. Especially when it comes from authority. Scrutinise and then evaluate. Even what *I* say – even what I'm telling you now. When you get to the point of telling me to go and jump in the lake, I'll know you've made it.'

Meg sighed. 'It's not that simple.'

'It *is* that simple. You make it that simple. Look, I said you're a strong woman: well, now you need to become a confident one. You mightn't realise, but you've already grown during these last eighteen months, from the moment you began questioning Colin's claptrap. It finally led you to leave him, didn't it?'

'Yes, and then he died.'

'That wasn't your doing, Meg.'

'Wasn't it?'

***

'MARTIN, HOW *IS* Tessie, really? ... Look, I'm her brother, remember, and I ought to know.' Frank Kane held the mobile phone tight against his ear. 'That bad? Oh dear God ... Do they have a diagnosis? Or are they still just guessing? ... They're sure it's Alzheimer's? ... Poor Tessie!'

Frank listened intently. 'How quickly? ... Really? You mean, just months? Weeks? ... Well then, she'll have to go over to Dympna. And soon – but at least it's a nursing home. Listen Martin, could you hold the fort for another while? I'm in the middle of filming here, and I can't really leave at this point. Every day costs a fortune' ...

'I'll be coming to Leeds to do Diane's wedding – you know, Dympna's granddaughter. Will you be there? We could have a family conference ... No? Sorry to hear that. Then I'll come across to see you in Tuam. I'll have talked to Dympna by then. Meanwhile, you'll hold the fort?' ...

'Thanks so much, Martin. You're a good man ... Yes, the Marines are that, aren't they – a few good men! Lord bless you, my lad. A great bloomin' nephew. We'll make it up to you.'

7

FRANK KANE TOSSED and turned in the warm Amalfi night. The hotel window was open to the balcony, and the whisper of the sea came up from far below. It seemed to whisper *Alzheimer's, Alzheimer's*.

Oh God, what will become of us all? Will I end up with it too? Doesn't Alzheimer's run in families? Dad and Mam? Never got a chance to find out, did we? Were we dysfunctional after losing them – with Tessie despising men and refusing to marry, and Eileen marrying that bastard in America who made her life a misery? And Seamus, for God's sake, mad as a hatter and persecuting asylum-seekers. No, sure he was daft from the start.

Well at least there's Dympna. She's sound as a bell. And her daughter and granddaughter – absolutely together people. Young Diane's so bright: looks like a model, too. That Philip's a lucky fellow, to be getting Diane. Must plan my sermon for the wedding – good Lord, it's nearly on top of me. Time does fly. Must keep the sermon short.

And Martin's sound enough, too – so there's hope for the next generation. In spite of that brute of a father.

Though he *can* get depressed. Hardly blame him. Well, there aren't too many descendants to carry on the Kane name. I certainly won't be having any.

Wish Nancy'd stick to her TV producing, though, and leave me alone about celibacy. God knows I'm trying. Struggling all my life. Always honestly tried. Those breasts of Nancy's don't help – that's for sure. 'Beware the good woman' – that's what they used to tell us in the seminary. Not the bad woman. The good one. It's the sheer goodness of the good woman that gets to the priest. So they told us.

Nancy's a good woman. But she keeps on about celibacy. Says the church is soon going to let priests marry – maybe the next pope will change the rules. Will I be the last of the celibates? Sort of dinosaur? I'd have made a good dad. Son like Martin, maybe. Or a granddaughter like Diane. Not going to happen now.

But what's the point nowadays? Celibacy – does it make me a better historian? Couldn't I present the TV programmes just as well if I were married – if I were a layman? No I couldn't – it's the white habit makes it work. Like that Sister Wendy.

They say celibacy's a witness – that there's another life hereafter. So do without in this one. Well, some of the others don't seem to be doing much doing-without – or witnessing – that's for sure. And do *I* do without much, do I, living in this fancy hotel?

Anyway, is television what I should be doing? Or

history for that matter? Is any of it a priestly ministry? Wouldn't I be better visiting hospitals or prisons?

Well I've still got prayer. Talk to God. As a friend I've had for years. And it does work. The only way. Every day. Only way for me, anyway. All I have left. Like, when I lie awake like this, and I can't stop thinking about Nancy. Jesus, give me strength now. Like you promised. *Sta principiis*, they told us – 'Stop it starting'. Turn your thoughts to something else.

Like what? Like Alzheimer's, maybe. Oh God, am I going to get it too?

***

'QUITE A BIT came in while you were out, Jack.' Des King handed Stokes a note. 'Call from Bantry – Ennis Hospital sent down a nurse from their heart unit, Mary Spillane. She ID'd the body. Absolutely no doubt, she says. It's the young fellow from the hospital.'

'I was hoping as much.'

'I think we all were.'

'I don't know why, but that wee bag o'bones is on my mind a lot of the time. Nearly as much as Hanging Tree Man. I wish I knew why. Bag O'Bones really got to me. Well, whatever he was scared of, he was bloody right to be scared. It got him in the end. Bigtime. Stokes sat down at his desk.

'Well, we don't quite know that yet,' Des King said. 'There were a couple of other things came in while you were out. The pathologist says there's no evidence of a struggle. She says she still can't go further than "death consistent with injuries from a fall". And probably won't *be* going further than that. It's here in the emails – I haven't printed it yet.'

'So it could still be just another suicide.'

'Yep.'

'So what else came in?'

'An email from Scotland Yard. They've absolutely nothing on Sheik Aboud. He's not, as they say, "known to the police". But they say they're willing to build up a profile for us, except it'll take some time since they'd be starting from scratch.'

'Tell them we'd be really grateful, Des. And say thanks. Is that the lot?'

'The note in your hand. An email from Doc Mansour.'

Stokes put on his reading glasses. 'Let's see – that jeans patch translates as *Sinbad High-Fashion Jeans*, he says. The rest simply says *100 per cent cotton*, and then there's the waist size and inside leg.'

'Not much help there, is there?'

'Don't be too sure, Des. You'd never know.' He pondered for a moment. 'Tell you what. Get that patch photo off to Interpol. ASAP. See if they can come up with anything. As you've heard me say till I'm blue in the face, it's the wee simple things that hold the clues.'

***

'JACK, THERE'S A couple of Paki's working for the sheik who've rented the house next to ours. And an Australian guy with them. I could get to know them. Would it help?'

'Pakistanis, Martin. Don't *you* go racist on us, now. Citizen O'Kane does enough of that for us all.' Gutman and Stokes were in their preferred corner at Buckley's. 'So tell us, how would you get to know them?'

'OK, sorry. Anyway these three guys work at the theme park. I saw two of them playing chess last evening in their garden, next to ours. One was this Australian – name of Colby, I think. Well, I play chess, not brilliantly, but they might be glad of an extra opponent. Whaddya think?'

'Wouldn't do any harm, Martin. Tell y'what, try it and see how you get on. It's odd – that theme park interests me far more than the computer plant. I wish t'God I knew why.'

'OK, then. I'll offer my chess services, and see how it goes.'

'Good man yourself. Sure there'd be no harm in trying. Oh and by the way, Deirdre's having a couple of people in Wednesday night. Des King, who works with me, and the wife. She's from Gaza. Would you come? It'd just be stir-fry and a drop of wine. And a bit of craic.'

'The stir-fry'll be OK. I don't do wine, as you've noticed.'

'Jeez, I forgot.' Stokes chuckled. 'Well then, you and Leila can stick to the stir-fry, and Des and I'll polish off the wine! Och no, there'll be lots else – tea, coffee, minerals. But tell me Martin, is life dreary without the wee drop?'

'I get by, Jack.'

'By the way, uh, Deirdre can be a wee bit, well in your face, if you know what I mean. She can ask the bluntest questions, and you never know what she's going to come up with. Don't take it badly if she – like, I mean she has a heart of gold. And a bloody great sense of humour.'

'Don't you worry, Jack. You forget the practice I'm getting with Aunt Tessie. She can be blunt as a sledge hammer. Not that I'm making comparisons, of course. But don't worry, I'll be the soul of diplomacy.'

***

MEG'S MOTHER BURST into tears at the kitchen stove. 'I'm doing my *best*!' she whimpered between sobs. 'Nobody ever thinks of me and my needs. I'm just a slave to you and that – child.'

'Mother, please.' Meg went over close to her, wanted to put her arms around her shoulders, but didn't. Her mother would have recoiled and muttered, 'Don't touch me!' She'd always been like that.

'And I hate being called Gran. It's so – *common*.'

'It's just that Grace calls you Gran. Would you like her to call you Grandma? Or maybe Martha?'

'Oh, just stop it. This is becoming ridiculous.'

'Look, Grace is in there with her teddy bear. I could ask her now.'

'Oh for heaven's sake leave it, will you? You're upsetting me now. Leave me alone.'

Her mother had been like that as long as Meg could remember. Solved all arguments by telling you to stop upsetting her. If you persisted she would up the ante, saying you were giving her a headache, or that she felt one of her 'turns' coming on – so you just backed off and let her be. Brilliant. Never failed.

And lately she had come up with a marvellous new one – 'I'm old and and I'm frightened, so just leave me alone.'

Fact was, Meg's mother wasn't all that old at all. On the other hand, maybe she had good reason for being the way she was, Meg thought. The colonel had never been exactly loving, either to wife or daughter. Maybe he had been too old when he got married. Bachelor soldier too long. Thought the house was Catterick Barracks. Never forgave his wife for not giving him a son who'd go to Sandhurst and keep up the family tradition.

And never seeming warm to Meg, who loved him to pieces, whose life revolved around trying to get his attention, if not his love. And then Father had been an idiot when it came to money, so there was always scrimping and making do, even on a colonel's salary. When he sold off half his pension for some daft investment, lost the lot, and then blew out his brains, Meg could hardly blame her mother for the way she was. She'd had to look after herself for years.

But at least Roedean had lived up to its motto – *Ex Fide Fiducia.* 'From Faith Comes Faithfulness'. Suddenly there was no money at all, and her mother was taking Meg away from the school. Roedean had come up with a scholarship out of the blue, just like that. The headmistress had sworn mother and daughter to secrecy. From faith comes faithfulness.

Meg could never forget Roedean.

'You might at least give me a hand with the potatoes,' Gran snapped from the stove. 'Instead of just mooning there. Why do I have to do everything around here? Oh God, why did you give me such a selfish daughter?'

***

'JACK,' DES KING called, as his boss came into the day room. 'Something here about those Arab jeans.'

Stokes crossed to Des' desk. The email from Interpol, was brief and to the point:

Re yr query on Sinbad High-Fashion Jeans. Item is manufactured by Mideast Cotton Company, in Jeddah, Saudi Arabia. Locally owned: no multinational input. Label identified as one issued within past six months, as label design changed six months ago. Although garments from this company retail throughout Saudi Arabia, Jordan, Syria, Lebanon, Egypt, Yemen, United Arab Emirates and Kuwait, so far this particular label sells only in Saudi Arabia. *Response ends.*

Stokes chuckled. 'Not much help, that patch, right?'

'OK. *OK*. Don't rub it in!'

'Wouldn't dream of sayin' I told you so, Des!' Stokes tapped his pen on the desk. 'So now it's definitely Saudi Arabia. Doc Mansour identified the accent and now the jeans patch confirms that. Alright then, let's look at what we've got so far. We've one scared boy, who becomes one dead boy, who came here from Saudi Arabia in the last six months, who mebbe went off the Cliffs of Moher, either shoved or jumped. Right?'

'And a suicide up in Tuam, out of Lebanon via Finsbury, leaves a note saying he can't go through with something.'

'Don't I know it. Still up a blind alley, though, aren't we? Martin says he checked and there's definitely nobody missing from the computer plant. Besides which, they're all experts in their twenties and thirties there, whereas our Bag O'Bones was only a wee lad. And Martin made discreet enquiries about the other two places, and there's nobody missing from there either. He's as near certain of that as makes no difference, he says. Coffee?'

'Hold on, I'll get it.'

When Des came back with the coffee, Stokes was standing and rubbing his hands. 'Just got an idea, Des. You know the picture? Wee Bag O'Bones? Why don't we circulate it to all the people working for the sheik?'

'But you said they're missing nobody.'

'Not the point, Des. If Bag O'Bones has been living around here, wouldn't the Arabs here know him? Socially, like? They'd all know each other, so they would. No, what we'll do is, we'll send around both pictures – Hanging Tree Man and Bag O'Bones.'

'They're both pretty horrific pictures, Jack. Hardly kosher to send them around. Not exactly standard procedure.'

'I'm past what's kosher, Des. And I'm past standard procedure – with that sheik, anyway.'

'But wouldn't we be showing our hand, then?'

'Aye, we would. But maybe it's time to.'

8

THE FOULEST CUP of coffee in Christendom must surely be the one they sell in the car-park café near the summit of Vesuvius. It tastes of rotten eggs.

'It's the sort of stuff Faust would drink in hell,' Frank Kane said with a shudder, as he tossed the coffee out on the blackened cinders. He looked at the lava all around: 'Well, I suppose we're in the right place for it.'

'We'll bring our own up tomorrow,' Nancy Harris said. She tossed her coffee away too. 'Tell me, Frank, are you really serious about a catastrophe about to happen?'

'I don't know. I truly don't. It's just that I've never felt like this before. I'm just wondering, as a historian I'd be rather finely tuned into events, wouldn't I? Am I subconsciously absorbing signals that I recognise – the way animals are aware of tremors before an earthquake?'

'What sort of signals?'

'Well, if they're subconscious, I'd hardly be aware of them, Nancy. But there's one thing I am aware of. There's a thing the historians call "the sunset factor". Have you ever noticed how, just before darkness falls, the sky gets suddenly brighter? For a brief moment? Or how a light bulb, before it fuses, glows extra bright? Well, before a disaster, people seem to live more intensely, more irresponsibly, more crazily just before it hits. As if they sense what's coming.'

'Like what?'

'Take Berlin just before the Nazis. It was a byword for depravity. Or take the Black Death that wiped out a third of Europe in the fourteenth century. There were orgies all over Europe, before the plague reached them.'

'But they knew it was coming. That's different. They were just having a last fling.'

'Not quite, Nancy. Most thought it couldn't happen to them, that the plague was something that would affect others, but never them. Still, they had their fling just the same. It was in the air.

'Right down there is an even better example.' Frank pointed down to where the Pompeii ruins lay under a smog cloud. 'Those people were at their most decadent in the period just before the mountain blew. Life was a round of orgies and feasting, vice and irresponsibility of every possible kind. That's what I mean by the sunset factor.'

'So,' Nancy asked, 'is that relevant today? Orgies and all that? And irresponsibility?'

'Yes. Just different kinds of orgies, Nancy. The orgy of guzzling oil as if there were no tomorrow, and brutalising the Middle East to get that oil. The orgy of piling up food mountains, then dumping them on the Third

World to ruin their economies. The orgy of squeezing the Third World for the last drop of debt.

'And look at the multinationals polluting the world, destroying the forests, wrecking the atmosphere, starting wars, as the oilmen do. These are the orgies of people who sense that things aren't going to last. They may not even be consciously thinking it, but their behaviour betrays it.'

'All right, team. Back to work,' Nancy called out. 'Don't mind Frank: he's on one of his downers again. Camera over here please, Tim. You here, Frank, facing the camera. Let's have a look. Slightly wider angle, Tim – to take in the bay. Ready, Frank? Sound. Camera.'

***

'I DIDN'T LIKE him, Jack.' Deirdre, big, buxom and bonny, could be brash when she chose. 'Did you see the way he ignored Leila and me?'

'Dee, will ya come off it. You're not suggesting he's –'

'Sure I wouldn't mind if he was. What'd be the harm in that? Could be, of course, or maybe AC-DC. But I'll tell you this, he took an eyeful of Leila's boobs. Thought we didn't notice. And my arse too – don't you know I've eyes in the back of my head? Good taste your Martin has, I'll say that for him.

'But did you hear the way he called me Ma'am? That was to put a distance between us. To make me older than him.'

The two were clearing glasses and plates into the kitchen.

'Jesus Dee, you're as touchy.' Jack was exasperated. 'You're so damn hard to please. I was hoping you'd take to him. Anyway, he did talk to you.'

'Oh he had a couple of gallant comments, alright. But he was only interested in talking to you men. Look, it's a type – they're all over the place. They see us as useful for serving and servicing. But no brains. Anyhow, it's typical of what comes out of the army – any army.'

Deirdre carefully loaded the stemmed glasses into the dishwasher, and then paused thoughtfully. 'Didn't you tell me he was with the Americans in Kabul, well, Afghanistan? I wonder what he did there. Maybe he was one of those who did the torturing?'

'*Dee!*'

'I bet he did, Jack. There was a lot of torturing went on there. Somebody had to have done it. I bet he was one of them.'

'That's just unfair. You jump to these conclusions. For no reason.'

'What about my intuition?'

'For God's sake.'

Actually, I'm sorry I didn't ask him. I might the next time.'

'Jeez I'd kill you, Dee. You're not serious are you? Tell us you're not.'

Deirdre tossed her unruly dark hair and grinned.

'Maybe I am, and maybe I'm not. You'll just have to wait and see, Jack Stokes, won't you now?'

***

EX FIDE FIDUCIA – 'From Faith Comes Faithfulness'. Motto of Roedean School. It was at the top of some letter to past pupils that had come through the mail.

Meg lifted it off the mantelpiece. 'Did I live up to that?' She showed it to Will Davis, who had just stood up from the sofa to go home to his wife. 'Did I live up to it when I walked out on Colin?'

'Don't torture yourself, Meg. It's over now.'

'Will, faithfulness means staying till the end. *Till the end*. It wouldn't have been that long, anyhow. The cancer was already in him when I walked out. But neither of us knew that.

'At least I went to see him in hospital every chance I could. He was different then. Gentle. The way I knew he could always have been. I remember once he took my hand and whispered to me, "I was very hard on you, wasn't I?" I just held his hand and squeezed. I cried, you know, then.

'Maybe, maybe if he had recovered, we could have made a new start. I'll never know.'

'Meg –'

'But I'll never forget the pain after he died. A hard, deep pain, just below the ribs, that stayed and stayed and stayed. It woke me out of sleep. It still comes sometimes.

When I see Grace's face – she's so like him. The eyes.

'I got relief once, walking in a shopping mall. I was just empty, in pain, not wanting to go home. Then I suddenly felt he was beside me. And the pain eased. Of course it was just my imagination.'

'Well, at least that pain is gone now. Thank heavens for that.'

'It hasn't.'

'Ah Meg. Don't tell me –'

'It's back, Will. I told you it still comes from time to time. I just try to get my mind off it.'

Will took her gently into his arms. 'Poor, dear Meg. What will we do with you?'

***

'NO JOY WITH those pictures, Jack.'

'Break it to me gently, Des. Christ, that's a wild day out there.' Stokes hung his dripping raincoat on the corner hanger, and sat down at his desk. 'And bring us some coffee, will ya?'

'Uniform boys went to all three places,' Des called across the room. 'Didn't get beyond the door anywhere – didn't get beyond the gate lodge at the castle – but they handed in the two photos to be passed around. No joy anywhere. They were told nobody recognised them, in any of the places.'

'I wonder were they passed around at all.' Stokes leaned back in his office chair, yawned and stretched. The dinner with Martin and the Kings had run on late enough, but then Deirdre going on about Martin afterwards had lasted into the wee hours. Should wait till weekends to invite people, Stokes thought. But that's Dee for you: she does things her way.

Des came over with the coffee. 'Thanks for last night, by the way. Your Deirdre can sure cook. Even Leila was impressed. As always.'

'I'll tell her that, Des. Now listen, I have an idea. Should have thought of it long ago. Wee Bag O'Bones was a Saudi, wasn't he? And the Tech Bureau took fingerprints, didn't they? So why don't we get them to send prints to the Saudi authorities and see what they come up with?' He snapped his fingers. 'Why didn't *you* think of that, Des? It's your job to think.'

'It's yours too.'

'Aye, but sure haven't *I* a hangover!'

***

A NEWSROOM COMING up to deadline always gave Meg an exhilarating sense of urgency, while at the same time the quiet click of keyboards was strangely soothing. Paradoxical things, newsrooms.

Time to head home. Meg felt a lot better lately, for Will's kindness to her. Maybe he'd drop around after deadline. One good thing about doing features is that you're not so tied to deadlines. And you don't have to stay until the small hours, as the hard-news people must. And none of the stress of those deadlines.

Meg switched off her laptop, eased it out of its docking station, clicked shut the lid, taking a momentary satisfaction in its chrome-yellow shell, strapped it into its carry-case, and stood up to leave.

Then she remembered the cardboard cylinder that had come in that morning's post. She pulled off the end lid and found a rolled-up poster inside. As she pulled it out, a letter fluttered onto the desk. It was from some crowd called COREcumbria – Cumbrians Organised for a Radiation-Free Environment. It was brief and to the point:

Dear Ms Watkins

Up here we have read your articles about Freshpark. We feel there are a few things that you still need to know, if you are to go on writing about it.

We would like to invite you to a public meeting next Thursday, at Barrow-in-Furness, where you would learn a few interesting facts. And there are some people we would like you to meet afterwards. They are people who could fill you in on a number of things.

We could put you up, by the way, or, if you prefer, we could find a place for you to stay. Let us know if you can come, at info@core.furness.co.uk.

Yours sincerely

Roger Postlethwaite

PS Please read the poem on the poster. And ponder

it. Also, attached are a few websites we would like
you to look at when you get time. Hopefully you
can come.

Meg unrolled the poster and discovered a Cezanne-
like painting of Scafell Pike in the Lake District, and
below it some poem by a Lake District poet, Norman
Nicholson. For the first time it really came home to Meg
that Freshpark was right on the edge of Britain's most
cherished beauty spot.

The poster would look good on her study wall up
at Mother's, Meg thought. She rolled it up and put it
back in the cylinder. She'd get to the poem later, she told
herself, as she walked to the lift. And she'd think about
Postlethwaite's invitation.

9

THE MOUTH WAS locked in a rictus of horror, as in Edvard Munch's painting, *The Scream*. Eyes were shut tight, clearly trying to blot out the terror that was closing in. The torso writhed in anguish. It was blue in colour.

'You've heard the expression "a hollow man"?' Father Frank Kane tapped the rib cage and turned to face the camera. 'Well, this is as near as you'll ever get to one. Looks like a man, doesn't it? Well, it once was, in a kind of a way. This poor devil was running from the wrath to come, only the Vesuvius ash engulfed him as he ran. In the course of centuries the ash solidified, and the chap inside rotted away, until all that was left was a man-shaped hollow.

'So, some years ago a smart Italian poured plaster into the hollow, let it harden, and then peeled away the ash. And, hey presto, a man-shaped plaster cast. But doesn't he look as if he's still running, two thousand years later? And can't you still see the horror in his face?'

Frank reached down and held the claw-like hand. 'What's so awful is that such horror may well be part of the normal course of world events. Some eminent thinkers believe that catastrophes are normal and inevitable. They are how our world changes, indeed how our universe changes. It's just hard on those who happen to be around when a catastrophe occurs. Like the dinosaurs.' He looked up. 'That all right, Nancy?'

'Go on to the next piece, Frank. Just keep doing it to camera. Though we might use some as a voice-over. We'll decide later.'

'Fine. OK, here we go.' He faced the camera again. 'It can't have been too pleasant for the dinosaurs. That was one mega catastrophe. Wiped out without a prayer. But consider the Native Americans – their disaster was the coming of the Europeans. Could they ever have conceived of what was to become of them? Or could they ever have staved it off? Or consider the destruction of Jerusalem in AD 70 (round about the time of Pompeii's destruction, actually). Jesus warned the people – *Weep not for me, but for yourselves and for your children*. Could that catastrophe have been avoided? Or the Black Death? Or the Ice Age? Or the Irish Famine? Or World War One? Or the *Titanic*? Or the Holocaust? Or Hiroshima? Or Dresden? Or 9/11? Or the Tsunami? Or New Orleans? Were they inevitable?

'We can't rewrite history. Or even wonder how else it might have been, *if* … But this much is certain: if the experts are right, and catastrophes are part of the life of the universe, then there must be another one due.

'That means two questions. Firstly, is the next catastrophe years away, or is it just around the corner? (And let us remember how the people of Pompeii weren't aware of any impending catastrophe – they had no idea that extinction was upon them, despite the warnings.)

'The second question is – if a catastrophe *is* at hand, can we do anything to prevent it? The answer to that is – no, we cannot. *Not if the Pompeii Syndrome rules.* Remember the Pompeii Syndrome? People facing disaster simply refuse to think about it, *because* it's unthinkable. So we cannot see it coming. Thus even if the catastrophe *is* preventable, we cannot prevent it because we're in denial. And the more awful the catastrophe, and the less we feel in control, the deeper we bury our heads in the sand.'

'Cut,' Nancy said. 'Silence, everybody, please. Fifteen seconds' silence please, while Mike is taping. Thanks everybody. Well done.'

***

DEIRDRE TURNED IN the bed and snuggled her head into Jack's curved arm.

'Jack,' Deirdre said after a few minutes. 'Could Martin be in the CIA?'

'God, woman, would ya give over. Would ya lay off that poor man.' A sigh. 'Where do you come up with these notions? That's the daftest I've heard in a while.'

'Now, listen to me for a minute,' Deirdre went on, unperturbed. 'He's over here how long? Three years, isn't it? He's in the one part of the country that's swarming with Arabs. For God's sake, he even works with them. Doesn't it all add up?'

'It does to you, I suppose. In your crab-like logic, I mean. Will ya ever –'

'Seriously. Jack. I'd call it lateral thinking. If I was the CIA, I'd want to know what was happening anywhere in Europe where Arabs are getting together. Well they're here, aren't they? Isn't that what's bothering *you*? So wouldn't it bother the CIA too? So what would they do? Get an undercover agent. And get him to work among the Arabs. Doesn't it all make sense?'

Jack snorted. 'God Dee, you really are away with it, love. Sure doesn't Martin spend all his spare time looking after that aunt of his? That's why he stayed over here in the first place – sure you know that.'

'Indeed I do. And can you think of any better cover than that? No Jack, it's my intuition again.'

'I thought you said it was lateral thinking.'

'How about lateral intuition?'

That made Jack chuckle. 'Go to sleep, will ya, for God's sake,' he murmured.

***

'HEY, JACK. GETTING somewhere. Message here from the Saudis. Via Interpol.'

Stokes carried his coffee across the room and peered into Des King's computer screen. 'I don't believe it. Wee

Bag O'Bones is on their database. Read it for me, Des – I don't have my glasses.'

'We've really got something here. He was part of some radical circle that the Saudis say is linked to one of the biggest terrorist groups in the Middle East. That's what it says here.'

'Keep going.'

'Let me see. His name is – Ibn al Khalil – hope I got that right. Anyway, he was at some junior training camp in the desert outside Kaf, which the Saudi police raided. That's how they got the fingerprints.

'He was arrested but later let go. There were no weapons at the camp, but the police are certain it was an initial training process for terrorists. The "spiritual" part – that's what it says here. I presume they mean the brainwashing part. The police had been keeping him under observation, along with the others who had been at the camp. Apparently he suddenly disappeared, about five months ago. They have no idea of his whereabouts.'

'*We* could tell them, so we could.'

'That's for sure.'

'So now, Mister Sheik, we've got a Saudi terrorist, junior one maybe, but a terrorist all the same, who collapses in terror right outside your front door. Well, your theme park's front door. Then winds up dead. What does that tell us about you, Mister Sheik? What's it tell *you*, Des?'

'That we have to get into that theme park. Right inside, not just where the punters go.'

'Got it in one. And how do we do that, Des?' Stokes folded his arms and leaned back in the chair.

'Warrant?'

'Judge Farrell wouldn't issue one. Not enough to go on.'

'John-Joe could issue a Section 29.'

'No, he couldn't. That's only when there's firearms involved. Or explosives. And even if there were, he still wouldn't do it. He's scared shitless of Flaherty.'

'So how do we get in?'

'T'tell the truth, Des, I don't rightly know yet. But I'll find a way.'

***

'LISTEN, MOTHER' – Meg was hesitant, as always when asking her a favour. 'I have to go back over to Freshpark for a couple of days. You know this thing I'm working on. Can you manage?'

'Well, I manage anyway, don't I? What's the difference? You're mostly down at that flat in Leeds anyway. I'm used to managing.' A sniff. 'When did I not? But you *are* neglecting your daughter, you know. As long as you realise that.'

The fact was, Mother wasn't such a bad manager, even if she did moan. She was good with the money Meg gave her for the household. She was loving to little Grace, and Grace loved her back.

More than she loves me, Meg occasionally found herself thinking.

'I'M AN OUTSIDER there, Jack. That's one thing I do know for sure. Thanks.' Martin accepted the proffered sparkling water.

'Tell us about it,' Stokes said. The two men were sitting in their usual corner at Buckley's.

'OK. You know there's lots of Arabs at the computer plant. Bright guys, I can tell you. Some of them are real wizards. Then there's the Pakistanis I play chess with; there's guys from the Lebanon; even a couple of Afghans. But there's only three westerners besides myself, and none of them's Irish. One's Australian and there's a couple of Americans. So we're sort of outsiders, because the others all have Islam in common.

'They're terrifically devout. The prayer mats go down five times a day – not on the shop floor either – there's a special prayer room set aside for that. And they have a shift system to enable them to do their prayers.

'I think they're good people, you know. Some of the hardest workers I ever saw, and believe me, a software plant's no easy place to work. They'd put the folks around here to shame.'

Stokes sipped his pint. 'And you've seen nothing would raise your eyebrows even this much?'

'Just when I think about it, uh, there's one thing I do notice. It's – it's the way the bosses and the workers get along together. Almost like equals. There seems to be great mutual respect. I mean, hey, it's great. But it's not what I'm used to in the States. Maybe that's just the military thing, still in me.

'And some of the technicians fly out regularly to Jeddah. I don't mean the sales people – these are technicians. What would they be doing out there? I mean, they're computer technicians.'Course, maybe they're just seeing their families.

'Hey, that's another thing. None of them have wives and kids here. None of them. Strikes me as a bit tough, to say the least.'

'Martin.' Stokes spoke quietly. 'Could you get us inside that plant? No, wait, could you get us into that theme park? That's even more urgent. I mean, behind the scenes, not just where the public gets to. I need that more than getting into the computer plant. Could you think of a way?'

'Let me think about it. Leave it with me. I might be able to set something up. But it'll take time to arrange. OK?'

'Don't leave it too long.'

***

THE CORECUMBRIA MEETING in Barrow was not overly impressive, and Meg found herself wondering why she had bothered to come. Granted the ballroom at the Ambrose Hotel was full, but there were too many beards, and Meg was inclined to suspect beards. They usually went with sandals, and sandals went with – well, Colin had been into sandals.

Meg sat at the back and took notes.

Much of the familiar grouches were aired again, mostly about the Irish Sea being polluted, and about radiation reaching the Arctic. The allegations seemed far-fetched: surely no British government could ever have allowed such things to happen.

And how could a huge corporation like Brit-Atomic, created by that government, with the future of Britain literally in its hands, dare to countenance the unbeliev-able things that were being alleged? It was always the same in controversies like this. The most serious allega-tions are the ones that get believed. Throw enough mud. Still, must keep an open mind, mustn't we?

The speakers were mostly from Greenpeace and Friends of the Earth as well as COREcumbria, of course. And a couple of unknowns over from Dundalk, on the east coast of Ireland.

An elderly doctor from Freshton spoke about ill-nesses in the locality, and obviously had an axe to grind. When he finally ground to a halt, there was no time for questions, and the meeting was over.

'Miss Watkins? Hello. I'm Roger Postlethwaite – chap who invited you. Glad you could come.'

Meg looked up. A tall, thirtyish man, high forehead, good looking, stood beside her seat. No beard. Not even sandals. 'Could I get you a drink? You're staying here tonight, I believe?'

They found a couple of armchairs in a corner of the

hotel lobby, away from the departing crowd, and Postle-thwaite brought a couple of pints of bitter.

'So what did you think of it, Miss Watkins?'

'Meg, please. What did I think? Well, there was nothing new. Nothing I hadn't heard before. But nobody ever backs up their allegations.'

'Maybe because we were preaching to the converted tonight.'

'*I'm* not one of your converts.'

'Supposing I put some documentation your way? A bit of proof? Would that help?'

Meg sighed. 'If you could come up with some, it certainly would. But based on the evidence I've seen so far, Freshpark seems to be efficiently run.'

'Do you know what the *Mirror* called it? "The world's nuclear dustbin."'

'That'd be the *Mirror*, wouldn't it?'

'The BBC used the same words. Miss Watkins, do you really know what goes on there?'

'They reprocess, I know that.'

'They're building up enough plutonium and high-level waste to wipe us all out. That's what goes on there. Look, could you stay another day? Or even two?'

'Why?'

'I'd like you to make two visits tomorrow – I'd take you myself, only I have to work. Would you take a look at the Freshpark visitors' centre tomorrow morning, and see what you think? And then I'd like you to drop in on my uncle, Doctor Postlethwaite, the old chap who spoke just before we broke up tonight. There's a few things I'd like him to show you. I could phone and tell him to expect you. How about it?'

'I'd have time for the visitors' centre, but then I've to head for Kendal for an interview. But I may come back over here again next week. Perhaps I could see your uncle then?'

'Here's his number. Give him a ring when you're planning to come.'

***

THESE BRIT-ATOMIC PEOPLE certainly know their public relations, Meg thought. Their visitors' centre at Freshpark was quietly reassuring. She should have come in here the first time she was up. To see how Brit-Atomic tells its story. Would Freshpark live up to its awesome appearance? Meg would never forget that first vision of the plant.

The visit began through an eerie, purple-tinged tunnel that eventually brought you inside a giant globe. It was early morning, so Meg was almost alone as she gazed at the scenes unfolding across the inside surface of the globe. Scenes transmitted by satellite of what was happening at that very instant all around the world. A hospital in India using electricity for an operating theatre and, well of course, a nuclear plant generating the required electricity. Point well made. Meg had to smile. Nine out of ten for that.

From there, Meg strolled past young women who smiled encouragingly, to a high darkened hall where dozens of sentences in foot-high white lettering appeared and disappeared on walls and floor. You could stroll among the sentences glowing on the floor at your feet, and try to read one before it faded and another one scrolled into its place.

Meg was surprised at the openness and balance of what she could manage to read. 'The government must take the initiative and terminate reprocessing at Fresh-park,' said one sentence, attributed to some Irish government minister called James Murray.

This was balanced by a statement saying that 'More people have been killed in conventional power stations than ever in nuclear power stations', while the opposite wall proclaimed that 'Even without accidents, nuclear power is already a killer'. This, in turn, was answered by a sentence along the floor that claimed, 'There is so much pollution from fossil fuels that if it weren't for our lungs there would be no place to put the pollution.'

As Meg climbed the stairs to the coffee shop, she felt struck by the balance of the display. It seemed as if their PR people were willing to let all sides have their say, and give them space to say it. This could indicate that they were utterly convinced about the merit of nuclear power, in particular its safety.

But was *she*?

At the top of the stairs Meg paused. Something was

niggling at her. She went back downstairs. For another twenty minutes she stood in the hall of the white sentences, watching once again the ebb and flow of opinions.

Got it. That's it, she thought. Why hadn't she seen it the first time? Most of the pro-nuclear opinions were from highly respected scientists and eminent names. People with clout – people you would heed. Ah, but the anti-nuke sentiments? Most of them were attributed to 'UK citizen', or 'Visitor to Freshpark'. Or to some unknown Irish politician. People no one here would pay attention to. Meg smiled wryly. Ten out of ten for subliminal PR, Brit-Atomic.

Cleverly done. But what did it all indicate? And why did they need to be clever? What if everything at Freshpark wasn't as flawless as that fabulous Freshton Manor where they had hosted Meg?

Meg's dormant critical faculty was coming quietly awake. Everything here now was beginning to seem overly plausible. Now she had to find the flaws, and she felt convinced now that there might be flaws.

Maybe I'm getting better at it, Meg thought. And maybe Freshpark isn't quite …'

***

HUMPHREY HODKINS LEANED back in his black-leather office chair and brought his fingertips together. The leather creaked slightly. 'My dear Miss Watkins. Ah. One might think the French are overreacting to 9/11. Or the London bombings. I mean, in siting missiles around their plutonium factory. On the other hand one might think the UK response is an under-reaction. Maybe the right measure lies somewhere in between.'

Meg was sitting in the Kendal office of Brit-Atomic's deputy director, ballpoint and notebook poised.

'What do *you* think, Mr Hodkins?'

'Ah, well, preparing for a terrorist attack presents a difficult balance. I don't feel best placed to judge whether the French have over-reacted or whether we have under-reacted.'

Meg sighed. 'But you're director of operations, Mr Hodkins.'

'Ah, yes indeed. But, ah, the people who have to take such decisions are the ones who are getting the best intelligence of the real potential of any threat. The government is in the position to do that: it determines our security status and forms a view on whether or not anything above and beyond what we have done so far, needs to be done. I mean, Freshpark's not the only site in the western world that could be potentially subject to a future terrorist attack…'

The plummy voice droned on, and Meg switched to automatic. She kept writing the words, but her thoughts were on those bombs at King's Cross.

'… our plants are robust and able to withstand significant major damage.' Hodkins was still at it. He leaned forward, lips pursed, fingertips still together. 'It's an anxious time for everybody, of course, and I don't think it is easy to remove anxiety like this with words.'

'You're certainly right there, Mr Hodkins.'

'My dear Miss Watkins, it's important I try to give you as much reassurance as I can. We have to be absolutely prepared for all measures resulting in emergency requirements, but there are some things I am not able to give answers to for obvious reasons. I do not want to make life easier for people who want to perpetrate such acts.

'But, I assure you, we have done a number of very specific things, with increased checks on vehicles entering the site, as well as vigilance at the perimeter fence and at the access gates. That sort of thing.'

Meg stood up, and folded her notebook. 'Thank you, Mr Hodkins. You've been most helpful.'

'Any time, Miss Watkins. Delighted to be of help.' He touched her elbow gently as he escorted her to the door. A courtly man.

As Meg stepped into the lift, a new emotion was nibbling at her. It was a sliver of doubt about someone like Hodkins, in a post of high responsibility. Meg might feel a growing confidence in herself, but she felt somewhat less in Humphrey Hodkins. Could there be others like that in positions of such huge responsibility?

10

DES KING CARRIED an email printout across to Stokes at his computer. 'Hey Jack, your sheik's as respectable as they come. So the Yard says.'

'So tell us what you got.'

'Well, the dad was Trucial Qumran's ambassador to Britain until 1981, after which the country became part of the Federated Emirates. So the boy more or less grew up in Britain. Played cricket for Winchester, would you believe? Apparently quite a sportsman: he got a Blue at Cambridge, whatever a Blue is. Rowed in that boat race. Supposed to be the quintessential English gentleman. Played polo with King Charles, actually.'

'Loaded?'

'Family's richer than God, and it's not just oil. They're one of the ancient families of the old Trucial Qumran, and a good chunk of the territory still belongs to them. They're part of the Emirate clan, I gather.'

'So how does our sheik use his money?'

'Well, he owns a heap of stuff in Britain, mostly computer plants. Both software and hardware. He's got a plant in Jeddah, Saudi Arabia, and two in South Africa. Egypt too. And he has a big trucking company in England, head-quarters in Manchester. And he's the man behind that transport museum up in the Lake District, at Coniston. He recently bought three fire-engines from Birmingham City Council, who were upgrading, and built a new annex to house them. Top-of-the-line vehicles. Dennis chassis with Rolls-Royce engines. Worth a fortune.'

'Who the hell'd want to see fire-engines?' Stokes snorted.

'You'd be surprised. There's anoraks come from all over the world to see them. Oh, and the sheik's a big contributor to the Conservative Party. Could mean a knighthood in a few years. But they say he gives nearly as much to Labour and the Liberals.'

'Keeps 'em all happy, I suppose. Makes sense. Tell us something: where did he live? Like, before he came here?'

'Mostly England. Still has a place on the Isle of Wight. But he's been more than ten years over here. Got citizenship and everything. Invested a couple of million in Ireland to get his passport.'

'Aye, I knew that. That fucker Flaherty behind it, no doubt.'

'No doubt. Though in fairness he wasn't Minister for Justice at the time. But Flaherty had the clout even then, and was in the passport game when it was the thing to be in.'

'So this here sheik, what else do we know about the scumbag? What's he been up to over the years?'

'He was abroad for quite a while. They don't know for sure where, probably travelling around. He certainly spent a while in Abu Dhabi. And in Saudi Arabia – Jeddah, I think. And he may have gone further east. It was just after that, he bought the place up near Tuam.'

'Castle Patrick. Aye, indeed. Where he lives behind the high walls.'

'Well now, let's be fair, there *was* an attempt to kidnap him.'

'Nobody ever got to the bottom of that, did they? Fringe republicans, they said at the time. Or could it have been staged, so as to justify the high walls now?'

'Could be. Anyhow, that's all they dug up for us, Jack. Except he's been a model citizen since he settled here. Friends in high places, of course.'

'You can say that again, Des.'

***

AS MEG DROVE back to Leeds, her mind went over and over the white words she had read on the floors and walls of Freshpark visitors' centre. Were the white words just whitewash? Or was Meg just being paranoid?

Whitewash? Those words couldn't be. Some of them written by such eminent people – nuclear scientists, top administrators, leading politicians. Wouldn't they know better than you? Who are you to question them? What would your judgment be worth in the face of all that experience?

And yet, and yet – remember the way the words were marshalled on the walls? Big names speaking up for Freshpark; mere nobodies knocking it. That's manipulative, surely? So if there's that kind of manipulation, is someone covering something up? Maybe the Big Names' words are out of context. Or maybe some of the Big Names have motives for saying what they do. Or maybe some are just downright wrong. People can be wrong. Just the same as – as you might be right. Might.

Trust your judgment, that's what the counsellor kept saying. It's what Will says too. You've got a brain as good as they have.

Or have you? Memories of a ponytailed nine-year-old in jodhpurs picking herself off the ground, and her father saying, 'For Christ's sake can you get nothing right? Couldn't you use your bloody head? Look, forget the jump, you'll never be any bloody good.'

He had always wanted a son. A son would have known how to use his head. A son would have judged that jump.

If only Father could have spent more time with me. It might have been different then. *I* might have been different. Well, how much time do *I* spend with Grace?

***

JACK STOKES COULDN'T sleep, and lay listening to Deirdre's even breathing. Just listening to it soothed him. Thank God she's doesn't snore like me, he thought. At least she says I'm a snorer. Sure I know I am: doesn't my own snoring wake me sometimes? I even hear my own snuffles as I'm waking up. Is that possible?

What if this Omar scrote *is* that bloody sheik? Why am I so obsessed with the sheik? *Am* I obsessed? Or is it just that gut feeling? Maybe if I called it intuition it'd feel better. Like our Deirdre does. Only she'd laugh at me – she's the one with the intuition. Monopoly on it, that one has.

God knows the Brits gave the sheik a clean bill of health. English gentleman and all that. That's what they'd say, but I bet they don't really think so. The only English gentleman is – an English gentleman. They see the rest as 'foreigners' no matter what school they went to. Or what good shots they are, or how they sit on a horse. But nobody'll dare say that, because of the money. What's this they say – when money talks, even the angels listen …?

But what is it bothers me about that man, when I haven't even met him? And why do I keep seeing poor wee Bag O'Bones from Bantry morgue? Why, whenever I think of the sheik, do I remember those bones? And the poor divil on the Hanging Tree?

Deirdre gave a sigh, turned towards him and curved herself into his back. If she were half awake she'd call that 'spooning him'.

***

THE SHADOWS OF the two cats moved gracefully

on the moonlit window blind, and they seemed strangely large. Jack Stokes slid the blind up and opened the french window to have a look.

One of the cats jumped straight into his arms. It was white, with faint stripes. Des King picked up the other one. It was white, too.

Far out in the moonlit wasteland something white moved. Stokes stared at it for a moment, then hurled the creature from his arms as far out as he could. 'Des, throw yours out quick. *Now*. Do it. And shut the window!'

'They're not cats at all, they're tiger cubs. Siberian tigers. That's why they're white. Look away out there. Can't you see the parent following the scent? It'll get here in no time. If it sees us we're done for. For God's sake put out that light, will you?'

The men sat in the darkened room and watched the creature move in the far distance. It moved with sinister elegance, sniffing slowly back and forward, following a zigzag trail, and coming slowly but ever surely closer. It was radiantly white in the moonlight and, as it neared the house, Jack could discern the dark tiger stripes.

But Siberian tigers aren't that white, are they, Stokes wondered, as he watched the creature's gradual approach. Well, this one is. Maybe it's albino.

The men grew silent as the tiger neared the window and they saw its massive sinews. Finally it was directly outside, tawny eyes gazing into the darkened room.

What could it see?

Each man could feel the fear in the room. There's only glass between us, Jack thought. God, we should have gone back to the other room, at least there'd be an oaken door between us then. It's too late now. Any move and the creature will see it. Just don't move. *Don't – even – breathe.*

The tiger's snout and whiskers now flattened against the glass. The steam of its breath began to fog the surface. Tawny eyes glowed.

Now it was beginning to press harder. The glass creaked and suddenly the house alarm went off. The ringing was deafening. Des started shaking Jack's shoulder in terror.

Cracks now appeared in the glass, running from the tiger's snout outward to the corners of the window. Jack tried to scream, but no scream would come.

The cracks were in the shape of a tree.

Now the cracks *were* a tree. The boughs of a black tree in the moonlight. Things hung from them – wretched, ruined, rotting, writhing things. The tiger's giant eyes, like two harvest moons, glared through the branches. The alarm kept ringing. Des kept shaking his shoulder.

'It's *alright*, my love.' Deirdre shook his shoulder again. 'It's only the alarm clock. It's *alright*.' She took her trembling husband in her arms. 'It's alright, love. It's over, whatever it was.'

'Did I scream?'

'No, but you gave one awful, dreadful groan. As if it

was your last. And the pillow's drenched.'

'Oh Jesus Dee, that was a bad one. I never had it this bad. Wish I knew what brought it on.'

'It's that terrorism beat, Jack. It's killing you.'

'Aye, it is, so it is.' Jack sighed. 'C'mere, will we take another few minutes? Just to get over this. Then we get up, nightmare or no nightmare. At least the real world's a bit better, Dee. Not much though, I'll admit.'

***

FRANK KANE WALKED alone along the Amalfi promenade, prayer book under his arm. The Italian around him was birdsong – a languid, liquid language. It was a warm evening and the youngsters were engaged in their favourite post-prandial pastime, parading in front of other youngsters, and watching the talent in turn. Not for the first time Frank marvelled at the exquisitely simple way they dressed.

Two gorgeous young women, both in white chinos and tight sweaters, sauntered past, arm in arm. A longing tightened somewhere in Frank's gut.

Well at least I still notice them, he thought. Please God I'll never be like Mossy Culligan. Same age as myself, but celibacy's dried him out like an old stick. I'll never forget that time in Galway we went for a few drinks, and I admired the girl behind the bar. Isn't she something, I said. What? says he. The girl, I said, look at her. Isn't she something? Arrah, says he, I left all that behind years ago.

Hadn't even noticed her.

God, don't ever let me be like that. Maybe that's what celibacy's meant to do? If you suppress sex for long enough you lose the whole thing. Is that what the Church intends to happen? That you dry out like some Egyptian mummy? Use it or lose it? Will that happen to me?

And the Vatican's going on more and more about celibacy. Not an inch. In spite of all the scandals, they won't give an inch. Could that be another sunset factor? Just before celibacy blows altogether, they screech about how it can never be done without. And then it'll just fade away.

Will I be the last dinosaur?

Or maybe, could I be having a personal sunset factor? Certainly celibacy's starting to bug me in a way it never did before. Is this me getting all worked up like the Pompeii folk, just before *I* blow? Oh dear God, strengthen me. Guide me. That I may see Thy will and do it.

Frank sat down on a bench on the promenade and opened his prayer book. The psalm was the *De Profundis*: 'Out of the depths I have cried to Thee, O Lord …'

***

'STOKES SPEAKING.'

'Hi, it's me. Martin.'

'Hello, Martin. How're y'doin'? Chess working out?'

'That's why I'm calling you. Look, these chess buffs are a real nice bunch of guys. Clean as a whistle, all just trying to earn enough to bring back to their families.

Maybe build a better house back home. I've seen pictures of the kids and all.

'But wait till you hear this. They were talking about terrorism the other night. I brought it up deliberately, and they were saying there's been some talk among the Arabs about an extremist group centred in Tallaght. That's near Dublin, isn't it?

'And they mentioned a name connected with it. Some guy called Omar. Ring any bells?'

***

GRACE WAS CRYING as her grandmother bathed her upstairs. Maybe soap in her eyes, Meg thought. But Meg stayed at her laptop – she needed to get further into this Freshpark thing, and anyway the grandmother did a far better job with the four-year-old than Meg herself.

Yes, it's still strange calling Mother 'Gran', Meg thought. But then children have a knack of giving names that stick. Well, actually she seems to be getting used to it, now. Just needs something to whine about when she feels like it. But at least she's looking after Grace, and doing it rather well. If she'd looked after me like that …

Meg noticed the poster on the wall across from her table – the one Roger Postlethwaite had sent her. Still just pinned to the wall: she would have to get it framed. That rugged Scafell Pike could have come from the palette knife of Cezanne.

She got up and went across to read the poem printed beneath. She read it over twice. Norman Nicholson had written a deeply disturbing poem:

The toadstool towers infest the shore:
Stink-horns that propagate and spore
    Wherever the wind blows.
Scafell looks down from the bracken band,
And sees hell in a grain of sand,
    And feels the canker itch between his toes.
This is a land where dirt is clean,
And poison pasture, quick and green.
    And Storm, sky bright and bare;
Where sewers flow with milk, and meat
Is carved up for the fire to eat,
    And children suffocate in God's fresh air.

Indeed it was profoundly disturbing. Hell in a grain of sand … a land where dirt is clean. Children suffocating in God's fresh air. Sometimes a simple poem can say things far more succinctly than a report filled with deadly-accurate data.

But was it a bit over the top? Children suffocating? Come on. Then Meg remembered the internet references attached to Postlethwaite's letter. She started Googling them on the internet, but was not particularly impressed. There was really little new in any of them. She had come across most of it already in her research. And of course websites are no better than the people who put them up.

All the same old accusations: according to one website, Freshpark has turned the Irish Sea into the most radioactive stretch of water in the world. Discharge pipes open into the sea beside the plant, it alleged, which daily pump two million gallons of radioactive waste into the Irish Sea.

One website said that Freshpark is storing enough plutonium on site to wipe out the human race. Worse still, there were accusations that Freshpark had already pumped out a quarter ton of that plutonium into the Irish Sea. This and a cocktail of other horrors were supposed to have embedded themselves in the silt and sediments of the Irish Sea, and to have contaminated the fish and shellfish of the region. One website told of lobsters caught in the Irish Sea with levels of radiation forty-two times greater than EU intervention limits.

Hell in many a grain of sand.

At least most of the plutonium was stored behind thick bunker walls. Far more worrisome, according to one website, was the liquid high-level waste stored right on the surface at Freshpark. It was supposed to be the most dangerous of all, being the most vulnerable and easy to release to the environment.

That's what these websites said, anyway. But could they be believed? Who were the people that put them up? Greenpeace? Friends of the Earth? CORE? All those Green parties? Didn't they all have axes to grind?

Anyhow much of this was at variance with what Meg had experienced at Freshpark and the apparently efficient, responsible people who were running it. And yet, remember the hall of white letters at Freshpark? Hadn't that been a bit too slick, to say the least?

Grace, complete with Boo, the teddy bear, climbed up on Meg's knee, redolent of shampoo. Few things are quite as lovely as the smell of a child, Meg thought. And a bathed child is an angel.

Then she thought of what it means to be dirty. People who would make the Irish Sea filthy, if those allegations could possibly be true, would be the really dirty people. Not the ones who don't wash, but the ones who would throw filth into our backyards. And the Irish Sea is everyone's backyard.

The websites might have been terrifying, *if* you could have believed them. But where was the proof? Then Meg remembered the packet of documents that Roger Postlethwaite had given her, which he said contained much of the evidence she needed.

'Gran's going to put you to bed now, my love,' she whispered to Grace. 'And I'll be up in a while to tuck you in. Love you, darling. Kiss and a hug for Mummy, now.'

After the child was gone, Meg lifted the fat manila envelope out of her briefcase.

***

FIVE HOURS LATER Meg was still reading.

'Would you like a cup of tea?' Her mother stood in the doorway.

'Eh? Oh, thanks, Mother. I could do with one just now. In fact I could do with a stiff brandy if there's any left. This is the most terrifying stuff I've ever read in my life. If this is the real Freshpark, then we're sitting on a time bomb. Every bit of this is documented. And there's evidence for every single thing here …'

***

BOO, THE BATTERED brown teddy bear, a creature of incomparable ugliness, kept his suspicious little remaining eye fixed on Meg, who sat on the side of the bed, watching her sleeping child. The two little heads were together on the pillow – Boo lay on his back; Grace on her tummy. The duvet rose and fell ever so gently. Meg wondered how the child could breathe with her face buried in the pillow like that. A wisp of fair hair lay across the spring lambs that forever leapt across the flowery meadows of the top sheet.

The intoxicating sweetness of a sleeping child touched Meg's nostrils. Warm young skin, shampoo, talc, breath. The scent of love. Oh *God*, Oh God, what am I *doing* letting *this* slide through my fingers? This, that will so soon pass? Is any career worth it?

Meg had a sudden longing to pull the child to her and hold her forever. Instead she lay down beside the little one, with her face too on the pillow, breathing in the incomparable scent of sleep. There was a snuffle somewhere down within the pillow and a snub little nose turned upwards seeking air. A sigh, a yawn, and a hand came out to rub the nose.

Meg noticed the nail on the little finger, and it brought her right back to those tiniest of tiny finger nails on that six-pound bundle in her arms four years ago – nearly five now. It was those finger nails with their tiny half-moons that had so fascinated both herself and Colin. 'There just has to be a God,' had been Colin's comment, after long minutes of studying their miniscule perfection.

'Mummy.' The child's cornflower-blue eyes were open now and the little arms reached out. 'Mummy, are you going to read me Harriet?'

'I am, darling.'

'Oh goody.' Grace wriggled with anticipation, and snuggled down on the pillow, clutching Boo tightly.

Meg lifted Daisy Meadows' book from the bedside table and opened it. '*Harriet the Hamster Fairy*,' she began.

***

'WHERE HAVE YOU put the tea, Mother?' Meg asked at breakfast the next morning.

'It's in the tin marked *Sugar*,' Gran snapped. 'Can't you *read*?'

Breakfast at Gran's was a function of considerable consequence. There was no standing at kitchen counter gulping down scalding tea before galloping off, as happened too often in Meg's own flat. Indeed there was no *sitting* at the counter either, at Gran's. One sat down to a proper table covered in a proper linen table cloth, upon which a proper white china teapot sat like a little fat man with one arm on his hip and the other pointing at the clock. None of your knitted tea-cosies either. Good heavens, no.

Everything was proper in Gran's kitchen, including the loose tea inside the teapot. The word *teabag* was unutterable within these walls. Teabags were common things. Indeed Gran was convinced they contained the sweepings from the warehouse floor. If you opened one you didn't find tea leaves – just a sort of dust.

Toast stood to attention in its silver toast rack, beside the Fortnum & Mason's *Old English Hunt* marmalade, long since decanted into its white china marmalade pot with the slot in the lid for the silver spoon to stick out. At this table knives were not inserted into marmalade.

'Come along, darling,' Gran said to Grace. 'Don't dilly dally or you'll be late for school.' She turned to Meg. 'Put the things in the dishwasher before you go, will you? *I* haven't time.'

'Of course I will, Mother.'

'And put on the alarm before you lock the door.'

Meg sighed. 'Of course, Mother. I always do.'

'You forgot once – don't you remember?'

'That was ages ago.'

'Humph,' Gran sniffed in reply.

Meg didn't really mind the sniff. She was tired but elated after a night spent lying beside her child. I'm going to find more time, she told herself. More time for Grace – I've simply got to. And I'll start this very Saturday. *Anybody here know what Saturday is?'* Meg said out loud, to no one in particular.

'It's my birthday,' Grace said, with her little wriggle.

'Good heavens, so it is. Well, we're going to have to do something very special for a very special little girl, aren't we?' Meg clapped her hands. 'I've got an idea! How about going to McDonalds?'

'Oh goodie, goodie!' Grace wriggled again for joy. 'And can I bring Boo?'

'You can.'

'And can Gran take me?'

11

'I'VE BEEN THINKING about that Pompeii Syndrome,' Nancy Harris said to Frank Kane. 'Did you come up with that yourself?'

'I did.'

The two were sitting over coffee on the terrace of Hotel Santa Catherina. Below them, Amalfi's beaked promontory brooded over the Mediterranean, and its reflected lights were golden serpents writhing up through the dark harbour water. The two younger members of the camera crew had headed down into the town after dinner.

'And people don't like to think the unthinkable, that's it, isn't it? Even when facing extinction?'

'Not just don't-like-to, Nancy. They seem congenitally incapable of it. Like a constant of human nature, down through the centuries. As a historian I see it all the time.'

'So why can't we face things?'

'It's something I'm still trying to work out. Maybe it's a way to stay sane – I don't quite know. Especially when it's something we feel we have no control over. Certainly the one thing I have learned from history is this: in every catastrophe that has ever happened, people have refused to see it coming.

'Look at Sodom, in the Bible. Lot warned the people but they wouldn't listen. Pompeii Syndrome. And you know what happened that lot – sorry, no pun intended. And the prophet Jeremiah's warnings were ignored, too. Pompeii Syndrome'.

'How about World War Two?' Nancy said. 'Didn't Churchill warn for years it was coming? But nobody wanted to know.'

'Absolutely. Pompeii Syndrome again. And look at the Holocaust, for heaven's sake. Hitler had vowed it in *Mein Kampf* fifteen years before. And he started the concentration camps in 1933, the moment he got power. And he made clear on *Kristallnacht* in 1938 exactly where he was heading. But you see, extermination of a whole people was unthinkable. And if it's unthinkable, you can't think it. That's the Pompeii Syndrome.'

'Makes you wonder, doesn't it?' Nancy sounded thoughtful. 'But do you really think *we're* heading for a catastrophe, and refusing to think of it?'

'I can't say I actually believe it, Nancy. But something's bothering me – something seems to be lurking at the back of my mind all the time, and I'm not sure what it is.'

***

'STRINGENTLY REGULATED – that's all I can really tell you.' Brit-Atomic's press officer addressed

Meg with mellow assurance as he brought the interview deftly to a close. 'All our discharges are stringently regulated to rigorous standards, to ensure that health and the environment are properly protected.'

Hold it now, Meg thought to herself. Words can do things they shouldn't. Like Colin's words used to.

She sighed. *Stringent. Rigorous. Properly protected.* Just words. Words strung together. And where you'd expect words to be pathways, opening up communication, these words seemed like boulders placed in your path to stop you getting any further.

***

DOCTOR POSTLETHWAITE CLIMBED out of his battered old grey Vauxhall Astra and looked across the Freshton rooftops to Freshpark. He looked gnarled. That was the only word that came to Meg. Late seventies – maybe more – and gnarled like an old oak.

'They're expecting us,' he said. 'I phoned.' He opened a little gate into the neglected bungalow garden and pressed a bell at the door.

A nervous woman in her forties opened it. She wore an apron. 'Come in, Doctor. You're welcome, too, Miss. He's in here.' She opened a door off the hall and a stale smell mingled with something medical.

The child was yellow. It was bald. It was tiny. It looked at them with the enormous eyes of ET. It said nothing.

'Mark's fourteen tomorrow,' the mother said. 'We'll be having a little party, won't we, Mark?'

Meg was in tears as they left.

'His father works at the plant,' Doc Postlethwaite said. 'Could be sperm damage. Could you face a few more? I've quite a few between here and Workington. And there's a hospital ward down in Barrow I'd like to take you to.'

By the time the day was over, Meg had vomited twice.

***

HORROR, RAGE AND terror surged through Meg as she drove back to Leeds. Horror at what she had seen. Rage at how Freshpark had misled her. Terror at what could happen to Grace.

What could happen to Grace? – the child was nowhere near Freshpark. *Doc Postlethwaite had told her what could happen.* It could happen to children far away from Freshpark, but it would come to them *from* Freshpark. It could come tomorrow. Or tonight. And it was something far worse than anything Meg could ever have imagined.

And Meg would never forget the sights she had seen on her rounds with Postlethwaite. But they were reality without this new Thing even happening yet.

Once again Meg felt that stone pain behind her ribs. It had been there when Colin died, and the pain had just stayed and stayed. Before that was the time her father had taken his life. She remembered how, even four months afterwards, she had been standing gazing out to sea from Roedean's cliffs, and heard her mother and the headmistress approaching.

'I think she's well over it now,' Meg overheard the headmistress say, as the two came down the path.

The headmistress could not have been more wrong. The pain was a smooth massive stone that just filled the space where the ribs ended. And didn't budge for two years.

And now once more that stone pain was back. First it had been for a father; then for a spouse; now it was for a daughter. For a daughter that could be irradiated this very night, even though she was far from Freshpark, and turn slowly and surely yellow. For a daughter Meg loved but could scarcely be with, so pressed would she now be to warn the world and head off the disaster that could come from Freshpark.

But now the pain was different. As Meg drove back to Leeds, it was slowly morphing into a stony anger.

From here on Meg's writing would no longer be just a newspaper series: it would be a mission, she told herself.

***

OLD DOC POSTLETHWAITE felt tired as he sat on the cliff wall across the road from his surgery, gazing out over the Irish Sea. He was tired after the day spent with Meg. He turned to look at the rooftops of Freshton, nestling in the hollow behind him. Beyond those roofs belched the evil chimneys of Freshpark. At seventy-eight the doctor was tired of battling – battling to save the lives of the children brought to his surgery, and battling to get rid of that Thing beyond the town which was eating away at his people.

He was tired of writing letters to *The Times*; tired of the endless trips to Barrow for those meetings of CORE. But more than anything he was tired from losing a wife to lymphoma and two daughters to leukaemia.

He was tired of waiting for the next catastrophe. The first had been more than fifty years earlier when, as a young doctor, he had been called in to the terrible fire at Freshpark in 1957, and had had to treat the firemen, or what was left of them.

The authorities had simply sealed up the whole reactor and walked away, leaving the reactor's interior molten until this very day. They left those towers with the knobs on top that looked like penises, reminding you of what still seethed down at their base, ready someday to ejaculate.

Postlethwaite had always wondered what the next great catastrophe would be. There had been so many smaller disasters at Freshpark – no, far from small, but like the earthquakes before Vesuvius blew.

Now he knew. Since the Twin Towers and the London bombs, he knew. One look at that devil's panorama, stretched out beyond the town, and he knew. Freshpark had changed its gender. It lay wide open, waiting to be penetrated. A nuclear whore.

The old man turned again and looked out to sea. The penetrators would come from there, skimming above the gilded waves at sundown. Or they would come from the east, across Scafell Pike and the lakes and fells.

Or perhaps they'd come from high above. The grizzled head turned to look up at a couple of vapour trails inching their way west across the evening sky. That's where they'd come from. One of those vapour trails would detach itself from the others and curl gracefully downwards. Who knew when? No one. But come they would.

***

'I'VE NEVER SEEN you angry like this, Meg,' Will said. 'By God, you're a changed woman. That's what you needed all along – now I realise it. You needed to be angry. Were you ever this angry in your life before?'

'Never like this. Will, I'm going to get those Freshpark bastards. They're holding the whole of England to ransom. The whole of Britain. We're wiped out if a plane flies into Freshpark. And they know it. *They know it.* The government knows it too but they're all hiding the facts, and they're doing sod all about it. I'm going after those bastards. Just you wait and see what I'll write for Saturday.'

'Meg, remember what Jessica Mitford said? They once asked her, do you ever get angry in your writing? She said, "Never. I just tell the facts, and the reader gets angry."

'That's what you'll do. You plan a completely new series. Just the facts, mind. Start with the less dramatic, the pollution, safety issues, the dishonesty, then the forgeries, all the different scandals. You don't have to rush them. One every couple of weeks. Just get it absolutely spot on. Draw your readers each time from bad to worse, and climax with the likelihood of terrorists flying into Freshpark. But just the facts, remember.'

'I've been thinking something like that. A series over the coming months. Eight or nine sort of tranches, maybe more, ending with what would happen if Freshpark was attacked by terrorists. That's if it doesn't blow up before I've finished. God, I can't wait. If only for Grace's sake.'

She stood up and clapped her hands together. 'Oh Will, I've never been so angry in my life. I could kill. And I've never been more terrified. But y'know what? Strangely, I've never been happier.'

12

OUR NEIGHBOURS FROM HELL was the headline for Meg Watkins' Saturday feature on Freshpark. 'We've all read the tabloid stories about neighbours throwing garbage and even human waste into other people's backyards,' the article began. "Neighbours from Hell", we call them. But what the Freshpark people throw into our backyard is infinitely more filthy. Our backyard is the Irish Sea, and the excrement they throw in there is evil, for it brings death. They are the true neighbours from hell.'

It mattered little that Britain had signed up to the Oslo-Paris Convention – about cutting radioactive discharges at sea: 'The Freshpark nucleocrats have found a neat loophole, because they don't actually discharge their filth "at sea": rather they discharge it "into the sea" – *from the land*. In this point they are legally in the clear, if hardly morally so.

'But,' wrote Meg, 'doesn't the Bible say, *By their fruits shall ye know them*? And what are the fruits of Freshpark? Mutated fish which the fishermen throw back because they daren't even show them, never mind sell them. Spray from the sea that dries into radioactive dust and blows into the houses. Beaches literally too dangerous to walk on.

'Monster lobsters that do all but glow. Pigeons flying in and out of Freshpark, grown so radioactive that they are known as "flying nuke waste", and dropping excrement that contaminates gardens and fields for miles around. Babies stillborn. Soaring leukaemia rates on the coasts around Freshpark and across the Irish Sea, and rotting the bone marrow of Freshpark workers' children.

'Of course government scientists have insisted that no leukaemia link has been proven. They tried saying it's because people came from all over Britain to work in Freshpark, and just *might* have brought an unknown virus with them. But that notion has been well and truly seen off.

'However, if the government insists that Freshpark's link with leukaemia has not been proven, the answer is that neither is it proven that there *is* no link. Surely with children's lives at stake, that is the argument that should prevail?

'Meanwhile the little ones continue to die of leukaemia, or to be born deformed. And we have a Brit-Atomic's health-and-safety director quietly telling Freshpark workers that "if someone is that worried, it may be the proper advice not to have a family". *His actual words.*

'Reports come and go, hypotheses are proved or disproved, but one thing remains and needs no proof: those terrible pipes from hell, vomiting their two-million gallons of filth daily into the Irish Sea.

'We call the pig a dirty animal. Well, the people responsible for these horrors must surely be the filthiest animals in all the world.'

***

JACK STOKES' MOBILE rang, as he cruised down the Galway-Tuam road. Martin Gutman's voice.

'Hold on till I pull in,' Jack said. 'Loudspeaker's gone wonky.' He eased the car over. 'Right, Martin. What've you got for us?'

'I think I know how you can get into that theme park.' The voice crackled slightly. 'I mean, right inside the works. Interested?'

'Am I what!'

'Eight OK at Buckley's? I'll fill you in then.'

'I'll be there.'

***

'HOW LONG HAVE you been living here?' Martin Gutman asked Stokes, who had just arrived into Buckley's. He kept his voice low.

'Not so long. Why?' Black Jack was puzzled.

'Have you been in the area long enough for people to recognise you? You ever wear uniform here?'

'Answer to both is no. I've only been in Tuam a few times, mostly to see your goodself.' Jack smiled. 'Or that aunt

158

of yours, of course. And I'm less than a year working out of Galway, so there'd be few there would know me either. Or what I do for a living. Why? What are you on about?'

'Next question. Can you handle a camera? I take it you can: I've seen the digital job you keep in the car. You can? Good. Then here's what we do.'

Stokes leaned forward to listen.

'It's like this, Jack. The *Irish Times'* man here is a buddy of mine. I already talked to him. He's going to do a story on the theme park, and he's taking you along as photographer. The camera'll let you right in behind the scenes. How about that?'

'Sounds good to me.' Stokes glanced out of the window. 'Listen, will we sit outside? There's nobody out there, and we could talk easier.'

'Sure, let's go. Oh God –' Martin suddenly grabbed Stokes' arm. 'Quick, Jack. Let's move. Someone I don't want to meet.'

'What the hell's bitin' you?' Stokes wanted to know, as they sat down at a bench in the last of the evening sun.

'It's that uncle of mine,' Martin said, by way of explanation. 'Well, my half-uncle. He's in at the bar.'

'How the hell could you have half an uncle?'

'Well, he's a half-brother of my real uncle.'

Stokes sighed. 'This gets worse by the minute.'

'Hold on and I'll get y'a drink.' Martin looked through the open door, caught Buckley's eye, raised a finger to signal for one pint, and turned back to Jack.

Jack sat with arms folded, a quizzical look on his face. 'Now about this here half an uncle –?'

'You know my aunt Tessie don't you? Who tried to murder you with the frying pan?'

'Could I forget?'

'OK, so she's my aunt, as you know. Now that TV priest – a sort of male Sister Wendy? Well, he's my uncle. Father Frank Kane. The two of them have a half brother from their father's first marriage. So he'd be my half-uncle, wouldn't he? Seamus Óg O'Kane.'

'You mean that fuckin' bollix is *your uncle*? Why didn't you tell me? I'm getting outta here, so I am. Or I might be dug out of him.'

'Hold on, Jack. *I* don't want to meet him either. Look, let me get your pint. Oh Christ, no –'

Seamus Óg O'Kane stood leering from the doorway, all paunch and little chins, a half-finished pint in his right hand, a chaser of whiskey in his left. 'I thought I saw ye come out. No escapin' Seamus Óg, eh? So who's your new friend, Martin? I'll sit down if ye don't mind.'

'This is Detective Sergeant Stokes.'

'Ah grand. I know all about you. Black Jack, the Great White Hunter, isn't it? Black and white like the bottle of scotch. Hah, I like that – good, eh? Well, Great Alien Hunter, anyway. And fair play to ye.'

Jack was aghast. How the hell could this creep guess what Jack did, even if he did get it skewed? 'I'm no alien hunter, Mr O'Kane. Just a garda.'

'Seamus Óg. Call me Seamus Óg.'

'Well, Seamus Óg, I don't know where you got that there notion. Like I said, I'm just a "polis-man".'

'Who're y'kiddin? Sure don't we all know you're the one goin' after the terrorists. Sure the dogs in the street know that.'

'Well, Seamus, if I was chasing terrorists, you wouldn't be making it easy for us, would you? All your inflammatory carry-on is making things nigh impossible for us. We can't ask a question or they're calling us racists.'

'Have you caught up with that sheik yet?'

'What? Who?'

'That Sheik Aboud. You know damn well who I mean.'

'What do you mean, have I caught up with him? What's to catch up with?'

'I'll tell you what's to catch up with. He's behind every bit of alien trouble in this country. I have a dossier on him would take the hair off your head.'

'Such as?'

'Did you know he was in Afghanistan, just before 9/11? Visitin' relatives – how are ye! You know he flies out to Saudi Arabia at the drop of a hat? You know who he meets there? Well, *I do*. And they're not the nicest. And you know who his friends are here in Ireland? Some of the most dangerous wogs in the whole bloody country. Oh, and there's his other friend, of course – our bloody wog-lovin' Minister for Justice. No wonder you can't touch the sheik. Come on, what's this you're havin'? A pint, is it?'

'No thanks, we'll be going shortly. But Seamus, you shouldn't be saying those things. They're slander anyway, and it makes things very hard for us.'

O'Kane gulped down his pint, chased it with the remaining whiskey, and caught Buckley's eye through the doorway. 'Two more pints, Tony,' he called out. 'And a sparkling water for the cissy, here.' He turned back to Stokes. 'You don't believe any of this, do you? Why don't you ask Mister CIA sittin' right beside you? He knows all about it. He knows more than you or I do, put together. Don't ye, Martin? Admit it, now.'

Martin just sighed. 'There you go again, Seamus. If you keep at it, some day somebody's going to believe you.'

'There's lots already do, nephew.'

'Half-nephew.'

'Arrah, sure I'll settle for a half one.'

***

JACK STOKES WAS close to tears when he got home. Tears of rage. Tears of frustration. Of bafflement. The normal reaction of normal people after an encounter with Seamus Óg O'Kane. It was infuriating to know that the dogs in the street knew what Stokes did for a living. Well, maybe not the dogs, but Seamus Óg certainly did.

Deirdre took one look at him and poured him a shot of Jameson. And one for herself.

'It isn't just that, Dee.' Jack sank into his armchair. 'That fucker says he knows all sorts of things about the sheik. Told me a few things and hinted he had lots more. No, he didn't hint it, he told me right out, so he did. And said that Martin knew lots. Mister CIA, he called him.'

'What'd I tell you?'

'I know that's what you think. But I doubt he is. To me he's just a troubled young fella looking after a mad aunt. And working hard for a living.'

'God, you're a simple soul, Jack. Too simple for your job.'

'You don't mean that Dee?'

''Course I don't. You're just a damn decent man, doing a damn difficult job. But listen, you're trying to get stuff on that sheik, aren't you? Well, if I were in your shoes, I'd go wherever I could get it, and that includes this O'Kane creep. Cosy up to him, and suck out all you can. Sup with the devil.'

'Aye, and use a long spoon! Cosying up to that fuckin' scrote would just about make me puke. But I'll do it if I have to. And maybe I do have to. Only thing is, he's off for a few weeks to his house in the Algarve.' Jack chuckled. 'Among what he calls 'the wogs'. So it's wait till he gets back, so it is.'

'Did he give you anything to go on?'

'Well he did convince me I'm not on a wild-goose

chase. Like, that I'm right to keep after the sheik. You know how Flaherty doesn't want me near his dear and darlin' pal. Even the Super would like me to back off. And there's times I feel maybe I should. That I've nothing really concrete to go on except a gut feeling.'

'*I* trust that gut, Jack. With good reason.'

'Och Dee, thanks love. Well, then, Seamus friggin' Óg, you've done us one big favour in spite of yourself. You've given us a reason for staying with it. For staying on that sheik. Know what that O'Kane called me, Dee? The Great Alien Hunter. He was poking fun, of course, but y'know what a hunter does? He sticks to the trail, and never lets up on his quarry. God bless you, Seamus Óg. And may you rot in hell.'

***

'ALL HELL'S BROKEN loose,' Will Davis said, as he came into Meg's flat and tugged off his jacket. 'You missed a damn good interview last night. With that Bertram Nicholls fellow. ITV news – a wonder you weren't on it yourself. You will be, mark my words.'

Meg chuckled. 'I hear Nicholls called me hysterical and ignorant. Well, he would wouldn't he? Do you know something? All my life I've tried to please. Tried to be the good little girl, and be liked. This is the first time I've deliberately got people cross with me. And it feels marvellous. There's a *Pinot Grigio* in the fridge, by the way.'

'Thanks. You're getting to them, Meg, you know that? When they howl like that, you're getting to them. I can't believe you've come so far in such a short time. I'm very proud of you.'

'Just you wait till I start on their accident record,' Meg called from the kitchen. 'Then you'll hear them really holler.'

'I take it their record's not brilliant?'

'It's a catalogue of horrors, Will. You've no idea. I mean, starting from the near meltdown in 1957 which could have wiped out Britain – it just goes on and on.'

'Like what?'

'How about 172 reportable accidents since 1957? How about inspectors threatening to close the place down, and saying there's "a serious safety-culture problem at Brit-Atomic"? How about magistrates convicting Freshpark officials three times in one year? How about sabotage?'

'That bad?'

'That's just the tip of the iceberg.'

***

'CHRISTOPHER ROBIN IS saying his prayers.' The old children's poem from A.A. Milne often occurred to Frank Kane as he knelt by his bedside to pray. He usually got a chuckle out of it – the thought of a grown man kneeling to pray by his bedside, just like a child.

But it had worked for Frank for years. And, as he often told himself, if it's not broken, don't mend it.

It wasn't the same as a child's prayers, though. It wasn't just *God-bless-Daddy-and-Mammy*, and nice little rhymes about guardian angels. And it wasn't pompous nonsense like *O-Thou-who-dost-vouchsafe-unto-us* …There was quite enough of that in the church services that Frank had to endure.

No, it was quite a different thing they had taught him in the Dominicans, and it seemed to work. You talked to God as a person, as a friend, and then you listened to him. You shut up and you just listened.

First you started by saying thank you for the good things that had happened that day. Then you came to the 'gimme' bit. Give me health, so I can keep on doing what I'm doing. Give me inspiration, to do it well. Give Martin a break, and give him the grace to handle Tessie. Oh, and help him with his depression. Give us success with this TV series we're finishing. And make it do some good. And get Nancy off my back about celibacy. Give me purity – but not yet, as St Augustine said.

But Augustine was right. I don't want to be a dried up old stick like Culligan. Keep me fresh, God. So that people like Nancy will enjoy being around me. No harm in asking that.

If you're going to put an end to celibacy, will you do it soon? But sure who'd have me now?

You could fix that too, God. If you wanted to.

Extraordinary thing is, when you pray regularly you find you're actually focusing on God as a real person.

You're actually talking to someone. The person you talked to last night, who's been waiting to hear from you again. It really is *I-and-Thou*, like Martin Buber said. A real person there, a friend waiting, then listening, then whispering. And it's not someone away up there somewhere, looking down. This person is right here, all around me, and even through me, within me.

I'm supposed to listen to you, now, right? OK, I'll go silent. Now you talk to me. I'm silent now. Speak Lord, thy servant heareth.

I'm quiet. I'm listening. Listening. So talk to me, God. Come on. I'm listening.

Listening ...

Listening ...

And then, before I finish, I want to ask your pardon for whatever I did wrong today. But especially for the things I should have done, but didn't. Like caring. Especially caring, really caring, about other people.

13

THE FRESHPARK NUCLEOCRATS: *Dirty, Dangerous, and Dishonest.* It was a drastic enough headline, but Meg's Saturday feature lived up to it. Or down to it.

'Dirty?' the article asked. 'We've already shown how dirty – how some of these nucleocrats must be the neighbours from hell, and the dirtiest animals on the planet. Dangerous? Our last article told of the lethal waste piling up and up while the children die. These people's dirt is dangerous.

'But *dishonest*? Yes, that too, and to the extent that I would not trust some of them to administer a piggy bank, let alone the most dangerous thousand-acre site on the planet.

'Freshpark's record of deliberate falsification and deceit has made it a pariah around the world. Independent analyst John Bartholomew has highlighted long-standing doubts about the probity and validity of Brit-Atomic's accounting practices down the years which, he said, masked the company's downward spiral to insolvency.

'Then we had the German government saying that a

particular press release from Brit-Atomic was "as reliable as its forged test results".

'That referred to Freshpark's biggest-ever scandal. They had been making pellets of nuclear fuel for Japan, Switzerland and Germany. Now nuclear fuel, more than anything else, is something that requires at least honest dealings. Yet certain Freshpark people deliberately forged quality and safety records on this fuel – not just once, but on thirty-one separate lots since 1996.

'Of course when the Japanese found out, they shipped the stuff right back. It was an international humiliation for Britain, and the government had to send a high-level team scurrying to Japan to grovel. It's a paradox: there are no more arrogant people on earth than the Freshpark nucleocrats and their government backers, but there are none more ready to grovel than they are, as soon as profits are on the line.

'But here's another paradox: there aren't any profits, nor are there likely to be (except for the golden handshakes given to certain directors). Freshpark will never, ever, make money. And the explanation of the paradoxical behaviour is this: arrogant people almost always have an equal measure of stupidity. It's what makes them arrogant in the first place.'

***

ONE OF THE studio cameras swung around to Meg like a tank turret and its red light came on. This was it, at last. Having to defend your thoughts in front of the nation. And she was dog tired, after a sleepless night of anticipation. And breakfast TV is the roughest of all.

'Outrageous,' Sir Bertram Nicholls was harrumphing. 'The tenor of your article is utterly outrageous. And insulting. Insulting to the British government. One might expect that from the Irish, but from you … !'

Meg tried hard to make her voice sound steely: 'Are you saying, Sir Bertram, that the nucleocrats have been totally honest in all their dealings?'

'There are – there are imperfections in all organisations. And there are always a few employees who – who will let one down. Must expect that. They've been sacked, of course.'

'Shall we perhaps list a few of these, uh, imperfections, Sir Bertram?'

'I don't see what –'

'Would you call lying an imperfection, Sir Bertram? Lying, falsification, dirty tricks, broken promises – would you call these imperfections? What about the lies told on television after a nuclear train crashed into a car at Romney Marsh? They said it never happened before, but it did, didn't it? In 1984, to be exact.

'Sir Bertram, have you heard what Japan's trade minister said about Freshpark's falsified Crox documents? He said, "With these new reports of dishonesty, our trust in Freshpark has collapsed." Well, so has ours, Sir Bertram.'

'Just one moment –'

'Or how about the fiddled figures used to justify the Crox plant? They lied to pretend it was financially viable – Alice-in-Wonderland economics, experts have been calling it.'

I can't believe I'm doing this, Meg thought. Hope Will's listening.

'Look here, young woman –'

But Meg wasn't giving an inch. 'And what about the crooked accounting practices that analyst Mark Lewis has shown up? And the use of clients' advance payments to hide the slide to insolvency?

'And the Brit-Atomic people lied again about the reason for closing down their Valox plants. And lied to their customers about how long their Thule reprocessing contracts would take, isn't that so?'

'They weren't deceiving anybody: they got that wrong themselves.'

'So you're saying they're not just liars – they're incompetent? That scares me even more, Sir Bertram. Our lives are in these people's hands.'

***

THE HOTEL DINING room at Rosedale Abbey had a stunning view over the Yorkshire Moors and Cropton Forest. People smiled and nodded as Meg made her way to the table where Will Davis rose to his feet. A loden-green silk dress, slit to mid thigh, wonderfully set off her figure and burnished hair.

'Isn't it amazing what one TV appearance can do,' she said to Will, as he held the chair for her to sit. 'Just now in the lobby, two people I've never met in my life came up to congratulate me.'

'I'm not the least bit surprised, Meg. That was no ordinary TV appearance – you just ran away with it. We've just discovered you're a natural. By the way, I've ordered champagne to celebrate.'

'I should be at home with Grace. I'm becoming a worse and worse mother by the day.'

'Now stop it. You need time off, like everybody else. And when do you get it? How long is it since you did something like this? Early days with Colin, I'd bet. Besides, your mother's just marvellous with Grace. Almost a mother to her. You've told me that yourself.'

'I know.' Meg sighed: 'It's what bothers me sometimes.'

***

'I KNOW you have very little time in Leeds, Professor,' Meg said, 'and that's why I appreciate your meeting me. But when I heard you were speaking at the university, I just had to see you.'

Professor Dieter Vogels bowed. He was tall, lean and old-worldly, with a face like an amiable hatchet. 'Happy to be of service, dear lady. Please.' He indicated a seat in the hotel lobby, which Meg accepted. 'Now, how can I help?'

'Professor, I'm aware you had a part in persuading the German government to wind down its nuclear industry. At least to *start* winding it down – I know it will still take years. Now you're not likely to be aware of it, but I'm engaged in a sort of one-woman crusade to close Freshpark, the site of our main reprocessing plant here.'

'I am well aware of Freshpark. Painfully so, I might say.'

'Well, the authorities here are getting very angry with me, because of what I am writing. It was alright at first, and people listened to what I had to say. But now I'm upsetting too many people, you see, and the people that run things don't like that. There are even doubts at my newspaper now. No one has said anything, but I can sense it. Although my editor is backing me to the hilt so far, and that's why I can keep going.'

'So how can I help?'

'Well if you could just tell me, what was the argument that swung it with the Germans in the end? Your most persuasive argument?'

Vogels smiled. 'You may not believe it, dear lady, but it was an argument from Wagner. From *The Ring of the Niebelungs*, to be precise.'

'The *Ring*? Really?'

'You remember what happened in the *Ring* cycle? The Rheingold should never have been taken out from where it lay beneath the Rhine, and should never have been made into that ring. And then the ring became cursed, so that it brought no benefit to anyone who possessed it, only death.

'Well, to me nuclear energy is that Rheingold – something deep in nature that should never have been released. And plutonium is the ring that was fashioned from it. All it has brought is ruin and death. It started with death in Nagasaki, and since then it has brought nothing but calamity and pollution, fear, illness and death, wherever nuclear power has been established. And it has never brought the riches that we dreamed of – instead, massive and mounting debts, and problems that will last for thousands of years to come. And again death. Much death. I really feel sometimes that nuclear power is cursed. Like the ring.'

'Is that not a bit anti-progress, Professor? I know I'm being devil's advocate now. But how do you answer that?'

'I would argue that nuclear power is simply too dangerous to share this planet with us. We have learned this at great cost, but we *have* learned it. That's not an admission of failure – it's new knowledge. And it's also what you call cutting your losses.

'I suggest that we put nuclear fission aside for now as unworkable, untameable. However, if and when science advances sufficiently, so that maybe fusion becomes practical, then perhaps we could look at nuclear power again. Though I fear we may have a very long wait indeed, and I wish the fusion advocates would admit to that.'

'So you're saying, Professor, I'm not mad in wanting

Freshpark closed?' Meg was relieved. 'By the way, I'm not joking: a lot of people in the nuclear industry are starting to suggest I'm mad. There have been letters to my editor; they've said it on television several times.'

'I'm afraid it is they who are mad. Especially with the present terrorism threat, it is utter madness to continue with nuclear power. As Britain is doing.'

'Are you saying a whole country can be insane?'

'My country was. For twelve years. Under Hitler. Countries can go insane, just as people can.' Vogels glanced at his watch.

'Thank you so much, Professor. Now, I know you're in a hurry and I don't want to hold you, but could I – if I emailed you a few queries, do you think you could find time to answer them for me?'

'By all means, dear lady. I should be delighted. Let me give you my card.'

***

IT WAS MARTIN'S turn to tell a joke. 'There's this New York lawyer,' he began, 'and some guy asks him how much he'd charge to answer three questions. The lawyer goes, "A thousand dollars". And the guy's like, "Isn't that a bit steep?" "Sure is," goes the lawyer. "So what's your third question?"'

It had been a chance meeting in Galway with Jack and Deirdre, and the three had ended up in the Skeff Bar.

Deirdre took a swig from her pint of Guinness. 'So Martin, can I ask *you* a couple of questions?'

'Deirdre, don't start now – please,' Jack said.

'Sure can, Ma'am. Fire at will.'

'Are you in the CIA?'

Martin smiled, as he took off his heavy glasses to polish them. He looked different without them. 'There's only one possible answer to that, Ma'am. If I was in the CIA, I'd deny it, wouldn't I? So the answer'd be no. And if I wasn't in it, I'd say no, wouldn't I? So, Ma'am, the answer's no. All the way.' He replaced the glasses – resuming his slightly owl-like appearance. 'Two more questions, and that'll be the thousand dollars.'

'Did you ever torture anyone in Kabul?'

'Deirdre, for God's *sake*!' Jack spluttered.

'Never did, Ma'am. You have my word for that. There were a few rogue soldiers did that. That's all it ever was.'

'Did you ever kill anybody?'

'That's something you never ask a soldier.' Pain tightened Martin's face as he closed his eyes momentarily.

There was a silence. Jack had his head in his hands. Martin took out his inhaler, and breathed deeply from it. Deirdre just sat there, waiting.

'It was accidental,' Martin said.

***

'WERE YOU EVER wrong in your life, Dee? *Ever*?' Stokes was getting cross as he brushed his teeth that night.

'I was once.'

'Were you, now? Never thought I'd hear that in a month of Sundays. So tell us – go on.'

Deirdre tossed her head and grinned. 'It was one time I thought I was wrong. And then I found I wasn't!'

Stokes had to laugh in spite of himself. But he was still cross with his wife for going on and on about Martin. 'What is it really bothers you about him, Dee? Is it just that he doesn't pay you much attention?'

'Now that's not fair, Jack. I wouldn't want his attention anyway. I just don't like him. *And I don't trust him.* It's intuition.'

'Och for Christ's sake. So what about *my* intuition? You've always said you believe in my gut. An' it tells me to trust Martin.'

'Now you listen to me, Jack Stokes. I do believe in your gut. But every now and then a gut feeling can be wrong. I think you feel it yourself about that fella. Deep down you really know you got that one wrong from the start. But you can't admit it, even to yourself.'

'Och, will ya get into bed and shut up for once.'

'I'll shut up. But you'll be sorry you didn't listen to me. And I'll tell you one thing for certain, Jack Stokes – that Martin fella's in the CIA. And he's up to no good here.'

***

IRISH TIMES REPORTER Kevin D'Arcy drove past the lined-up tour buses, and pulled into the car-park at The Great Eastern Theme Park in Ballybrit. He reached across to the glove compartment for his notebook. From the other side Jack Stokes climbed out, a couple of high-end digital cameras slung around his neck.

'Should get a good picture story out of this,' D'Arcy said. 'That's if you can handle the cameras like Martin says you can.'

'Well, as the fella says, I'll be doin' as good as I can. But don't you forget to ask the things I mentioned. Come to think of it, we're both imposters, so we are. Like, with me taking press photos and you asking police questions.'

'Could you get in trouble for this? I mean, sort of impersonating?'

'Working undercover's quite legit. Anyway I checked this with the Super. They give us a lot more leeway in our section – maybe we have to bend the rules a wee bit, seein' as what we're dealing with.'

Mr Nahyan seemed slightly nervous as he received the two men in his plush manager's office, but he made them welcome and offered coffee.

'How about we do a bit of a tour first?' D'Arcy suggested. 'Then I'll know what questions to ask when we do our interview. And Jack here can get his pictures at the same time.'

'That's fine. If you'll just follow me, gentlemen …' Nahyan led them out to the crowded central plaza of the park. It was alive with young people – clusters of whooping teenagers, parents with little ones, young couples, and the noise was deafening. The men blinked in the bright sunlight.

'My God, this is a right success story, isn't it?' Stokes said. 'And it's grown since I was here last.'

'When was that, Mr Stokes?'

'Very first day. I was here for the opening.'

'And you got some fine pictures that day?'

'What? Och, aye, surely.'

'And what have you in mind for today?'

'Well, I'd like to get outdoor shots of the children, and indoor flash pictures of some of the rides. Specially the faces on the wee ones – they're always great. But what I'd really like are some behind-the-scenes shots. Like, what makes it all happen, how they control everything, how they maintain things.'

He turned and faced Nahyan. 'D'you know what took my fancy most, the first time I was here? Those models of Westminster and power stations like Ardnacrusha. And Moneypoint. They tell me the models are all built here on the spot, and there's more to come soon. Now that's what I'd really like to get pictures of – you must have some fantastic technicians.'

Nahyan's face tightened slightly. 'I'm afraid, Mr Stokes, all our workshops are out of bounds. Even to me, believe it or not. They're a separate little empire to themselves. With a separate manager.'

'But, why on earth – ?'

'If you think about it for a moment you will understand. We have brought here the most highly-skilled model makers in the world. Literally. That's how important this theme park is intended to be. But of course such people have techniques that must be kept very secret, otherwise well, everyone would be copying what we are doing. Think about it: it makes sense, does it not?'

'Aye. Maybe it does make sense.' Stokes nodded thoughtfully.

PART TWO

14

S HEIK KEMAL ABOUD stood with the Minister for Justice beside the helipad at Castle Patrick. The helicopter's rotor blades were lashing whips.

'Goodbye, Minister. Always glad of our weekends together. By the way, a little something for the party coffers.' The sheik pressed an envelope into the minister's hand. 'Or for yourself – wherever it's most needed. By the way, the envelope is beige, not brown, you will observe. Ha, ha. Not at all, don't thank me – can I ever forget your help? Thanks to you I'm an Irish citizen. A real paddy, eh?'

'Not in those robes, you aren't, Kemal,' Flaherty said. 'More like Jesus, if y'pardon me saying so.'

'But a very tall Jesus. Ah yes. And not quite so poor, *n'est-ce pas?*'

'No, not quite so poor, thanks be to Jesus – or thanks be to Allah, I suppose. No, we're all glad you're not poor, Kemal.' The Justice Minister chuckled as he deftly slid the envelope inside his jacket.

He shook hands, ducked under the rotor and climbed into the white-and-gold machine. Everything white and gold – Flaherty liked that. Even the leather seats were white. Good taste, the sheik had. Flaherty appreciated good taste.

The whine of the blades grew shrill as they faded to a ghostly parasol, the wash plucking at the sheik's white robes. The helicopter moaned and hauled itself high above Castle Patrick. As it lowered its head and thudded away, the sheik was still waving.

***

SHEIK ABOUD FINISHED waving, but stood watching until the helicopter was a dot in the sky. He strode briskly into the castle, turned down a passage towards the closed-off east wing, went through two electronically-controlled doors, to the great ballroom where Omar al Naim was waiting.

The Minister for Justice had never visited the east wing. And never would. Nobody ever went there except the sheik's closest retainers.

Omar al Naim bowed at the sheik's arrival, his reflector shades glinting. He was as tall as the sheik, but his black *jalabi-ya* and head-dress contrasted with the sheik's white robes. Two young men stood hesitantly to one side. Omar presented each, and Sheik Aboud bowed slightly. '*Mar-habah, ekwah!*' he said, patting each shoulder as he did so. 'Welcome, my brothers! Welcome to *Beit al-Shuhadaa*. The House of Martyrs. By coming here, you prove that you are ready for the Jihad. You have proven that you have overcome the love of the world and the abhorrence of death.' He waved towards the strange structures in the ballroom. 'Tell them,' he said to Omar.

'Gentlemen,' Omar began, 'You will notice I am speaking English to you. In fact it will always be English here, because that will be the language of your training. It is the international language of aviation. Now, you already know why you are here – to fly and to die. This is your part in the Jihad, which is an obligation on each and every one of us. And you are privileged to have been selected out of thousands who would willingly take your place.

'Your first duty is to learn to fly, and I am your instructor. But this is a unique flying school – here you learn to fly without ever leaving the ground. We have twenty-three willing young martyrs like you already trained, who return here each day to refine their skills for the moment when the call will come. You may be the last we shall train, because the call will come soon.

'What you see in this room are four aircraft simulators. One replicates the simple cockpit of a single-engined training plane – a Cessna 150. The second simulator is the cockpit of a modern twin-engined light aircraft – a Piper Apache. The third one, that large structure at the left end of the ballroom, has been especially built to replicate the cockpit of a Boeing 737-800 series jet, and the one beside it is an exact replica of the Airbus A320 cockpit. These are the ones on which you will do your final training: the 737 and the Airbus are the workhorses of most European airlines.

'These last two simulators are computerised to enable the trainee to fly into any European airport. But – and this is where they differ from all other simulators in the world – they are also specially programmed to simulate flying into Freshpark, as well as into fourteen British nuclear power sites, plus seventeen of the biggest European nuclear sites. Including, of course, Cap La Hague, which we call "the Freshpark of France".'

The sheik spoke. 'Do you know how Freshpark and Cap La Hague differ from almost all other nuclear plants? No? Ah well, perhaps you should know at this stage. These are the two sites that take in spent fuel from the rest of Europe – indeed from the rest of the world. These two places are the nuclear dumps of the world. Once those dumps go up in smoke, that smoke will terminate the West.'

He gestured with evident respect to Omar. 'This is the man who will train you to fly into the key nuclear facilities of Europe. Salute him now, for he is the man who will write the history of the world.'

***

'MY MOTHER ALWAYS said red hair was a sign of bad breeding. How about that, Will?' Meg struggled to push some stray hairs back into her clip, as Will sat down across from her in the canteen.

'She actually told you that?'

'Oh yes. She often said it.'

'Where'd she get that idea?'

'Oh, she maintained it must have come through my father – the hair, I mean, not the idea! "It's from those ghastly Watkins people," she'd say. She had this notion red hair meant Scottish or Irish blood, which she thought wasn't quite kosher. She was frightfully class conscious. Still is.'

'But your father had lots of class, hadn't he? Wasn't he a cavalry officer or something?'

'He was in one of those Guards regiments. Coldstream, I think. But I wouldn't mind Mother. She always had ridiculous notions and she had to find some way to look down on him.'

'Tell me about your father.'

'What's there to tell? He fought at Suez, and Aden, I think. And later in the Falklands. I think he got the DSO there. Or some medal, anyway. He was quite a hero, I believe. Never said much about it. I learned most of it when *The Times* ran his obituary.'

'But what was he *like*?'

'*The Times* said he wasn't just a career soldier. They said he fought because he believed the fight was necessary, and that he never, ever walked away from wrongdoing. I think I remember those words. Something like them anyway.'

'No, what I'm asking is, what was he like as a man, as a person?'

'I don't know, really. He was so remote, so silent. So old, I suppose. It was my mother who did the screeching in our house: I suppose that was enough for all of us. Anyway, he hadn't much feeling for me.'

'Tell me Meg, who sent you to Roedean?'

'How do you mean? My parents did, of course.'

'No. I mean, who actually made the decision?'

'Um, I suppose it was Father. Yes, come to think of it, it had to be. Because I remember Mother saying, "I don't want her going to that school and coming back to tell me what to do." She must have been against it.'

'Who arranged the riding lessons for you? You told me you used to ride a lot.'

'I suppose Father set them up. Well, yes, because he used to take me to the stables. And then growl at me for not being much good. He always wanted a son, you see.'

'How do you know that?'

'Mother always said it.'

'Yes, she would, wouldn't she?' Will sat up and stretched his arms. 'You know, I think your father loved you to bits. And I think your mother was jealous of that.'

'God Will, don't talk such bullshit. You never knew my father. *I did*. And you haven't met my mother. How can you –'

'Listen to me for a minute. Your father sent you to Roedean, yet you told me there wasn't a lot of money.

Would he have made that kind of sacrifice if he didn't love you? And weren't there ballet lessons as well as the riding? So, alright, he didn't talk much to you – ever hear of the strong silent type? Stiff upper lip and all that? He was a military man, remember. Did he ever express any real interest in you? Or did he just ignore you?'

'Well, I once heard him say education's the best investment of all. And he'd give out to me about my posture. He'd tell me straighten my shoulders, and pull in my tummy "till it touches your backbone" was the way he'd put it. I used to think – that's what he'd tell a son.'

'Nope. He had a beautiful daughter, and he wanted her to walk like a queen. It's clear as day, Meg. The man loved you. Probably more than he loved his wife.'

'Good God.'

'And if that's the case, your mother would have to be jealous, wouldn't she? If she's the character you've described to me, anyhow. With him spending that money on you, when there was so little. And taking you riding – spending all that time on you. She'd have done anything to keep you two apart, wouldn't she? Like telling you he'd never wanted a daughter. Oh, and one other thing. Was your father good-looking?'

'What? Uh, I suppose he must have been. People said he was, anyway. Of course he was old when I remember him. But my aunt once told me he was very handsome as a young man – "dashing" was the word she used.'

'And do you take after him?'

'Maybe. I don't really know.'

'Of course you do. And it's another reason for jealousy. You were better looking than your mother, since you take after those ghastly Watkins people, as she put it. Of course she was jealous. Could you really blame her?'

'You know what she said just the other day, Will? She said to me, "You were always good at English, you know." But she never, ever, told me that as a child. She never praised me. Mostly told me I was selfish and stupid. And I believed her. Still do. Often when I came back from ballet, I'd want to show her my steps. She'd always say, some other time, I'm busy now. She wasn't much of a mother, in some ways.'

'And yet you say she does pretty well at mothering Grace?'

'That's what's so strange – yes, she seems to do alright. Rather well, actually. I have to admit that.'

'That's because she's not jealous of Grace. That's your real mother coming out. The one she could never let you see. Do you think you could accept that, after all you've been through? It would help, you know. Help *you*. What is it the French say? *Comprendre tout, c'est pardonner tout.* To understand all, is to forgive all.'

Meg sighed. 'Don't say any more, please. I – I just need to think this through.'

***

MEG LOOKED PALE when she sat down at her desk

the next day. It had been a sleepless night. Will's words had whispered around within her head – 'loved you to bits' – 'wanted you to walk like a queen' – 'more than he loved his wife' – '*comprendre tout ...*'

And her father's sparse words had chased each other through her sleepless brain – 'till it touches your backbone' – 'education an investment' – 'she's *going* to Roedean.'

And then Meg remembered how her father had once asked her to come for a stroll with him. Only the once. She, who had always craved his attention, had by then grown into a snooty teenager, home on holidays from Roedean, and no longer vying for her father's love. She had sensed the old chap trying to work up to asking her to come with him, trying to get the courage to ask, but she gave him no help. And when he finally did ask, she told him No. Oh God.

A few tears came. And then Meg got to thinking of her father's final days. Half his pension lost, and the shame of it. Roedean unpayable. And no one to turn to – wife locked down within her own wretchedness; daughter away at school. The loneliness. The hopelessness. The bleakness. The service revolver.

Now the tears came in floods, unstoppable, drenching the pillow. By morning Meg's rib cage ached from the violence of it.

But now she knew she had once been loved.

***

SHEIK KEMAL ABOUD sat among cushions at one end of the Castle Patrick ballroom. Gathered around him were twenty-five young men. The Arab youngsters reclined easily on cushions on the floor; the nine westerners seemed less used to the cushions.

The scene was that of a holy man surrounded by his disciples. Omar al Naim sat to the sheik's left, slightly behind him. As always Omar's dark robes contrasted with the sheik's white ones, and he wore his usual reflecting shades. Both wore the *tabiya* head-dress. The young people surrounding them wore mostly jeans and tee-shirts, but three were in *jalabi-yas*.

The sweet smoke of bakour hung in the air.

The sheik's dark eyes held everyone's. He spoke gently, but with uncanny fervour, which somehow softened his patrician accent. 'I am talking to you every few days, my brothers, so that you may maintain your spirits and keep faith with your commitment. You have all undertaken to die, although not all of you may be finally chosen this time. You die so that the Great Satan may also die.

'America, the Great *Shaytan*, the Great Satan, has brought hunger, pestilence, war and wickedness to the world. He has raped our countries with his tanks to take our oil. He has seduced our children with his evil culture. He has stripped our men naked in his prisons and humiliated them beyond belief. He has laid bare our women with his infidel fashions. He has destroyed our children with his sex tourism. He has spread his filthy philosophy of instant gratification among our young. He has provoked war between our peoples, so he can sell his tanks and guns. He has given our people over to the Jews. And all to make money for those Jewish Wall Street bankers.

'God demands that the Great Satan be brought down. But the Satan is waiting, and the Satan is wise.'

The sheik brought his palms together. 'But not as wise as we are. The Satan expects us to strike again at New York and Washington. We will not do so. We will take the destruction where it is not expected.

'Remember, my young brothers, this Satan is not just America. Satan is the West. So we strike at the West's underbelly, which is Europe. As we did in London. But this will be a million times greater. In one blessed day we will put an end to Europe, flying airliners simultaneously into nuclear centres in Britain, France, Belgium, Germany, the Netherlands, Sweden, Spain and Switzerland.

'We may not succeed in all our strikes, but if we can cause at least Freshpark and Cap La Hague to erupt, much of Europe will come to an end. You already know how these last two targets differ from all the rest, because of the plutonium and the high-level waste they store there. That is what will put an end to Europe.

'And I do not have to tell you that the wide arms of God await you after the deed, and the abode he has prepared for you will be beyond your dreams.'

Sheik Aboud turned slowly to look into each pair of

eyes. 'But remember what I said to you: any young man among you who feels he is not yet ready for death, has only to say so, to Omar or to me. Such a one will leave here with honour, as one of our young men did some weeks ago. He is now where he needed to be. And so may you be, if you so decide. You too may leave with honour. That is my promise. You will return to a place where you will have all the time you need to prepare for when the next call may come. As come it surely will.'

The sheik rose, and all the young men rose too. 'I leave you now, my young brothers. Omar will direct your practice. Remember, practise constantly. America is wondering at what flying schools we now train our pilots. This room is our flying school – it is all we need. With these machines, which America invented, you are becoming expert pilots without ever leaving the ground. Practise, practise, my dear brothers. And may God be with you in the cockpit. *Allah yiekremak.*' The sheik glided from the room.

Omar clapped his hands. 'Those scheduled for training take your places now. The rest of you return to work. There's a minibus going to Galway and two of the Humvees will take people to Trucial Software.'

15

'YOU'VE BEEN OUT at that Hanging Tree again, haven't you?' Deirdre said.

Jack Stokes sighed. 'I have, love. How'd you know?'

'I always know when you've been out there. There's that look in your eyes. Jack, I don't mind, honestly. But are you sure it's good for you? D'you even know why you go there?'

'God, if I knew that I'd be a lot wiser. It's just I seem to be able to do a bit of thinking there. Maybe, maybe even get a bit of inspiration.'

The children had eaten and the two were re-setting the table for their own meal. They sat down and Jack held the plate for his wife to ladle the stew.

'Is it the Tree that affects you?' Deirdre asked. 'Or what hung from it?'

'Both really. When I go out there I find myself thinking of all the poor divils that hung from it down the years. I know it's ridiculous, Dee, but then I start thinking how the Tree itself has been terribly wronged over all those years. Perverted from the task God gave it. Bearing fruit. Well, maybe just acorns. I dunno. It's not an evil tree, but evil's been done to it. Terrible evil.'

'My God, you're a bit of a poet now, Jack. Or maybe a mystic or something? I suppose now you're going to tell me you talk to the Tree!'

'Know what, Dee? Sometimes I nearly do. There's an old stump I sit on, and I sort of meditate. And I often come away a bit more tranquil. Even sometimes with fresh ideas what to do next. Could it be the Tree? Or all those poor hanged fellas trying to guide me? Or am I just goin' nuts?'

'I don't know, love. But there's one thing I do know and it's that my Jack Stokes is a million miles from going nuts. He's the sanest man I know.'

***

'ONE OF THE really great war films,' Frank Kane was saying to camera, 'was *The Dam Busters*. It told how scientists developed a special bomb to bounce along the surface of the water, and to sink at the exact spot that would destroy the Möhne Dam in Germany.'

A small crowd had gathered near Pompeii's south gate to watch the filming.

'Well, many years later I got to know an old artist who lived on a bluff above Möhne Lake. He remembered clearly the night the Lancasters came, and he had been able to look down and watch the dam go. He told me something I never heard before.

'He said there had been a village below the dam. Set right down in the valley, with the dam wall towering high above. The parish priest of the village was forever warning that the Allies would surely bomb the dam. But the people treated him like Jeremiah, and nobody would listen.

'In fact, in the end the SS called him in and accused him of undermining morale. They threatened him with arrest and a concentration camp.

'He of course drowned with all his people when the dam went, and a wall of water came down the valley.'

Frank turned to face the Pompeii gate. 'You see,' he said, 'the Pompeii Syndrome is not confined to Pompeii. It is alive and well today. Nearly three decades ago Mount St Helens in Washington State was swelling upwards at the rate of three metres per day. Governor Dixie Lee Ray ordered the local sheriff to clear everyone out. Many refused to leave.

'There was an old man called Harry Truman who rented out fishing boats on the lake beneath the mountain. I actually rented from him, while I was doing summer work as a priest at nearby Longview. I remember Harry had a pink Cadillac of which he was very proud.

'Anyhow, he refused the sheriff's orders to move. So now he and his pink Cadillac, and about forty neighbours, lie beneath the cubic mile of mountain that blew off Mount St Helens.

'The Pompeii Syndrome is thriving. Disasters happen

to others, never to us. Since a catastrophe is unthinkable, we do not think it. We're like rabbits caught in lights. A bird facing a snake.'

Frank paused, while the camera continued to roll. 'People sometimes ask me, as a historian, if I think we are facing another disaster today. My answer is, I simply do not know.

'But this I do know. If a catastrophe comes, it won't be global warming. It won't be Aids. Nor pollution. It will be anger. Global anger.'

'Cut!' Nancy Harris called.

***

'WHAT DID YOU mean when you said *anger*?' Mike Stewart wanted to know. 'How can anger be a catastrophe?'

'Here's how, Mike. Remember the late George W. Bush saying the West is hated because it has freedom? And that the rest of the world is envious of that freedom?

'Well, he was wrong. The West is hated for what it has done with that freedom. Because it has misused its freedom and its power, to exploit the rest of the world. We have ruined the Middle East to be sure of cheap oil. We've used monstrous trading laws to exploit the Third World, so we get cheaper coffee. We've squeezed them for debt until they've literally died of starvation.

'Do you know that one of the big sportswear companies paid a celebrity the equivalent wages of 30,000 of its workers in the Far East? Children who ruin their fingers hand-sewing trainers for our youngsters. Paid him that just for his publicity.'

'Who's having coffee?' Nancy interrupted. 'Don't know if it's fair-trade.' The team was sitting around a table in one of Amalfi's seafront terrace restaurants. It was Nancy's treat.

'Espresso for me, please, Nancy.' Frank was on a roll. 'That's just an example. But worse than any of that, we've violated cultures around the world with our violent films, our child pornography, our drugs and alcohol, our internet, our malls and supermarkets, our shopping mania, our risqué fashions, our sex tourism. Even our fast-food outlets.

'Do you realise that many in the East see these things as a virus? A virus takes over an organism and gets its host to help it propagate. That's how Islamic people feel when they see their own children spurn their ancient culture, opting for the worst of the West. They feel the West is a virus that is destroying their culture and that it must be eradicated.'

He turned to Mike. 'Do you know Wagner's *Ring*?'

'Well, "Ride of the Valkyries", I suppose. *Apocalypse Now*. Right?'

'There's a lesson for us in the *Ring*. Wotan was king of the Gods, and couldn't understand why he was hated. He was hated because he had used his supreme power, not for justice, but to break his promise to the Giants, to cheat the Dwarves, to manipulate the Humans, to deprive the Rhine Maidens of the gold that was theirs, and to treat his own daughter Brünnhilde unspeakably.

'In the end he built Valhalla, the mightiest fortress ever conceived, where he and the Gods could be safe forever behind eternal walls, safe from all the enemies their selfishness had created.

'But they weren't safe. They could never be. In the end Valhalla burned to the ground, and we had the Twilight of the Gods.'

Frank looked around the table. 'Sounds familiar, doesn't it? Cheating; broken promises; manipulation; exploitation? The West does it all, on a far more monstrous scale than Wotan. The only thing that hasn't happened yet is our Valhalla burning down.

'We're the Gods of Valhalla. We live like gods, compared to the rest of the world. And we hide behind walls clutching our nuclear thunderbolts. And we're utterly indifferent to the sufferings of anyone else. That's why we're hated, just as the Nordic Gods were.

'I was thinking too, the Nordics had their great Tree of Life – *Yggdrasil* I think they called it – the World Ash Tree. It was the Pillar of the Universe: it grew in and through everything, holding together all existing things. But on the other hand the people of Pompeii had a Tree of Death – Pliny's pine tree that rose into the sky above Vesuvius and brought extinction to them all. I was wondering – could we too have a World Tree of Death, its branches growing and spreading above us at this very moment? And could that tree be – Global Anger?'

***

DIRTY, DANGEROUS, DISHONEST, AND DUMB, ran the headline over Meg Watkins' latest piece on Freshpark. The opening paragraph set the tone:

'When knaves are also fools, we need to beware. We already know that some of our nucleocrats are dirty, dangerous and dishonest. *But what if they're dumb as well?*

'Then we truly are in trouble. Because if some of the people in charge of the world's most dangerous place are themselves stupid and incompetent (as well as dishonest), then what, besides prayer, can save us from the almost unthinkable consequences of their stupidity?

'And yet that is the only conclusion one can draw from the evidence – court prosecutions and press reports of breaches of safety, management incompetence, a culture of complacency, the lack of central control of safety, falsification of safety records, carelessness, preventable accidents, pollution of the sea, the fouling of the air and the ruination of beaches.

'What of the transporting of plutonium right across the world's oceans, in the teeth of terrorists who need just a few kilos to make an atomic bomb? Is that not incomparably stupid?

'What of the hundreds of cubic metres of high-level waste lying on the surface of Freshpark? Or the stockpiling of over 100 tonnes of plutonium powder, so toxic that inhaling 80 micrograms is fatal?

'And the people in charge of these horrors have been condemned by the Nuclear Installations Inspectorate for their lack of safety management on the site – a situation so menacing that the same inspectors have had to threaten to close down Freshpark.

'And the Trade and Industry Secretary Jay Clarkenwell has said, "The events [at Freshpark] show a fundamental flaw in the management at Brit-Atomic, and that has to change."

'Dr Henry White, of Friends of the Earth, describes the faked Crox safety tests as "a damning indictment of a management culture that has led to the aggravation of problems rather than solving them."

'Dirty. Dangerous. Dishonest. *And Dumb.* That is an accurate description of at least some of our nucleocrats. A confidential memo leaked to the press has described Freshpark management as "so shell-shocked they can no longer understand the gravity of their problems".'

This, Meg wrote, had led to drastic demoralisation and disaffection of the staff at Freshpark: 'Local Labour leader Frank Deeney, who used to be a trainer there, has described many of the staff as depressed and punch drunk: "People working there feel as if everybody's kicking them," he said.'

The demoralisation had even reached the point of sabotage in two cases, where control cables had been deliberately cut, and where foreign objects were inserted into nuclear rods with potentially horrendous consequences.

'If these are the workers, who needs enemies?' Meg asked her readers. 'Which brings me to the next investigation I am planning, on the real enemies out there. I mean the terrorists. It's only a matter of time.'

***

'SO, ARE THERE any questions?' Sheik Kemal Aboud asked.

Around him the young men were silent. Then a hand went up. The accent was Texan. 'Sir, with respect, the containment walls around the reactors at Freshpark are seven feet thick. How do we get a plane through that, to reach the reactor?'

'A good question, Wayne. The answer is, we don't. Let me explain. You may have heard of the Maginot Line. It was a line of fortifications which the French built in the nineteen-thirties to keep the Germans from invading. It was made of massive concrete walls, tank traps, cannons, gun turrets, underground forts. The French believed it was impassable. And they were right.

'So Hitler didn't pass it: he went around it. There was a space between the Maginot Line and the coast, and he went through that. Simple, was it not?'

Sheik Aboud leaned back on his cushion. 'We do the same. We don't bother with Freshpark's reactors, which are out of use anyhow. What we hit are tanks of high-level nuclear waste that sit on top of the ground inside a flimsy building.

'Those tanks don't have seven-foot containment walls. Their walls are hardly more than a few tens of centimetres thick. Their contents have to be kept permanently cooled and agitated, to stop them from boiling dry.

'If an airliner hits those tanks, the mile-high fireball will send that nuclear waste into a plume that will devastate Britain, far more effectively than any meltdown at the reactor, even if we could achieve one.'

The sheik brought his fingers together. 'That Maginot Line concept is crucial in all our planning. Another instance of it: they have almost impregnable security at Heathrow and at all the great airports. So we don't use the great airports. We go around them – we board our planes at little airports, like Galway or Knock here in Ireland. They'll have security certainly, but nothing like Heathrow. I fly my own jet out of Knock, so I should know.

'One more example. The Freshpark people boast of their 15-foot razor-wire perimeter fence. And their guard dogs, and their magnificent nuclear police force. Fine. But we fly over their fence. We wave at their guard dogs. And thumb our noses at their nuclear police.

'Think of it – the only defences Freshpark really has *are a couple of bored people at a Knock Airport X-ray machine, and two or three little stewardesses on an aeroplane.*

'Even the X-ray people can't do a thing, because we won't be carrying guns on board. Nor even plastic knives.

We use whatever is already on the plane. Remember we have people working on the maintenance of these planes, in all the airports where the flights originate. They have access to the planes, and can place whatever we need on any one of them. Besides, we may also use whatever we have on our persons – simple ordinary, everyday things. You would be amazed what can be achieved with a pair of spectacles. Think about it. We shall talk about this again.

'Just another instance of the Maginot concept. Always remember: imagination is the key. As is simplicity. As the Americans themselves would say, "Low tech – high concept!"'

A young man raised his hand.

'Yes, Mustapha?'

'Sir. What about the new hardened doors they are putting on the cockpits? How can we get through a door like that?'

'A good question, Mustapha. There are two answers. Firstly, many airliners in Europe have yet to get those new cockpit doors. It will take many months, perhaps years, before all planes have been retrofitted, and by then our aims, God willing, will have been accomplished.

'However, for the present, if you are on a mission and you see there is a hardened door – you recognise it by the keypad mounted on the door, that looks like a mobile phone – then you simply abort the mission, and behave as a normal passenger. That is our procedure as of now.

'But if it's one of the older doors, it's relatively easy. All you need is to turn a key in a lock, and walk right in to the cockpit. And there are ways of getting a key.'

The sheik paused and thought for a moment. 'But those hardened doors really do present a problem, and it's one we're still working on. We know that the keypad works by punching in a code number, a number which is changed periodically. Now, we already have people in place in the relevant airlines who will be able to tell us those codes within minutes after they are changed.

'But that's not enough, because the code doesn't actually open the door – rather it sounds a buzzer in the cockpit indicating that someone is waiting outside. One of the pilots then checks a screen above the door, which shows who is there. Or just uses the peephole if it's an older plane. If satisfied, the pilot opens the door from inside.

'There is our problem, and we're still trying to find a solution to it. We believe we're close to one, and it may be a very simple solution. More on that later. Remember that nothing, Mustapha, is impossible, given a little imagination, and planning. And God's will.'

***

'WE CAN'T SEARCH either place, so we can't,' Stokes told Des King. 'We've no grounds at all to go in. I wish to God we had.'

'Tell you what we *could* do, Jack. We could get a

bunch of the uniformed lads in there to check everyone's papers. Immigration and all that. In fact we could get GNIBS – y'know, the Immigrant Bureau – to order it.'

'Now you're talking, Des. But we'd have to do both places at the same time. Tuam could handle the computer plant, and our fellas here could take the theme park. At least we'd pick up some data to be going on with, Stuff we could check through Interpol, FBI and the Yard – the lot.

"Course, y'know what I'd really like to check out? That bloody sheik's place, Castle Patrick. But we haven't a hope in hell of getting in there. Fuckin' Flaherty'd have a fit.'

16

THE ROOM IS windowless and darkened. There are no spotlights to dazzle the eye: the enormous model of Freshpark nuclear plant is softly lit, much of it from within. The model includes shoreline and sea. Three young men are gathered around the model, their boyish features reflecting a little of the soft light from the model. Two are darkly Mediterranean, and one has a shock of fair hair.

A technician speaks with a Glasgow accent. 'The fence, here, is fifteen feet high. It runs all the way around.' The fence glows brighter for a moment, as the man touches a button on his zapper. 'There is a second fence inside that. Between them is a clear perimeter several yards wide.' The perimeter lights up momentarily.

Lights pick out a small river snaking through the compound. 'That's the Freshton River,' the technician says. 'And those buildings along its banks are the old Valox reactors – you'll recognise them by their four big cooling towers. The domed buildings beside them are the reactor housings.'

The four domed structures become transparent, showing the rod-filled cores within.

'Over here are the two original reactors. People used recognise them by their tall towers with the bulge at the top. This one's where the fire was in the '50s. The core is damaged to an unknown degree, so they have never yet been able to get the fuel out.

'They tried dismantling it a few years ago but had to back off until they solved a load of technical problems. But they did take down its contaminated tower lately. That's Thule over there, by the way. And the rectangular building right beside it is the Crox facility.

'Now this is what I want you all to take note of. Do you see that low structure, sort of L-shaped, almost at ground level? That's Unit X-24 – and that's what you'll be aiming for. But that's enough for today. I'll tell you about it in our next session.'

'Can I ask a question?' It was the fair-haired Texan youngster.

'Sure.'

'So where do you get all this information? I mean, about what's where at Freshpark?'

'Oh that's quite simple. We've got men in there. Been feeding us stuff for years. Not that we need them any more, though. Every single thing is on the internet now. And in public record offices. Even the site plans for Freshpark. Right there for everyone to see.'

***

'OMAR, THIS IS Doctor Mujib.' Sheik Aboud gestured

to the slight, balding man in a well-cut business suit. 'He is a structural engineer who has worked extensively in Pakistan's nuclear industry. He is also one of us.'

Omar bowed slightly, and Mujib did the same. His eyes recalled those of Picasso. His smile was warm.

'Dr Mujib will be with us for several days,' the sheik continued, 'to help us evaluate our plans. Above all, to ensure that they are as effective as humanly possible. This, Dr Mujib, is Mr Campbell, our chief technician. And these are two of our more senior young pilots – if you will pardon the paradox. Well, our more mature young pilots. I have asked them to sit in with us – I don't think we need trouble the others with more details than are necessary for their performance.'

Mujib bowed. Everyone sat down at a table facing a screen. Dr Mujib opened his laptop and switched it on. He pressed a button on the table and an electronic projector in the ceiling clicked on, the screen glowing blue.

The man spoke quietly, but with authority: 'Let us be clear from the start, my brothers, on the threefold purpose of this training which our young men are undergoing. It is firstly, to bring about the largest number of deaths that is humanly possible which, with God's help, will be numbered in the hundreds of thousands, possibly millions. Secondly, to render uninhabitable as much as possible of the western world. And thirdly, to ensure that what the westerners call their culture will be a memory from the past.'

There was a murmur of approval.

'It is incredible but true, that much of this is within your reach. And it is so because you will be using the West's own strengths against itself. Two western strengths in particular – its nuclear power, and its civil air power. The West would like to keep them separate: our function is to bring both powers together in a way that will put an end to the West. And we do it quite simply, by flying their aeroplanes into their nuclear plants.

'For this morning, let us concentrate on the Freshpark assignment which some of your pilots will be taking on. You already know that the most satisfactory targets are the twenty-one high-level waste tanks. These contain enough caesium 137 to bring about a nuclear-radiation effect one hundred times that of Chernobyl.'

A map of Freshpark appeared on the screen behind Dr Mujib. An L-shaped structure glowed red near the centre of the map. The cypher X-24 appeared beside it.

'The most important point,' the speaker continued, 'is that these tanks are among the less protected of any of the targets within Freshpark. And they are set in a straight line, on each arm of the L. Together they contain some 1,500 cubic metres of high-level waste. As you know, these tanks must be kept constantly cooled and agitated to prevent them from boiling dry. This waste is so lethal that one minute's exposure, at one metre distance, guarantees death. Imagine the effect of an immense plume of this waste spreading across the skies of Britain and Europe ...'

A murmur of appreciation rippled around the table.

'A Boeing 737, weighing 70 tonnes, and with almost full tanks containing 26,000 litres of fuel, would be sufficient to take out one arm of the L. The plane would, of course, have to be on a long haul to be carrying a full complement of fuel. The scenario would be something like this:

'The aeroplane approaches the tanks from almost exactly due south, and slides into the second or third tank, here.' A cursor arrow moved up along the bottom arm of the L-shaped building. 'One-third of the fuel explodes immediately with the force of many tonnes of TNT, rupturing the tanks directly in front and behind the point of impact. The remaining two thirds of the fuel emulsifies, creating a fireball a mile high, spreading to many times the wingspan of the plane, which then combines with the caesium 137 and carries it into the air.

'The aeroplane crumples like paper on impact. The engines however, being made of sterner stuff, each having a mass of several tonnes, should continue forward to penetrate one tank after another.

'After this, all is in the hands of God. With westerly winds and the right temperatures, the caesium plume should rise vertically, and then start shearing, bringing its contents down on the north of England. Rain, of course, would be the greatest gift of the Almighty, as it would flush far more of the materials to the ground, where they could do their lethal work.

'Remember, if only one tank is breached, and the contents released, it would mean the evacuation of 28 million people from up to a thousand kilometres from the site. And we could hope for as many as nine million cases of cancer.'

'*Inch'Allah!*' The murmur was spontaneous around the table.

'Now, of course, in a best-case scenario, there are a number of truly wonderful things that we might also hope for, God willing. The first is that the fireball might spread to reach the plutonium store, directly north of the tanks. If that were to happen, our cup would be full. A plutonium plume would be the most lethal thing we could ever dream of.'

'*Inch'Allah!*'

'And now, my brothers,' Dr Mujib said, 'it is time for us to pray to the Almighty, that all these things may come to pass …'

***

TO HAVE BEEN loved and never to have known it. To know now that you were once cherished, that you mattered terribly to someone, and that you had never realised it. All this had brought a whirlwind of mixed feelings to Meg.

There was grief – acute grief at the love she had failed

to recognise, and that was gone now forever. There was a strange shift in feelings for a father she had loved so hard when she was a child, who had never seemed to return that love. But he *had* returned it. Could Meg perhaps try to love him differently now if he were still alive? A two-way love? But he wasn't alive. Could you love someone who didn't exist? Or did he still, in some way? And if so, could he be aware of Meg's new feelings? The old unanswerables.

But there was joy too. Almost rapture, to know that you were once loved to bits. That you must have been worth loving. Or even if you hadn't been worth it, that the love was there anyway. No, of course you were worth loving. And someone, a long time ago, had recognised that. To know that was sheer joy.

And that joy threw the shoulders back, 'sucked in the tummy to the backbone', pushed out the breasts, tossed the head high. Meg mattered back then, and by God she must matter now.

She could almost believe now that the television success had been no fluke. And that those articles which had so stirred things up, had done so because Meg was bloody good at what she did. Maybe. And that her anger was her most effective weapon, if it could make her write like that. Maybe, indeed. And that Will had been right when he told her how effective she was. Maybe. That 'maybe' was enough to bring Meg close to euphoria at times.

But more than anything, Meg was starting to under-

stand how uncannily like her father she was in one crucial aspect – that's if *The Times*' words were true. She was
doing precisely what her father would have done. She
too was fighting because she believed the fight was necessary, and she would never, ever give in. Just a different
enemy this time.

***

SHEIK ABOUD SAT in silence with closed eyes, and
hands in his lap. Then his eyes opened and gazed upon
the rapt young men. 'My brothers, God commands you
to go forth and kill,' he said. 'There was a time when the
Jihad was something a man of Islam might take up or
not as he wished. But now, since the troops of America,
the Great Satan, are actually defiling our sacred Lands of
the Two Sanctuaries, the Jihad has become a *fard'ain*. An
individual duty on every single Muslim who lives and
breathes.

'Thus no one can be without sin who does not take
up the Jihad. Until the Americans are removed from all
the lands of Islam, and until the filthy polluting culture
of Disney and Playboy and Murdoch and McDonalds
and Coca Cola and Wall Street and drugs and alcohol
and child pornography is uprooted from every corner of
the Muslim world, no one is absolved from sin, except
those who fight to root it out.

'My brothers, you must learn to kill. You must learn
how to slaughter with gladness in your heart, knowing

217

that what you are doing is the holy will of God. And when God grants you a slaughter, whether it be cutting the throat of an airline stewardess, or strangling an infidel passenger, or wiping out an infidel city – you should rejoice, and perform it as an offering to God on behalf of your father and mother, for they are owed by you.'

The young men listened in silence, their eyes shining.

'Remember always that when a slaughter is bestowed upon you, it is a gift from God, and when you fulfil it you have worshipped God.

'And lastly, let us remember the words of our great scholar of the Jihad, Abdullah Azzam: "Glory does not build its lofty edifice except with skulls. Honour and respect cannot be established except on a foundation of cripples and corpses."'

'*Allahu akbar!*' Someone whispered.

'*Allahu akbar!*' Many of the young men whispered in reply.

Everyone stood as the sheik rose from his cushion and glided from the room.

Omar clapped his hands. 'Assignments, gentlemen!' They gathered around him. 'Achmed, Mustapha, and Kevin – pilot training, Boeing. Karl, Yoshimuro, Salman – pilot training, Airbus.

'Site-model study: Youssef, Abd and Wayne, you take Freshpark. Your instructor is waiting. Jeremy and Din, you take Cap La Hague. Let's go, gentlemen.

'Dwight, Hussein, George. You've got Neckar West-

heim. That's Germany. And Nadir, Patrick, Aadam
– Neckar Two for you …'

***

'WILL, CAN I ask you something? Am I going a bit
crackers on the Freshpark thing? People are starting to
hint that I am. Even around the newsroom.'

'Let's call it an *idée fixe*. A tiny bit of obsession, perhaps.
But that's what makes you such an effective journalist,
Meg. I wish they were all as obsessive as you – we might
get a bit more done around the *Clarion*. Anyway, I'm right
behind you, obsessive or not. Don't forget that.'

'Will, are you behind me because you believe in what
I'm doing or because you're my friend?'

'Oh for fuck's *sake*, Meg. That doesn't even deserve
an answer. Just don't start that sort of thing, doubting
yourself again. Look, I have to go.'

After Will left, Meg wanted to kick herself for having
asked such a thing. The flash of anger had surprised her
– she'd never seen that before. Well, ask a stupid question
… And where was this wonderful new confidence that
she was so proud of? Pull yourself together, she thought.

17

'I CANNOT DO it, my Sheik,' the young man said. 'I have been reading our scripture as you said we should. And it says be kind to the Christians and the Jews. The People of the Book. "Say to them, we believe what you believe. Your God and our God are one." Sheik, I cannot kill these people.'

The young man stood before Sheik Aboud's desk. Omar stood to one side. There was silence for some moments.

'Can you kill yourself?' the sheik asked quietly.

'My Sheik, I found that in the Koran too. In 4:29 it says clearly, "Do not kill yourselves, for God has been most merciful to you." Please believe me, Sheik, I was willing to die. I *am* willing to die. For the Jihad, for you. But not by my own hand. God says *no*.' The young man trembled as he spoke.

Sheik Aboud came from behind the desk and put a calming arm around the boy's shoulder. 'It's alright, Khair. It's alright. I respect your honesty, young brother. And I am grateful for your courage in sharing your thoughts with me. Think nothing of it – if you feel it's not right, then you must not do it. I still respect your courage in offering yourself in the first place. And your faith in God that brought you among us.'

Khair's shoulders shook as he started to weep.

The sheik became brisk. 'Now cheer up, young brother. I am a man of my word. Today is Monday: There's a flight out of Shannon on Wednesday at seven in the morning. Omar here will give you your passport, and provide you with tickets to Paris and from there to Kuwait. The helicopter will leave at half past three on Wednesday morning to take you to Shannon. You will file the flight plan, Omar? Good.

'There's just one thing I ask you, Khair. Will you promise me to stay away from the others before you leave? I don't want them to get upset – you can understand why. Perhaps you might like to spend a day in Galway, to buy a few presents for your family? Yes? Good. And you can sleep here tonight: Omar will collect your clothes and things.

'Now don't be despondent, Khair. You remember young Ibn who left us some time ago? He left for the same reason as you – he could not bring himself to kill. He is now where he needed to be. And happy. Do not fear. Your time for heroism will come, sooner than you can ever imagine.' Sheik Aboud put both hands on the boy's head: '*Ma a el salama*,' he said gently. 'Go with peace, little brother. *Fi hifd ellah*.'

***

'FRANK,' NANCY HARRIS said. 'How'd you like to do one more in the series? I floated an idea with Leeds, and they're all for it. So maybe we don't wrap yet. That's if you're agreeable of course.'

'Well, tell me about it first.'

'Look, that Pompeii Syndrome's a winner. I've told Leeds about it. I've suggested we do one more in the series. About the Pompeii Syndrome in all the great disasters.'

'God Nancy, we'd have to start travelling the world again.'

'No, we wouldn't. We'll have lots of cuts from the films we've already done; then there's clips from the archives; and we could do a bit more on location here – after all it is the *Pompeii* Syndrome. Oh, and they'd want to thread a studio discussion through it as well. What do you think?'

'I'd be willing to try it. So how long more would we stay on, after we finish with this one?'

'A week or two would do it. Just basically you teasing out your concept of the Pompeii Syndrome. Here in Pompeii itself. That's all we need. The rest can be voice-over, and you can do that in Leeds.'

***

MEG CLICKED HER email icon as soon as she sat down at her desk in the newsroom. She clicked *Send/Receive* and waited. She enjoyed the anticipation of watching the emails pulse in from the top of the screen, pushing one another down screen like cattle through a gateway. And there was the name, right there among the emails – *Dieter Vogels*. She clicked on it.

Dear Ms Watkins

In answer to your specific questions:

1. The scenario is of a deliberate crashing of an airliner into Freshpark, breaching and setting fire to a number of the high-level waste tanks in building X-24. Is this a credible scenario?

Yes.

2. How far could the plume travel and still remain lethal or dangerous, and how wide might it become?

The larger the thermal input into the source of the dispersion, the higher the plume (chimney effect). The higher the plume is rising, the farther it can travel, which can be thousands of miles. The terms *lethal* and *dangerous* have to be better defined. Any additional exposure to radiation increases the risk of cancer and genetic defects, and larger doses have larger effects. In other words, wherever, at whatever distance people get exposed to the plume, there will always be negative health effects.

3. What might the plume contain, and where might it dump its contents?

Strong rain would bring down a significant share of the contained radioactivity, in particular, soluble radio-elements like caesium.

4. What could be the worst possible physical/medical effects

*on people (a) living nearby, and (b) living 100 miles away
– within Minutes? Hours? Days? Months? Years?*

Just to fix the orders of magnitude: unshielded, the high-level radioactive waste delivers a lethal dose at one-metre distance within one minute. However, people exposed could die a slow, unbelievably horrible death over months. (It took a Japanese worker who was exposed during the accident at Tokai-mura in September 1999 almost seven months to die.)

The less-exposed people might die thirty years later. Actually, some might not die, but their grandchildren or great-grandchildren might die because of genetic effects which might show up only generations later.

Others might develop certain types of cancer within a few years (thyroid; leukaemia).

5. What numbers of people might be affected in a worst-case scenario?

Hundreds of millions, of which hundreds of thousands to over one million could develop lethal cancer. Richard Garwin, (the "father" of the US H-bomb, a very pro-nuclear, but brilliant scientist), told a conference of the Irish Academy of Sciences in 2002 that from only one single Freshpark tank, containing 150 cubic metres of high-level waste, the result would be four times that of Chernobyl – that is, 120,000 cancer deaths. Garwin is probably the strongest scientific witness you can get. And let us remember that there are twenty-one such tanks at Freshpark.

6. What might be the long-term geographical effects? Could a region be left uninhabitable?

The consequences could be absolutely dramatic, if the largest share of the radioactivity released actually came down in the North of England. Yes, it could be rendered permanently uninhabitable. Or if the wind were from the east, this would happen to Ireland.

7. How would the above scenario change if, instead of breaching the high-level waste tanks, the airliner were to breach the vaults containing the powdered plutonium?

That is very difficult to say. The key question is how much plutonium would be effectively dispersed off site. There are some 100 metric tonnes in the form of plutonium oxide stored at Freshpark. It takes only a few millionths of a gram inhaled to cause lung cancer. In other words, that's enough to poison the entire human race several hundred times, if the plutonium were administered equally to each living human being. So the question is only how much could/would end up in the bodies of human beings.

Plutonium oxide (PuO_2) is a powder. How much plutonium would get airborne? What would be the local/global distribution? Those are not questions I could answer in a brief memo.

8. Is there anything else I should have asked?

What about precautionary measures? For example the distribution of iodine pills? Very surprising in this case since the key isotope (not the only one!) would be caesium and not iodine.

What about fire-fighting after the impact? (I talked to a top professional firefighter who said it would probably take a full week before they could even get on site.) What about medical care in the aftermath? And who will have to be paying for all this medical care? Who would carry political responsibility?

I hope this is of some help.

With the best wishes for you and for the success of your enterprise.

Sincerely – Dieter Vogels.

MEG CLICKED ON *Print*, and across the aisle the laser printer started churning. She went over to pick up the sheets. With this authority as a basis for her next article, maybe now people in high places would really pay attention.

And perhaps Will Davis wouldn't get doubts. Meg suspected he was starting to have them, even if he was keeping them carefully to himself. But Meg, for the first time in her life, didn't have doubts. Even if the carpet were pulled from under her, as it might be, she had no doubts any more.

***

THE HELICOPTER SANG through the moonlight at 2,000 feet. The moon glinted on Lough Corrib as the machine moved south above its eastern shore, then over Galway City and out across the bay, rising to cross the Burren Hills. In the rear seat Omar tapped Khair's shoulder and pointed: the young man could just see the outline of the Aran Islands to his right. There was little speaking because of the engine noise, and both men wore ear mufflers.

Khair was finally happy after so many sleepless nights. They were sending him home as they had promised, and he would neither have to kill nor die.

Black Head looked like a great whale nosing into the Atlantic, and there was a white edge of foam around it. The white lighthouse showed clearly in the moonlight, its light flashing reassuringly.

Just south of Corofin the helicopter banked to starboard and headed towards the ocean. As the coast slid away beneath, the pilot dropped to a few hundred feet above the water, flying due west. Now there was only the Atlantic.

Yet still the helicopter flew west. Within the cabin no one spoke. Down below, the ocean shone in the moonlight like a mackerel's back. There was a stillness in the cabin.

And still they flew west. And still no one spoke. Khair sat deathly still. An urgent odour of excrement crept through the cabin.

The note of engines and rotor changed subtly as the helicopter began to climb. It climbed for several minutes.

The rotor rhythm changed again and now the helicopter was hovering. Omar clicked open his safety belt, pulled a harness from under his seat, put it on and closed the fasteners. He was now anchored to the floor by a lanyard. He took off his ear mufflers and motioned to Khair to do the same.

He held out a canvas bag to Khair. 'Empty your pockets into this,' he said, loudly to be heard over the engine noise. 'Everything. Including your passport.'

The boy obeyed.

'Is that everything, Khair? Nothing left in your pockets? You sure?'

Khair nodded.

Omar reached over and slid back the door. The pulsing howl of engines and rotor was now almost deafening. The cabin grew cold, and the air had the freshness of the sea.

'The time of heroism has come, Khair,' Omar said. 'Undo your safety belt. God go with you.'

The boy sat frozen.

'There is no time, Khair. Go, please. It will be over very quickly.'

Khair did not move. He was weeping.

Omar leaned over and unclipped Khair's safety belt. He lifted him under the arms and forced him backwards towards the open door. The boy went into the air, hurtled downwards, and ended up with his fingers clutching the rim of the cabin floor.

Omar unclipped the emergency axe from its cradle

under the seat. He brought it down smartly on the clutching fingers of the boy's left hand. The four fingers fell into the cabin as Khair slipped away.

Omar picked up the still twitching fingers and tossed them out into the air. The door clunked shut. He took a box of tissues from under the seat and wiped the blood from the cabin floor. He then wiped the seat where Khair had been.

The helicopter dropped again to five hundred feet and turned for the coast.

***

WILL DAVIS PUSHED his flat screen sideways on its moveable arm, yawned, stretched, and looked at his watch. 'I've four minutes to news conference, Meg. Look, I just want you to do me a list of the Freshpark topics you've still to deal with. The whole seam must be nearly worked out by now.'

'Far from it, Will. It's like subatomic physics. The further into it you go, the more you find there's still to find. Let me tell you what I'm digging out –'

'Haven't time now, Meg. Just do me that list, will you? Oh, and another thing. Brian's taking my place for a couple of weeks next month when I take the children to Scotland. Soon as the exams are over.'

***

'THE MINISTER, PLEASE. This is Sheik Aboud.'

'May I ask what it's about, Sir?'

'I'm a close personal friend. The Minister will take my call, I am certain of that. Just say who I am please.'

The authority in the voice must have worked, for Mick Flaherty came on. 'Kemal, you old scoundrel. What are you up to?'

'Good morning, Michael. Listen, your police are really bothering us. They've been into Trucial Software, asking questions. And the theme park as well. There's one man in particular who's been making a nuisance of himself.'

'Who's that, Kemal?'

'A Sergeant Stokes.'

'Jack Stokes? They say he's a good man. Well regarded.'

'Perhaps so, but he has been extremely intrusive. And quite unpleasant. And, as you well know, my operations here are completely legitimate.'

'I know that, Kemal. Provide a lot of employment, too.'

'Well, people here feel that Stokes is a racist. It could look bad, with so many people here from the Middle East. Especially with that O'Kane fellow stirring things up, the way he has been doing this last while. I'd be very distressed to think the police were also racist.'

'Aw, I doubt if Stokes is a racist. I don't know him personally, but he has a very fair reputation. I wouldn't worry about him if I were you, Kemal.'

'Call him off, Michael. Will you do that for me?'

'I'll talk to his superiors, Kemal. I promise. They can rein him in if need be.'

'Call him off, Michael.'

'I'll do the best I can, Kemal.'

'Call him off, Michael.'

***

'BESIDE ME ON the desk as I write this,' Meg typed into her laptop, 'is one of the most pathetic little tourism brochures I have ever read. It's entitled *Village Walks in Historic Freshton-on-Sea* (with the subtitle, *Cumbria's Seaside Village*). On the beautifully sketched cover, children romp happily along a jetty out over blue water; a fisherman brings in his lobster pots; a sunny, sandy beach beckons; and a seagull hovers overhead.

'It suggests the dream of a tiny fishing and holiday village under blue skies.

'Yet I know what comes out of those blue skies. I know that no local children would dare romp on that jetty – some would be too sick to romp anyhow. I know how that beach has too many times been declared off limits; how that blue sea is the most radioactive in the world; how those lobsters almost glow in the dark; and how that seagull is nuclear waste on wings, from flying in and out of Freshpark.'

I'm getting good at this, Meg thought. When I've really researched the facts, and I'm absolutely sure of them, then my head's as good as any. As long as the facts are in there. And then my writing can really get going.

'Freshpark is what the brochure fails to show – those

dark towers rising beyond the village rooftops, sending their sinister, silent smoke into the sky. Nor does its cover show the chimneys with the bulges on top that have struck fear into the hearts of people for fifty years; nor does it show the fifteen-foot razor fences that keep the public at bay.

'Nor does it show the railway hidden in a cutting behind that beach, which carries radioactive filth from all over the world to Freshpark.

'When I first caught sight of Freshpark not that long ago, I was awestruck. I thought it a stunning silhouette of power and invincibility. Now I realise it is a silhouette of failure. Every tower and chimney in that panorama resonates of failure. Brit-Atomic's failure. Failure to make a single penny in fifty long years. Failure to be clean. Failure to come clean. Failure to be safe. Failure to tell the truth. Failure to be honest. Failure to keep promises. Failure to care about its neighbours. Failure to care about the people it's supposed to serve. Failure to face the future intelligently.

'Even the most impressive of Freshpark's silhouettes are symbols of failure. Those tall chimneys with the bulges on top are Freshpark's first reactors, now seething and sealed and shut down, where fire came close to contaminating huge areas of Britain more than fifty years ago. It is significant that one of those chimneys has lately gone. Yet even now they can't dismantle the molten Pile No. 1, because it might spontaneously catch fire.

Decommissioning experts see the project as extremely technically demanding – "perhaps the most challenging decommissioning project in the UK", as an official paper puts it.

'That giant golf-ball silhouette is the so-called Forward Gas Plant which was so forward that it never really worked, and was finally abandoned. The four huge cooling towers are for the Valox reactors that are now shut down because they are useless, and because no one wants the military plutonium they produce. That square block is the vitrification plant which they keep hoping will turn high-level waste into some sort of glass, but which has never worked properly. And now it has even been sabotaged by Freshpark workers.

'Freshpark is one colossal symbol of failure. But perhaps its most terrific failure has yet to come – a failure that could end the world as we know it.'

Meg ran a spell check, then clicked on *Save*, then *Close*, then *Log Off*, and shut the laptop. If we could only shut Freshpark that easily, she thought.

***

'SIR.' THE CHIEF technician touched his cap to Sheik Aboud. 'I've just been working on something that could be helpful, Sir.' There was a slight Scottish inflection to his accent. 'You know the plutonium they've got at Freshpark? Seventy tonnes – no, it's up to a hundred now. Well, I've confirmed that the door to the vault is the same steel the British use in their tanks and armoured cars. Now, granted it could be breached with oxy-acetylene, but it would take time, and there wouldn't *be* time.

'But I found out there's a few portable anti-tank guns on the market that could penetrate such armour. There's a wee beauty called the *TOW 2*, that sits on a tripod, and you could carry her in an ordinary van. She can be bought, and I believe I know where. And if we can't get that, there's another called the *Milan*. Nearly as good.'

'Praise be to God.'

'So we may have the choice then of stealing the plutonium, or blowing it up. Or maybe a bit of both: we only need about 30 kilos for an atom bomb. A lot less if we get a few extra bits and pieces like neutron reflectors.

'But we can surely blow the roof off. It's only fifteen inches of reinforced concrete, so a bomb could take it right off.

'The problem is getting the plutonium up in the air so the wind will carry it. If there was a way we could get a kerosene fire going in the vault, that should do it. I think it's worth looking into.'

'The plutonium.' The sheik nodded his head in reverence. 'The most lethal substance of all. God be praised.'

'You see, Sir, once it's in the air then people should be able to breathe it into their lungs. That should do nicely. Remember 80 micrograms is fatal.'

18

'DES.' BLACK JACK Stokes looked up from his computer screen. 'Sure a helicopter couldn't fly the Atlantic, could it?'

'God, no. They're just short-haul things. Maybe there's special ones for the long haul, but I never heard of them. Why?'

'There's something here from IAA – you know those reports out of Shannon? Well, seems this here Air Canada pilot was heading for Shannon, and his glide path took him on a curve well to the north because of the runway he'd be using. Anyway he claims he saw a helicopter without navigation lights, about two and half thousand feet. Just glimpsed a silhouette – it was quite a distance away. But Des, the odd thing is, *it was heading west!*

'I think the poor man got a bit of a fright. Like I mean, a hundred miles out over the ocean and heading west. Next stop America. A helicopter? Come on! A kind of Flying Dutchman up in the clouds. I'll take a bet on it, that fella gave up the drink for a while after that. I would, I can tell you.'

'How long ago was this?' Des was all interest.

'Last Wednesday, 3.42 in the morning.' Stokes paused, as a thought struck him. Then he slapped his hand down on the desk. 'Des, I want you to do something for me. A couple of things. First, would you find out where do they file flight plans? It's probably Shannon. Find out, anyway. Then will you find out what helicopters filed flight plans for last Wednesday, the day your man saw his ghost helicopter. Will y'do that right away?'

'Sir!'

'I wish you wouldn't go on with that "Sir" thing, Des. It's gettin' a wee bit tiresome, so it is.'

'Sorry, Jack. I'll try to remember. Sir!'

'Oh, for Christ's *sake* …'

***

THE WHITE-AND-GOLD LEARJET came in over the gorse and gently touched the tarmac at Knock Airport. Its engines rumbled as it slowed, then it taxied to where a helicopter in matching livery waited, rotor just starting to turn.

A car came across from the airport building, and two men climbed out, just as the plane door opened and its steps folded down. Sheik Aboud bent through the doorway, came down the couple of steps and strode across to the helicopter. A young man followed with two suitcases.

One of the airport men raised a hand in greeting. 'Morning, Sheik. You're welcome home. Good trip, I hope?'

'Excellent, Damian. But I'm tired, I can tell you that.'

'Er. Nothing to declare, I suppose?'

'The usual, Damian. A few bottles of cognac for the infidels! That's about it.'

'Good, so. Have a nice trip home, now.' He saluted and both men climbed into their car.

As the helicopter lifted off, the sheik turned to Omar al Naim, beside him in the back. 'How is the training, my friend?'

'They're all nearly ready. There's not one who can't handle a Boeing at this stage. But the hardest part is actually hitting the facility. Knowing exactly where to hit, so as to ensure the greatest possible havoc – it's different at each plant. That's where the models are such a help.

'And even when our trainees know where to hit, getting them accurate is the problem. So, now that we've finished the flying training, we're concentrating on the final dives into the plants. That simulator software is a gift. It gives us pretty well every single nuclear plant in Europe.

'But the one big problem we still have are those hardened cockpit doors. They're installing more and more of them, and we're still helpless against them.'

'Not any more,' the Sheik said.

'You mean, we've solved the problem?'

'A very simple, low-tech solution, my friend. Jeddah suggested it. I will explain it to you later – you'll need to look at some diagrams. And we may have to speed things up,' the sheik went on. 'That's what they told me in Jeddah. Seems the CIA is aware of some threat to Europe, and that it could be nuclear. And of course I had to tell Jeddah about the police here getting restless. Anyway they said they might ask us to move at very short notice. This I must ask you, Omar. Do you still insist on taking one of the assignments yourself?'

There was a moment's silence. 'I have made up my mind,' Omar said. 'It's my destiny now.'

'I shall miss you, dearest, dearest boy. More than I can ever say. But you already know how much.' He reached out and took the other man's hand in his.

***

ALL EYES WERE on Sheik Aboud, who sat with closed eyes, hands folded on his lap. Then the Sheik spoke: 'A *hadith* from the collection of al-Bukhari says that no servant of God who dies could want to return to the world again.

'But there is one exception. The *shahid*, the martyr. For when such a man sees the bounty of martyrdom, he will want to return to the world and be killed again.

'You have heard people quote that verse from our scripture which says we should not kill ourselves? And that is right and true. Killing myself would be flinging my life back in the face of God, who gave me that life. You remember Issam who walked away from us and hanged himself from a tree? He is of course in Hell now.

'*But martyrdom is not killing ourselves* – it is the making of ourselves an oblation to God. It is doing the absolute will of God, leaving to Him the moral consequence of what we do.

'Martyrdom is our own private act of worship, and utterly pleasing to God. There is no other act like it.

'As Abdullah Azzam once said, "Islamic history is coloured with two lines: one of them black with the ink of the scholar's pen; the other one red with the martyr's blood. It is even more beautiful when the two become one, so that the hand of the scholar which expends the ink and moves the pen is the same as the hand which expends its blood and moves the people to action.'

Sheik Aboud stood up in the silent room and slowly opened wide his arms. 'Remember always, my brothers, that if we are not killed, we shall die anyway. Why not choose the most honourable death of all – to be killed in the way of Allah?'

'*Allahu akbar!*' the youngsters murmured.

***

SHEIK KEMAL ABOUD was walking in the grounds of Castle Patrick with a handsome young Jordanian. Their feet scrunched on the gravel path between the trees.

From a bough above them a chaffinch sang. A rich aroma of earth after rain rose around them. The evening sun slanted through the beech leaves, making diamonds of the raindrops on each blade of grass.

The sheik put his arm around the lad's shoulder. 'Do you believe what I said, Achmed? About the joy that awaits the martyr?'

'Every word, my Sheik.'

'Would you be willing to die very soon, if I asked you to? I mean, sooner than you expected? If it would further the Cause?'

'You need only say the word, my Sheik.'

'You would go straight to Paradise, Achmed.'

'I believe you, my Sheik. With all my heart.'

'Then, Achmed, my dear young brother, I have a task for you. A very special task indeed.'

The chaffinch's song had changed into its staccato warning note.

***

DES KING PUT down the phone and clapped his hands. 'We got him, Jack!'

'Got who?' Jack Stokes looked up from the papers on his desk.

'The sheik!'

'You mean – ?'

'I do. He filed a flight plan from Tuam to Shannon for 3 a.m. last Wednesday. Same day that pilot saw the ghost helicopter.'

Stokes was silent as he took in the news. Then he rubbed his hands: 'Well, Allah be praised, as the friggin' sheik himself would say.' He thought for a moment.

'Right Des, we haven't nailed him yet. We've just the word of a tired pilot who thinks he might have seen something, but isn't too sure.' He thought for a moment. 'Wait a minute now. When did wee Bag O'Bones come up in that net?'

'Give me a minute and I'll have it for you … Yep, here it is. March the twelfth.'

'Right. Ring Shannon again, and find if the sheik filed a flight plan any time around then. Especially March eleven. And then find out if they have a record of the time of arrival. Actually do it for both those flights, if there *are* two – for last Wednesday and for March eleven. Wouldn't it be interesting if they both took a while longer than they should?'

'I'll get right on to it.'

Stokes stood up to go. 'And there's one other thing you could do for us, while I'm in Tuam. I'm heading up there now. All those names and details the uniform boys took at the theme park and the computer plant, get them off to the Yard and Interpol. Oh, and Europol as well. Include all the details we have – place of origin, where they lived before they came here. Anything the boys came up with.'

'And we'll see if there's any convergence, right?'

'Got it in one. I'm off now. You hold the fort?'

'No problem.'

Stokes paused at the door. 'Know what Des? If a trawler could just manage to fish out another bag o'bones, and there was another nicely-timed flight plan, jeez, we'd be doin' rightly, wouldn't we? Then there'd be a pattern.' He sighed. 'Asking a bit much, I suppose.'

***

'JUST BACK OFF a tiny bit, Meg.' Will Davis paused to pour wine into Meg's glass. 'That Freshton-by-the-Sea piece was absolutely brilliant. Trouble is, it was so brilliant it's got the nucleocrats all riled up. They were on to Upstairs this morning, I gather. Kershaw stood his ground, of course, and he'll stick by you. As *I* will.

'It's just, as managing editor, he's got a lot on his plate right now. So let's not make it too hard for him.'

'You want me to back off completely, then?'

'Goodness no, Meg. Far from it. Just go easy for a week or two, until the nuclear crowd simmer down. Then we hit them again. Alright?'

'Not for too long, Will. I'm getting stuff now that's really scaring me to death. And it has to be aired. You know what I've been telling you, about terrorists going after Freshpark? About what could happen if they do? Well, it's worse than I ever imagined. It's almost unthinkable. I can't sit on it. The nuke people know all about it, but they're not saying. Afraid of panic – I'm certain that's the reason. But somebody's got to say it. And nobody's saying anything, but me.'

'Ten days, Meg. Give them ten to cool down. That's not too long to wait, is it?'

'As long as the terrorists wait that long.'

***

OMAR AL NAIM'S earphones crackled as he sat in the co-pilot's seat in the white Agusta helicopter.

'He's just left,' a voice said. 'Looks like he's headed for the Tuam Road. As expected.'

19

THE TOYOTA PRIUS hissed through the rain, northwards along the road to Tuam. Traffic was light. The helicopter, 2,000 feet above the road, was just part of the scenery. Occasionally it looped out over the fields but always circled back above the road again. Omar's eyes followed the car below.

Jack Stokes relaxed as he drove. He loved the murmur of that hybrid engine. He felt elated at the progress they were making, getting close to that sheik.

Achmed Maktum sat in a dark-blue Opel Astra, facing south on the hard shoulder, just below the Anbally Inn. Rain streamed down the windscreen, matching the tears streaming down his cheeks. His lips moved in prayer: '*Allahum aftah li kul al-abwab* – Oh God, open all doors for me'. He whispered it over and over.

Omar watched the tiny outline of the white garda car below, as it dropped speed to enter Claregalway, and followed its passage through the village. There was a silver car behind it now, a larger car than the Prius. Where had that come from? One of those SUVs. It was driving closer than it should. People ought to be more careful.

The garda car accelerated as it left the village. It slowed occasionally as it encountered the several curves in the road, and then accelerated again into the Anbally straight.

Achmed's car phone beeped. He reached down and touched a button. Omar's voice: 'One minute and a half. Ready, Achmed?'

'I'm ready.'

'… One minute. Fifty seconds. Thirty. Ten. *Go*, Achmed, and God go with you.'

The car pulled out and roared off down the highway.

'Bring it up to exactly one-thirty,' Omar's voice said. 'Hold it at one-thirty. Hold it. Hold it. Centre of your lane. Keep it there. Hold it. *Hold it*. NOW, pull across. The white police car.'

Stokes was thinking of that ghost helicopter out over the Atlantic. Maybe poor wee Bag O' Bones never came off the Cliffs of Moher at all. A blue car was coming towards him at speed, a plume of spray in its wake. It crossed the white line and came straight across. Stokes stomped on the accelerator and the Prius shot forward. There was a bang as something hit the right rear corner of the Prius, which careened across the road, demolished a low, loose-stone wall, narrowly missed a moving tractor, and finished upside down in a field.

Jack Stokes hung from his safety belt, smelling petrol. His chest was in agony. He fumbled to switch off the ignition.

Voices: 'Turn the car over!'

'Jaysus, there's only three of us.'

'Turn it – c'mon *try*, for Jaysus sake. Oh Christ, the one on the road's on fire … Christ, there's two cars out there!'

Then oblivion.

***

THE CAMERA CREW were not pleased about having an extra couple of weeks added to their tour of duty. Cameraman Tim McLeod was particularly upset that he wouldn't be seeing his little daughter.

'Tammy's been counting the days,' he was saying. 'I promised her I'd be home for her birthday.'

But no one would dream of crossing Nancy Harris. Besides, they liked her. Nancy was a natural leader.

However, as a consequence of their displeasure, the two younger men were having somewhat more than usual to drink at dinner. So indeed was Frank, and so was Nancy. The somewhat lubricated conversation now turned to the subject of Frank's celibacy, a source of permanent fascination to the team.

Sound engineer Mike Stewart wanted to know if Frank had ever 'poked' a woman.

'No, Mike,' Frank said. 'Never, as a matter of fact.' He laughed. 'Though if I had done, I wouldn't tell you!'

'Would you like to?'

'What do *you* think, now?'

'Well,' Mike shrugged. 'You could be into boys.' He shook his head. 'No, that wouldn't be you, Frank.'

Nancy cut in. 'Not a chance, Mike. But what I want to know about Frank is, how does he cope with all the women in his life?'

'No, what *I* want to know,' Tim said, 'is how he pulls the chicks in the first place. We've seen the way they flock around you, Frank. What's your secret?'

'It's a habit, Tim.'

'Whaddya mean?'

'A white Dominican habit.'

'Aw, come off it, Frank.'

'No, really. Priests seem to fascinate some women. Maybe it's because they're forbidden fruit. Or because women see them as a challenge.'

'That's not why they come after *you*.' Nancy had no hesitation. 'Look, *I* see you as a challenge. Of course I do. But that's not the whole story. What women look for is warmth and caring, far more than looks. You've got the lot, anyway. But you care about people, and that's what brings the women around. It's more than your looks. I know what I'm talking about.'

The booze was making Mike dogged. 'But how do you manage without, y'know, without sex, Frank? I mean, let's face it, it's part of life. I accept you do without it. I take your word for that. But how? D'you not dry up?'

'Mike, love is a lot more than sex. And I get lots of love. From people I've tried to help or comfort. And whom I've actually loved. And – yes, from some of those lovely women, too!' He sighed. 'Sometimes I think, maybe I gave up the love of one woman, and got the love of a lot of women in exchange. I just hope I'm right.'

'Aye, but it's not the same.' Tim McLeod shook his head. 'It's not the same at all.'

Nancy clapped her hands. 'An announcement everybody. A special announcement. As you know, Frank was to do a wedding in Leeds next week. But now it seems he has to go to Ireland after the wedding – urgent family business.

'So guess what? We can all go home till Thursday. I asked Leeds, and they're paying the fares. How about that, everyone?'

There was a cheer and Tim McLeod got up and hugged Nancy.

***

'YOU'RE ONE LUCKY man, you know,' Mr Thorne, the consultant, was saying to Jack Stokes. 'You should be dead. You realise that, don't you? No, don't try to sit up, for God's sake.'

'Am I badly hurt?'

'Badly bruised. A bit of concussion, and two cracked ribs. The seat belt did for your ribs. But, Sergeant, it saved your life, so what's two cracked ribs in that scenario, eh?'

'So what happened? I take it this is the Regional?'

'We prefer to call it the University Hospital now.

You're in the ward, not the morgue – surprisingly. You should be dead, you know. Five others are.'

'Oh Good Christ. Was I to blame?'

'Apparently not. Some young lunatic, speeding as always. Nicked your car and ploughed into the one behind you. A mother taking her three youngsters from school. All four burnt to death, plus the other driver. That's if they weren't already dead. I sincerely hope they were. The cars were welded together.'

'God, that's – that's just awful. Oh Christ. The poor things.'

'By the way, your assistant, Guard King, has been in a few times. Actually he left your mobile phone with the nurse. There's a text message on it for you, he says. I'll have it sent in. Now you must take it very easy. I'll be in to see you in the morning.'

A young woman came in with the phone.

'Would you switch it on, please, Nurse?' Stokes said. 'And if you wouldn't mind getting me the message that's on it. Just hold it where I can read it. Aye, thanks.'

The message was brief. It said:

Jack –

Mar 11 flight-plan? Yes.

Longer thn estmd flight time? Yes in both cases (by approx 45 mts).

Two of names sent to Yard = members of that Finsbury fundst club.

Gt well soonest. Th wont let me in t see u. But wl come soon as alwd

– Des

'THANKS NURSE,' Stokes said. 'Now would y'do us a wee favour, an' delete that message, please? Thanks, Nurse.' He closed his eyes in thought. His chest hurt.

***

ON THE FLIGHT to Leeds the next day, Frank found himself bothered by Tim's words – 'Aye, but it's not the same.'

There were times when something could niggle at Frank's mind, and when the niggling started, it could go on for days. It could be triggered by a few words uttered in all innocence, but that resonated somehow with Frank. Or a sentence or two he read in a magazine, or heard on the radio.

He took out his prayer book to read Vespers, but the words niggled through the tranquillity of the psalmist's prayer. 'Aye, but it's not the same.'

Maybe it was the prospect of doing Diane's wedding that was bothering him. Weddings sometimes upset Frank, seeing all that joy and love and intimacy, and that hope for children and family life, things he could never now experience. But then that's what a vocation involves.

Aye, but it's not the same.

What sort of fragility was in him, which made him

so vulnerable to a few words? It was nearly always something about celibacy, wasn't it? Or else something about priestly ministry.

The stewardess was saying something.

'Beg pardon? Oh sorry. Yes. Yes, thanks, I'll have coffee. Milk, no sugar. Thanks, Miss.'

Look at those legs. Right up to the navel. Here we go again. Remember as a student asking old Father Barden would I ever be free of sexual thoughts. He said yes, after you're eight hours in the grave.

Open the prayer book; try the psalms again. *To you, Lord God, my eyes are turned: in you I take refuge; spare my soul. I have called to you, Lord; hasten to help me …*

Aye, but it's not the same.

Does every priest go through this? Never know, will I, because none of them would admit it if they did. Would *I* admit it to anyone? Certainly wouldn't.

This brooding's an awful thing. Was that how it all started for Tessie? Could this be the start of Alzheimer's? No, sure I've had this for years. But anything can trigger it.

If it's not celibacy, it's ministry. Am I really ministering? Should I be a hospital chaplain, helping people to die well? Or working in the prison, like Padre Mario in Rome? At Regina Coeli. He's a real priest.

Nancy says your ministry's where your talent is. Maybe she's right – women have this insight. Maybe history is the only talent I have, or nattering on TV. Stewardess saying something.

'Huh? Oh, no, Miss. Thanks. But I'd take a glass of water, please – sparking water, if you wouldn't mind.'

Try the prayerbook again.

… the Almighty works marvels for me. Holy is his name! … He puts forth his arm in strength …

Aye, but it's not the same.

***

'THEY'RE NOT ORDINARY police, Meg.' Will Davis sounded worried. 'They're the Nuclear Police. They're answerable to no one but the AEA, the atomic energy people. They're armed, and they've got incredible powers of search and arrest. They can enter any house at will, and they can arrest anyone just on suspicion. If they're on to you, you bloody well better watch out. And the union won't be much help.'

'So what exactly did happen, Will?'

'Well, they asked to see me, two of them, and they wanted to know where you were getting your information from. That was about it.'

'But, as *you* know, it's all public-record stuff. I hope you told them that? Internet, public-record offices, the newspapers, the environmentalists, or whatever I manage to drag out of the Freshpark creeps in interviews. All I've done is draw conclusions from that. So what's biting them?'

'Maybe they just want to shut you up. That's the feeling I had. Let's face it, Meg – those, ah, conclusions of yours have been ruffling some feathers, to put it mildly. Oh, and another thing they said was that you could be putting ideas into terrorists' heads.'

'Oh for God's *sake*, Will!'

'Look, *I* know it's nonsense. The terrorists have the ideas long before the rest of us.'

'You can be sure of that. And I want to get the same ideas into the public's mind to make them aware of what could happen. So they'd do something about it, like pressurising the government to shut Freshpark. Or at least to bury all that high-level waste in a proper and safe way. Anyway Will, nobody's going to shut me up. This stuff has got to be said. Should have been said long ago. You'll back me, won't you?'

'Now when did I ever not back you, Meg? Didn't I put you on to all of this? Alright?'

In spite of her brave words, in spite of her certainty about what she was writing, Meg realised, as she left, how fragile still her newly-won confidence really was. And how fragile would be Will's support, if push ever came to shove. He might like her – she was even beginning to suspect he might love her – but he loved his job too. What kind of choice might he make?

Was this the bottom starting to drop out, that Meg had been dreading? There had to be a catch somewhere. *There always was.*

***

'WHAT I WANT you to do Des, is talk to the fore-man at Dempseys.' Jack Stokes grimaced as a twinge of pain hit his ribs. 'Ask him would he find out, discreetly, if anybody accidentally spilled paint on my car when it was in for servicing.'

'Paint? On your car?'

'Just ask him, right? But don't make a meal out of it.'

Des King pulled his chair closer to the bed. 'Jack. What's this about? You're up to something. I know that look.'

Stokes shifted to make himself more comfortable. The old chest still hurt, but nothing like a few days before. 'This might be daft, Des, but one of the fellas who got me out of the car came to see me yesterday. Damn decent of him, so it was. A young farmer, one of the Millanes from near Anbally. Anyway, before he left, he mentioned that while they were rolling the car right side up, he noticed a blob of red paint on the roof. As if somebody had spilt a can of paint and hadn't cleaned it off properly.'

'Could it have come from the field?'

'He said no. And anyway I remember noticing it my-self as I got in the car. Just before the accident. I meant to ask the garage, but sure I forgot, with all that happened since. Until your man mentioned it.'

'Well then, sure, it could only have been the garage.'

'Aye. That's just what I want you to find out. Was it?'

20

MEG SAT WITH Doc Postlethwaite on the sea wall across from his surgery. It was the old fellow's favourite spot. An orange disc of sun balanced spinning on the rim of the sea behind them. To their left, beyond Freshton, loomed the chimneys of Freshpark.

The doctor was depressed. 'They've their heads in the sand, my dear,' he was saying to Meg. 'They just keep saying it can't happen. So there's going to be total bloody chaos when it does happen.'

'You believe it will?'

'I *know* it will. And the government knows it. But they don't want to tell the public, because they think the public wouldn't know how to face the reality of it. They're afraid people all over Britain would panic. And maybe they would. But it's nothing to the panic there'll be when the whole place actually blows.'

'How do you know the government knows it?'

'Because I've been to meetings – Oxford Research Group and the like – where government officials more or less admitted it. It's generally accepted now that no one can stop a plane going into Freshpark. If the terrorists decide on it, and follow through with their decision, their probability of success isn't a thousand to one, or ten to one, *but almost one to one*. Ninety-five per cent chance of success, to be precise – that's the expert estimate. As good as certainty. They're certain to succeed if they attempt it. And after 9/11 and the London bombs, it's only a matter of time until they do attempt it.'

'So it's all about dealing with the aftermath?'

'Well, if they refuse to shut Freshpark, then, yes, it's about dealing with the aftermath. But, because the catastrophe will be so vast, the government hasn't faced that either. Do you know there are no nationwide emergency plans for anything like this? Imagine, there are no plans for dealing with a nuclear plume hitting London! Do you know that the police have no training in any of this? Or that ambulance men have zero training for this, and zero radiation tolerance?

'Do you know that firefighters have to withdraw from radiation fires after seven minutes? A fireman here told me that. He says it makes them totally ineffective if anything hits Freshpark. But if they stay longer than seven minutes, they're cooked anyway.' The old man turned to look at the last speck of orange sun, touching the horizon. Then it was quenched, and in that instant the sky seemed to flash green for the briefest of instants.

The doctor remained gazing out to sea. 'You asked me am I depressed,' he said, without turning. 'Yes, I am depressed. I've fought all my life against Freshpark. I lost so many patients to it. I lost my wife to it. And my children. And now it seems I'm going to lose my country to it.'

***

DYMPNA MANNING WAS at Leeds airport to meet her brother. She looked older, Frank thought, and maybe a bit tired, but the face was kindly as ever. And that smile, which Frank remembered from the years Dympna had reared him, after the car accident that had taken their parents. Dympna had been mother and father to him then. To all of them, to himself and Tessie and Eileen. But Frank had been her favourite.

'How's Chris?' Frank asked.

'Chris is great. He's looking forward to seeing you. And a game of chess. You know he's retired and sold the practice, don't you?'

'You mentioned that in the letter. He's not bored or anything?'

'Busier than ever. He still looks after the patients here, and they love him. And he keeps the books now, which is great – there's so much paperwork nowadays. But he's just brilliant with the old folks. He's as good as a chaplain. More like a priest than a doctor.'

The niggling pain started in Frank's stomach. Better priest than me, he started thinking. No. No. Forget it. *Sta principiis.* Stop it starting. He pulled himself together, tossed his bag into the back seat of Dympna's VW mini-bus, and sat in.

'And how's the prospective bride?'

'Diane's blooming. She's going to look absolutely stunning tomorrow. She and young Philip were over last night and I never saw Diane looking happier. You know I still can't believe I'm grandmother to a nineteen-year-old.'

'I hear Martin's not coming.'

'He can't, Frank.' Dympna put the minibus in gear and eased out of the parking space. 'He was on the phone the other night. Says poor Tessie's getting worse by the day. He has to have someone in the whole time now, when he's at work. And he's out an awful lot of the time. Sometimes he doesn't get home till all hours, he says. That computer plant takes so much of his time. I don't know why.'

'I'm going over to see him and Tessie after the wedding, Dympna. To see for myself how bad things really are. Not that I think Martin's exaggerating. But you know he suffers from depression, don't you?'

'Oh I know that. He's been over here a couple of times to see me. But it's just on and off. Mostly he seems alright. It's that asthma gives him a hard time. He never had that as a boy. Remember he came over with Eileen a couple of times from America? He was a lovely young-ster. So considerate, for a child.'

'Well he certainly is no child now. He's a fine six-footer, that's for sure. How old would he be now, Dympna?'

'He must be twenty-eight or nine. It's hard to believe, isn't it? Time just flies. Tell me, do you think his depression's getting worse?'

'I honestly don't know. Maybe yes. I get hints of it over the phone. But sure Tessie'd depress anyone with her antics. Y'know, I think his depression started in the Marines. Or soon after he left. Something happened there – we've all guessed that. But we're not sure what, and of course Martin won't talk about it. You know that as well as I do.'

'Well, Frank, if he's not all that together at the moment, he shouldn't have the responsibility of Tessie. I'd be glad to have her over here with me. You know that, don't you?'

'I do, Dympna, and it's awfully generous of you. It means a lot to us all. I'll pay my share, of course, from the TV salary. The Dominicans won't grudge me it. They're a pretty understanding bunch.

'Anyhow, I'll see how Tessie is when I get to Tuam, but it's my guess it won't be long before you'll have her here.'

***

THE ENGINE NOTE changes slightly, as the Boeing 737 leaves cruising altitude and starts its descent. The cockpit windows show the floor of cloud towards which the plane is gently moving.

'We're just a hundred miles out from Manchester,' Omar tells the young pilot in the left seat. 'Now punch in those Freshpark co-ordinates. Do it now. Good. But you don't actually make your turn north until you're just thirty miles out.'

There is silence in the cockpit. The song of the engines rises and falls in a gentle cycle.

'We've already passed south of the Isle of Man,' Omar says. 'You make your turn exactly three minutes from now.'

The quiet descent continues. Coffee shimmers in a plastic cup with the slight vibrations.

'Now!' Omar says quietly.

In one move hands turn and pull the wheel slightly, feet adjust the rudder, and, as the plane banks shallowly to the left, the cloud floor tilts in the left-hand window and the sun moves across the cockpit.

'Straighten up, now,' Omar says. 'Engage computer direct for Freshpark. Switch off transponder and radio. We're now a rogue plane – Manchester will know there's something up, but they won't be sure what for a few minutes – so that gives us a little time. Descend at max possible until 500 feet, to get below radar.'

The plane is now descending at an alarming angle, and the engines' note is rising.

'Ease back a little,' Omar says. 'Three thirty max. You don't want to take the wings off.'

The plane starts to buffet as it enters the cloud layer, and a grey glow surrounds the cockpit.

The buffeting eases. They emerge from the cloud, above a pewter sea.

'Level out at five hundred.'

The sea comes up until the flecks of foam seem just under the wings.

'Now!' Omar says. 'Full throttle.'

The plane leaps forward. A shadow to starboard is the coast of England. The sea is now a grey blur.

'Eight minutes to target,' Omar says. 'This is the dangerous bit – depends how quick Manchester are on to us. And how quickly they act.'

The coast is closer now, a five-hundred-mile-an-hour blur. That's Barrow-in-Furness to starboard.

Directly ahead are the tall towers of Freshpark. Distant. Now they fill the windscreen.

'Line up with Valox Three tower. That one! Now hold it steady.'

The towers tilt slightly.

'Hold it steady,' Omar says. 'There's X-24. The L shape. Go for it. *SLAM IT IN!*'

The cabin lurches and the windscreen goes black. The two men sit back in their seats and breathe deeply. The younger man's hands are shaking.

'We'll try it one more time,' Omar says. 'We'll come in from the south-west this time. Are you up to it? Or how about some fresh coffee first?'

***

JACK STOKES SMILED wryly. 'Deirdre here thinks I'm getting paranoid about this whole terrorist thing, Martin.'

A coffee machine rasped nearby, and a dozen conversations bounced off the hard walls of the hospital canteen. The three were drinking coffee, Stokes resplendent in a red dressing gown. He still looked shaken.

'That's not fair now, Jack,' his wife said. She turned to Martin Gutman. 'I just want him better soon, and out of here. The kids are lost without him. But he's lying awake at night. The nurses told me. I know my man and I know what's keeping him awake. That's no way to get well.' She looked around. 'Isn't the noise here awful?'

'I know what you're all thinking. That *I'm* thinking they're out to get me. Well, boys and girls, maybe they just are. Listen here to me: remember that paint on my car? I was driving a marked car, so I was. Do y'understand? And where did your man work? The man that nearly killed me? You know damn well where he worked – Trucial Software. It's getting to be a small world, now grant me that much at least.'

Deirdre sighed. 'Jack. *Jack.* That poor divil got himself killed. He was coming home from work, for heaven's sake. How could he have been trying to kill you? Killers don't kill themselves.'

'They did at the Twin Towers,' Martin said quietly. 'And they did in London.'

***

IT HAD BEEN a few years since Frank Kane last visited Cawood. Mostly Dympna had taken the train to

London to meet him, or had come out with her husband to visit him in Rome. So he was seeing her Yorkshire Haven retirement home for the first time in some years. He liked what he saw.

It certainly lived up to the name *haven*. It was clear that Dympna and her husband put a lot of care and love into it. The old folk smiled at Frank, and even the few who sat staring into space looked contented. There was no smell of overcooked cabbage or stale urine, often the hallmarks of grudging care.

'Are you sure Tessie won't disrupt all this?' Frank asked. 'Martin says she can be a handful.'

'I wouldn't worry about it, Frank. That's only a passing phase. They get awfully quiet after a while. Far too quiet, I'm afraid. Look at Jean across there: she's got Alzheimer's. Not a budge out of her most of the time. It's sad, really. No, Frank. Tessie won't be a problem.'

It's sad that Chris and Dympna only had the one child, Frank was thinking. I've often wondered why. Maybe there was just never time for more, with her nursing in Leeds, and Chris running a busy medical practice.

Or maybe a physical problem? They've never mentioned one. Not my place to ask.

But they must have been bloody great parents. Daughter's well-adjusted, that's for sure. No wonder, getting that kind of love. And the granddaughter's as together as they come. Lucky the man that's getting her.

Was never the same for poor Martin, with that brute

of a father, and Eileen not able to cope. Could that be the root of Martin's depression, I wonder? Or of his asthma?

***

'OMAR,' THE SHEIK asked, 'can you manage without the Freshpark model for a short while? And the simulator software?'

'We can, but it won't be easy. What's the problem?'

'Changes at Freshpark. Details have just come in, so we have to update the model. Technicians from the theme park will be here after lunch to fetch it to the workshops. They say it could take a couple of days.'

'Changes? What kind of changes?'

'They have built – or are building – a wall around the X-24 complex. Possibly forty metres high. That's the main change.'

Omar was silent for a moment as he pondered the information. 'Kemal, that is about the worst news we've had since we began here. Do you realise what this means?'

'Tell me.'

'It means a drastic change in our training, at least for Freshpark. It means that our aircraft will have to dive almost vertically into X-24, or at least steeper than forty-five degrees. None of our pilots are trained for that.'

He thought for a moment. 'Actually it confirms one thing. *I'm* going to have to do it. I'm the only one who could. Do you realise the wings will probably come off the plane in a dive like that?'

'I WOULDN'T WORRY about the Alzheimer's,' Chris was telling Frank. 'Just because it's hit Tessie doesn't mean you're going to get it. I've known lots of families where it singled out one sibling. No, I wouldn't worry if I were you. Another little drop?' He reached over for Frank's glass. 'It's an XO – rather good, isn't it? They claim it's got real Napoleon in it. Just a tincture of course, these days. Gift from a former patient. Dympna? How about you?'

'More than enough here, thanks love.' Dympna put a finger across her Waterford brandy snifter.

It had been a pleasant dinner: paté and a Sauternes to start; chicken breasts covered in a delicious seafood sauce, a Chardonnay from Chile, and a cognac to round it off. Dympna hadn't lost the touch, Frank observed. They were relaxing now over the cognac, on the little garden patio outside the dining room.

'I was always more concerned,' Dympna said, 'about the mental health thing. I mean, you know we deliberately stopped after one child?'

'I didn't, actually. What I did know was that Eileen had a breakdown in Portland. But I'm sure that was from the awful time Robbie gave her.'

'They diagnosed schizophrenia. And she died in a psychiatric hospital. Did you know that?' The liquor was evidently loosening Dympna's tongue a little.

'No, I didn't.'

'Nobody talked about it at the time. But Robbie let it slip when I went over for the funeral. I kept it to myself.'

'Dear God. No, I never knew that.' Frank contemplated his glass. 'Could that explain Martin? You know, the depression he's been suffering over the years?'

'There could be plenty of other reasons for that,' Dympna said. 'Did you know that his father used to beat him with a walking stick when he was only two?'

'I always knew Robbie was a brute. He ran the family like he was still in the Marines.'

'No, but did you know it went on all through Martin's childhood, until he started growing as big as his father? Then it stopped.'

'It's a wonder Martin didn't kill him.'

'The poor boy got very religious in his teens. Used to spend hours in the local church. Of course the father despised him for that. Used to sneer at him. But Martin just took it.'

'The poor little kid. I never knew the half of it.'

'Hardly anybody does. Even now. Martin doesn't talk about it. Though I did get some of it out of him.'

Frank finished his cognac. 'I suppose it was a relief for Martin to get away to the Marines.'

'Oh, he just loved it. I heard him say that – he was over here a few times on leave – though he never gave many details about his work. I suppose they weren't allowed to. But the amazing thing is, for a big tough Marine, he stayed so gentle and caring. And he's still like that in the way he deals with Tessie.' Dympna sighed. 'I just wish I knew what exactly happened, to make him leave the

Marines, I mean. I thought he'd make it his life.'

Frank's brow furrowed. 'Can I ask you something, Dympna? You said you were worried enough not to have more children? Was that on account of Eileen?'

Dympna hesitated.

'You should tell him, dear,' Chris said.

'You don't know this, Frank, but maybe you should. You were twelve when the accident happened. You know, to Dad and Mam. You remember you were away at school in Newbridge when it happened?'

'Could I forget!'

'Do you remember me writing to you, a month earlier – just after you went back to Newbridge after the holidays – to tell you Mam was in hospital?'

Frank nodded.

'Well it was Ballinasloe she was in, but I didn't tell you that. You know what Ballinasloe means, don't you?'

'What was the diagnosis?'

'Schizophrenia.'

'Dear God.'

'And there's something else you may not know – when the accident happened it wasn't our Dad was doing the driving.'

'D'you mean – ?'

'It was one of the theories. But we'll never know.'

***

SUPERINTENDENT JOHN-JOE MORAN looked worried. 'They're saying your behaviour could be construed as harassment, Jack. No, worse, they're actually *calling* it harassment. It's the word HQ used.'

'You mean the word Flaherty used! Right? Flaherty, high-and-mighty Minister for Justice. And you know where he got the word from? Of course you do.'

'You may well be right. We know the sheik's got Flaherty in his pocket, but we've both got to live with that.' He tapped his pen on the desk. 'Listen, Jack. I want you to ease off for a bit. I know your brief is terrorism. But this is the west of Ireland, Jack. Not the most likely place for terrorists, you'll agree. Who would they want to terrorise around here?'

'That's just what I'm trying to find out.'

'Well, just take it a bit easier, will you? Remember you're still shook from the accident. So don't go pushing yourself. And Jack, a low profile, alright? Forget the warrant for now. Alright?'

'It isn't alright, Super. I already told you about the helicopter. Well, I've got more for you now. Remember those names we got, when we checked papers at the theme park? And the computer plant? Well we sent them off to Scotland Yard and Interpol. And d'y'know something? The Yard knew two of the names.'

'Terrorist records?'

'I wish t'God. No, but two of those fellas lived in London before they came here, and belonged to some

Arab fundamentalist club there – *Al*-something or other. But the point is, this particular club is seen as extremist, so the police have a watching brief on it. That's how they had the two names.'

'Well, it's a bit more concrete than most of what we have. But just go a bit easy, will you? Low profile, like I said. And don't get up the sheik's nose. Remember he's got more clout than you. Or me.'

'There's one more thing, Super. The Yard tells me they're now nearly certain this Omar character's in Ireland – *virtually certain* are the words they used. But they've no idea where, or what the bastard's up to.'

'Well, do they even know what he looks like?'

'They haven't a clue. It's just a name that keeps cropping up. But we've already heard he could be up around Dublin. Tallaght, maybe. Here's hoping he stays there!'

21

'WILL DAVIS IS worried about you, Meg.' Science editor Brian Mottram sipped his coffee. 'He thinks this Freshpark thing's getting to you. You *are* depressed, you know.'

It was early morning and the staff canteen was relatively quiet. A good time to talk, Meg thought gratefully, because you didn't have to yell above the clatter and the chatter.

'I'm more than depressed, Brian. I'm scared out of my wits. Our world could end.'

'Tell me.'

'I'm convinced the terrorists are going after Freshpark.'

'You mean, you have a gut feeling?'

'More than that. A conviction. I have enough facts, not actually to prove anything, but when I put the facts side by side and look at them together, it all points to one thing. They're going to do it.'

'So let's see your facts.'

'Alright. First of all, the Americans in Afghanistan found terrorist blueprints of nuclear plants.'

'Good God. Freshpark?'

'Seattle, actually. But it means they're thinking of hitting nuclear plants. Let me ask you something, Brian. If you were a terrorist, where would you strike next?'

'Not sure I follow you.'

'Alright. Let's say I'm a top terrorist leader. I've destroyed the Twin Towers, and I want to hit America again. Where do I strike?'

'Where they're not expecting?'

'Exactly.'

'I take your point, Meg. They'll strike Europe. Probably Britain again.'

'Now you're talking. Keep hitting America's closest ally, the one that's still fighting in Iraq. Destroy us if they can, or at least cause such havoc that Britain will finally shy away from any further support of America. The way Spain pulled out of Iraq. That's how you get at America.'

'Keep going.'

'Next question. How do you cause the maximum havoc? Bombs in the underground aren't enough any more – you have to up the ante. Let me read you something, Brian.' Meg took a news cutting from her briefcase. 'Just listen to this: "Today we see the use of home-made improvised explosive devices; tomorrow's threat may include the use of chemicals, bacteriological agents, radioactive materials and even nuclear technology." You want to know who said that?'

'One of the usual suspects, I suppose.'

'None of the usual suspects, Brian. It was the head of MI5 herself.'

'So it'll be a nuke plant next?'

'Of course it will. But which one? Well, which would you choose, if you were a terrorist? The one that has piled up plutonium and radioactive waste from all over the world. The one that has practically no defences. The one with feckless management. The one on our east coast, so the prevailing west wind will devastate the country.'

'Freshpark?'

'Where else? What amazes me is that no one's done it yet. But you can rest assured that if all this has occurred to me, it has also occurred to the terrorists. They'd be fools not to go after Freshpark. Wouldn't you, if you were a terrorist?'

***

NIGHTMARE was the banner headline on the front of the *Yorkshire Morning Clarion*'s Saturday feature section. It was in red across a lowering sky above a silhouetted Freshpark. The standfirst read:

> 'Last-century technology built our nuclear plants to withstand the accidental impact of a jet fighter. Could they withstand the deliberate high-speed ramming of a modern airliner twenty-two times heavier? Unlikely, explains science writer *Meg Watkins*.'

The story spelled out the grim statistics: 'Even the world's most solidly constructed nuclear containment buildings were designed to withstand only the accidental impact of a Phantom II jetfighter. A Phantom weighs 26,309 kilos, whereas the Boeings 767s that slammed into the World Trade Centre in New York weighed more than seven times as much and carried fifteen times as much fuel.

'It gets worse. The latest Airbus A-380 weighs twenty-two times the weight of a Phantom, and carries fifty times as much as fuel. There is no known structure in the world, except maybe the Pyramids, which could survive a high-speed encounter with a monster like that.'

One can't blame the plant designers, Meg explained. When most nuclear plants were constructed back in the 1960s, giant wide-body airliners simply did not exist. Nor did suicidal terrorist pilots. So research at that time would have reckoned the probability of an airliner crashing into a nuclear plant at one in seventy million in a given year. As close to zero as makes no difference.

'The Twin Towers changed that forever. It's no longer a question of chance or accident, but of whether or not terrorists will go after Freshpark. And if they do, all they need to attack are the flimsy tanks of high-level waste sitting in a dilapidated building.

'If they do so decide, one of Britain's top nuclear engineers estimates a 95-per-cent chance of success, once they are committed to the final run to the target.

'So the only odds are whether or not terrorists will

attack. And with the level of malice out there, and the incredible and obvious vulnerability of Freshpark, those odds must be very low indeed.

'Mohammed El Baradei, head of the International Atomic Energy Agency, says that nuclear terrorism "is not just a remote possibility – it's a clear and present danger." Up to now, he says, "we did not take into the analysis the possibility of an aerial attack by a large aircraft."

'Now we must.'

Meg's article quoted Ed Lyman, president of America's Nuclear Control Institute, as insisting that nuclear plants 'were not designed with this kind of attack in mind, and it is foolish to make statements, like some in the industry have, that plants could withstand that.'

Meg left her readers with three final thoughts. 'One: The Prime Minister has said that further terrorist attacks on Britain are almost a certainty. Two: Two hundred flights a day pass within 50 miles of Freshpark. Three: Freshpark is less that five minutes flying time from many of these flight paths. *Some flights are only two minutes away.*'

* * *

'SOMETHING'S GOING TO happen, Martin,' Jack Stokes said. 'And soon. I haven't the slightest doubt about it. And I haven't a fuckin' clue what it is.

'But I know in my bones it's got something to do with this sheik. If I could get that search warrant I'd know a helluva lot more. Another one? Christ, you and your sparkling water. Alright, *be* like that.'Long as I don't have to.'

Stokes caught the barman's eye. 'Same again, Tony. We'll make a man outa this fella yet!'

The barman brought the drinks and Stokes handed him the money. 'Kinda quiet today, aren't we?' he said to Martin Gutman. 'Bit depressed?'

'Tessie's reached the end, Jack.' He sighed. 'I haven't told you much, but she's – Jack, I can't handle her any more. You've no idea. And Mary, who comes in to look after her, she's had her fill of Tessie.' Martin sighed again. 'So I'm afraid it's Leeds.'

'What's Leeds, exactly?'

'An aunt of mine owns a nursing home there. Tessie's sister.'

'How about money?'

'Dympna Manning – that's the sister – says she'll take her as one of the family. And of course Father Frank will contribute. I mean, he earns a lot from those TV programmes, and the Dominicans will let him use some money for this if he asks. They're decent like that. Everything's planned.' Suddenly Martin looked weary, almost tearful. 'It's just, I didn't expect it all to happen this soon.'

'Will you be taking her soon, then?'

'Could be any day now. I already talked to Dympna, and she says whenever we're ready. Hey, sorry, I'm going on about my troubles. You've enough of your own with that terrorist thing. Do you think you'll get your warrant?'

'I hope t'God I do. And soon.'

'Something's going to happen, you said?'

'Something is, Martin. Jesus, I wish I knew what, though.'

***

'I WANT FRESHPARK shut down,' Meg said quietly into the studio camera. 'And there are millions of others just like me, who want it shut.'

'But even if they shut it,' the presenter said, 'the lethal waste will still be there. What will shutting Freshpark achieve?'

'Well, firstly, it'd mean they wouldn't be bringing in more spent fuel from around the world, to create even more waste. And secondly, they could then put all their efforts and money into finding out how to store the waste safely. Underground? I don't know. That's what they should be studying. But first shut the place down. That's a start.'

'That's complete nonsense!' snorted Sir Bertram Nicholls, who had sat simmering in his chair at the far end of the table, mouth opening and shutting like a goldfish. 'It's just your sheer, downright pigheadedness.'

Meg turned on him: 'I'm not alone in demanding it, and you know that. Apart from the enviromentalists, there are millions of ordinary citizens who want it shut. Members of parliament want it shut. As well as most of Europe, whether or not they have power stations of their own. The Norwegians want Freshpark shut. The Danes. The Dutch. The Swedes. The Irish government wants it shut, too.'

'Don't mind *them*!' Sir Bertram erupted into his favourite topic. 'As I've said before, the Irish are ignorant, hysterical and envious too. Envious of Freshpark. They envy what we have and they haven't got. What matters is that the British people want to keep Freshpark. We want to keep our nuclear industry. I foresee the day when Britain will be totally nuclear, and when electricity will be so cheap, it won't be worth metering.'

The presenter turned to Meg. 'Do you have an alternative to nuclear, Ms Watkins? I mean, a clean alternative?'

'The cleanest power is the one *that we don't use*. I'm talking about energy conservation. Look, what sense does it make to go on using light bulbs invented a century ago, and break our hearts finding power to light them, when we have those new high-efficiency ones that cut consumption by 80 per cent? Wind power could provide a third of our electricity, or much more if we cut consumption first. And we could harness the tides, like the French did at Rance. Then there's wave power, if there was only money for the research. There's all kinds of biomass and solar power, that could work even under our grey skies.

'Look, I'm no expert, and I'm not pretending to be. But there *are* experts, and nobody's bothering to give them their head. No one's encouraging them to try. And there's no money for them if they do.'

'What about fusion?'

'The experts say it's still fifty years down the line. What we need are solutions now.'

Sir Bertram snorted. 'I don't suppose you're aware that harnessing the tides could pull the moon closer to the earth? Or that all those windmills could change our wind patterns and damage our climate?'

'Oh for God's sake, Sir Bertram, will you stop peddling science fiction!' Meg was out of patience. 'Why don't you tell us the moon's made of cheese? Anyway, this whole debate's got hung up on energy sources. We're locked into talking about supply, instead of demand.

'Look, it's not actually electricity we want, but heat and light, and trains and television. *The things electricity provides*. So let's look at *them*. As I said, why aren't we talking about effective insulation and lighting? That alone would cut the need for a few nuclear plants right away.

'We should be using our imagination and our intelligence instead of banging away at getting more and more electricity, without thinking of how we're using it up.

'Besides, the fact is, Freshpark's not about making electricity, it's about taking in the world's dirty washing and laundering it, reprocessing it. So electricity's not even relevant to the discussion. It's not the reason they keep Freshpark going. And profit isn't the reason either, because there *is* no profit. They don't know themselves why they keep it going, except that it's hard to back out. There's only one thing that *is* certain – the terrorists are going after Freshpark.'

'There you go again with your outrageous scaremongering!' Sir Bertram's face turned purplish as the camera swung towards him. 'And worse still, you're putting dangerous ideas into the heads of terrorists.'

'Those ideas are already in their heads. They're way ahead of us. What I'm doing is making the public aware of what the terrorists are already thinking. And all the details and site plans the terrorists need are already in the public domain, in local libraries and on the internet. That's where I got them. By the way, was it you who put the nuke police onto me?'

'What? I did nothing of the sort! But – but maybe it's time for something like that. You're a hysterical and dangerous young woman. And – and grossly irresponsible!'

Meg was angry, and rather enjoyed the sensation. 'You call *me* irresponsible, Sir Bertram? What about the irresponsibility of deliberately lulling the British people into a false sense of security, when terrorists are almost certainly eyeing Freshpark? They'd be fools not to. This very day two hundred commercial flights will pass within five minutes' flying time of Freshpark. Some within two minutes of it. One slip of security, on just one plane, and

Freshpark blows. I believe no one has even dared to calculate the consequences.'

She lowered her voice. 'But much of Britain will be gone forever.'

'Hysterical scaremongering. And damned ignorance. My advisers assure me our defences are absolutely – absolutely first class. Everything has been considered very carefully, and, uh, robust and stringent arrangements are in place. We've got the RAF at Coningsby, especially for guarding Freshpark.'

'And can they get there in five minutes? In *two* minutes? Coningsby's in Lincolnshire. They couldn't reach Freshpark in *twenty-five* minutes. But five minutes is the maximum they're ever going to have. More likely two. The fact is they can never get there in time.'

'My dear young woman, the likelihood of a terrorist attack is so minimal, so utterly minimal, that it can quite simply be discounted. And that is also the view of the British people. They want their Freshpark. They want to live the normal comfortable lives that electricity enables them to lead.'

Meg spoke quietly, even wearily: 'Did you even *hear* what I said? There's *no* Freshpark electricity any more. None. But there's plutonium and high-level waste, and that's going to destroy us.' She sighed. 'What I will never, ever, understand is how people under a volcano can go on living normal comfortable lives, and be totally blind to the destruction about to come upon them. Do they make themselves blind because they don't dare to see what's coming? Could that be it, I wonder … ?'

***

'MORE TEA, JACK? *Dara!* – *Maeve!* – stop that! I said *now*! Your father needs a bit of peace and quiet before he goes to work.'

'Thanks, love.' Jack held out his breakfast mug. 'Y'see, what's bugging me about the whole thing is, what could terrorists be wanting with Ireland? Like, I mean, we've no enemies, like America has. Who'd want to blow us up? What's there to blow up, anyway?'

'Are you starting to think maybe it's a wild-goose chase?'

'Jesus, no. There's this Omar character. His name keeps cropping up. But he's like a bloody shadow. Hey, hold on a minute – would you turn that telly up? Quiet, Dara. I want to hear this.'

The woman on the TV was talking about terrorism. What was she saying? ('Quiet, Dara! D'y'hear me now?')

'… Only a matter of time before a plane goes into Freshpark,' the woman was saying. 'If you were a terrorist, what would you go for? You'd be a fool not to go for Freshpark! Where else, for God's sake? It makes sense – sense, if you're a terrorist, I mean. And where would you start from? Do you know where I'd start from? Not Heathrow. Not Gatwick. Not Frankfurt. *I'd start from Ireland.*'

Stokes put down his tea, and stood up to move close to the screen.

'Why Ireland, Ms Watkins?' the presenter asked.

'I'd start from Ireland because airports like Galway and Knock are relatively tiny places, laid back in terms of security, and not too concerned with terrorism. And they're right, in a way. Who'd want to blow up Ireland? Ah yes, but what they forget, and we forget too, is that Freshpark is just forty minutes flying time from Shannon. And even less from Galway or Knock.'

'There you go again,' some elderly, pompous, purple face interjected. Looked as if he should be wearing a monacle. 'Absolute rubbish. There is no better defended place in the whole of this United Kingdom than our Freshpark Nuclear Plant. Robust and stringent security. And let me tell you –'

'Turn it off, Dee? I've heard enough.'

'What is it, Jack? What's wrong? Is everything alright?'

'No, Deirdre, it isn't. Leave me alone a wee minute. Just let me think.' He spoke almost to himself: 'I think I understand now.'

***

FATHER FRANK KANE stood up from the television and turned to his sister. 'Where's that broadcast from, Dympna?'

'Liverpool. That's the *This Morning* programme. Been going for years.'

'How do I call the studio? I need to talk to that young woman. Maybe I can catch her before she leaves.'

'Directory enquiries – that'd be quickest. Hold on, let me do it for you.'

***

MEG STOOD WAITING by the studio lift, gazing out of the window at the miniature British Isles anchored in the dock water below. In past years she had often seen the TV weather people step like giants from one island to the other as they promised fair weather or foul.

She stared down at the spot where Freshpark would be located. Where will the death plume drift, after Freshpark blows? Will it go east across the Lakes and the Fells, or will it drift southeast down to Leeds and Cawood, to Grace and Mother?

I'm going to have to get them out. But where to? Who knows where the wind will be blowing when it happens? Nowhere's safe.

Or could bloody Nicholls be right? Could I be just hysterical and daft? No. I know it's going to happen. Doc Postlethwaite knows. The government knows, but they're afraid to panic people. It's as clear as that finger writing on the wall in the Bible.

It has to happen. Freshpark sits there saying, come and get me, I'm here for the taking. That I know in my bones. I couldn't be more certain of it.

No, I'm not daft. They're the daft ones, everybody,

living under the volcano and saying it's not there.

One of the studio secretaries came out on the landing. 'Oh good, you're not gone yet. For once I'm glad that lift is slow. There's a call for you. You can take it in my office if you like.'

'Thank you.' Meg followed the young woman and took the proffered phone.

A mellow, slightly Irish-accented voice at the other end: 'Good morning, Miss Watkins. My name is Frank Kane. You – you just might be familiar with my YTV documentaries. On Channel 4.'

'Father Kane? Of course I know you. And I think the world of your work.'

'Thank you. Thank you indeed. Look, I've just watched your interview, and I'm quite disturbed by it. I didn't know anything about your crusade until this morning. You see, I live in Rome. In fact I'm flying back to Italy later this week.

'Look, I've something to ask you. Would there be any chance you could come out to see me? Something you said this morning, something you said absolutely matched what I've been working on myself. I think you could be of real help to me if we could meet and maybe work on this together. And I think I might be able to help you too. I get the feeling you could do with some help right now. Would I be right?'

'You would be, Father.'

'So could you come? I mean, this week?'

'I'll come as soon as I can get a flight.'

'Naples, now. Not Rome. You see I'm working out of Amalfi at the moment. I should be back there about three days from now. And look, ah, I can't really pay for you to come. I'm a mendicant friar, and all that!' He gave a gentle chuckle. 'But I'll ask my producer. She'll get the money from YTV.'

'My paper'll pay, Father. Don't you worry about that.'

'Well, we'll see. And you'll stay at our hotel in Amalfi. Would you like me to book you in?'

'Do, please, Father. Just as soon as I let you know my flight. I'll need your mobile number, by the way.'

22

'SIT DOWN, JACK,' John-Joe Moran said. 'What's on your mind? Oh not again. I know that look.'

'Super – we've got to get into Castle Patrick,' Stokes said.

'Not a snowball's chance in hell, Jack. And you know it.'

'I want a search warrant. And I want it yesterday.'

'We've still nothing to go on, for Christ's sake.'

'We've lots to go on now, Super. All right, it's circumstantial. But look at what we have now. I mean, when you see it all together. Look. Shannon radar has a record, Wednesday, the eleventh March, of an unidentified something at 2,000 feet, which then goes off the screen. And then Bag O' Bones is picked up by the fishing boat, twenty-two hours and thirty-six minutes later, a hundred miles west of Black Head.

'And the sheik's crowd files a flight plan, Tuam-Shannon, for 3 a.m. Wednesday, March eleven. And the trip takes forty minutes longer than it should. All this within twenty-four hours. Super, that wee Bag o'Bones never came off a cliff. No cliff would be high enough for the state he was in.'

'Did the pathologist say that?'

'Didn't have to. Come on, John-Joe.'

'It's all still circumstantial, Jack. You know better than that. We've been over it before.'

'Wait, John-Joe. We've the same thing again, May eighteen. Or nearly the same. This time an airline pilot sees a ghost helicopter heading west over the Atlantic at 3.35 a.m. Sheik files a flight plan for 3 a.m. same morning. And it's forty minutes late getting into Shannon.'

'Still circumstantial, Jack.'

Listen, I have to have that warrant. I have to get inside Castle Patrick, and I need a forensic examination of that chopper.'

'*You* listen, Jack. You have me half convinced, in case you didn't know. I'm on your side. But Judge Farrell simply won't grant a warrant on what we have. You know what he's like – he'll want real, hard evidence. Besides, we'd be in the shit with Flaherty if we made any move against the sheik. Remember what he said: anything, *anything* to do with the sheik has to go through him.'

'*You* could do me a Section-29 warrant, couldn't you?'

'Now you're really joking, Jack. Where's the firearms to justify it? Or explosives? And even if there were, I've Flaherty to live with. And my career to think of.'

'We have to do something, Super. Some bad things have been happening, and we both know it. And there's worse to come.'

'Tell me something, Jack. Why all this sudden urgency? You've known most of this for a while.'

'Something really big is going to happen in Ireland, Super. Or going to come out of Ireland, I don't know which. And I don't know what. Something really big, and really bad.'

'I know. I *know*. Your gut is telling you, I suppose.'

'Yes it is, John-Joe. *Yes it is.* An' I've a theory or two, even if I can't prove anything yet.'

'Better find some proof, then, hadn't you? And I mean *proof*.'

* * *

'MEG, YOU'RE GOING to have to back off a bit more.' Will leaned back in his leather office chair. 'Upstairs have been on to me. But I gather Brit-Atomic were on to them. Upstairs just wants you – *us* – to be ultra careful. And diplomatic. I gather that 'Nightmare' piece gave the nuke boys nightmares. And what you said on TV didn't exactly placate them.'

'It was all true, Will. You know that.'

'Of course I do. And it's bloody frightening because it is all true. But that's not the point. The point is they say you're putting ideas into terrorists' heads.'

'And I say I'm not. I told you before and I'm telling

you again, the terrorists already have the ideas. That's if they're any bloody good at their job. I'm just putting the ideas into ordinary people's heads, about what they're really facing and don't know it. And that's what the nukies are scared of. They don't want the public to know. They don't want the pressure the public would bring, if the public really knew. For Christ's sake don't let's stop now.'

'Take it easy, Meg. Calm down. You're at your best when you're furious, as I'm always telling you. But – but maybe this isn't the time for furious.'

'Just a couple more pieces, Will. I'm learning more and more about the dangers every day, and honest to God I can't sleep for what I know. For what the government knows. People have got to be informed about what's being kept from them.'

'I understand that. Look, I'm just asking you to cool it for the next three weeks. I'm away for two of those weeks, as you know, in Scotland. So just take it easy while I'm away, that's all I'm asking. Keep up the research, and write your stuff. But print nothing till I get back. Unless something really urgent comes up. Alright?'

Meg sighed. 'Whatever you say. But if it is something urgent? Are you leaving me to decide?'

'You and Brian Mottram can decide together. He's standing in for me. He's got a good head on his shoulders, and he knows his stuff. Upstairs'll stand over whatever Brian passes. Anyway, if there's any doubt, you can always get me on the mobile.'

'That's fine. We'll do it that way. Hold on a minute Will – I've never seen you this uptight. What's really bothering you? Is there something you know that I don't?'

'Yes, there *is* something I know, Meg but you know it too. Maybe it's just time you thought about it. You're aware of the law brought in a while back, about revealing nuclear secrets? You can get seven years in jail, not just for that, but for uttering anything that might endanger nuclear safety. Give that a bit of thought while I'm away.'

***

'GOD IS GRACIOUS to me,' Sheik Kemal Aboud said, 'to have given me this mission. To be called upon to bring the West to its well-deserved end is the greatest privilege I can conceive. Our peoples have longed for such a happening ever since the so-called crusaders sacked our cities, and humiliated us in every century since.'

'Not that you yourself were ever humiliated,' Omar said. 'Your wealth would have insulated you.'

'Not so, my friend. I know I come across as the quintessential Englishman, apart from these robes. But have you any idea of the price I paid for it?'

'Tell me.'

'The humiliation of being an Arab at a British public school. You cannot even imagine the sneers and jeers at my faith, at my semitic face, at the few little customs I tried to hang on to. The mockery about our supposed harems and homosexuality.'

'But you came through it.'

'Oh, I came through it. I came through it by becoming more disgustingly English than even they were. It helped that my family lived in Britain, of course. And I hid my hate. I hid it so deeply that some of those boys still regard me as their friend. Many went up to Cambridge with me and some are in high places in Britain today. My wealth of course has been available to them.

'But I hate them. I can hardly tell you how deeply I hate the – the whole foul brood. I long for the moment when Winchester School lies in ruins, along with the rest of England. Can you imagine, Omar, what joy it is to be preparing that ruin today, and to know that it is the absolute will of God?'

***

'DEAR MS WATKINS,' the email said, 'You'd better take a look at this.' Nothing else, except for the attachment. The sender's name meant nothing to Meg.

But the attachment certainly did. To begin with, it was marked *Top Secret*. It was a confidential document prepared for the House of Commons Defence Committee, by world-renowned nuclear scientist Naom Wasserstein, detailing what would happen if a jumbo jet were flown into Freshpark. And those details were utterly terrifying. Wasserstein was predicting 'a disaster of historic proportions.'

'We'll have to go with this,' Meg said to Brian Mottram. 'If we've got it, the other papers most likely have it too. We can't afford to wait – can't take the chance of being scooped.'

'We'd better ring Will. I hate disturbing him, but he'd want to hear this. What's his number?'

Brian dialled, then shook his head: 'Probably no coverage. Isn't he in the mountains? What now, Meg? I say we run with it.'

'I'd go with that. There's forty minutes to deadline. I can write it as a news story. Will you ask the news desk if they'll run it? Ask them to hold fifteen inches for me.'

'We've got to check if it's authentic.'

'Absolutely. It's on official Commons letterhead, but that doesn't mean much. But we can find out very quickly through Higson. He's our closest MP, and he's on that committee. Would you ring Higson, and I'll get on with this?'

***

MARTIN GUTMAN WAS waiting at Knock Airport when Father Frank Kane came off the British Airways flight from Manchester. As always the thick-rimmed glasses gave Martin the look of a large and gentle owl.

However he looked healthy in spite of the asthma, and didn't seem in the least depressed, which was no mean achievement in a life shared with Tessie. He treated Frank to a powerful bear hug. There was something reassuring about the hug.

What a lovely little airport Knock is, Frank thought. Always enjoy flying in here. Feel so welcome. Feel I'm home, with the gorse lining the edge of the runway. Still some yellow blossoms left. There always are. How does the saying go? 'When the gorse shall cease to bloom' – meaning never. Or forever.

So relaxed here, compared to Manchester. Just a couple of people sitting around the coffee shop and a couple of planes sitting around the tarmac. That's some plane over there, that white-and-gold one. Somebody's executive jet. Who could afford that around here? Certainly no one when I was a boy. But sure planes like that didn't exist then, anyway.

'So how was the wedding?' Martin asked.

'Martin, she looked an absolute dream. I wish you could have been there.'

'I wish I coulda been. But there wasn't a chance in hell.' Martin pulled the gold Suzuki Jimny out into the road.

'Tessie?'

'Ah, Frank, she's out of it. Really. I never saw anybody go down so fast. And then she'll come to herself for a while, and that's worse, because then she knows something's terribly wrong. And she'll start weeping and asking me what's happening her.'

'You've help, of course?'

'Up to now, yes. Mary Madden comes in before I go to work. You remember the Maddens from High Street?'

'Sure I knew Mary as a child. I used to hurl with her

brother. Good people. Well got.'

'Mary will have to quit soon. She can't take much more.'

Both men were silent as they drove towards Tuam. Frank drank in the landscape. A mild sun caressed the fields, which showed yellow-green through chinks in the dry-stone walls. A solitary cloud drifted across the blue.

Home, Frank thought. This used to be home. Coming home to Tessie. Golden Tessie with the wide-open arms and peals of laughter and the jokes and the lust for life and the Morgan sports car she loved. What a beauty Tessie had been.

And the way she carried herself. Like Granuaile. Aren't the Kanes supposed to be descended from her, the pirate queen? Just an old tale, probably. Well, whether that's true or not, the men couldn't keep their eyes off Tessie.

Though why did she never marry? Could it have been what happened to Mam? Tessie would have known, surely. Or maybe she was too busy with the local politics and her law practice.

All the boys tried to catch her. Every eligible bachelor in Tuam. In the whole bloody county. Tessie was famous. And a tough cookie. The politicians respected her. Flaherty was scared of her, because she could see right through him. Weren't they on the county council together? Think so.

Wonder does she realise he's Justice Minister now? It

must break her heart if she does. Tessie had such a passion for openness and honesty. Hated our half-brother Seamus for being such a scoundrel. I see Martin's taking a quiet puff from his inhaler.

'How's the asthma, Martin?'

'I get by.'

'Are you taking anything for it?'

'You bet. I'm on medication. Seems to work most of the time. 'Specially when I use this.' He indicated the inhaler in his left hand.

And now Tessie's dwindling away to nothing, Frank thought. Like what happened to Alice in Wonderland, growing tinier and tinier. Golden Tessie. She doesn't deserve this. I dread what I'm going to find.

'Does our Seamus ever call around?' Frank asked.

'Almost never. He'd be far too scared of Tessie. You know how much she loathes him.'

'We all know that. Can hardly blame her, can you?'

'But he might turn up if he hears you're around. He was away at his place in Portugal, but I hear he's back unexpectedly. So maybe he'll come sniffing for news if he knows you're here. You know what he's like.'

'Then just keep it quiet, Martin, like a good man.'

***

TERRORIST ATTACK on Freshpark could wipe out North of England ran the headline, above Meg's byline. It was on page one, above the fold.

The story spelled it out clearly: 'A report by Naom Wasserstein, world-renowned nuclear expert, has told the House of Commons Defence Committee that such an attack "would leave 200,000 square kilometres of land totally uninhabitable … a catastrophe of Armageddon magnitude."

'Wasserstein says it is clear that the British government and its nuclear administrators have been warned, time and again, that nuclear plants are sitting ducks for terrorists. Nevertheless both government and the nuclear industry *"consistently ignore or even reject these warnings."* His words. Our italics.

'Wasserstein warns the House of Commons Defence Committee not to rely on government or the nuclear industry: "Far from looking for ways of reducing the threat, these bodies simply refuse to admit that the threat even exists."

'The British nucleocrats' paralysis is echoed by the U.S. Nuclear Regulatory Commission, whose position, according to a Washington attorney, is that "since it's not possible to quantify the probability of a terrorist attack, it's not necessary to examine the consequences of an attack or to mitigate those consequences."

'And the terrorists do not even have to cause a nuclear explosion. All they have to do is hit the above-ground waste at Freshpark. Wasserstein: "One of the world's most vulnerable nuclear targets for terrorists is the X-24 facility at Freshpark. Within it are 21 steel tanks con-

296

taining high-level radioactive waste, in the form of liquid that requires continuous cooling and agitation to prevent it boiling over."

'What wreaked such devastation at Chernobyl,' Meg wrote, 'were the mere 27 kilos of caesium-137 that were released into the air from the fire. But the high-level waste in these Freshpark tanks contain 2,400 kilos of that same caesium – that's one hundred times as much.

'But the kernel of Wasserstein's message is – don't trust the government, and don't trust the nucleocrats. For they simply *cannot be* trusted.'

* * *

THE BIG OLD Georgian house on Tuam's Cathedral Street looked just as Frank remembered it from childhood, and on all those visits home, down through the years. The door needed a lick of paint, and the windows too, but otherwise just the same.

No, not the same. For this time there was no Tessie on the steps with eyes wide in joy, arms wide for the hug she had ready for Frank. No Tessie at the door at all.

Even on this early summer afternoon the hall felt cold and damp. It smelled of urine. Frank's nose wrinkled: couldn't Martin do better than that? Or that Madden woman? Surely …

Martin seemed to read his mind. Or saw the nose wrinkling. 'She wets herself, Frank. Only sometimes, but, y'know, like everything else it's going downhill. But I've found a way to handle it for the moment. If I get her to the bathroom in time, she can manage for herself.

'So I just go, "Potty time, Tessie", and she comes along like a lamb. I do it regularly when I'm at home here. She's grateful to me, I think.'Least, she always comes. And I'm getting Mary Madden to say the same when she sees it coming. *She's* starting to get the hang of it too.'

'Where is Tessie?'

'She's right here.' Martin opened the living-room door to the left of the hall.

Frank's eyes filled with tears. The curtains were drawn, leaving a chink from which a pencil of sunlight slanted through the dust motes to put a spot of light on the fawn carpet at Tessie's feet. The glow from the spot touched Tessie's face from below, so that the bottom of her nose and chin and eyebrows were lit.

She sat at the far side of the flickering grate, in the high old winged chair that Mam had always used. She seemed only half the size she should be.

Tessie's left hand moved slowly up and down her right arm, from wrist to elbow and back. It was the only movement. The eyes didn't move: they seemed fixed on the dark corner opposite.

'Tessie? Tessie, it's me, Frank.'

The eyes didn't move.

Frank went over and put his arms around her. She had that smell that old people sometimes have. He felt the wool of the shoulders – Frank looked and recognised a white

Aran cardigan he had once brought her from Donegal.

Someone stood up from the gloom of the room. 'Hello, Father Frank. You're welcome home. 'Tis great to see you again.'

'Ah, Mary, I didn't see you there. How are you? How're all the Maddens?'

'They're all great, Father, thank God. And you're looking well yourself. Those foreign parts must be agreeing with you. Well, I'll be off now, Martin. I'll see you both in the morning. Bye, now.'

'Bye, Mary.'

'Potty time, Tessie,' Martin said gently.

Tessie's eyes focussed slightly, and she made a move to rise. Martin helped her gently out of the chair and walked her slowly from the room.

Frank sat down and started to weep.

***

THE DOORBELL RANG and Martin got up to answer it. He and Frank had been sitting on either side of the fire, Frank with a tumbler of whiskey, Martin with a cup of coffee. Remnants of a Chinese takeaway were on the table. Tessie was safely upstairs in bed. It was a mercy she slept soundly.

'God bless all here!' Seamus Óg O'Kane bustled into the room, all belly and chins. 'Sure an' how's me little brother?'

'Your little half-brother,' Frank replied. 'And I'm bigger than you.'

'As you keep telling me.' Both men laughed.

'Something to drink, Seamus?' Martin asked.

'Whatever you're havin' yourself, Sir.' Seamus gave a chuckle.

'I'm drinking coffee. You wouldn't want that.'

'Ah no, I would not – you're right there. Gimme what *he's* havin'. A nice, large John Jameson. No better man.'

Seamus eased himself into Martin's chair, reached down and threw a couple of turf briquettes on the fire. 'Cold these nights, isn't it? For early summer. Freeze the balls off a brass monkey, hah!' He rubbed his hands. 'Ah, sure, the weather's gone to hell altogether. So how've ye been, little brother? Thanks Martin, thanks.' He took the proffered tumbler, and Martin sat over by the table.

'How's politics?' Frank asked, for something to say. Their common father was about all he had in common with Seamus.

'Grand, thanks be to God. Ah, grand, yes. I'm kept very busy, alright.'

'I hear you're busy with those asylum-seekers,' Martin said quietly.

'Indeed I am. And rightly so.' Seamus' carefully cultivated folksiness was getting better with the whiskey. 'D'y'know how many blacks there are down in Ennis now? Jesus, you walk down the street there and you'd think it was darkest Africa. There's three hundred and twenty-nine bloody blacks in Ennis. Would you believe that? And Gort's full of bloody Brazilians – about a thousand of 'em there. All I can say is, thank God we're surrounded by water, or we'd be swamped altogether. I'll have another drop if y'don't mind.' He held out his tumbler to Martin. 'Arrah sure, bring in the bottle will ya? Just leave it here.'

'Why are you on about this, Seamus?' Frank asked. 'Is it to get votes?'

'Now there you do me wrong, Frank. The people are up the walls about all the dilution when the intermarryin' starts. Dilution of our Irishness. Of our blood, for heaven's sake. To say nothing of the jobs they're taking.' He took another gulp from his whiskey.

Haven't seen him drink this quickly before, Frank thought.

'D'y'know, Frank, the Irish used to be the whitest nation in the world? Sure, d'y'know why all those Americans all want to be Irish? To have Irish ancestors? I'll tell you why. Because the Irish never married the negroes. So if you were Irish, you were sure you were white. Pure white. Did y'ever know that?'

'You're sounding like Hitler, Seamus.'

'Bejaysus, oul' Hitler had his points. Not that I'm fascist, mind you, or anything like that. But I'll tell ye this, we're not goin' to be the white Irish much longer. We're goin' to be the fawn Irish. Or the golden-brown Irish. D'ye want that?'

Where did this fellow come out of, Frank wondered. How can he be a brother of Tessie and me? And Dympna? Well, a half-brother. Was his mother as awful as that? Never heard much about her. Before my time. Naturally.

'… And the people won't wear it,' Seamus was saying. 'Most of the people in this country are up the walls over the blacks and the Arabs swampin' us. They want me to stand up for them.'

'I thought it was your job to lead, not just follow what people want.' Martin spoke quietly, but Frank had the impression he was winding Seamus up.

'*I* want it too,' Seamus snorted. He held the bottle poised, glass in the other hand. 'Listen to me, you. You know as well as I do, this place around here is crawling with bloody Arabs. They're everywhere, and you know it, because you work in their bloody computer plant. They're just taking our jobs.'

'Seamus, nobody can work in that computer plant without special training. It's highly specialised, so they have to bring in people who are qualified. I just work in the office there.'

But Seamus wasn't into listening at this stage. 'It's that bloody emir or sheik that's bringin' them all in. An' nobody can stop him, because he's got that fucker Flaherty in his pocket. Minister for Justice, how are ye! Minister for Passports, if ye ask me!'

'Seamus –'

'An' did ye hear about the mosque? There's a mosque in bloody Galway! Did ye hear that? That shouldn't be let. Fellas hollerin' from minarets. Shouting down the Angelus, for Jesus' sake. Insulting our holy religion!'

That was too much for Frank. 'Seamus. Seamus, show some respect! Those Muslims are our people, and they're entitled to their mosque. And don't you use words like that when you don't mean them. "Our holy religion", will you come off it! That kind of hypocrisy might go down with your constituents, but don't try it with me. Not with me, Seamus. I know you too well.'

'Ah yes. Like all the clergy, you think you own the fuckin' religion. Well let me tell you, you've no monopoly. It's our bloody religion as much as yours. An' I'll tell y'somethin' else. I know my Bible as well as you. An' I know the Jews threw out the Samaritans, and I know God told them to massacre the Hittites or some fuckin' crowd, I forget their name. So's they wouldn't pollute the nation.'

'I don't believe I'm hearing this.'

'I'm not saying I'd massacre the crowd here. No, I wouldn't go that far. But I'll tell you one thing: there's millions out in Africa an' places like that that're goin' to eat us out of house and home. There's a fella called Hardy or Hartley or something – a class of a scientist – an' d'y'know what he says? He says we should drop atom bombs on those fellas in Africa, to put them out of their misery, an' get down the numbers on the planet. There's too many, y'see.'

'Seamus,' Frank said, 'I think you've gone mad.'

'*Me*, is it? *My* mother wasn't mad. I inherited nothing in *my* genes. How about yours?'

Frank stood up. 'Jesus Christ, Seamus. I'll be dug out of you. How dare you!'

'Calm, now. Calm. Woah. Priests can't go losin' their temper, now, can they – ?'

The door opened and Tessie came in. She was in a bathrobe, and one hand was inside it. 'Get out, you!' she hissed at Seamus. 'Get out.'

'Tessie, now, listen –'

Tessie's hand emerged holding a kitchen knife and she lunged at Seamus. He knocked over the whiskey bottle as he scurried out through the door. It didn't much matter, for the bottle was nearly empty.

23

'WHAT THE *HELL* were you thinking of, Meg?' Will Davis was yelling down the phone. 'What the fuck got into you? I told you to back off Freshpark. How dare you publish that! How *dare* you!'

'Will, we had to decide –'

'Listen, I've had enough of your ego trip. This time you've dumped us right in it, you idiot. Have you any idea what you've stirred up? Top Secret, from the Commons Defence Committee? And you went off and *published* it? Have you ever heard of the Official Secrets Act? Well, you will now. *They are wild.* You heard what they said on the News? They're going to take action, they said. Were you fucking well out of your fucking mind?'

'Will, please –'

'I'm coming back tomorrow. Don't you dare touch a keyboard till I get back. Did you get that?'

***

'THERE WAS A bishop in Germany many centuries ago, whose name was Hatto. A man both evil and greedy.'

It was Sunday, and Father Frank Kane was preaching a brief sermon during eleven o'clock Mass in Tuam Cathedral. When Frank had turned up for Mass that morning, the regular priest had invited him to celebrate the Mass along with him, and to address the congregation. It was normal courtesy to a distinguished visiting priest.

The people listened with more than usual interest, for this was the famous TV personality, as well as being one of their own, of whom they were proud.

Frank fixed his eye on his half-brother as he spoke. Seamus Óg O'Kane, county councillor, prominent local politician and nationwide campaigner, was in a front bench of the cathedral, looking as if he belonged there. He exuded devoutness.

'This Bishop Hatto,' Frank went on, 'had bought up all the corn when he saw it was going to be scarce, so he could sell it at a huge profit. But when the famine came to the land, the poor besieged his castle, begging for alms.

'So he appointed a day, and bade the poor go to his great barn, where he would provide them with food. So when the barn was full as it could hold, of women and children, young and old, he set fire to it and burned them all.

"I'faith 'tis an excellent bonfire!" quoth he,
"And the country is greatly obliged to me,
For ridding it in these times forlorn
Of Rats that only consume the corn."

'Well, that night he slept like an innocent man, but Bishop Hatto never slept again. The next morning his portrait had been eaten out of its frame by rats. And then a man came running to say that rats had eaten all the corn in his granaries.

'And then another man came running to say, "Ten thousand rats are coming this way – the Lord forgive you for yesterday!"

'So the good bishop took himself off to his island tower on the Rhine, where no rats could possibly swim the fast, deep waters.

But they have swum the river so deep,
And they have climb'd the shores so steep,
And up the Tower their way is bent,
To do the work for which they were sent.

Down on his knees the Bishop fell,
And faster and faster his beads did he tell,
As louder and louder drawing near
The gnawing of their teeth he could hear.

They have whetted their teeth against the stones,
And now they pick the Bishop's bones:
They gnaw'd the flesh from every limb,
For they were sent to do judgment on him.

'Of course not all bishops are like My Lord Hatto,' Frank

said, and the congregation grinned. 'I doubt if His Eminence here in Tuam would do a thing like that.' Now there were distinct chuckles.

'But seriously, dear friends, we behave like Bishop Hatto every day of our lives. We leave the poor of the Third World to starve. We don't consume them by fire. We leave it to Aids and hunger to do the consuming for us.

'And we are grateful for that, even though we don't admit it to ourselves. For if the people of the Third World took their full share of food, and increased and multiplied too much, our comfortable lifestyles would be at an end. And that we cannot and will not permit.'

Frank caught Seamus Óg's eye. 'Only yesterday I heard someone in this town say that Aids and hunger had the necessary function of bringing Africa's population down to manageable levels. And the person who said that is not alone.

'He had an eminent predecessor, one Charles Edward Trevelyan, who said more or less that at the time of the Irish Famine. Trevelyan, Assistant Secretary to the Treasury, said the Famine was a natural and necessary phenomenon to bring the Irish population down to an acceptable level. And what was his role? He was in charge of famine relief.'

There were no smiles now.

But Frank had one further point to make: 'There is another way in which we resemble Bishop Hatto. He fled to his tower, but the rats got through all his defences and reached him in the end. We in the West, both Europe and America, are like Bishop Hatto, telling our beads and hiding behind our defences – our oceans that surround us; our laws against asylum-seekers; our world-trade organisations that keep us rich and the world's poor poor; our military might that holds the Third World at bay; our high fences around our nuclear installations; the thick walls of our World Bank.

'But the avenging rats will get through in the end. They will get through, to do judgment on us, just as they did on Bishop Hatto. *They always do.*'

There was silence in the cathedral.

Frank glanced at his watch. 'Let us now profess our Faith. I believe in one God, Father Almighty …'

***

'I'M TAKING YOU off the story, Meg.' Will Davis didn't sound angry any more. Just wretchedly uncomfortable. 'Sorry, but I've no choice. I came in to tell you myself, even though it's Sunday morning.'

'You can't, Will. This is life and death. You can't take me off it.'

'I don't have any option. I'm sorry.'

'Don't do this to me, Will. Just don't. *Don't.*'

'It's not me, Meg. It came from Upstairs. The nuclear police were on to them again. They've even threatened to arrest *you*, by the way. There's been a lot of hassle apparently, that none of us knew about. Upstairs won't wear it any more.'

'Couldn't you stand up for me?'

'I already did, Meg. Time and again. Please believe me. It's over, I'm telling you.'

'It's not over. Not until we're all blown to hell, it's not over. Or until they shut down Freshpark. Will, can't you understand?'

'It's over, Meg.'

'Like hell it is. I'm keeping going.'

'Well I'm sorry, but not on our payroll.'

'So you're sacking me?'

'You know better than that. I'm a union man myself remember? Besides, I know what the NUJ would do if I did. No, I'm putting you on City Hall. Mike Bruce's beat. As from Monday.'

'Then it's goodbye, Will. It's been good working with you. And thanks for all your help. You're not a bad person – far from it.'

'Meg –'

'Bye, Will.'

'Don't …'

'Remember you once said, I'd have made it when I could tell you to go and jump in the lake? Well, read my lips …'

***

'THAT WAS SOME sermon, Frank.' Martin spoke with enthusiasm. 'I never heard the place so quiet.'

'I was preaching to myself as much as to them. I'm living the same lifestyle as they do. A lot better than many, at least right now.'

The two men were walking home down Cathedral Street after Mass. People passed them by and smiled and nodded.

'You know, Martin, I missed the most important thing of all when I was talking about the West's vulnerability. There wasn't time to say it. It's this: no defences will save us. Nothing. Only a change of heart. What they used to call "repentance" in the old days.'

'How d'y'mean?'

'You know what they say makes humans different? Different from the other animals? Tools. That's what a lot of anthropologists say. *Homo faber* – man the maker. Tools have brought us where we are today.

'Now what's the ultimate tool? Weapons. Weapons give us the ability to kill. To dominate. To keep the Third World at bay, enforce its dependence on us, and maintain our monopoly of all our other tools. And to keep the world's resources for ourselves, so we don't have to share them. Without weapons, we'd have to share.'

A black S-Class Mercedes hissed down the street, Seamus Óg at the wheel. He saw the two men and gave a curt nod. Frank waved back.

'But you know, I don't agree,' he went on. 'I don't

agree that tools are the ultimate mark of man. There's another view. Another view of the origins of human nature. Some scientists who've studied primitive man conclude that the basic act which makes us human is the sharing of food. Those creatures evolved into humans at the very point when they started to share food. There's a lot of evidence for that.'

They stopped at the door of their house.

'That's what we've just been doing, Martin. That's what Communion is. Sharing the Eucharist, sharing food. It's what the Jews do in their Seder meal. The Muslims do something similar after Ramadan. But those are just symbols of what it is to be human, to share our food.'

'That's the conversion we need, Martin. *From weapons back to sharing*. A conversion to a global politics of sharing our food with the starving, away from a politics of using weapons to prevent that sharing. From being inhuman – literally, non-human – to being truly human.

'But we need this conversion, this repentance, not to get the terrorists off our backs, but because it's right. And it won't stop the terrorists anyhow. To tell the truth, I don't know if anything can stop them now.'

Martin took out his key and opened the door in thoughtful silence.

***

THE HELICOPTER STRUMMED through the sky, high above the hill of Knockma, a few miles outside Tuam. The pilot would hardly have noticed the two tiny figures hiking through the bracken towards the top. The figures stopped to watch it descend towards a distant grove of trees in the plain below. Towers and grey battlements rose above the trees. The helicopter disappeared from view but they could still hear the dying whine of the engines.

'That's the sheik's place,' Martin Gutman said. 'Castle Patrick.'

'Would that be him in the helicopter?'

'No. He's off in Jeddah at the moment. Left yesterday. So I heard.'

'What's he like to work for?' Frank Kane looked every inch the outdoors man in his olive-drab army-surplus shirt and a pair of Martin's green wellies.

'Fair enough employer, I'd have to say. And gives a lot of work around here. Wages are OK.'

As the sound of the helicopter faded, the men could hear a skylark singing high above.

'What's he like? As a man, I mean?'

'We hardly ever see him out at the computer plant. Bit of a recluse, really. Flies in and out in that helicopter. I think he spends a lot more time at his castle and at a theme park he has down in Galway. It's only in the first phase, but they say it's going to be big internationally. Really big.' Martin stopped and took a puff from his inhaler.

'You alright, Martin?'

'I'm fine. Honest. Just need a shot of this from time to time.' He gestured down towards Castle Patrick. 'Y'know, Frank, there's a cop here has a thing about what goes on down there. He says no locals ever get inside. And that it's all a bit mysterious. He's asked me to keep my ears open at the computer plant. Jack Stokes is his name.'

'Could he be right to worry? You know, with all this talk of terrorism?'

'I think he's a bit over the top, to be honest. He's one of those Northern Ireland guys, and you know how they can go on. Like terriers. Though I like the guy. We take a drink together. He asked me to stay close to a couple of Pakistanis who work at the computer plant, so I oblige him. I play chess with them and an Australian who lives with them. But I haven't learned a thing that would worry me. They're OK guys.'

The men reached the top of Knockma and paused for breath beside the immense pile of loose stones that crowns the summit. A hill in its own right – a hill upon a hill.

'Must be a few million stones here,' Frank said. 'Hard to believe our ancestors lugged every one of them up here five thousand years ago.' He lifted one. They were all shapes and sizes. 'Imagine, this stone was actually held by human hands, three thousand years before Christ was born. Isn't that something?

'And down there, you know, where those fields fade into the distance, could be the site of one of the greatest battles of our pre-history, the first Battle of Moytura. We only know it as myth, but according to the myth, the battle wiped out a whole nation. People they call the Firbolgs.'

Frank leaned back on the hill of stones. He put his hands behind his head and gazed out over the plain. 'Do you know, Martin, there's something about that myth that really moves me: a few brief hours of battle and a whole nation wiped out. I've been studying catastrophes a lot lately, the actual historical ones, and there were an awful lot of them. I'm coming to the conclusion that that's the way things happen. The normal way.'

He cupped his chin in his hands. 'But do you know what? I have a sort of premonition that there's another catastrophe coming. And that it's just around the corner.'

'What kind of catastrophe?'

'I've no idea. No idea at all.' Frank shook his head. 'Except, I heard a woman on TV the other day, and she's convinced terrorists are going to wipe out a nuclear plant. It really hit me – and I think maybe that could be the next catastrophe. I've actually arranged to meet her.

'Look, maybe I'm crazy. Maybe it's just me. I've been working hard on those catastrophe documentaries, and perhaps it's getting to me. Some of it can be quite awful, you know. Mass deaths, massacres, extinctions, people dying of sheer terror. Men withering. It's not pleasant stuff. But it *is* history – it all really happened. Ah, sure, don't mind me.'

'You're kinda down, aren't you?'

'I suppose it's Tessie, and what's happening to her. And what's going to happen. Her own private catastrophe. You know she loved Knockma? Did you know that? She used to bring me up here when I was little. Said it was the gathering place for all the faery folk of Ireland. It was her favourite place in all the world.

'That's why I wanted to come up today. I'm glad I did. Will we head down?'

'Sure.' Martin stood up. 'Anyway we both know Tessie hasn't much longer. Much longer here, I mean. The doc says she'll have to go into care almost immediately. So I'll be taking her to Leeds very soon, in a week or two. I'm arranging time off work.'

He stopped for a moment, and faced Frank. 'Y'know what makes me feel bad? Real bad? I've told her she's going on a month's holiday. And she believes me. But *I* know she's never coming back. Never.'

The men threaded their way down through the bracken. A grouse burst from the undergrowth and flapped noisily to safety.

'What will you do when she's gone, Martin?'

'Haven't really thought about it.'

'You could stay on here, you know. Stay on in the house. We could arrange something. Would you like to go on living in Ireland?'

'I haven't thought much about the future.'

'Wouldn't you be better thinking a bit about it? I

mean, the future's going to come, isn't it?'

'Certain about that, Frank? Didn't you just say something about a catastrophe?'

***

WHEN MEG CAME up the stairs to her Leeds apartment, the first thing she noticed was the door swinging on its hinges.

She felt faint when she saw the debris inside. Her filing cabinet lay open; papers littered the floor; sofa and chairs were ripped abdomens with their guts spilling out.

Then she saw that the computer was gone from her desk. But only the CPU – the square box containing most of the works. They had left screen, keyboard and mouse. That's how Meg knew it hadn't been thieves: thieves would have taken the lot. Well thank God at least they didn't get the laptop. That's where all the real stuff was.

The phone rang. Meg's mother was in tears. 'Meg, it's awful. The police smashed everything, they cut open things, they broke into the walls.'

'They did it here too, Mother.'

'And they left Grace screaming. She's only stopped because she's in shock. The poor little thing is shaking like a leaf, here in my arms.'

'Oh Grace! Put her on to me, Mother. It's all right, darling. It's all right. Mummy'll see you soon. Don't be upset, my lovely Grace. Mummy'll see you soon.'

Meg's mother came back on. 'They said they're going

to arrest you, Meg. Better not come to Cawood – that's why I'm ringing. Hide somewhere. For a while. Grace and I will manage. We'll be alright, I promise. We will, Grace, won't we, sweetheart? And so will Boo. Say good-bye to Mummy, now.'

24

FRANK KANE SAT in a garden nook at the Santa Catherina Hotel in Amalfi. His short-sleeved white shirt and black chinos were simple but elegant. The scent of bougainvillea was balm. Frank was both tired and elated after the day's filming across the peninsula at Pompeii. It had been a good day.

A stone cupid eyed him impishly from a grotto across the garden. The yellow of the lemons, nodding against the blue Mediterranean sky, was the flag of Sweden. Or Tipperary's colours. Or County Clare's, for that matter. How was it that yellow and blue together had such a magic? Was Vermeer the first to notice it, with his *Women at a Spinet*? Or his *Girl with the Pearl Earring*? It's in nearly all his paintings. And it was lemon yellow, not chrome yellow or any other hue, that Vermeer loved. Together with the blue. Frank could see why.

Dinner would be welcome, with Nancy Harris' wit, and the camera crew for company. Great they got on so well. Frank sipped his martini. Far below, the white beak of Amalfi sipped the indigo waters of the Mediterranean.

It was framed by the lemon trees' brilliantly-burdened branches.

Frank's mobile phone rang, and he tugged it from his shirt pocket. 'Miss Watkins? Hello. You're coming, then? ... Oh? Oh dear, I'm sorry to hear it. Did they take much? ... You don't mean – ... So now no job? My heavens, this has been one bad day. So what are you going to do? ... You mean, without funding? How will you do that? ... And who'll publish them? ... Wait a minute, let me think. Let me think a minute. Listen, carefully. Have you thought of doing it as a book? ... Yes I realise that, but we could *find* one. We could find a publisher. A book like that – it's a wonder they haven't come looking for you already.

'It's too late tonight, but tomorrow I'll ring my agent in London. You'll have a publisher, believe me, and soon. Meanwhile, get on that plane and come out here. Borrow if you have to. We'll refund you. Now, you'll come? Promise?'

***

'THEY'LL BE ON to us within the week,' the sheik said. 'Both the CIA and the British. It's unfortunate, but there it is.' He turned from the computer on his elaborate desk. 'Jeddah wants us to strike immediately. Sit down by me, Omar.'

'We can certainly hit Freshpark,' Omar said. 'I have everything ready. And *I'm* ready. But the other European plants – we don't have our men in place, and it would take several more weeks. Better disperse them: let them reassemble wherever Jeddah decides. What do you think?'

'We have no option, Omar. But are you still determined to go into Freshpark yourself?'

'There's no one else can do it now. With the new walls around X-24, I'm the only one who could dive a plane in. None of the others are trained for that.'

'Omar. My dear boy. I wish it didn't have to be this way.'

'I wish it too, Kemal.'

'You know I'd be glad to die with you, don't you? Except I've further work to do. You understand that? Otherwise I would be beside you when you do it. You do know that?'

'I have never doubted it, my friend.'

'You know, I even thought of using the Learjet on one of the other plants, but it would be far too light to have any effect.'

'I understand that, Kemal. I have never, ever doubted your courage. Or your dedication to the Cause. But I will miss you. No, that's not quite right – I won't be there to miss you. But you'll miss me, won't you?'

'More than I can ever say, my beloved friend.'

Both men stood spontaneously and embraced. Neither of them could speak a word.

***

'YOUR ROOM ALL right, Meg?' Father Frank asked.

'I can't believe it. I'm not used to this. The view!'

'Well I told you YTV's paying for it, didn't I? I asked them, and they said yes. I'll tell you why in a moment.'

Frank sat with Meg in the cliff garden of the Santa Catherina Hotel, high above Amalfi. The sea whispered, hundreds of feet below the parapet.

Meg looked even better in the flesh than she had on television. There's an innate assurance that comes from good looks, yet she hadn't sounded that assured on her last phone call – quite the contrary. Anyhow, here she was and she was certainly good looking. Frank had that uncomplicated admiration for a beautiful woman which genuinely celibate men often manifest.

'A drink, by the way? Or a coffee?' Frank asked.

'A cappuccino, thanks.'

Frank signalled the waiter. *'Due cappuccini, per favore.'* He turned to Meg. 'Now, to brass tacks. You tell me you got out just ahead of the posse? And they've ransacked your place? First question: have you done anything wrong? I mean, have you been revealing nuclear secrets or security secrets or anything like that?'

'Nothing that's not on the internet, or common knowledge anyway. Well I did publish a document marked *Top Secret*, but even in that there was nothing really new. It was simply authoritative because of its author. And all the other papers ran with it too. It's my conclusions they don't like. That Freshpark's going to be blown up.'

'And your paper's dumped you because they don't want trouble?'

'That's about it. Well, no, actually *I* dumped *them*.'

'Let me think.' The wicker chair creaked as Frank leaned back and put his hands behind his head. 'Right. First, if we get you a top international publisher, you'll have clout behind you. Real clout. First thing the publisher'll do is hire a lawyer to get those police off your back, so you can continue your work.

'I've just had an idea. Did you clear up your apartment after the raid?'

'I just ran, Father. I was so scared and upset. I rang a neighbour from the airport, to get the door fixed. The neighbour's a friend.'

'How long ago was that? I'm Frank, by the way, forget the "Father" bit. Alright?'

'Fine. How long ago was what?'

'That you phoned your friend?'

'Just hours ago. I was lucky to get a seat right away to Naples – er, Frank!' She smiled slightly.

Frank pulled out his mobile phone. 'Ring the neighbour. Ask her has she cleared up your flat. If she hasn't, tell her not to.'

'But why ever –?'

'Trust me. I'll explain in a minute. Here, give her a call.'

Meg did so, paused, and talked briefly. She turned to Frank. 'She's got the door fixed and locked, but that's all.

She's too scared to clear up yet, in case the police come back. So what's this about?'

'Just an idea. You know I work for Yorkshire Television? Actually it's why I asked you out here. I've an idea that might interest you – and them. But we'll talk about that later. Right now I want to suggest to our local newsroom back home that they film the mess in your flat. It could be useful later, maybe to put pressure on the police. Get them off your back. Would you agree to that?'

Meg nodded, and Frank lifted his phone again.

* * *

'WE'VE SO MUCH to learn from them, Jack.'

'Such as?'

'Tolerance, for one thing.'

Jack almost choked on his pint. 'Tell me anything else, Des. But *tolerance*? The Muslims? Will ya come on, now.'

The two men were having an after-work pint at Galway's Skeffington Arms. As usual, the talk was about Islam: there seemed no getting away from it these days. But this was different: usually Des kept his personal views to himself.

'How much do you know about them, Jack? Really?'

'Only what I pick up by way of work. And what I read in the papers. But I'm aware of all that Sharia stuff. Stoning, and the like.'

'Those are the extremists – the equivalent of us burning witches. Do you know when we burned our last witch here in Ireland? 1895. Unofficial of course. But we did it. Thought the woman was a changeling. Happened in Tipperary.

'What about us locking pregnant women away for the rest of their lives? That was done in our parents' lifetime – in *our* lifetime, for God's sake. What about raping children in orphanages all over Ireland? Canada too. Do you think ordinary Muslims would do that? They absolutely love children.'

'Well I surely hope they're not as bad as we were.'

'Remember last year I went to that wedding in Gaza? Leila's cousin. Remember?'

'I remember you said you got no strong drink!'

'True, but no matter. That visit was a turning-point for me. The people who took us into their homes were the warmest families I've ever met. They really meant it when they welcomed us. I kept comparing it to the West's dreary have-a-nice-day claptrap. Such hospitality and genuineness. And real tolerance of me as a Christian.

'I found myself thinking: we must be doing something really terrible for terrorists to emerge out of such tolerant people as that.' Des pulled at his pint. 'Do you know where the greatest tolerance in history existed?'

'You're going to tell me.'

'In Andalusia, under the Muslims. In the Middle Ages. That's when the Jews, the Arabs, the Christians and even the Goths all lived in harmony. It was an oasis for freethinkers. There were women poets, and women judges –'

'Where'd you learn all this?'

'I'm, uh, doing a course. Islamic Studies, with the Open University.'

'Christ, that's the first I heard of it. C'mere Des, you – you haven't joined them, have you? The Muslims, I mean? You haven't become one?'

'No, but I go to the mosque with Leila from time to time. It's here in Galway. Only a couple of rooms, but do you know what? I have never seen people pray as they do there. I mean, they *pray*. If prayer puts you in touch with God, then these people must really be in touch with God.'

'Take your word for it, Des.' Jack chuckled. 'But if I catch you smuggling a prayer mat into the day room, I'll know the truth, heh?' He stood up. 'Right, I'm off to Tuam. Martin's got a couple of ideas for me. Got them off some uncle of his that was visiting. You'd never know what could come in handy.'

***

IT WAS AFTER midnight when Stokes climbed into his replacement Toyota Prius and headed back south out of Tuam. The wind was in the trees and a half moon scudded among long, ragged clouds. His mind was pondering some notion Martin had picked up from his priest uncle – that catastrophes are part of the normal working of the world. So could we be heading for one now, he wondered.

But sure aren't there catastrophes in everybody's life? Getting cancer's a catastrophe for the one who gets it. A head-on collision is another, he thought, at the very moment some idiot crossed the solid centre line and roared by. Only difference is the numbers affected, like in a tsunami or an earthquake. And sure we'll all be gone in the end anyhow. When the time comes.

Aye, the real catastrophe is when the end comes *before its time*. Like all these poor young boys topping themselves these days. Like at that bloody Hanging Tree. As the Prius hissed down the road to Galway a memory of those blackened branches came to him. Spontaneously Stokes swung the car to the right at the signpost, and headed down the side road that would take him to the Tree. As usual, he wasn't sure why. He was never quite sure why. As if the Tree summoned him.

The road ahead glinted fitfully as the half moon came and went. At one point it came half up out of a line of scudding cloud and, as it sliced through the cloud, it was the dorsal fin of a great white shark.

Twenty minutes later Stokes was picking his way between the trees, his flashlamp illuminating the slippery remnants of last year's oak leaves on the faint track before him. They looked like tiny decaying children's hands. As he reached the clearing he switched off the flashlamp and just stood and gazed. For a few moments the moon gazed back through the bare ruined branches of the Hanging Tree. Then it scurried behind a cloud, leaving the clearing in darkness.

As his eyes got used to the darkness Stokes found the old tree-stump and went across to sit. Above him the oak leaves conversed with the fitful night breeze, the boughs nodding agreement.

But the Hanging Tree never moved at all. It had no leaves to catch the wind.

Some tiny creature rustled among the carpet of leaves. Something squealed briefly, a distance away. Wings flapped somewhere above – perhaps an owl.

Deirdre had once told Stokes that when the ancient Celts cleared a woodland, they always left one great oak tree in the centre of the clearing – the *crann bethadh* – and it became their Tree of Life. It was sacred, with its roots reaching to the Lower World and its branches reaching towards Heaven.

But here before him, Stokes thought, was a Tree of Death. For a moment he imagined it groaning under the full harvest of its strange fruit – all of those lush, abundant, elongated, humanoid, rotting things that had ever hung from its boughs. Remains of those wretched Croppies whose screams had echoed through the forest as they were dragged here after 'Ninety-Eight; and later of those silent ones who, down the two centuries that followed, had crept here of their own will, bearing their own personal rope. Once more the words of Billie

Holiday slunk through his brain –

> Here is the fruit for the crows to pluck
> For the rain to gather, for the wind to suck
> For the sun to rot, for the tree to drop
> Here is a strange and bitter crop.

But they don't mind by then, no, not by the time they rot and drop. They're long past minding. Only the onlookers mind by then, and they only mind the smell.

No, the awfulness is at the beginning. Whose is the greater anguish – the man who's dying to live, but has his head forced inside a noose and feels the rope closing on his neck before that awful *THUNK* that snaps it?

> *Bhí caipín bán air in áit a hata*
> *Agus róipín cnáibhe in áit a charbhat.*

Aye, indeed, the white cap in place of his hat, and the hempen rope in place of his cravat.

Or is the greater anguish that of the man whose life has grown so unbearable that he inserts his own head in a noose that he tied for himself? When life itself seems more awful than the prospect of a rope strangling that life away? Like all those youngsters throughout Ireland who felt precisely that way in the past few years, and acted on it. Some at this very Tree.

A twig snaps in the darkness, somewhere away to the

right. Some creature of the night. Another twig snaps, nearer this time. And another. Then the sound of something – no, some*one* – making a way towards the clearing. Faint shuffle of feet through undergrowth.

Less faint now.

A dim figure enters the clearing only a couple of metres from Stokes. It seems to have something hoisted on its shoulder. It pauses, then turns and makes directly for the Tree.

There's movement now in the darkness beneath the Tree.

Stokes switches on the flashlamp, and gets a momentary glimpse of a white shirt with dark epaulettes on the shoulders. Jeez, a garda? A white face yells something incomprehensible, something foreign, then turns and disappears into the darkness. Stokes makes to follow, then, realising the futility of it, tugs out his phone as he hears the crashing in the undergrowth growing ever fainter.

After a brief phone call for assistance, he turns the flashlamp on the Tree. A length of orange clothes-line has already been looped over a horizontal bough, but no noose has yet been tied. An aluminium step ladder stands beneath the tree.

***

FRANK AND MEG sat at a café table in the tiny main square of Amalfi, in the shadow of the crags that soar above the town. Hordes of youngsters perched like starlings on the long, stepped ramp leading up to the cathedral. They even chattered like starlings.

Frank put down his coffee cup, leaned back and put his hands behind his head. He did that a lot. He seemed to choose his words carefully: 'When I listened to you on TV the other morning – it was just by chance I happened to hear you – anyway, something you said resonated with me. You asked the exact question I had been pondering for a long time, certainly ever since we started this TV series we're doing. But, unlike me, you answered the question.'

'And that was?' Meg eyes were wide with interest.

'Let me explain something to you first, Meg. We've been doing this series – *Great Catastrophes in History*. It's not finished yet, so you won't have heard of it. But I've found that the one thing that comes up, over and over again, in every catastrophe in history, is that people are always caught unawares. And especially when the omens are so clear that people couldn't possibly be unaware. Yet in almost every case they are. Or rather, they're in denial.'

Meg nodded.

Frank caught the waiter's eye. '*Due limoncelli, per favore.*' He turned to Meg. 'You'll like this – made from the lemons here. Anyhow, I've pondered the question, and brooded over it. I mean, it's been like that from the very beginning. People refusing to see the destruction that's staring them in the face. Sodom and Gomorrah, for heaven's sake. Didn't Lot break his heart trying to warn them?'

'Or the Black Death. Or the Holocaust,' Meg said.

'Indeed. The greatest man-made catastrophe of them all. We've done one of our series on it. The catastrophe was there, staring them in the face, yet the Jews in Germany and all over Europe, were sure it couldn't happen. Even when it had already started. You see, it was unthinkable. I call it the Pompeii Syndrome – the people in Pompeii saw death coming and just went on about their business. Extinction was unthinkable.

'That's actually the key word – *unthinkable*. But I couldn't believe when I saw you on TV saying exactly the same thing. However you were talking about something quite different. A catastrophe that hasn't yet happened. Freshpark. That hit me so hard, because I've had this strange premonition of a coming catastrophe. Yet I never thought of Freshpark. Dear God, Meg, if you're right …'

'Yes,' Meg said slowly. A hand went up to her mouth. 'Yes, indeed. I'm not sure I realised the full significance of that remark when I made it. But I do now – yes, the Pompeii Syndrome. Of course. I understand now: I understand that creep Nicholls and those Freshpark people. The government, too. And the ordinary British people. It's unthinkable, *so they cannot think it*. Even the government cannot think it. They're all in denial. Oh heaven help us all. We don't stand a chance do we?' Tears came into her eyes.

Frank leaned over and gently touched her shoulder. 'We do stand a chance, Meg. You see, we have something they didn't have at Pompeii: it's called television. We can cut through the Pompeii Syndrome. If it's used rightly, television could make people finally think the unthinkable. Even the unthinkable about Freshpark.

'And you and I are going to do just that. That's why I asked you out here. By the way, how's the limoncello?'

'Tastes like cough mixture!'

'We'll get you a cognac.'

***

MEG LIKED WATCHING the filming. Frank looked gothically beautiful in his long cream-coloured habit with the hood thrown carelessly back and the deep mandarin sleeves and the vertical lines of the scapular. Why was such a stunning outfit wasted on celibate friars, Meg mused. He was one of those saints you see carved on the doorways of York Minster. If he spread his arms wide, you'd expect the Pompeii dead to arise.

'Cut!' Nancy Harris called. 'Coffee, everybody.'

Not frightfully friendly, that Nancy Harris, Meg thought. Certainly a bit cool in the jeep this morning. Cool? Cold. Well sod her: I don't need that. And I needn't take it. Not any more. Oh, well, maybe she was just preoccupied, planning the day's filming. Maybe. Huh.

Frank was coming across the grass towards Meg, carrying two plastic cups. Gorgeous material that Dominican habit. Pure wool, must be. And spotless. How do they ever keep them clean?

He handed Meg a cup. 'You don't take sugar I've noticed. Now, while we have a chance, let me sum up what I told you last night. You're not too tired?'

'Not at all. By the way, that Nancy doesn't seem very friendly. Is she a bit of a cold fish?'

'Nancy?' Frank was surprised. 'Nancy's alright. You just need to know her better. She's grand, and she does a fabulous job of directing.'

'Maybe so, but she doesn't like *me*.'

'Give her time, Meg. Anyhow, let's go over my idea. As I told you, we're just finishing this series on *Great Catastrophes*: the present one's on Pompeii, and then we're doing a sort of round up of catastrophes throughout history. But it never occurred to me, or to Nancy for that matter, that we should do one on the present day. Indeed, on a catastrophe that hasn't even happened yet, but could happen.'

'That *will* happen.'

'After what you told me last night, I'm inclined to believe that. *Quod potest deficere, aliquando defecit.*'

'Sorry?'

'Thomas Aquinas – "Whatever can fail, sometimes will." Just the Murphy's Law of the Middle Ages. You'd probably call it Sod's Law. Anyway, what we're going to propose to Leeds is that we finish the series with one further one on Freshpark – "the catastrophe to come".

I've already talked to Nancy, and she'll back me on this.

'Now, if we get the green light from Leeds, I want you on the team as consultant. Full-time, and on the payroll. I don't know if I made that clear? I'm sure the money would help right now, wouldn't it? But it's in our interest. There's no one knows more about the Freshpark threat than you, so we need you. How about it, Meg?'

'Well, alright. If I can get along with that Nancy, I suppose. But we'll have to move very fast. I mean that, Frank. I honestly think there's very little time left.'

***

'THEY WANT YOU off the case, Jack.' Superintendent John-Joe Moran breathed deeply. It hadn't been easy getting it said.

'Who do?'

'Dublin. Flaherty, to be precise.'

'I fuckin' knew it. That fuckin' sheik's been at him.'

'Jack –'

'Anyway, how can they want me off the case? There isn't one. There's no case to take me off. But there might be soon. Y'want to hear my news?'

'Look, news or no news, they want you moved off the whole terrorism beat. They're saying you have a bee in your bonnet about it. You're getting everyone upset; you're getting your colleagues upset; you're getting that sheik upset.' Moran fiddled with his ballpoint. 'And you're getting me upset, if you want the truth.'

'So you're taking me off it?'

'As of now, Jack. Exigencies of the Service demand it, as they say.'

'Well, fuck you, John-Joe. I thought you'd do better than that.'

'I've no option, Jack,' Moran said coldly. 'I do as I'm bid. And watch your language. Oh, and you might call me Superintendent, if it's not too much to ask.'

'So you don't want to hear my news, then – Superintendent?'

''Course I do. But it'll make no difference. I told you, my hands are tied. What've you got, anyway?'

'Hanging Tree Man Number Two – fella with the epaulettes. They found him.'

'Dead or alive?'

'Drowndead.'

'Where?'

'Lough Doon. Trout lake a few miles from the Hanging Tree. A fisherman found the body floating.'

'Well, that's it then. Case closed.'

'Indeed it's not – *Superintendent*. Remember I said he looked like a garda in the darkness? The epaulettes? Well, they were there alright but he was no garda. One of the Knock airport people identified him: he was one of the sheik's two chopper pilots. *Now* can I go back on the case?'

'No you can't. You heard what I said – my hands are tied. But with this kind of news there'd be nothing to stop you scrabbling away on your own. Seeing as those eejits in Dublin never thought of putting anyone in your place. Long as *I* don't know, of course.'

'You won't regret it, John-Joe. We're nearly there. Can I keep Des?'

'Off the record, yes, Jack. And I can see you're nearly there. That poor dead chopper pilot might fly you right in.'

***

AMALFI'S REFLECTED LIGHTS writhed golden in the dark harbour, as Meg gazed down from her balcony in the wee hours of the morning. There had been no sleep. The call to her mother had left her unnerved: the police had called again, and Grace was frightened and calling out for Meg.

And how do I go back, Meg was thinking. What if the police are at the airport? It's seven years' jail for disclosing anything that could prejudice nuclear security, or for even being reckless about security. Grace will be twelve when I get out. *No*, Freshpark will have blown long before then. Oh God. Don't panic. I've got to get Grace and Mother away before it blows. I know people are saying I've gone mad. I'm not mad. My heart's starting to thump. Hasn't done this for ages. I've nowhere to go – can't stay here. Nowhere to take Grace and Mother and just hide from the police, no, hide from Freshpark. Nowhere to go. Don't panic. Maybe I *am* mad. Oh God, my heart hasn't thumped like this for years…

From below came the quiet sound of a throat being

cleared. Meg leaned over to look. On the balcony below was the faint figure of a man in a light-coloured bathrobe, leaning on the balustrade, gazing silently out over Amalfi. As Meg watched, the figure straightened and brought the hands behind the head.

The very sight of Frank gave momentary ease to Meg's thumping heart. Then the thumping started again. She felt as if something was going to burst. And now she was trying to get her breath.

At that moment, Frank turned and looked up. He peered for a moment, and then whispered, 'Meg? Is that you?'

Meg started to weep convulsively. She couldn't even whisper a reply.

'Meg. That's you, isn't it?' Frank could hear the weeping now. 'Would you like me to come up? Meg, I know it's you. Just answer. Would you like me to come up?

'Meg, I'm coming up. Let me in when I knock.'

25

FRIDAY 11.40 A.M. Jack Stokes tapped on John-Joe Moran's door and entered in a state of high excitement. 'Super, we've got something big from Scotland Yard, here. If this comes through, we'll be getting that search warrant.'

'You're still off the case officially, Jack. So if this is an email, I don't know how you got it. Dublin told me they were stopping your security clearance.'

'Well, they haven't yet. Super, will ya just listen to this? Will ya?'

'Go on.'

'Omar's here in County Galway. The Yard says it's all on some Arab grapevine that's usually reliable, and he's supposed to be planning something soon. Either here or in Britain. They're pretty sure of it. But there's more. Remember the names we sent to England? Two turned out to be members of some Finsbury radical group, re-member? Well, this here's what's new: one of them turns out to have been in Saddam's Republican Guard, and may have turned terrorist after the Americans disbanded the Iraqi army.'

'You said, *may* have.'

'They're pretty certain it's true, but they just want the Iraqi authorities to confirm it. We'll know in a couple of hours.'

'Alright, Jack. Let's see what we have that's new. One: sheik's chopper pilot tops himself. Two: Omar's right here. Three: we've a confirmed Iraqi terrorist working for the sheik – well, *if* he's confirmed. Could be one and the same, Omar and this Iraqi, we just don't know yet. But all this together certainly puts a different complexion on things.'

'We'd get our search warrant, wouldn't we? I mean, add that to all the chopper's unusual trips, and so forth. In fact, you could issue a Section 29 yourself. You could cite an emergency.'

'Same as always. Where's the firearms or explosives? And I wouldn't do it anyway, Jack. I've a career here, and Flaherty would tear the balls off me. No, we'll wait till Judge Farrell gets back, and go the standard route. He's due back tomorrow night for God's sake, and we'll go for the warrant right away. He'll sign on this evidence if, as I said, Iraq confirms for us.'

'So when do we go in? I'd say about four in the morning. They wouldn't be expecting us.' Jack rubbed his hands with glee. 'And maybe we'll catch that friggin' sheik with his pants down.'

'Not confirmed yet, Jack. Don't count your chickens. And don't forget: you're still off the case – officially!'

FRIDAY 10.45 P.M. Martin Gutman was drinking pints in Buckley's. That was unprecedented. Jack Stokes was drinking pints, too, but that wasn't unprecedented.

The two men had different reasons for drinking. Stokes was celebrating the coming warrant, having had the terrorist confirmed by the Iraqis. And Martin Gutman was in a depression about having to take his aunt to Leeds.

'I can't look her in the eye, Jack,' Martin was saying. 'I've told her it's only for a month. Just a holiday. But she's never coming back, y'see. *I* know that. And to tell the truth, I think she knows it too. She has that look of somebody going to her execution.'

'Will ya stop, Martin.'

'No, really. She's sort of resigned. It's awful. Not even mean to me any more.'

'Sure you're only doing what y'have to.'

'I've had my fill of doing what I have to. I thought doing-what-I-have-to was over.'

'How d'you mean?'

'Jack, you know what happened in the Marines.'

'No I don't, as a matter of fact. You never told me.'

'Did I not?' Martin took a long pull from his pint. 'I never told you about shooting up that column in the Kush?'

'No.'

'I never told you about flying this A-10 at a whole column of stragglers and blowing them all to hell? A-10's a tank-buster, y'know.'

'So what happened?'

'They were women and children. That's what happened.'

'Oh God.'

Martin put his head in his hands and started to weep. Jack laid a gentle hand on his shoulder. 'It's alright, Martin. It's alright.'

Martin looked up with tears running from his eyes. 'It's *not* alright. They showed me the photos later. I'll see them for the rest of my life. That's when I turned. That's when I turned against the whole damn thing. The fucking cunts – they're destroying the world. Just for Wall Street. We have to stop them.' He started to weep convulsively.

'You never told me you were a pilot,' Stokes said quietly.

'Didn't I? Well, I was. A-10. Twin-engined tank-buster. Jeez, that was some motherfucker. One burst from the Gatling could take out a whole column. Some motherfucker. Jeez.'

'C'mon, Martin. I'll run you home. Leave that – you're not used to it. When are you taking Tessie, by the way?'

'Fuck. Lemme think. Monday morning. Check-in's 8.15. Plane leaves 9.30. Oh God, Jack, I wish I didn't have to do this. She won't be back, y'know. Only she doesn't know it. Or maybe she does.'

***

SATURDAY 8.25 A.M. The queue moved forward and Martin and Tessie reached the check-in desk at Knock Airport. The screen above said *BA 7724 Manchester/Düsseldorf.*

Martin handed over tickets and passports but kept a firm hold on Tessie's arm. She stood there vacantly.

'Ah yes, Mr Gutman,' the young woman at the desk said. 'This is the Miss Kane you phoned about? Well, don't you worry, she'll be called first. And yourself, of course. And you've got two seats near the front. The toilet's just forward of that.'

'Thank you,' Martin said. 'You've really been very kind.' He coughed and brought his inhaler to his mouth.

'Are you all right, sir?' the young woman asked.

'Fine. Just routine. But thanks.'

The woman sent the bags on their way and beamed at Tessie. 'You'll be grand, Miss Kane. Don't you worry at all now.' She handed Martin the boarding cards and tickets, tucked into the passports. 'Have a good flight! Ye'll both be grand.'

As they approached the security check, Martin noticed two of his chess partners in the small queue ahead – Colby, the Australian, and one of the Pakistanis. Colby looked around and Martin gave him a nod and a brief 'Hi.' With Tessie on his hands, there would be little opportunity for chat.

The security check was no great trial to Tessie. Martin put his inhaler, a bunch of keys and some coins on the X-

ray tray and simply guided Tessie through the little security gateway. She bridled momentarily, but then came
through. The woman in charge smiled at her.

'Potty time, Tessie,' Martin said. He took her to the
ladies' lavatory and waited outside. When she came out,
he led her into the paper shop and then through the tiny
gift shop.

Tessie looked vaguely at things, but she was only half
there. They sat down opposite gate two and waited. A
certain extra bustle about the desk indicated something
was about to happen.

'British Airways announce their flight BA 7724 to
Manchester and Düsseldorf – now boarding at gate two,'
a woman's voice said over the loudspeaker. 'Would Ms
Theresa Kane please present herself for boarding. Also
anyone with children, or persons with a disability, please
come forward now.'

Martin led Tessie to the gate, presented the boarding
cards, and guided her through the door to the tarmac.
The ground was damp and the air smelled of rain. But
there was no chill in the air.

A British Airways Boeing 737-500 stood a short distance away. Martin recognised the distinctive flat-bottomed
engine nacelles that seemed almost to touch the ground.

There was a sudden roar of jet engines and he turned
to see Sheik Aboud's white-and-gold Learjet rocketing
down the runway. Tessie waited patiently while Martin
watched it rotate and lift steeply into the sky.

He turned to lead her towards the steps at the Boeing's forward door. Tessie climbed the steps as if she were ascending the gallows.

As they stepped into the cabin, a stewardess greeted Tessie with a smile and led her to a right-hand aisle seat only two rows from the front. Martin had the seat next to her.

As they settled in, he noticed the two emergency flashlamps clipped to the bulkhead by the cabin door, just aft of the cockpit. A tiny red LED lamp blinked on one of them, indicating that it was charging. The other evidently was not.

Martin saw a stewardess go in through the cockpit door. It was one of the older-type doors, without a keypad. The stewardess simply took a key from around her neck, inserted it in the slot on the door knob, and the door swung open. There was a momentary glimpse of green-glowing dials and screens, and someone's arm in a short-sleeved white shirt.

***

SATURDAY, 9.50 A.M. The unpredictable Galway traffic means Jack Stokes arrives late to work. He picks up his mail and goes over to the coffee machine. Maybe coffee will keep him awake after a sleepless night. He has been lying awake thinking about Martin Gutman being a pilot. Most likely nothing to it. But Deirdre was all agog when he told her. Urged him to check it out first thing.

Bloody old machine hasn't even reached the boil. Jack goes through his mail while he waits. Usual circulars, and some handwritten stuff. Probably anonymous. He'll see later.

Watched bloody pots never boil. But at last the coffee starts dribbling out. Stingily dribbling, hissing and spitting. What a pest of a machine. Stokes adds sugar and powdered creamer, carries his coffee to his desk and sits. He switches on the computer screen, takes a scalding gulp from his cup, clicks on his email, then clicks on the security option. The screen asks for his password: he types it in and clicks OK. *Entry not authorised*, the screen says.

'Hey, Jack.' Des King sits down at the next desk. 'Super wants you. Right away, he says.'

'And I want *him*,' Jack says through his teeth. He heads across the hall to Moran's office. 'What's happened to my email, John-Joe?'

'Sit down, will you?'

'I will not. Listen, did Dublin withdraw my authorisation?'

'Well, they said they were going to, didn't they? I told you, they've taken you off the terrorist beat. But don't you worry – you can head the search detail when we get that warrant. I'll stand over it.'

'Listen, John-Joe. Just take my word for this, there's something I really have to check. Probably nothing, but I can't take a risk. Trust me, I'll explain later. I have to get through to the FBI, asap. You just have to believe me, alright?'

Moran stares at him for a moment. He reaches for a pad of *Post-It* notes, jots something, and hands it to Stokes. 'Use my password,' he says.

This time Stokes gets through to the confidential link to the FBI. Options come up on the screen, and he clicks on the one marked *Security Check*. In the *Subject* field he types in the words, 'Martin Gutman', and clicks on *Send*. The screen clears.

Come on, come on. FBI *come on*. Stokes paces the room, comes back to his desk, peers at the computer screen, thumps the desk. The thing is starting to feel urgent. What if – but it's hardly likely. I know Martin well, for God's sake. But I can't take a risk. Come on, come on.

He carries his cup to the coffee machine, then notices that it's still full. Comes back to his desk. He lifts the phone, then puts it down again.

'What's got into you, Jack?' Des comes over to the desk. 'Later!'

'That bad?' Des stays behind Stokes, watching the screen.

Come on. Come on, FBI. Come on. The Super comes across the hall, and stands behind Stokes. He says nothing.

The screen clears. First thing comes up is a black-and-white photo. Martin Gutman. Mugshot, bit younger looking. Military uniform. Then the text:

Gutman, Martin Dominic. Capt, US Marines, April 1997 thru April 2003. Graduated as pilot, qualified for twin-jet aircraft. Flew A-10A anti-tank aircraft out of Kabul. Honourable discharge, April 10, 2003, on health grounds. Due to nervous breakdown, following erroneous aerial attack on civilian refugee column north of Kabul, Aug. 31, 2002, from which fully exonerated. **New information (as of yesterday 3 p.m.):** Gutman now believed to have returned to Afghanistan after discharge, and to have got involved with a terrorist network there. Present exact whereabouts uncertain, but is now believed to have entered the Irish Republic. May be using pseudonym **Al Naim**. (Note: *naim* in Arabic means 'sleeper'.) Sometimes calls himself Omar, or Omar Al Naim. – *30*

Stokes says nothing, but punches in a number on the desk phone, puts it on loudspeaker, and asks for Martin Gutman.

'I'm sorry,' a young voice says, 'but Mr Gutman's not at work today. He left this morning for Manchester.'

I'm going to faint, Stokes thinks. He looks up at the clock: 10.12. The aroma of coffee hits his nostrils, then a whiff of his own armpits. He seems to be moving in slow motion. He turns to the Superintendent and Des King. 'Listen, fellas, I think this is called red alert. Something like that. Would yiz just do what I ask, without questions?'

There's something in Stokes' face that makes both men nod.

'John-Joe. Get Knock airport. Tell them to recall the 9.30 flight to Manchester. Could be a terrorist on board. No, forget Knock – call Dublin, find whoever handles things centrally. And Des, get through to the RAF, any way you can. Tell them there's a plane approaching their east coast with a possible terrorist on board. No, *a terrorist*.' He put his head in his hands. 'Christ, no. They could shoot down a planeload of people. Look, we have to tell them anyway.'

The men hurry off.

***

10.20 A.M. THREE high-viz red Dennis fire engines move out from the Coniston Transport Museum in Cumbria's Lake District and, one behind the other, take the road south. Behind the vehicles are two white Mercedes ambulances.

Three miles down the road, at Torver, the convoy forks right onto the A593 which leads to the Cumbria coast. The vehicles switch on their sirens and blue flashing lights.

***

10.25 A.M. TESSIE sits in her seat gazing vacantly forward. Martin is holding her hand. He looks at his watch, takes his hand away, removes his heavy, horn-rimmed glasses. From inside one of the spectacle sides he slides out a long, razor-sharp blade, with the curved ear-piece as its handle. He puts the blade into his left-hand shirt pocket. From the right-hand pocket he takes out his reflecting shades and puts them on. He takes the inhaler in his left hand.

He leans over to Tessie. 'Potty time,' he whispers gently.

She gets up slowly, and he leads her the few metres to the toilet door, which is just to the left of the cockpit door, and at right angles to it. Martin opens the door, leans in to help her enter, and closes the door. He waits outside.

Sitting in the front row, directly aft of the door, is Colby, the Australian. Martin nods to him.

Exactly five minutes later Martin Gutman walks down the plane to find a stewardess. 'My aunt's in the toilet,' he explains. 'She's not been well, and I think I heard her fall.'

The stewardess, a fair-haired young woman, turns to accompany Martin. As they hurry forward, the Pakistani man, farther back in the plane, falls into the aisle in a severe and loud epileptic fit. The other stewardesses rush to help and everyone turns around to watch.

The stewardess with Martin lifts the little flap on the toilet door, finds it already unlocked, and pushes in the door. Martin leans in, inhaler in hand, gives her a shot of Mace in the face, and then cuts her throat with the razor-sharp blade. He pushes her on top of his already-dead aunt (whose throat dribbles its last measure of blood), takes the key from around her neck, and pulls the door closed.

He puts the key into the cockpit door-knob, turns it, walks in behind the two pilots, and closes the door gently behind him. He claps his hands so that both pilots turn to look. The one on the left is a young woman, the sight of whom gives Martin a momentary shock.

Each pilot gets a shot of Mace into the face, and each doubles up, gasping. Martin carefully cuts each throat. He drops the security bar into place inside the cockpit door, hoists the woman out of her seat, lays the limp body on the cabin floor, and slides into her place.

Through his trousers he feels the warm wetness of the blood-soaked seat. A sweetish butcher-shop smell permeates the cockpit, mingling with the stench of excrement.

Martin briefly checks the various computer screens: the plane is some minutes past top of descent, on autopilot, already down to ten thousand feet, and decending at a thousand feet a minute.

He punches in the coordinates for Freshpark. He flicks the radio and transponder switches to *Off*.

Martin banks the plane to the left in a wide, gentle circle, which brings it finally on a northerly course. All the passengers might possibly notice would be the cloud floor tilting slightly beneath the port windows.

However no one notices anything, since all are intent on watching the Pakistani man, whose epileptic fit continues dramatically. The stewardesses are doing their best to help.

The Australian, Colby, gets up from his seat and

stands in the passage outside the cockpit. Like everyone else he is looking down the aisle at the man having the fit. He turns to the bulkhead behind him and lifts down one of the two emergency flashlamps, unclips the lens, revealing the recessed barrel of a gun. He gives three taps on the cockpit door, then folds down the back-facing stewardess' seat and straps himself in.

Immediately Martin puts the wheel forward in the steepest possible 300mph dive. There is a ferocious buffeting as the Boeing enters the cloud layer. Then there is the pewter sea hard below as the plane levels out at 500 feet. Martin pushes the throttles to full, and the plane leaps forward. There are screams from the cabin and the dull thump of low-velocity gunfire. That would be Colby, holding the pass.

***

10.31 A.M. STOKES pounds the desk with his fists. What else to do? What else *can* I do? Oh God, Martin, don't do this to me. 10.32 now. What to do? RAF? Des is handling that. I could try calling direct. Might be faster. While Des takes the central route. Coningsby, that's the base that covers Freshpark.

'Get me RAF Coningsby – urgent. Aye, connect me. That Coningsby? Hello? Irish police here. Red alert. Plane with possible terrorists aboard, approaching your coast … No, I've no registration for it. But it'll be British Airways, probably a Boeing 737 … Look, we'll *try* and get the registration.' Clock reads 10.35 …'Our ID? Will ya listen – this is the Irish police, anti-terrorist division, Jack Stokes speaking … No, it's not a hoax. Listen, you'll hear it officially in a minute from your end. I'm just saying get ready, that's all … No, there's no time to ask Downing Street … Oh for God's *sake*! Look, just get ready. Standby – d'y'know what standby means?'

Des is back. Oh, God no, his face says it all. Des: 'I got through: it's Manchester handles it. They've tried to contact the plane. It's not answering.'

***

10.37 A.M. AS the Boeing hurtles northwards, the coast of northwest England slithers by in the murk. Then it recedes away to the right. That would be the expanse of Morcambe Bay.

Now directly ahead is Barrow-in-Furness docks. Glimpse of that Pintail nuke ship. Town flashes by underneath. Boeing at 500 feet, flying almost due north along the coast. White shoreline hurtling below. Start steep climb now, to 2,000 feet.

The thump, thump of Colby's gun.

Shouts: 'C'mon lads, he's out of ammo.'

A scream, as of an animal butchered.

Now silence back there.

A massive thud hits the cockpit door. Then another. It's the thud of some heavy object, perhaps a trolley turned on end, perhaps used as a battering ram.

A pause. Silence.

The thuds begin again. Now they takes on a regular rhythm, and the chanting of *heave - heave - heave* comes clearly into the cabin.

Through the windscreen, far ahead, Freshpark's smoke straight up, then curling east.

Heave – THUD – *heave* – THUD – *heave* –

Martin can hear the door cracking behind him. Security bar should hold a few more seconds. All that's needed.

Heave – THUD – *heave* –THUD – *heave* –

Tall towers tiny yet.

Freshton come and gone.

Towers now filling windscreen. Keep Valox Three to starboard …

Heave – *THUD* –

Door cracking.

Yielding?

Sound of cursing bodies pushing through some gap behind Martin. Push wheel forward for dive. Steep. *Steeper* … Straps hold Martin in place in the near-vertical cockpit. Two bodies hurtle downwards past him and slam against the instrument panel. A pilot's body slithers down to join the heap.

Far down there the circular wall – opening seems so tiny, just like the model. Insert plane into it. Tanks in there. Wings fluttering but still on. Just about. *Now vertical.* Opening now bigger, BIGGER – will we fit? *Will we fit?* Coming up, coming up – *IN*.

The wings sheer off; a fireball soars. The walls are a chimney that forces the fireball vertically up and up and up. Already it has risen to 5,000 feet and down within the walls it has engulfed seventeen out of the twenty-one tanks of high-level waste.

Twenty-two minutes later the first Tornado F3 jet from Coningsby streaks through the caesium plume moving south-east from Freshpark.

PART THREE

The issue is nuclear. There is no question that the next generation of terrorists, rather than going for small, little dramas, will go for the big one. They now understand that the way to get the world's attention is not strapping bombs to themselves in a pizza parlour, but to do something so horrific it gets you into the *Guinness Book of World Records* for terrorism. That takes years to plan – and it will be nuclear.

– Richard Holbrooke, former US Ambassador to the United Nations and US Special Envoy in Bosnia and Kosovo, quoted in *The Guardian*, 22 November, 2001

S ATURDAY, 11.08 A.M. '…One moment life was going on as usual. Just hours later it was all over. There was nothing. No living thing. No Pompeii. Just a smooth and smoking plain of grey-black ash.'

'Cut,' Nancy Harris says. 'Nice going, Frank. Let's have coffee, everyone.'

As the four sat on a couple of broken pillars cradling their coffee, Frank tugged his mobile phone from his deep habit pocket and switched it back on. Almost immediately it rang.

He pressed the green answer-button and put it to his ear. Whatever he heard made his eyes open wide in horror.

'Are you alright?' Nancy leaned across to him.

Frank shook his head. It was as if he had been struck dumb.

Meg stepped lightly down the little Pompeii street, still with the cartwheel grooves worn into the ancient stone. Cartwheels? She felt like *doing* cartwheels. How could happiness come so suddenly, during a single night? A night with a beautiful man. And the hopes that had been uttered. The sun was warm on her hair. She smiled and the smile felt strange, as though the muscles were out of practice. Well, they were, weren't they? I'll smile again, she told herself. I'll smile a lot. So will Grace and so will mother.

She turned the corner into the forum and stopped. A little group was clustered around Frank's white-clad figure, as if he was ill. He sat on a stone pillar, his head bent into his hands. Meg started running.

'Frank. Frank. It's me, Meg. Frank, what is it? What on earth is wrong?'

Frank's face came up out of his hands. The eyes were pools of horror. 'The catastrophe,' he said. 'It's come.'

***

11.14 A.M. DOCTOR Postlethwaite stood with his back to the sea wall, looking out across the roofs of Freshton below him. Beyond the rooftops rose a wall of flame where Freshpark's chimneys should have been, purple smoke writhing through the flame. It seemed to extend right across the site.

Freshton's church tower was silhouetted against the flame, and the old man remembered that famous picture of St Paul's Cathedral outlined against the smoke and flames of the Blitz. Above the flames, a higher wall of smoke as wide as Freshpark itself had turned the sky greenish black, and was extending towards the southeast.

God help the people of Sandforth, the doctor thought. They're right in the way.

A burnt-wool smell touched his nostrils, then caught his throat and made him cough. A distant roar, as of an opened furnace door, came from across the rooftops.

The doctor had been in his surgery when he heard the plane go over. He had understood immediately: a plane that big, that low, going that fast and in that direction, could mean only one thing – the thing he had so long dreaded.

He had gone straight to the front door, had taken one look across at Freshpark, sniffed the wind for direction, and had come right back in.

'Dress as quickly as you can, Blanche,' he had told the pregnant young woman in his surgery. 'Come across to the waiting room right away. Your husband's there, isn't he?'

There were three people in the waiting room. A man older than the doctor, a young woman with an infant, and a handsome fellow in his thirties.

The doctor nodded to all three. 'Trevor, better get to the plant. There's trouble, and they'll need all the firemen they can. I'll see Blanche home. Listen, I want you others to go straight home. No time to explain. Go home, close windows and doors, pull the shutters and curtains, get in the shower and keep it running. Celia, you've Freddy at the school? Fetch him home. Tell them all to go home. Tell them I said it. And don't anyone try to leave town. Worst thing you could do is be out in the open. Besides, you wouldn't get far anyway. Roads'll be jammed.' .

As the people filed out, Doc Postlethwaite put his

hand on the pregnant woman's shoulder. 'Trevor's a brave man, love.'

'He is, Doctor.' She was starting to weep.

'Just pray he'll be all right. Nothing else we can do for the moment. Except pray. Come on, Blanche, love. I'll take you home.'

And now Doc Postlethwaite was back outside, watching his world come to an end. Time to go in and turn on the shower. Indeed. Whatever good a shower'll really do… maybe wash away the particles.

Well, it's been a worthwhile life.

* * *

11.22 A.M. SANDFORTH'S a pretty village, with its three pubs clustered in the centre – a lot prettier than drab Freshton. Even though Sandforth is only a couple of miles from Freshpark nuclear plant, you'd never know it, as there are hilly green fields full of cows between the two places.

The three youngish people having tea and toasted sandwiches outside the Rose and Crown had a professional look about them – the two men in dark suits, the woman power-dressed in navy blue. Obviously there on business, perhaps a meeting down at the nuke plant. Their silver Jaguar XJ sat sleekly across the street. The squawk of morning television came through the open pub door.

They had heard something like distant thunder from over the fields, and had wondered briefly what it was.

Freshpark, very likely. You'd never know what they'd be up to over there.

One of the young men cracked a joke, and the trio laughed heartily. Someone capped it with another joke and they all laughed again. The sound of the television had changed, and the TV voice had an edge of urgency. But the trio didn't notice.

The young woman stood up, lifted her handbag and strolled elegantly into the pub. Just inside the door she stopped, listening to whatever was being said on the big television screen to the left. A minute later she called sharply to the two men outside. They got up and came into the pub.

Less than another minute later all three scurried out and across to the Jaguar. It lurched out onto the road, one of the men jumped out and threw some coins on the pub table, and jumped back in.

With a screech of tyres the Jaguar swung around the little roundabout, and down towards the main road.

As it pulled out onto the highway, it nearly collided with a fire engine racing northwards, blue lights dancing and sirens howling. Two more identical engines were right behind it, followed by two white Mercedes ambulances.

As the Jag sped off, other people were tumbling out of their houses and into their cars. A man came out of the little grocery store up the street, and started frantically rolling down the shutters.

Further up, a man ushered an older couple out of Charlie Pyle's Bookshop, locked the front door, and hurried to the nearby car park. One by one, all three pubs were closed and locked.

The coins stayed on the table in front of the inn.

Five minutes later the village was silent and empty, except for a black-and-white border collie sauntering down the street. It lifted its leg at the lamp-posts, indifferent to the plume of greenish smoke passing overhead.

***

11.29 A.M. THE barriers at Freshpark's main gate swung upwards to let the three fire engines roar through, followed by the ambulances. A couple of guards waved them urgently on: the others were gazing blankly towards the wall of flame and the smoke roiling twenty times higher than the cooling towers. The fire engines slowed slightly and then dispersed on their various assignments.

The leading engine, followed by the ambulances, swung sharp left along the western perimeter, and screeched to a halt outside the plutonium vault, the top of which which rose only ten feet above ground level. One fire engine pulled sideways across the road to shield the view from the main gate. At the same time the two guards outside the building were mown down by automatic fire before they knew what was happening. The sound was drowned by the roar of the conflagration.

Both ambulances slewed around the fire engine and stopped. Two men opened the rear doors of one and lifted out a *Tow-2* anti-tank weapon which they set up on its tripod facing the armour-plated doors of the plutonium vault. Two other men stood by with acetylene torches, blue flames already at the tips.

A single *Tow-2* armour-piercing missile quickly had the doors hanging from their hinges; a second one flattened the inner armoured door. Six of the crew rushed in with machine pistols, followed by the men with the acetylene torches.

Minutes later the men were loading flasks of plutonium oxide into the second ambulance, each carefully embedded in its bird-cage container to keep it separate from the others.

When the ambulance was filled to capacity with plutonium, it drove with flashing lights back down to the main gate. The guards immediately waved it through.

Back at the plutonium vault the fire engine started up, a hose was reeled out and into the vault, and the engine started pumping the contents of its 1,800-litre tank down into the remaining almost 99 tonnes of plutonium oxide. Except that it pumped kerosene instead of water.

Once the pumping was complete, four men went to the remaining ambulance and lifted out a massive bomb, packed into a wheelie bin, which they pushed deep into the vault. They came out, climbed into the fire engine and drove across the compound to join the other fire engines which were using their kerosene-filled water tanks to create random fires and cause maximum confusion.

It was only then that some Freshpark security guards, in the midst of the confusion and flames, became aware of the bogus firefighters. They began shooting at two genuine Workington City fire engines that had just arrived through the main gate.

During the shooting, the bomb went off inside the plutonium vault, lifting off the roof and sending a blazing kerosene and plutonium plume thousands of feet above Freshpark, to meet and mate with the west wind.

***

12.10 P.M. AT nineteen, Diane could hardly believe she was married. Yet here she was in the Lake District with her husband of a few days, hiking a forest trail high above Newby Bridge.

This was as good as it gets. The Swan Hotel, right by the ancient bridge where the river surges out of Windermere; the swimming pool just inside the lobby; gorgeous food; and the prospect of fantastic lovemaking that night.

Her man beside her now; a blue sky beyond the trees; the sun filtering through the beech leaves and warm on their bare arms. Not a soul around.

On their left as they climbed the track towards High Dam, a series of little waterfalls tumbled and sparkled. This would be the stream that once fed the old Stotts

Bobbin Mill far below. It's wonderful the way a chuckling stream can seem to reflect your joy.

Hand in hand the young couple emerged from the trees at High Dam, crossed the little bridge where the water tumbled from the grassy dam wall, pulled off their backpacks and spread a rug on a knoll beside the lake.

Diane opened her backpack and took the foil off the ham-and-cheese sandwiches. Hot tea from the Thermos set the cups steaming. Milk already in. Neither took sugar. They drank in the view with their tea.

'Notice something?' Diane said. 'There aren't any birds.'

'Now that you mention it …'

They sat quietly, listening to the silence. Not even a lark in the sky above them. Diane looked up. A slight haze had crept over the sun.

They munched their sandwiches and contemplated the sylvan scene around them. The sky grew hazier, and the haze was greenish yellow.

'*The sedge is withered from the lake, and no bird sings,*' Philip said.

'What's that?'

'Just a poem I remember from school –

> Ah! What can ail thee, knight-at-arms,
> Alone and palely loitering?
> The sedge is withered from the lake,
> And no bird sings.

'It's about this fellow who meets some *belle dame sans merci* – some spooky bitch who puts a spell on him. Come to think of it, this place is kind of spooky. Come on, Diane, admit it. You did cast a spell, didn't you?'

They sat in silence. Then, spontaneously, they both stood up. They stared at one another, eyes wide. Diane turned to gaze at the lake, from whence the sparkle had faded. She looked at the silent trees, then at the hazy, birdless sky. 'There's something about this place, Philip,' she said. 'I don't like it. Let's get out of here.'

'OK, come on, let's go.' He shoved everything back into the bags.

'Hurry!'

He helped Diane's bag onto her back, and swung his own over one shoulder. They set off stumbling and slipping back down the track that led to Stotts Bobbin Mill and Newby Bridge. By the time they got to the main road they were half running, Diane was crying, and Philip had his arm around her.

'There was something awful up there,' Diane whispered. 'I really felt scared. Look, I hate everything around here. Let's pack the car and move on.'

'That's fine by me, love.'

They were running down the road at full speed now. A Volvo came from behind at unusual speed, slithering around them with screeching tyres.

As they rounded the corner to the hotel, people were tumbling into cars and roaring off. They saw a six-year-old girl being pushed into the back seat of a red Audi. Her doll fell on the road and the child howled. The driver slammed the door on the child, and drove off, leaving the doll lying on the road. It was one of those Barbies or Cindys like the ones Diane used to play with as a child. This doll was in a white wedding dress and veil. Another car drove over it.

'What the hell's happening?' Philip yelled at a man who was hurrying past. The man ignored him.

'Come on, Diane. Let's get our things.' Philip took her arm. 'Take it easy, love. Don't lose it on me, now.'

'Leave our things. I just want to get out of here!'

They raced past the hotel to the car park. It was empty. Even Philip's BMW was gone. The sky was greenish yellow, and Diane started to scream.

***

12.17 P.M. MARTHA Watkins brought her silver Nissan Micra screeching to a stop outside the school in Cawood. As she ran inside, two women were hurrying out, each dragging a bewildered child. Grace was in the hallway, clutching her teddy bear and trying not to cry.

'Gran's going to take you for a little drive, darling,' Martha said, lifting her and going straight back out to the car. It took seconds to strap Grace into her seat, and the Micra sped away at considerably more than the speed limit.

Thank God she'd had the radio on, Martha thought. She had been paying it little attention, it was just for background, when she heard something about a plane hitting Freshpark. They had interrupted the programme to announce it.

Just as when the London bombs had happened, she immediately switched on the TV and sat down, duster in her hand, to watch. But there weren't any pictures, just a breathless announcer saying how an airliner had flown into Freshpark, but no one knew yet if it was an accident or an attack.

The woman said something about a radioactive plume moving east-southeast. Martha kept on listening. But it was when the woman said that 20 mph winds could carry the plume over Leeds within five hours that something clicked in her head. Leeds, Cawood – the same thing.

She had dropped the duster and run out to the car.

Head south, that's what we have to do now. Out through Camblesforth, and then down the M18 past Doncaster. Just keep on going, to get away from this – this plume. Whatever it is they're calling it.

'Are you alright, love? Grace? Are you alright? Yes, I know, love. You're a brave little girl. Everything's going to be alright.'

Wonder has Meg heard yet? She'll be beside herself. Oh God, my tablets. Can't go back now. This sort of thing's what brings on the blood pressure. Well, got to keep going. Mustn't grumble.

'Grace, my brave little girl. Don't worry, we'll be fine. And so will Boo. Shall we sing a nice song?'

***

12.47 P.M. DYMPNA Manning got up from her desk, walked through the hall of Yorkshire Haven rest home, to the lounge where her husband was watching the events on television. The screen showed wall-to-wall flame and smoke. A helicopter churned across the screen, black against the glare.

'You haven't changed your mind, Chris?' Dympna asked.

'Not unless you have, my love. No, we stay. We couldn't move the old dears anyhow – it would kill them.'

The screen changed, to show aerial views of a grid-locked motorway.

'Anyway,' Chris added, 'how could we get anywhere, even if we wanted to? Look at that.'

'How long have we got? I mean, before – before it gets here?'

'They're saying it could reach Leeds just after three. That's if the wind doesn't change. I'm afraid, though, it's not expected to change.'

'And what's to happen then? You do know, don't you? As a doctor, I mean.'

'My dear Dympna, I really don't. Nobody knows for certain. I mean, we know what happened in Chernobyl, but the circumstances were never like this. Just pray it doesn't rain. That's the main thing.'

'Why?'

'Because rain would wash everything out of the plume, right down on top of us. Caesium something or other. And something called strontium. That would not be nice, and that's an understatement. I just wish they had given us those iodine tablets. On second thoughts, they'd be useless if it's caesium.'

Chris shook himself, and made a point of rubbing his hands cheerfully together. 'Anyway, we'll take all the precautions. We'll shut every window, pull the curtains, get the old dears into the bathrooms, and – and spray them with water, I suppose. For as long as it takes. You can rely on me!'

'That's the one thing I'm sure of, Chris.'

***

'I WANT TO wee-wee, Gran.'

'But you did, love.'

'I want to, again.'

'That's all right, love. We'll just get out of the car. You can do it right here, between the cars.' Martha sighed. 'I never thought we'd be going to the loo in the middle of the M18. I think I might have to go too.'

The cars had been stalled for hours. The radio had said the motorway was locked solid as far south as Rotherham.

As Martha helped Grace out of the car, the murmuring of hundreds of car radios filled the air. There was obviously nothing anyone could do but listen to whatever the radio could tell them, about what was happening further north. She noticed that the sky had clouded over. It was starting to feel cold and damp.

Martha helped the child back into the car, this time in the front seat, and climbed into the driving seat beside her. No need for Grace to sit in the back: she wasn't going anywhere. Martha turned on the car radio: '... reporting that Freshpark is one vast conflagration,' the announcer was saying. 'Firefighters can get nowhere near the flames, and have had to withdraw from several areas of the plant to which the fires have spread, where they are now out of control.

'Fire has disabled the cooling facilities for the high-level waste tanks. The result is that the remaining tanks, those which had survived the airliner's initial impact, are now believed to be boiling over, and catching fire from the nearby flames. This means that a radioactive plume continues to emerge from Freshpark, and is moving to cover much of northern England.

'It is believed that a plutonium vault to the north of the tanks is on fire, but this has not been confirmed.

'Reports are coming in of bogus firefighters having infiltrated Freshpark, where they have been causing considerable confusion, as a result of which several genuine firemen have been shot dead by security guards.

'There is also the likelihood that the bogus firefighters may have been the cause of the fires spreading.

'In the last few minutes the Meteorological Office said the wind may shortly veer to the north, which means it could carry the radioactive plume southwards. There is also a possibility of rain, which could bring the radioactive chemicals down from the plume …'

A sort of wail welled up from the surrounding cars and trucks, and horns blared as if that alone could manage to break the gridlock. People began moving past the car window. Then there were more of them, pushing, shoving, cursing, crying.

'Come on, Grace. We have to start walking, my love.' Martha had difficulty opening the door, because of the people bumping into it, until a burly man with a large belly placed his body in the narrow passage and stood his ground until she got the child out, still clutching Boo.

'Just follow me, luv,' he said to Martha. 'And give me the little girl.' The accent was Leeds, Martha observed, ever so slightly working-class. She followed him as he pushed his way between the cars, until they came to the steep, grassy verge on the edge of the motorway.

'Let's climb up and see if there's a way through up here,' the man said.

At the top of the slope Martha felt faint at the vision she beheld. A river of humanity, flowing inexorably southward, curled around the stalled vehicles as water curves around rocks. Even the northbound lanes were full of stalled cars and lorries: obviously the exits farther north were jammed too.

'No way through here,' the man said. 'And we can't walk along this incline. Tell you what – we'll go back down to the centre divide. There'll be a bit more room there. I'm Eric, by the way.' He held the child like a light doll in his right arm, and extended the left in greeting.

'How d'you do, Eric. I'm Martha, and this is Grace, my granddaughter. Say hello to the gentleman, Grace.'

Grace shyly turned her head away and hugged Boo tighter.

The centre divide was jam-packed with wailing children and stony-faced adults, many with mobile phones jammed to their ears, others with earphones. But there was less pushing and shoving now – just a mass of refugees shambling southwards, some lugging carrier bags, and some tugging wheelie suitcases.

'The wind doesn't *have* to veer north, you know,' Eric said. 'These Met lads get it wrong half the time, you know.'

'I pray God you're right.'

'But they really should stop these broadcasts. It's not helping at all. All it's doing is causing panic. I mean, look at this.'

***

GRACE AND BOO were asleep in Eric's arms. The people trudged on in silence, their gait that of refugees

377

in Second World War newsreels. All they lacked were the handcarts piled high with bits of furniture, and the dive-bombing Stukas screaming above. In place of the Stukas, helicopters churned up and down above the lines of fleeing humanity.

And instead of muddy tracks between Picardy hedgerows, these people trudged down a motorway between unending alleys of stalled cars and lorries. But the faces held the same expressions of blank despair.

The sky had darkened.

Martha had got to the point where hips and knee-joints and feet had all merged in one dull ache, where fatigue had reached a peak and then faded into a dull routine, where one foot went in front of the other because it had nowhere else to go. There was no thought of what lay ahead, nor of the home left behind: shock had numbed thought.

A helicopter clattered overhead, heading south above the motorway.

When the rain came, it came suddenly and in torrents. Within seconds people were drenched and shivering. Eric took off his jacket and wrapped it around Grace.

The young man in front of Eric adjusted his ear-phones. 'Oh God,' he shouted suddenly, 'the wind's turned. It's coming this way!' He started to run, elbowing his way through the people in front of him.

People around began running, and there were shouts of 'It's coming after us! It's here!' Within moments

Martha was being carried along in the crowd, in spite of herself, as the rain roared down.

Her feet trod on something soft: she looked down and realised it was a woman lying on her back. There was no time to know if she was alive or dead. It was the woman's soft abdomen she had stepped on. Martha had the ridiculous thought that it was just as well she wasn't wearing high heels. Ridiculous, because she hadn't worn them for years.

What had been a river of people flowing between the cars was now a torrent, a terrified torrent of drenched humanity. Martha was carried along, sometimes held up by the bodies beside her, sometimes her feet hardly touching the ground, sometimes stumbling across prone bodies, sometimes slipping in blood, or shit, or rain-washed vomit.

She lost sight of Eric and Grace. 'Grace! Grace, where are you, love?' she screamed.

A man in front of her grabbed what might have been his wife and hugged her to himself as he ran. Then Martha saw the glint of a pistol against the woman's head, heard the bang and saw the woman's head explode right beside her lover's head. The head slid downwards. Two children were running in front of him, a boy and a girl, about eight or nine years old. The man shot the boy in the back of the head and the child went down. The little girl turned, horror in her face. As she too slid downwards her left eye was a well of blood where the bullet had entered. Martha had to jump across the body. Then the man put the gun to his own head and there was another bang.

A helicopter clattered by, going north this time. It was heading towards the greenish clouds massing in the distance.

***

THE THREE YOUNG people sat in their silver Jaguar, jammed in the very centre of the old stone bridge at Dutton, as the green clouds roiled overhead. It had been a hair-raising drive down the A595, one of the worst main roads in the country, with its hills and hairpin bends and narrow villages to negotiate at high speed, in a frantic effort to escape to the south.

But there is no escape to the south on the A595. Since Cumbria projects westwards into the Irish Sea, the only thing to the south is water. So the road perforce swings east at Whicham, with the result that it now carried the Jaguar straight into the widening plume from Freshpark. And with all the fleeing cars coming up from Barrow-in-Furness, the road ahead was clogged.

So the young people sat in their silver Jag at Dutton Bridge, where they waited and wept and were irradiated.

DAY 2, PFE

'THE PRIME MINISTER'S going to speak, dear,' Dympna called. 'Come and listen.'

Chris slid into the armchair across from her and turned up the sound.

Sir Anthony Ware looked as suave and relaxed as ever, the silver hair sleek and groomed. 'I am speaking to you from Gibraltar,' he began, 'where, as you may know, we have moved your government for a very brief period, until the emergency is over. This is solely to ensure that the United Kingdom continues to be administered effectively in the interim. All services are fully operative within Britain, and we are in constant communication with all parties, to ensure that this continues to be the case.'

The PM was sitting at a desk, complete with pens and telephones, and a flat computer screen to one side. Reassuring red leather-bound volumes lined the wall behind him, as though somewhere between those sumptuous gold-embossed covers lay the remedy for what was happening.

The camera moved in and the Prime Minister's face filled the screen. Never had he looked more caring.

'And now my fellow Britons, I have to ask you something. Please return to your homes, I implore you. There is nothing for you in the south of England. No place to stay, not enough tents to house you, not enough food in the supermarkets, and no way to transport it. If you continue to head south you will create chaos.

'Will those of you who see or hear this broadcast, please pass my message along urgently to others. And those on the roads who hear this on radio please do the same. If you can no longer manage to move your cars, just go to your nearest railway station. There are trains running non-stop to take you back home. We can look to the cars later.'

Sir Anthony's expression now became grim. 'And now I have to tell you that, on my orders, the Ministry of Defence has established a *cordon sanitaire* across England and Wales, stretching from King's Lynn, in Norfolk, through Wolverhampton to Aberystwyth, cutting all north-south traffic. All roads in the area, even the smallest, have been sealed off for the period of this emergency, and no vehicles or persons are to be allowed to pass through, with the exception of police, military, and emergency personnel.

'This may at first seem a harsh measure, but I assure you that, on careful consideration, you will see its merit. You will realise that the government, in ordering this *cordon sanitaire*, has *you* in mind, your ultimate welfare, the ultimate good of the nation.

'There now remain to us three tasks – to grieve for the deceased; to care for the survivors; and to hunt down those who did this, this *thing*. I cannot find words for it.

'Good-bye, and remember I am fully in touch, and

fully in control. I will be addressing you soon again. And your government will be returning very soon indeed. Meanwhile, I wish you the strength to get through this tragic time, each and every one of you.'

***

JACK STOKES WATCHED as the Tuam and Galway fire brigades doused the last embers of Castle Patrick. Gutted. Deliberately. Not a clue remaining. Twenty-three bodies charred beyond recognition. It was the same down at the theme park: bodies there too, but not yet counted. And the same at the computer plant – more bodies there – but again everything burnt to a cinder. The sheik, having vanished into air, into thin air, had left not a rack behind.

But his revels were not ended. His evil smoke was moving south over Britain. When winds blow south-wards, Stokes thought grimly, they can soon blow west-wards. Over Ireland.

Ireland was in an uproar. The Taoiseach – prime min-ister – had flown his key ministers to Rome in the gov-ernment jet, leaving his deputy, the Tánaiste, in charge. The government was operating for the moment out of the Irish embassy to the Vatican, on Rome's Janiculum Hill.

The ferries were jammed with people trying to get out of Ireland. Even the ferries that usually sailed to Britain had been diverted to Brittany and Spain. The ferries had refused to take cars, and had packed the holds with passengers. All planes had of course been grounded, right across Europe, since the attack on Freshpark.

It was mostly the wealthy, selfish Irish who had got away, because they could pay the prices demanded by the gougers who had grabbed most of the tickets.

A terrifying sense of being trapped had swept the country and there had already been a rash of suicides, especially of young males.

Stokes pressed his mobile phone. 'Deirdre? Are the wee ones all right? Oh, thanks be to God. Look, I'll be home in half an hour, but I'll only have a few minutes. Everything's happening all at once – tell you when I see you. Bye, love.'

As Jack Stokes drove down the road to Galway, it struck him for the first time what it means to live on an island. Even one as big as Ireland. You cannot easily get off an island. It's just an illusion that you can. That's because only a relatively few people want to get off it at any given time.

Stokes used to take it for granted – flights out of Shannon to wherever – to London or Paris. Ferries to Cherbourg, with the kids and the car. Europe your oyster. But when the whole nation wants to get off the island, you're trapped. Like in the Famine. *You can't get off an island.*

And we're only four million. What must Britain be like, with sixty million trying to get out of it? Oh Jesus, maybe we'll soon find out.

'YOU LOOK TANNED, m'boy,' Doctor Postlethwaite said quietly. Sadly. He put his stethoscope down on the table and turned away for a moment to hide the pain showing in his face.

'That's about what it is down there, a tannery,' Trevor said.

'What's it like, Trevor? Really?'

'I never thought hell existed until now. You can't get within a thousand yards of the flames. You feel cooked before you even get to hold the hoses. And they don't reach, anyway. Nowhere near.' Trevor sighed. 'It's worse now than yesterday. The fire's spreading everywhere.'

'How long do you spend with the hoses?'

'We were doing the regulation seven minutes and then moving back. Handing over to the next man. But that's gone now. We just stay with it.'

'That could be dangerous.'

'We're dead anyway, Doc. Aren't we? Tell me we're not!'

The doctor sighed. 'Trevor, we're never dead till we die. Look, I want you to go home now. Go home to Blanche. And try to get some sleep.'

***

WHEN DIANE AWOKE, the hotel was silent. Not a door banged. She looked at her sleeping partner. His head was handsome in sleep. It had been a night of desperate lovemaking.

And then Diane remembered with a lurch why it had been so frenzied. The car gone. The empty hotel. That evil sky. The mobile phone dead. The horrors on the TV.

She snuggled into the warmth of her sleeping husband, and hugged him with the tightness of terror. We'll make love again when he wakes, she thought. It's all we've got left.

***

JACK STOKES STOOD watching CNN, a cup of tea in his hand. Deirdre sat with Dara and Maeve on her knee. The children were unusually subdued. They knew that whatever it was, it was serious.

There was nothing to be got out of the other channels. Obviously orders had been given to censor their news, to prevent further panic. A bit late in the day for that, Stokes thought. Anyhow CNN from the satellite seemed to be carrying more real information than the others.

That Octavia Nasr was telling how Freshpark was totally out of control, that fires were spreading and burning more fiercely than ever. Firefighters and equipment could get nowhere near the conflagration. The lethal plumes of caesium and plutonium were pumping out at ever higher rates, and had now covered most of the North of England, and as far south as Stoke-on-Trent. The torrential rain that accompanied the plumes meant that the whole area, cities and countryside, was now steeped in caesium 137, strontium 90, and plutonium powder. Experts were saying the entire region would probably have to be declared permanently uninhabitable.

'However, and this is a source of immense relief for Britain, due to an emerging cold front, the wind last night swung back to its original west-northwest direction. This means that for the moment London and the south of England have been spared. And Ireland so far remains untouched.

'Unfortunately, of course, it means that the plumes are now heading directly towards Holland. They should reach Amsterdam within hours. If the winds continue in the same direction, the plumes will cut a swathe across both Holland and Germany, taking in Essen, Düsseldorf, Cologne and Frankfurt.'

Jack Stokes turned to his wife, strangely shy. 'Deirdre? D'y'remember – remember we used to pray a wee bit together? When we first got married? Like, before all those scandals? Would you – d'y'think we could – ?'

Deirdre nodded. There were tears in her eyes. Jack moved across and sat on the arm of the chair, put his arm around her shoulders. The little ones on Deirdre's knee looked around, wide-eyed.

'What'll we say, Dee?'

'Dunno. Wait, what about the *Our Father*? It says "Deliver us from evil", doesn't it?'

'Alright then. All together – *Our Father, who art in heaven, hallowed be thy name …*'

Both wept as they prayed.

DAY 6, PFE

IT TOOK MEG and Frank almost a week to reach Cawood, Yorkshire, with all European flights grounded, and most cross-channel connections suspended.

A bit of influence from a friend of Frank's, high up in the Italian foreign ministry, had secured scarce places on European trains and ferry.

By the time they got to Cawood they had passed through an England that was unrecognisable. Impassive soldiers stood at every corner, charged with enforcing the new martial-law decree. Railway stations crawled with blank-faced refugees, many being physically forced onto trains to take them back to the north.

Meg had heard a woman with two young children screaming, 'But you're sending us back to die!' She had thought of her own daughter then.

Leeds was like a city under plague. Shutters were down; curtains were pulled; the streets echoed to occasional footsteps. The taxi driver who finally agreed to take them to Cawood told tales of shut supermarkets, looting and shooting, food running out, and an epidemic of suicides.

***

MARTHA WATKINS' 1930s-era semi-detached was silent and curtained. She looked a decade older when she finally opened the door to her daughter. Both women wept.

'Where's Grace?' Meg asked.

'She's in here.'

Grace sat motionless at the kitchen table, eyes blank. Meg hugged her, but she did not react.

'She hasn't spoken for days,' her mother said. 'Since we got separated in a panic on the motorway and she lost her teddy bear. She said her last words when I collected her from the police. What she said was, "Boo's dead, isn't he, Gran? And we'll be dead soon, won't we?" No, don't worry, she doesn't even hear us.'

Martha noticed Frank for the first time. Meg introduced them.

'A cup of tea, Father?' Martha asked him. 'There's no milk, I'm afraid …'

'Thanks. I'd love some.' Frank sat down at the table. 'Look, I'm going to try to get my sister's family out to Italy. That's if they'll come. If I could manage to get you all out of here as well, would you come?'

Both women nodded.

'Phones working?' he asked. 'No? Well I didn't expect so. And my mobile's not working. At least it wasn't on the way up. Let's try again.' He pulled his phone out, dialled, and put it to his ear. He shook his head. 'Alright, now. Let's see where we start …'

DAY 11, PFE

DYMPNA MANNING SAT at a table in the lounge, cupping her chin in both hands. 'She must be dead, Chris. She'd have rung by now, wouldn't she?'

'But the phones aren't working, dear. I keep telling you that.'

'No, Diane's dead. I mean, she was over there. Newby Bridge is near where it happened.'

'She's a strong girl, my dear. And she has a good man with her. Both resourceful. I wouldn't give up hope. Certainly not.'

'But she'd have come back to check on us, wouldn't she?'

'She probably couldn't, dear. It's chaos out there, and the plume would have destroyed her if she'd tried to travel through it. My guess is they're gone up to Scotland. That's what would make sense.'

'Would you try the police, Chris?'

'How can I, without the phone, dear? Anyway there'd be millions of people trying to contact them. And a lot of the police must be ill by now.'

Dympna looked around at the old people, sitting motionless in their chairs in the darkened lounge. 'How are we going to feed them, Chris?'

'I'll head out and see what I can forage. Don't you worry.'

'But aren't we supposed to stay inside? They said there's particles and gases still in the air.'

Chris stood and rubbed his hands briskly. 'It's food that matters now. I'll take my chance on the particles. Just trust me – alright?'

'I'm so frightened, Chris. I've never been as frightened in my life.'

***

'ARE YOU EATING, Trevor?' Doctor Postlethwaite asked as he put away the stethoscope.

The young fireman shook his head. 'Nothing stays down, Doctor. For days now. Blanche is up the walls. And she's worried about my face, too. Just look at it.'

Postlethwaite had been trying not to look. Earlier there had been little ulcers on mouth, tongue, inside cheeks. Then the mucous membranes had begun coming away in flakes, like pastry. Later the face had turned brown, but now it was greyish white, and pieces of skin were flaking off. A small piece from the left cheek came away in the doctor's fingers.

He turned away to hide his tears.

***

GULLS CRIED AS they rode the breeze over Galway Bay. Jack Stokes looked up at the white clouds sailing in from the Atlantic across a blue summer sky. Their shadows moved over the Burren Hills, south of the bay. The distant silhouette of Black Head had a rim of white foam where it touched the indigo Atlantic.

Never had Stokes been more aware of the beauty of the world around him. Or felt more sad. The lines from Padraic Pearse, remembered from school, came into his mind:

> The beauty of this world hath made me sad,
> This beauty that will pass.

He looked up at the gently moving clouds. They were like little white cottage loaves against the blue sky – round on top, flat underneath. Stokes shuddered: if ever those clouds turned around and came the other way, death would come out of that blue sky.

He climbed back into his car on the Salthill promenade and switched on the one o'clock news.

'... and both archbishops of Dublin have called for prayers that the winds will continue from the west until the danger is past,' newsreader John Murray was saying.

'The King of England has refused to take refuge with his government in Gibraltar, and has moved north with a small entourage into the affected zone. King Charles said today he will remain with his people until the crisis is over. "For as long as it takes," the King said.

'A ferry belonging to Irish Continental Lines has been turned back on reaching Roscoff in Brittany. The authorities there have refused to allow any further refugees to disembark. They claim that orders to that effect have come directly from the French government.

'Among the refugees on the vessel is Mr Seamus Óg O'Kane, the prominent campaigner against asylum-seekers ...'

As Jack Stokes flicked off the radio, he smiled for the first time in days.

DAY 31, PFE

THE PRIME MINISTER had never, in all his long years of power, looked so paternal, thought Dympna, as she watched him on BBC television addressing the nation.

'I am speaking to you from Downing Street,' Sir Anthony said, 'to which, as you know, your government has now returned. I am speaking on a matter of grave import for the Nation.

'As you know, the heroic people of Brit-Atomic have succeeded at last in getting control of the fires at Freshpark, at tragic cost to themselves. They will be honoured forever. Their names will live to be written with those who have died in our other world wars. For this, let us not be in any doubt, *is* a world war.

'Because of their heroism, the wind may soon blow where it will, without causing us further harm. As you know, during several crucial days the prevailing wind blew continuously from the northwest or west, thus saving that part of Britain that lies south of Birmingham, and leaving Scotland only slightly affected. It was only after the radioactive plumes were exhausted that the wind direction changed, so there was no further harm that the wind could bring us.

'However, I must now tell you something I had hoped I would never have to say. Most of northern England probably cannot be lived in for many generations to come. We will not be able to grow our crops there or raise our animals. But above all, our people can no longer live there. We have to declare it, at least for the present, uninhabitable.

'This is the principal reason for the shortages that now afflict us. There are other causes as well, notably our problems with transportation and infrastructure, which we are working so hard to overcome, and will overcome soon, provided we all pitch in and abide strictly by the rationing regulations.

'Regrettably, our problems have been exacerbated by the vast amount of fraud that is taking place, especially in the sale of contaminated frozen food.

'Of course, as you know, our greatest problem is water. With so much of our water sources contaminated beyond use (for the moment, that is), it is vital that we adhere to the extremely strict water rationing that is now in place. I cannot emphasise enough that children must never be deprived of their ration of water, and that the dying may not receive more than their allotted portion, even to relieve suffering.

'Now, there is something I must ask you to consider along with me. Thirty million people live in the zone that is now declared uninhabitable. Or rather, *did* live there, for now they must leave. They must be moved soon if they are to survive at all.

'On your behalf I asked our fellow nations in the European Union if they would take some of our people.

I have to tell you that, in spite of our rights as European citizens, all these governments have refused to accept more than strictly limited numbers. They have cited emergency circumstances and the numbers of their own refugees from the affected parts of Holland, Germany and Austria. They insist there is no way they can or will accommodate thirty million people, or even a reasonable portion of that number.

'Australia, New Zealand, Canada and South Africa have undertaken to accept some millions of our people. For this we are grateful. As we are to the United States, which is also accepting several million.

'But let me ask you this. How do you transport even half a million people across the world? The very largest airliners can carry only a few hundred. We would need ships. And where would we find those ships? And how many ships would be needed, and how long would it take? Even the largest ships can carry only a thousand or two, whereas we must transport thirty million.

'Even if we were to use all available transportation, we would still have many millions of people with simply nowhere to go.

'What would be more natural then, than that we should look to our sister island across the Irish Sea? An island with only four million inhabitants, and large tracts of only lightly-populated countryside? An island that has emerged scot-free from what must be history's greatest catastrophe?

'I asked the Irish government if it would be willing to receive our people. I am sorry to have to tell you that they have refused. They gave their reasons, and indeed offered to accept token numbers, but, in essence, they said no.

'Now I want you to carefully consider this question. Where are our people to go? *There is nowhere else.*

'Therefore, in view of these circumstances, at five o'clock this morning, on my direct orders, troops of the Third Parachute Regiment, and a battalion of the King's Own Scottish Borderers, proceeded south across the border and entered the Irish Republic. Although there has been some token resistance, I am relieved to say that the outcome has so far been relatively peaceful.

'We shall begin to settle our people in Ireland as soon as it is safe to do so. That, of course, may not be for some time, and I would ask you all to be patient.'

'I ask you to pray to Almighty God for a peaceful outcome, for the safety of our young men, and that the Irish will come to understand that there was absolutely no alternative left to us.

'I conclude with that unanswerable question: what else could we have done? Where else could our people go? I leave you now with the ancient prayer, *God save Ireland.* And may God bless England. Good night.'

YEAR 53, PFE

THE BOOK YOU have just read was written more than fifty years after those apocalyptic events of the first decade of the twenty-first century. I, the author, Alice Watkins, was born just nine months after those events.

I have based it partly on the notes and journals of my late mother, Meg Watkins, on conversations I had with her down through the years, on newspaper reports from that time, on letters received, and on interviews with some of those who survived, and their descendants. My mother, of course, was a journalist, and kept extremely effective notes.

I too, am a journalist, and I have written this simply to tell how things really were at the time. Or rather, how I think they might have been because, of course, I have had to imagine many of the scenes and sometimes guess at what might have happened.

I hope at least I have given you the essence of those times. I wrote this book to try to show people today how a world came to an end.

Firstly, Britain as it was then, more or less ceased to be (as did Ireland, for different reasons). With the whole northern half of England rendered uninhabitable, with 23 million (the final figure) rendered homeless and rejected by continental Europe, with refugee camps throughout southern England where, as in Palestine, whole families live in squalor to this day. With the deaths that began three months after Freshpark and grew over the following years to a crescendo of millions, and with the horrific mutations and birth deformities that ensued (and continue to this day), society simply could not cope.

Add to this the ferocious and brutal guerrilla campaign waged by the Irish in revenge for what they saw as the invasion of their island.

The attempt on Britain's part to forcibly settle a few million of its homeless in Ireland – there was nowhere else to put them, except Scotland and Iceland, which could not contain anything like the numbers in need – was met by resistance, not by a few IRA fanatics, but by an implacable nation that carried a savage guerrilla war across to Britain and to this very day continues it, making a purgatory of whatever wretched life is left in Britain.

The mistake Sir Anthony Ware made was his belief that Ireland's military was in essence a peace-keeping force which served the United Nations. In this he was correct, but he did not consider the fact that the Irish military was also trained in guerrilla warfare, precisely as a deterrent to any invader.

The result was that after the Irish army's token stand at Drogheda, only a stone's throw from the site of the Battle of the Boyne, the soldiers simply faded away. And then the real war began, the guerrilla war, in which most of the nation took part, led by its erstwhile military officers.

In Ireland itself, events such as the Curragh Massacre, where a tent city of 'Freshies' (as the refugees from the Freshpark plume became known) was wiped out by Irish natives, led quickly to the notorious ethnic cleansing, where so many native Irish were uprooted by Britain, and forcibly moved to the west of the country, beyond the Shannon. Although this was to leave room for the Freshies, it was seen by the Irish as a repeat of the plantations of earlier centuries, where people had been sent 'to hell or to Connacht'. The Irish proceeded to take a terrible toll on the new 'planters'.

***

IT WAS THE end too, of Europe as a potential world power. The EU could hardly have survived Britain's anger over the rejection of its refugees. It was reciprocated by the fury of Holland, Germany and Austria, which blamed Britain for the uninhabitable swathe that to this day stretches from Amsterdam to Vienna.

But Europe, like Britain itself, came to its end principally because of economic decline. The decline stemmed from the devastation; from the crash of the stock markets everywhere; from the food and water shortages in Britain and the Continent, amounting in some areas to famine, particularly in Britain; the French riots at Cap La Hague which spread throughout France and then into the rest of the continent; the growing death toll, first from leukaemia and later from thyroid and other cancers, from heart diseases, still births and massive suicide rates.

In the end civil society practically ceased to function, particularly in Britain, where the south of England had to cope with many millions of displaced people, in conditions of chaos and famine. But such conditions were replicated, at least to some extent, in many of the affected parts of Europe.

The rest of the world was affected by a significant increase in cancers, but much more by the growth in illness and mortality rates from other causes that could not be directly linked to the Freshpark catastrophe, but most probably were. Millions died from various forms of flu, because of lowered immunity: it was similar to the impact of Aids. All this eventually weakened nations even more than the Aids epidemic of the earlier part of the century.

***

THE UNITED STATES, like everywhere else, was affected in a similar way. It was also held to ransom by the plutonium stolen from Freshpark, which was later used in the nuclear bombs that wiped out Seattle and Chicago.

Quite apart from that, the US became a classic instance of the 'sunset factor', gleaming brightly as the world's only hyperpower before fading with astonishing rapidity.

Historians trace the decline to the theft of the presidency in the year 2000. That was when the Republican Party, in what amounted to a coup, managed to halt the vote count and install a president obedient to the oil companies and to the concept of a 'New American Empire'. The succession of pathetically inept 'petroleum presidents' that followed, in thrall to the oil interests and crassly ignorant of the rest of the world, eventually led America into the wilderness.

After the failure of its adventure in Iraq, and its other attempts at empire building in Iran, North Korea and Latin America, the US turned increasingly in on itself with its Homeland Security campaigns, leading to the gradual but inexorable erosion of those very freedoms that had created America, until finally it had become tantamount to a totalitarian state.

Yet that did not mean the US stopped meddling abroad. The world's greatest military power continued to exhaust itself and alienate its own young people through paranoid pre-emptive invasions of little countries that were suspected of challenging that power; in worldwide pursuit of the last few drops of the globe's now-exhausted oil reserves; and in chasing the Islamist shadows that led it a dance around the world.

America became the last of the mammoths, thrashing wildly amid the circling tormentors which its tusks could not reach, and sinking inexorably into the slough.

The Islamist Jihad eventually receded, but not before it had achieved the ruination of the West. Islamism had been galvanised by hatred of the West, and once the West was no longer a power worth hating, the Jihad faded. The

Islamists have not yet achieved their worldwide caliphate governing the whole of Islam, but who is to say it will not eventually come about in a revived Jihad?

Which leaves us with the two superpowers of today, now squaring up to each other – China and India – who, with their weapons of mass destruction, their plutonium plants and their massive military might, seem to have learned nothing from what happened in what once was Britain, more than half a century ago. The world again seems to be heading for catastrophe, so it seems that the Pompeii Syndrome is alive and well. As Brecht once put it, 'Human beings learn as much from catastrophes as laboratory rabbits learn about biology'.

***

BEFORE I FINISH, let me tell briefly what happened to the members of my family who feature in this account.

I will start with Meg Watkins. After finding her mother and daughter back home in Cawood, Meg managed, with the help of Frank Kane, to bring them both out to Italy, and later to New Zealand – they had relatives there – where they settled in a place called Okaihau on the North Island. Meg gave birth to me slightly less than nine months later.

I just about remember Frank Kane, who was my father. He came all the way to New Zealand with Meg, her mother and her daughter, with the intention of returning to his order in Europe once he had seen them safely settled. But when it became clear that my mother was pregnant and that he was the father, he saw it as his duty to marry, and asked the Vatican to dispense him from his vow of celibacy. I think that by then, anyhow, he was deeply in love with my mother, and she with him. My mother once told me it had begun as a one-night stand in a hotel in Italy, and that he had been a genuinely celibate priest until then.

My father never returned to the *Great Catastrophes* series back in Britain – in fact the series itself was never finished. He was invited to take up work with an Auckland television station, where he made a considerable reputation. Unfortunately he died six years later, from one of those strange flu epidemics that regularly decimated the population in those years, like repetitions of the Great Flu of 1918.

My mother said he always remained a man of prayer, and actually taught her how to pray, in a way that changed her life and helped her through many crises.

Dympna Manning and her husband decided they could not leave the old folks who were in their charge, so they simply stayed on in the Freshified Zone, and continued to run the retirement home. There were terrible times of hunger, indeed famine, and of course flu epidemics, as well as the cancers that were the direct result of Freshpark.

One by one the old people died. Chris and Dympna

died within a year of each other, both from radiation-induced heart diseases. At that point there were five of the old people left. I do not know what became of them.

The Mannings' granddaughter, Diane, went with her husband to live in Scotland, where they both died within a couple of years, having been massively exposed to radiation during their honeymoon.

Hopes were high for my grandmother, Martha Watkins, and my half-sister, Grace, once they reached New Zealand. It was to be the start of a new life. Unfortunately both died horrible deaths. Martha Watkins died three years after arrival, having shrunk to a sort of skeleton, due to a once-rare cancer that had become frequent among Freshpark survivors.

Grace was eleven when she succumbed to leukaemia. My mother told me of the other sufferings my half-sister endured, even before she became ill. She was of course one of the Freshies (quite a few came to New Zealand), and, as a Freshie, she was ostracised. Her schoolmates were afraid to come near her because she was 'contaminated'. They would not physically touch her or sit at the same desk with her. The only occasion they did touch her was when they threw her into a windowless school-basement cellar to see if she would glow in the dark.

Maybe the children were right. For in the fullness of time I myself married one of the Freshies. James was a truly lovely man, about nine years older then me, gentle, kindly and humorous as so many of the northern English used to be. But both our children were frightfully deformed. I won't go into the details here. One died in the first year of life. Mercifully. The other, unfortunately, lingered until the age of fifteen. We had to squeeze him to empty his bladder.

And James himself died eighteen years ago, from Non-Hodgkin's Lymphoma.

Although Jack Stokes was not a member of the family, after all my research he seems like one. Unfortunately the following is all I can tell of what happened to him later. His wife and his children perished in one of those ethnic-cleansing massacres that followed the invasion of Ireland. Some ten months later he hanged himself, 'on a tree in a clearing in a wood near Tuam in County Galway'. That's all the letter said.

My mother passed away in 2037. To her dying day she campaigned against everything nuclear, and lived to see much of the world abandon the nuclear generation of power. Except of course, India, China and the United States.

I remember once asking my mother if the Freshpark catastrophe could have been prevented. Her answer was *no*. As long as Freshpark remained open, with all that high-level waste and plutonium stored on site, the only defences it could ever really have had were a couple of bored people at an airport X-ray machine, and a couple of stewardesses on a plane. And that could never have been enough.

Indeed nothing can ever be enough as long as the Pompeii Syndrome holds sway. Which it still does. And always will.

THE END

ACKNOWLEDGEMENTS

I WAS STANDING in the forum of Pompeii, looking towards Vesuvius, one June day in 2002, when I
said to Catherine Thorne, 'I know now what my next
book will be.' Neither of us guessed that it would take five
years of research, and that things would emerge from that
research that would give many sleepless nights. The result
is this grievously troubling book. Fiction, yes, but based on
reality – the reality of what could happen tomorrow. Or
even tonight. What strengthens my conviction is the calibre
of the people who have advised me, and who have helped
me write this book, and I thank them here. In particular
I single out Mycle Schneider, of Wise-Paris, international
consultant on energy and nuclear policy, adviser on nuclear
security to the UK Committee on Radioactive Waste,
former adviser on nuclear security to the Belgian, French
and German governments, who was an almost inexhaust-
ible source of information and documentation. He took
me to stay at his Paris home, and later came to my home to
work on the material with me. He finally read and passed
the manuscript as scientifically credible, as far as fiction can
be. I must also thank two of Britain's top nuclear specialists
– physicist Dr Frank Barnaby, who painstakingly answered
my queries; and nuclear engineer Dr John Large, who met
with me at Oxford, answered my queries, and shared some

valuable insights and suggestions. I am grateful to certain personnel of British Airways who shared their concerns with me, as well as their technical expertise. One is a senior airline captain. They cannot be named. I am also indebted to the Oxford Research Group, which invited me to its seminar on nuclear security, and shared subsequent documentation with me. A number of books were of immense help, and I have drawn liberally upon them. They include Malise Ruthven's *A Fury for God*; and Rohan Gunaratna's *Inside Al Qaeda*. Although my own book in no way refers to Sellafield, I found extremely helpful Harold Bolter's *Inside Sellafield*; and Colum Kenny's *Fearing Sellafield*. Also extremely helpful were *Voices from Chernobyl*, by Svetlana Alexievich; and *Doomsday: Britain after Nuclear Attack*, by Stan Openshaw, Philip Steadman and Owen Greene. Also outstandingly useful was *The Stoa Report*, from Wise-Paris. I am indebted to Carlin Music Corporation, for permission to quote Billie Holiday's famous song *Strange Fruit*; and to Faber & Faber Ltd. for permission to quote Norman Nicholson's poem, *Windscale*. I am utterly astonished at the number of people who shared their expertise to help me make this book accurate, and who read and commented over several years to help me refine the text and get it right. I gladly thank Dr Brendan Thornton for his medical expertise, Garda Inspector Paul Hogan and Det/Garda Albert Kelly and others of their colleagues for their police expertise, all of which was so generously shared. I thank Ali Boushnaf who generously helped me with the Arabic in the book. My thanks to Seamus Cashman, whose editing and publishing skills guided me through a difficult moment with the story. Others who have helped, guided and encouraged me in the writing of this book over the last five years include Catherine Thorne, my brother Dermot Rice, Kieran Ruan, John Murphy, Jim Watkins, John Madden, Carole Madden, Marjorie Quarton, Derek Boate, Bernie Healy, Jean Borreye, Gemma Mawdsley, George Mawdsley, Patricia-Ann Moore, Corrie Kirby, Dr Harvey Wasserman, Christy White, Dr M.F. Grehan, Gerry Curran, Colum Quigley, Claire Connelly-Doyle, Joan Lonergan, Eddie Collins, John Brophy, Miriam Donohoe, John Murray, Tom Lauwers, Julie McAuliffe, Mamar Marzouk, Victoria Bruce, Emmet Stagg, Leon Agnew (Leon spent many, many hours with me, speaking, out loud, Jack Stokes' utterances, and emending them so as to get the Northern Irish 'voice' just right), Kevin Hendrick, Deirdre Grimes, Erin McGrath, Victor Davis, Aedrina Stewart, Dan Minchin, Barbara Minchin, Dick Ahlstrom, Roger Porritt, Fiona Newcombe, Tom Griffin, Michael Lewis, Rosa Lewis, and Gordon Baker. And especially to James Moore, without whose help this book might not now be in your hands. Also to all members of the Killaloe Hedge-School Writers' Group and the Killaloe Readers' Group who listened to my reading of extracts from the book and gently commented and guided me over the last five years. I must also thank IT specialist Eugene McDonagh, who rescued me so often when I was about to put my fist through my computer screen. A special thanks to my agent Jonathan Williams, a very good man indeed to have on one's side. The biggest thanks of all are to those at Mercier Press, who chose to believe in this book – to Mary and Clodagh Feehan, Brian Ronan, Patrick Crowley and Rebecca Whitney, to my editor Isobel Creed, whose skill both enhanced and tightened the text in a way that astonished me (and who knew how to bargain with an author – 'if I let you keep this phrase, will you give in on that?' Secretly I call it horse-trading). And to Catherine Twibill, for her stunning gifts of design. I also thank Nuala Ahern, for her enthusiastic encouragement from the very beginning, and for the initial contacts which gave me the start I needed. And I must mention some most generous people who, many, many years ago, guided me towards a start in writing – Gordon Thomas; Peter de Rosa; Bunny Carr; and Howard Long, Professor of Journalism at Southern Illinois University, Carbondale. But especially three wonderful Dominicans, Father Reginald Harrington, Father Austin Flannery and Father Mark Healy. *(If I should forget you, let my right hand be forgotten.)* Of course, in spite of the unprecedented amount of input from so many people, none of the persons mentioned here are to be blamed for anything whatsoever written in this volume. All of it is solely my responsibility. But feel free to visit me in jail.

– *DAVID RICE, Feb 2, 2007*